D1413124

Brilliance

By J.G. Lynn

Prologue

My life has never been phenomenal. I am always searching for a purpose, a meaning in my rippled existence. I cannot seem to surmise why, considering the prosperous evidence I am not truly human. Yes, my inhabitance is Earth and yes, my Province conspires on Earth as well. I am not from space. I am absolutely not an "alien" either. But instead, I am known as a Clockwork. There are many individuals around the world that are just as intriguing as me. Essentially, the Province is divided into three sections: Exols, Clockworks, and Creators. All of the Province inhabitants are considered "Beings" because we are unlike any ordinary human on this planet. We are all gifted with special abilities. I am considered a Protector because I was gifted with the potential to become invisible and to create force fields from my inner spirit.

Exols, in our seemingly native culture, are notorious for being considered Gods due to their freakishly gorgeous complexions. Every Exol is gifted with beauty, regardless if they are male or female. They have deep, aqua-blue eyes with gold surrounding their irises. Their palace sits on a cascading waterfall on a foreign island somewhere on Earth. Exols govern the Province with peace and virtue. They solely believe in not using violence because it is against the way they are constructed. Exols are not meant to fall in love due to any cataclysmic effects that will conspire within their children. All of them are extremely powerful although they are meant to shadow their abilities to follow their peaceful virtues. If they bore a child, the child will become twice that power and they will be able to overthrow the whole Province and the mortals. Due to their inability to have children, they are naturally born from the Spiritually-Bounded Waterfall known as *Innocence.* As water flows down, it crashes into the rocks, creating bubbles in the moonlight that conspire together to create a fetus. The fetus grows in the waters, absorbing the spirits that grant them their abilities. It takes approximately five months for a fetus to grow into a fully functional adult body.

Clockworks are unfortunately not born so beautifully. We are born from two parents and at least one family needs to have a bloodline of a Clockwork in order for the child to possibly become one as well. Clockworks are the opposite of the Exols, we were created to protect the world from any dangers that could impact the Province and the mortals.

Creators are practically Clockworks that experienced the harsh end of life's cruelties and they wish to become something more in this lifetime. They wish to create a new life in their unhappy worlds. Me, and my young sixteen-year-old mind truly believed they were nothing. They were just there... At least, that's what I thought.

I am Esther Green, and this is how I was Chosen to be the Protector of Brilliance in the cataclysmic demise of Earth.

Chapter 1. I Saw Him

My bedroom was dark as the night sky; the rain tapped quietly on my wooden window pane. I sat on my old frayed mattress, envisioning the memory of my father chasing me down the short, narrow hallway into my bedroom as we both laughed playfully. He passed away a year ago from lung cancer. He knew he was getting sick but he never told me nor my mother. My father wasn't a Clockwork, so he always had a difficult time trying to connect with me. He was unsure how to raise a dangerous child that honestly had no idea how to use her abilities half the time. But he managed.

On the other hand, my mother was a Clockwork. She was considered a Boundary because she was able to view the future and see passed individual's motives. But as she aged, her abilities began to fade just like how her hair has to gray. It boiled in my soul that we weren't able to keep something that made us ourselves even as we became elders. If I could change one thing, it would be that entirely.

I remembered the day of my first Annual Autumn Ball. I stood in the mirror, admiring myself. I looked beautiful and I felt radiant. Everything about myself was eye-catching and I adored it. My hair was perfect and my face was absolutely gorgeous. I reached up, gently touching my cheek. I felt like a woman even though I wasn't, but I so greatly admired the feeling.

"You've always been beautiful, Esther," my dad said, appearing in the doorway. "You just didn't notice it before."

I turned around, looking at him in his tuxedo. "Looking good, Dad."

He grinned. "Sorry I've been weird lately. I'm just drained."

"From what?" I asked.

He shrugged. "It's nothing, really. Let's just focus on having fun tonight." He scratched the back of his head and walked away. I smiled, following after him.

If only then I noticed the hints of his nearing death. I blamed my mother constantly for not being able to fight her aging so she would've been able to view the future. I was so angry, frustrated, and disgusted by the fact I couldn't have done anything to stop it. I was meant to be on this Earth to make a change, but I couldn't even save my father's life.

I picked up a crinkled piece of paper from my bed that was damped in tears. It was the last letter my father ever wrote to me.

Dear Esther,   Dec. 3rd

I wish I could be there for you when you need me. I will be in a way you won't necessarily expect though. Sometimes I wish I could spend my final hours with you, but for someone so fragile with feelings, I couldn't possibly comprehend the pain I'm causing you.

I remember five years ago when I was brushing your hair in the mirror and you looked up at me with such innocent eyes and you said, "I want to be someone someday."

I looked down at you with a smile saying, "You already are."

Years flew by quickly and you were once again standing in front of the mirror; this time with a beautiful forest green dress on. And in that moment, I knew you had finally become a woman. Your eyes still held such an innocent look, but I knew you were a strong, determined young lady. You walk with such confidence it warms my heart to see you so brave. I love you so much.

But Esther, as a child, I always knew you wanted a place in this world. You will find it. I believe in you. And I know, as brave as you are, you will succeed.

I felt the overwhelming surge of pain flood my heart like a tsunami. Annoyed by my sadness, I created a fiery force field, surging with orange flames that ignited the letter. The letter perished into a pile of ash onto my knit comforter. I dissipated the force field with a flick of my wrist. My heart wrenched with despair in what I just did, but I knew I had to move on from this. I had to start my life from scratch. My father would not want me to mope in piles of my own brood. I stared up at my ceiling fan, sucked in my chest as tears poured down my cheeks.

"Give me a reason," I meekly stated. "Give me a reason why I'm here."

Suddenly there was a knock at my door. "Esther?" my mom said, appearing from behind the door.

"Yeah?" I asked, losing concentration on being invisible.

"We need to talk."

"Okay?"

She walked over to my bed and sat down. She looked into my eyes sympathetically. I knew this was a bad sign. "I don't want to risk people finding out about your abilities. Or about Clockworks for that matter. Just don't use your powers and especially not in public, okay?" She paused. "I'm not stupid, Esther. I know what you've been doing lately. Locking yourself up in your room, using your abilities to refrain from the grief of your father. Possibly the use of them in public, too."

"Okay." I tried to stop myself from arguing.

"Esther, I don't want to lose you. We can't let the Exols find out about you using your powers, especially in the presence of mortals."

"Why does it have to be like that though? Why can't the mortals know about us? How am I going to protect myself?" I asked, finally letting the volcano inside me boil out.

"We are to live amongst each other in harmony. If they know about us, more negative people will come along with more violence than there already is. We are to protect this world and keep it in balance."

I rolled my eyes. "That's so stupid, Mom! I don't even—."

"You're acting like a foolish teenager that has no respect, Esther!"

I sighed. "I'm sorry... I just don't know... I'm sorry." I turned on my side, facing the opposite direction of her. I shouldn't have to deal with this.

She sighed, tucking my hair behind my ear. "Your hair is beautiful, darling. It's so long and soft. Reminds me of mine when I was younger." Now my mom was trying to soothe everything over with a useless compliment. She gave me an awkward hug. "Love you." I heard her walk across my room, shutting the door behind her.

I exhaled, closing my eyes. "Please let something exciting happen tomorrow. Please."

The next morning, I stood at my turquoise locker in the flooded hallway of students as they pushed and shoved, yelling obscure obscenities. Annoyed by the students, I rolled my eyes and continued to place my books in my locker.

Suddenly, my locker slammed shut and I quickly recoiled my hand away from the fast-moving metal. My body tensed up and I could feel my soul burning with the desire to form a force field.

"Awe, sorry Esther." I heard that putrid, whiney voice that only indicated one thing… Becca Smith. My own personal bully. Yeah, sixteen years-old and apparently her lowering a self-esteem of another individual is still comedic in her own, twisted personality.

"Yeah and what do you want from me today, huh?" I snapped at her, moving away from my locker to stare menacingly into her dark, green eyes.

She gave me a wicked smirk, shrugged her shoulders and danced to the opposite side of my locker. "Oh nothing. I just wanted to see if you were, ya know, done crying in class about your dad." I continued staring at her, resisting the urge to catch this wicked bitch on fire with a simple flick of a force field. "It's been a year honey," she pursued. "I got over the death of my parents from a vicious car accident within less than a month."

I gritted my teeth as the rage coursed inside of me. Oh, how much I wished I could throw a punch into her throat. "That only proves how heartless you are, Becca."

She laughed, swinging her head back and her long blonde hair danced dramatically around her round face. "Yeah but you still have a mom but yet you act like the world treats you so dirty. It doesn't, pretty spoiled girl. You may live in a trailer, but I live in a one-room, dirty ass apartment with my musk-smellin' grandmother. Now you tell me who's really heartless? Your mother couldn't even come to my parents' funeral when we were friends. When our moms were friends. That stung and it will forever sting. But yet, I'm the

8

heartless one?" She smiled, her green eyes showing disinterest in observing me as I stared at her with daggers reflecting in my eyes.

"Becca, that was 9 years ago when we were kids. And you hold so much of a grudge about that to where you don't even care about our friendship. You love trying to torment me over one small act. And that to me is bull."

I knew it was wrong of my family to not make an appearance at the funeral. The only reason why my mom didn't want me to go was because she didn't want me to understand death. She was always so overprotective of me and I could never understand why. I thought it was pretty ridiculous that Becca decided to ruin our since-birth friendship. It was also hard for my mother to lose Becca's mom like that. They were pretty close and Becca's mom use to always babysit me. It was genuinely hard for her. But my mother's protection over me outweighed her love for Becca's mother. As terrible as it sounds, it was the cold truth. Obviously, Becca thinks it was an excuse.

"Whatever, Esther. You and your family could die if all I care. Maybe you'll understand then."

I was about to harshly retaliate but the bell rang and Becca brushed my shoulder before I could say another word. I stood in the hallway, staring down at my combat boots. Damn, I hated her and I hated this life that I had to somehow live every day in. Becca would always be rude to me. My mom would always overprotect me to where I couldn't seem to breathe. My dad was dead and only a memory now. I was forced to live a normal human life although my abilities were coursing through my skin, eager to show its power. I would always be unhappy until I met a purpose but honestly, I didn't think it was even near.

I made my way through the hallway with students constantly brushing against my shoulders, rushing to their classes without even acknowledging my presence. They laughed, chattered as they hurried by with the others around them. Man, must've been nice to have friends.

I slipped into my classroom as the final bell rang. My teacher, Mrs. Banks, gave me a glare as I made my way to my desk, only a couple seconds late. I ignored the eyes on me in the classroom. Everyone knew me as the "weird girl". Although I did nothing to be weird, or to be labelled as weird, I still received the name because I didn't care to interact with anyone. Nothing against the girls here, but I couldn't relate to getting my nails done, getting my first car or dying my hair. All of that was only an image. An image shouldn't matter. A soul should matter. But the humans didn't focus on the soul, they focused on what they could see.

I glanced around the square classroom and all four rows of wooden desks were equally placed apart from each other. I sat in the middle of the room but it was enough for me to get the perfect view of my classmates and the chalkboard. I tapped my pencil against the desk and observed the teenagers around me. There were three girls in the corner of the room that laughed as they pointed at people falling asleep in classroom. I rolled my eyes. My eyes trailed towards two football players that sat in front of me. I heard them whispering, "Does he even try to lift?" And they pointed towards a scrawny boy that hadn't matured yet.

I questioned if these were the kids of the future but yet they are so focused on their image. There was more to the soul that should be questioned. The souls in this room were washed out, bland or nonexistent. It was upsetting, but I truly believed that was why I simply couldn't connect with any of them.

My heart began to clench and the feeling was all too familiar. I was alone. I have no friends. No purpose to life. I was simply just a powerful vessel sitting in a classroom of normal teenagers. I desperately wished I could show them who I truly was so they could sit back and admire my power. Everyone would be eager to be my friend then, and I would never have to feel that same emptiness again.

Spontaneously, Becca busted through the classroom door, breathing heavily. Her eyes were wicked and fearful. "I saw something." Her voice croaked as she took a big gulp, continuing to hyperventilate. The hairs on the back of my neck stood up and I clenched my palm on the desk, trying to fight the unbreakable urge of my own curiosity. Mrs. Banks rushed over to Becca and held her body close to her. All of the students had their mouths dropped open in disbelief. They typically didn't see a mental breakdown on a regular basis, so I completely understood their concern.

"Becca," Mrs. Banks said calmly, "Slow down and tell me what happened. Are you hurt? Do I need to contact the office?"

"There… There were people… A woman and a man, in the

girls' restroom. They fucking shattered the mirror without touching it!" she screamed.

My mouth dropped open and my blood started coursing through my body. I could feel the own heat of my fear rising up into my throat. What the actual hell. I instantaneously dug into my bookbag, trying to find my phone. I texted my mom right away, explaining what happened.

"Becca, you know that couldn't be true. How old were they?" Mrs. Banks asked.

"Late thirties. I saw it with my own eyes Mrs. Banks… They turned to look back at me and they gave me a wicked grin. Then the man created a portal out of purple gases and they disappeared."

Well, shit. That gave me my answer. It had to be Creators. No Clockwork would ever want to cause hysteria like that on a random human. But how were there Creators in Erin Springs? And why were they here? Not trying to bash my own town or anything, but our town didn't have much in it.

Mrs. Banks called the office immediately without saying another word. She put down the phone and looked at the class, analyzing all of our faces and most of the faces mirrored back in disbelief. No one believed Becca. I, too began to look around the classroom and people were rolling their eyes and saying, "Crazy Bitch" underneath their breaths. I chuckled, but only because I hated Becca with a burning passion and this was a historical moment for me. Becca scoffed and sat down in her seat, glaring at anyone that looked at her in a wrong way. She then looked back at me, her eyes narrowing even further. She studied my features, trying to read into my expressions to see if I believed her or not. If she saw a glimmer of me believing her, there would be a chance of exposure to the Provinces. So, I decided to make her feel even worse about herself so I wouldn't risk any connection to the Province. I mouthed, "Crazy Bitch" at her and she gritted her teeth.

"I'll so get a hold of you, don't tempt me," she hissed under her breath so Mrs. Banks wouldn't hear. I only laughed. I wasn't afraid of her.

The rest of the day at school was no different than any other ordinary day. The only difference was the constant ridicule Becca received and everyone mocked her, saying that Becca "sees dead people". I thought it was hilarious. She deserved it. Becca also had to see a counselor every Tuesday after the incident today. The only positive about this situation was that every human was still blind to the secret world that they will never know about. I wished they would know so I wouldn't have to hide who I am, but oh well. I could only dream, right? Anyways, I was kicking back on my recliner, reading the newspaper. I usually only read it for the comics, but I decided to read the whole thing today. My eyes glossed over the pages and then I saw an alarming headline, *Bombings in Texas? Terrorist Group in Action?*

My overwhelming curiosity and eagerness compelled me to scan the pages even harder, analyzing every sentence formatted by the journalist. In the picture, I could see a figure dancing near the flames of a burning building. I could see a faintly charred body in the background. My heart began to race. This couldn't have been an accident. Especially with the event today with the broken glass. The Creators were definitely up to something.

"Mom!" I yelled, desperate for more answers. She trudged into the living room, drying off a pot with a soiled rag.

"Yes, honey?"

"Have you been reading the paper? Or, even watching the news lately?" I questioned her, watching every muscle in her body flinch at the question. I already knew what that meant. She was hiding something from me. "What are you not telling me, Mother?"

"It is not my place to say, Esther. My ability isn't given to me to try and change the future. The future is inevitable."

Okay. Wow. Great response there. "What are the Creators conspiring? They usually are never in the public eye. Are the Exols doing anything about this? There are already some casualties with whatever is going on. We need to do something about this!" I automatically snapped, standing up while glaring at my mother. I waited for her response.

"You know we aren't to use our abilities in the public eye, Esther."

"I don't care! Whoever these Creators are, they killed innocent people. Weren't we created to protect the mankind? Shouldn't we stand against this? They should be standing in front of the Exols, awaiting their punishment!" I screamed, my voice getting hoarse with my raging emotions. My mother sighed, collapsing on the couch across from me. She looked defeated as she placed a hand over her forehead.

"There's so much more, Esther. So much you don't know... And with me losing my abilities as I age, I can't give you all the answers you're looking for. Primarily, you're not ready to hear about your future. That is something I vowed when you were born. I would never tell you your future because I trust you will do the right thing and bypass whatever path I may see. It changes every day with every choice you make. But what I can say right now, stay out of this Esther. It's not your battle and I want to keep you far away from this as much as I can."

"What do you mean it's not my battle?" I snapped. "Why can't I do what I'm meant to do and that's to keep this Earth safe? I can't make forcefields or make myself disappear for no reason! I was created to fight. To protect. So, I never understand why you prevent me from doing what I want to do?"

"I'm just trying to protect *you*, Esther. Forget about the other people. The only human I ever cared about protecting was your father and I couldn't even do that. Now, I want to keep you safe."

My rage grew to its breaking point. I threw the newspaper on the floor and stomped down the hallway to my room. I slammed the door shut as hard as I could and plopped onto my bed. I closed my eyes, allowing the warming fondle of becoming invisible overtake me. Just again, laying on my bed and crying about the same shit when I just wanted to kick some ass and call myself a hero. But the same person that prevented me every single time was my mom. It was whatever, just a normal typical life for an average weirdo. I gently placed the covers over my body, closing my eyes as tears tickled my cheeks. I knew as soon as I fell asleep, I wouldn't be invisible or miserable anymore. It was okay though. I needed to sleep.

My eyes began to flutter open. I glanced around, surveying my surroundings. I was in the middle of a dark, foggy field. The mist seeped its way through the trees in the distance, almost like a cloud above water. I heard a snap of a twig in the distance and I instantaneously whipped my head around. In front of me, there was a large muscular body with tattoos imbedded in his biceps that I couldn't recognize in the darkness. He had gauges in both of his ears and a single piercing above his eyebrow. His jawbones were chiseled and clenched.

"Hello?" I merely croaked.

"Esther... I've been looking for you." His voice was deep and intimidating.

"Looking for me?" I questioned.

"Yes... I've been searching for all the Four Souls from the Prophecy written by Brilliance. But since I'm the Wise, I unlocked a part of my brain that allows me to tap into your dreams. I've been watching all of your dreams, searching for any evidence of where you may live, where you may be hiding away at."

My heart began to burst out of my chest. "Wha—what do you mean? Four Souls? Brilliance?"

He let out a chuckle and began rubbing his chiseled jaw with his massive hand. "Oh Esther, you are certainly the curious one. And because of that I will love slaughtering you, even if you are not the one Brilliance will Choose. The clock is ticking, Esther... Brilliance is thriving to be alive in one of the Souls." He began to walk around me, staring me down with his deep, dark green eyes. "But to answer your questions, there are Four Souls Brilliance can Choose to Protect it. The Soul of the Spiritual-Human, the Exol Child, Half-Blood and The Wise. Bril—" Suddenly, his speech broke off as the ground beneath us began to rumble. The scene in front of me began to dissipate rapidly and the image of the man standing in front of me was no longer present.

I opened my eyes, sitting upright in my bed as my heart raced a million beats per second. In the darkness of my own bedroom, I saw a gold light glimmering above me. I glanced at the ceiling and I created a total of seven force fields in each and every corner of my room above me. With one flick of my wrist, all of them vanished before my eyes. "Now, what was that?" I questioned. There was no way any of that made sense. I never heard of this, "Brilliance" and I certainly never heard of any description regarding these Four Souls he claimed exist. It had to be just a dream. The Exols would've notified the Provinces of the existence of Brilliance and most certainly, my mother would've told me if somehow, I was a part of whatever I dreamt of.

I rolled over in my bed, pulling up my sheets. I stared at my rusty, dirty hardwood floor and tried to forget about the strange dream. Each of the particles of dirt on the floor reminded me of space and the existence of all things unimaginable. As I was fading in and out of consciousness, images of pure darkness and the stars flooded through my mind as if I was flying through space. In the distance, I could see Earth. I squinted my eyes and flew faster, darting through space. I broke through the threshold of the atmosphere and made my way to the United States. At this point my body felt like it was no longer mine. I had a gravitational pull controlling my body and I flew straight into New York City, passing Oklahoma. Ahead of me was an old building sitting tightly against other buildings. The sign read *Rizzoli Bookstore* as my body slowly came to a stop. I levitated above the sidewalk and I was gracefully floating slowly into the doors of the old bookstore. It was two levels with a grand staircase, truly magnificent in its vintage way.

"Estheeeerrrrrrr...." I heard an unrecognizable, intoxicating voice whisper my name from the second level. My body was gently placed on the hardwood floor. I felt a pull, but it was coming from my own soul this time. I placed my hand on the dusty handrail and gingerly made my way up the stairs. My own curiosity and my own desires washed over my body like a tsunami. Everything in my entire Being was telling me to keep going, keep following whatever this mysterious voice was.

"Esther!" my mom screamed, instantly jolting me awake in my bed. I stared at her wild, fiery-red hair as she stood in my doorway. "You're late for school! Get up and go!"

I groggily stared at my clock. It was eight in the morning. Last time I woke up it was only a little passed midnight. The wicked dream I had only felt like it lasted two minutes, but it was hours that I slept. I got up out of bed and went to my closet quickly, throwing on a flannel and some jeans. I then proceeded to head out the door with my bookbag.

The autumn air was prickling my cheeks with its frigid, windy air. I thought about my dreams and what they truly meant. *Brilliance? The Rizzoli Bookstore? The man that claims he is the Prophecy of the Wise?*

I continued to run down the street as the leaves fell in astonishing colors around me. I felt cleansed today. I felt happier even though nothing changed in my life. This was the first time I felt like this since my father died. I didn't care I was late to school, I only loved to run in the moment because I was able to feel the Earth's breath against my cheeks. I could see the sun through the orange leaves, shining on my face. It created the balance between the warm and the cold. It felt like everything was aligning itself in a purposeful way. I had no idea why I felt like my soul had been cleansed, but frankly I didn't mind it at all. If I could, I would choose to be happy like this every day.

I finally made my way to the school. I smiled, excited to start my day in order to finish it faster. In the back of my mind I also knew I wanted to research the Rizzoli Bookstore. I trudged up the marbled steps and made my way into the double doors of the school building. Teenagers flooded around me with the sounds of rustling papers, immense amounts of chuckling and talking to one another. As each student passed me, I studied their faces. Each of them appeared to be infused with felicity. Something in my soul felt peculiar since last night. I was almost happy for the people around me, living their lives to their fullest potential since they were only just regular humans. I always despised them for not having to live conspicuously and always having to conceal their own identity for a governmental Province. I was once yet again submerged in my own self-doubt, but almost in a more enthusiastic way. Before, I had no desire to be alive if I could not be who I was and show the world who me, Esther Green truly was. But now, my whole entire Being was whispering the slightest of murmurs, evoking my soul to the fact there was *something more* and that same *something more* will shine its own light. It will execute itself in a way that I will be who I was meant to be.

Boy, I just wish I wasn't alone. My mom was here but she was never truly *here*. She was completely okay with living away from the darkness the world possessed. I knew the Province wanted our people to believe there was stability amongst the humans and also within our own home. My heart was telling me that was not the case. I continued to study each of the humans. They would not be capable of protecting themselves if shit fell apart before them. There was war between them, just like how I believed there could be war between the Provinces if the Creators couldn't essentially get their shit together. And my mom couldn't shelter me if that was the case. I wanted to help mend the world together again, like a clock set in time with full focus on the passing hands. As the hands ticked to each number, it represented Clockworks mending any broken sector to time. That was why we were labeled as Clockworks because we were meant to correct time. Essentially, all ticking hands had the chance of becoming corrupt.

"Hey Esther." I heard Becca's voice behind me. I turned around, immediately noticing her posse of four girls that followed her around like lost puppies. "Who are you gonna sit with at lunch today, boo? Your bookbag?" Her group of friends erupted into a unison of hysterical laughter.

"Maybe," I stated calmly, continuing to walk to my first period class with her and her friends following closely behind me. "But at least my bookbag is more real than those four leaches that can't seem to be apart from you."

Becca chuckled. "At least they were there for me when my parents died."

I rolled my eyes as I still proceeded to my classroom. I brought up my middle finger and flicked her off before I went into the room. Even though she hated me for not going to her parents' funeral, I still tried my best to ignore the pain her comments gave me about it. Creating a tough image proves my strength to succubus's like her. They just wanted to suck the life out of their victims and bring them all the way down until they perished like ash in cool wind.

I sat down in my wooden desk and pulled out my books. Everyone else was getting settled in their seats as well. Once the bell rang, my teacher instantaneously shot up in her seat and clasped her hands eagerly together. "Boys and girls, I am proud to announce we will be receiving a new student here in a couple short moments. I expect everyone to be on their best behavior and treat the new student with a great deal of respect." She shot me a stone-cold glance. "And that means definitely do not flick them off either, Ms. Green. I saw the stunt you pulled outside before you came in. See me after class."

I eagerly bit my lip, thinking about the possibility of getting a detention. I wouldn't mind, but I knew my mom would.

Suddenly, the knob of the door in our classroom jiggled and I could hear all of the students turning their attention to the new kid. I never looked up once, but I could hear him make his way around the desks with another series of footsteps trailing after him. I paid attention to the wooden linings in my desk and repeatedly tapped my pencil. Finally, I picked up my head and instantly, our eyes locked. My heart began to race and my palms simultaneously began to sweat as his electric, ocean-blue eyes stared directly into mine. He furrowed his brows, almost as if he felt a similar vibe of static electricity that seemed to course between the both of us. He was incredibly handsome and honestly, I have never been attracted to anyone like this before.

"Well, introduce yourself honey," said a woman with the same raven-like black hair as him. I almost didn't notice she was standing right next to him until now. It was probably his mother.

"Hello, I am Damion Lee Storm. I will go take my seat now." He gracefully made his way to the seat a couple rows over and a few desks back from my own. He never broke his stride. Even when he sat down, he made it seem like it was effortless when he wedged himself between the chair and the desk. I continued staring at him, observing every aspect of his chiseled jawline, his shaggy jet-black hair and his piercing blue eyes. He didn't look at me again after he sat down. I frowned. He probably didn't like me and he probably already thought I was the weird girl without even knowing me. I pushed the negative thoughts out of my head and tried to focus on my teacher's lecture.

As I was attempting to concentrate on the lesson, I could still feel this indomitable desire to crane my neck around and stare at the boy. It felt like my entire body was rioting against me, wanting so desperately to gravitate itself to Damion. Damion... Even his name sparked an electrifying sensation on the surface of my skin. *Who even was he? And why was I reacting like this?* I broke my own resistance and I finally turned around in my seat. To my alarming surprise, he was already staring me down in bewilderment. His ocean blue eyes locked with my hazel almost as if it were a tsunami releasing, the tension finally broken as our two souls were linked together in some impossible way. At least, that was how it felt. But to him? I wasn't too sure, since he finally broke his eye contact with me and stared eagerly at his desk, avoiding all contact. I observed him even though I knew I was a creep for continuing to stare but I couldn't help myself. I watched him as he nervously plucked at the skin on his forearms without looking at me.

"Miss Green, is there a reason why you're not looking at the front of the classroom?" asked Mrs. Banks.

I quickly snapped my head around as murmurs and the light chuckling of students erupted my soul into immediate embarrassment. I could feel my cheeks getting warm but I quickly eradicated the feeling and immediately coated my emotions with my typical, snarky attitude. "I mean, anything is better than this boring class." I rolled my eyes at Mrs. Banks.

"Keep it up Esther. I certainly can't wait to talk to you after class," she said as she stared at me with daggers in her eyes.

I was not scared of Mrs. Banks and certainly not any other teachers in this school. One thing about Clockworks was that we exceeded in all preliminary schoolings. The way our souls were constructed allow us to retain information faster than the average human. Because of this, it was nearly impossible for me to get a terrible grade in any of my classes. So, no matter how much trouble I could get into, my grades would never be affected. My mother didn't appreciate my thought process on school in the slightest. Even if I did so happen to get a detention, I would be more scared of my mother's harshness than a teacher.

The bell finally rang and everyone began to pack up their school books and migrate out of the classroom for lunch. I knew I had to stick around for whatever Mrs. Banks wanted to give me as a punishment, but I wasn't alone either. Damion stayed back as well.

"Esther, I'll deal with you in a second. Stay in your seat," she said aggressively.

She swiftly made her way over to Damion's desk with a huge smile plastered on her face. "Anything I can help you with?" Her tone was automatically changed, almost annoyingly higher in frequency.

Damion looked up at Mrs. Banks and a small grin pulled at the corner of his lips. "I did have a slight question. I noticed that some of *your* students were throwing paper straws in the back of the room. Why did you not hold them back from class either? We are attempting to promote decent behavior here, are we not?"

She stepped back, stunned. "I'm *sorry*? Who do you think *you* are?"

Damion smiled, beginning to pack up some of his books on his desk. "I'm just saying, if you punish one, punish all." And with that, his things were already packed up and his bookbag was slung across his shoulders. He effortlessly made his way out the door. He was mysterious. Elegant. Quiet, but confident with his words. I never met a human with such adequacy and ability to promote social order in the fair way, not Mrs. Banks twisted 'I don't like you' sort of way. But what if he wasn't a human? What if he could potentially be a Clockwork? I definitely had an eager desire to gain more knowledge on him. And why was I so drawn to him also? I've met a couple Clockworks from my mother's friend group before but I never had a vibe like this when I first met them.

"Welp, am I free to go?" I asked, clasping my hands together on my desk.

"Well, I guess." She stood in the middle of the empty classroom. Her expression showed that she was still confused on what just happened. "But Esther, you're one of my top students… You need to get your behavior under control. There's no one here that will hurt you so don't always try to cover yourself with an image you are not."

I knew she was right, but what she didn't know was that I simply couldn't relate to the students here. They tormented me and tried to lower my own self esteem but I would never let that happen. I grabbed my bookbag and left without saying anything to Mrs. Banks. I quickly walked passed her with my head down, trying to ignore locking eyes with her. As I walked out of the classroom, I felt a hard object collide into my nose, knocking me onto the floor. I frantically glanced up and my blood began to boil…Becca.

"Did ya like that?" she taunted.

I could feel a single trail of blood trickle down my nose. "I am going to hurt you." I instantaneously sprung up off the ground, creating a single invisible forcefield coated over the surface of my skin. If she was able to throw another punch, my skin wouldn't adhere to any of the damages. I brought up my fist and collided it into her jawline. She doubled back, but then quickly regained herself. Her group of friends were chanting behind her. She brought up her hand and slapped my face. I could only feel the vibration of the slap, but not the pain due to the forcefield. I gritted my teeth. At this point every fiber of my Being was telling me to grab her by the hair and continuously punch her in the face for breaking my heart on the mere subject of human friendships. I brought up my fist again, readying myself to completely annihilate her with all the drastic emotions coursing through my body.

Suddenly, I felt the vibration of intensely robust arms pull mine back from attacking Becca. Although my forcefield coated my body, I felt tingling electric shocks course throughout my entire core, sending puzzling sensations from head to toe. The strong mass continued to pull me further and further away from Becca and I started screaming. I desperately wanted to go back to her and finish all of the pain she caused me over the years. I looked up at the strong mass as it pulled me back. I noticed the familiar electrifying ocean eyes and the strong, chiseled jawlines. Once he pulled me far away from the crowd, he released me. In fast movements, I turned around so I could stand in front of him.

"Why would you do that? She hit me!" I screamed, studying his reaction.

"What you were about to do to her is wrong. You can't sink into someone else's despair. Don't give her what she wants you to give her. You're only feeding her energy." Damion stared me down and studied my reaction as well.

Defensively, I grabbed my arm and held it over my chest as if it were a defense mechanism. "Okay, well, um, you're not wrong there…" My voice trailed off as I spoke, annoyed at the fact this so-called social justice warrior out here was reprimanding every poor behavior he came into contact with.

"What's your name?" he said, quickly changing the subject with a grin.

"I… uh… Esther. Esther Green, actually."

"Nice to meet you, Esther. I'm Damion. Damion Storm, actually." He grinned wider at his own joke.

I had no choice but to smile but quickly I dismissed my smile. I felt awkward. I wasn't one to strike up just a random conversation without a meaning. "Well, I should probably get to lunch." I turned around, quickly turning my head so I wouldn't have to bare looking into his electric, ocean eyes. I couldn't understand why he affected me the way he did. I wanted to learn more but this didn't feel like the right time.

"Alright, Esther. I'll see you around."

I sat in our community park, right underneath my favorite willow tree. I heard the rushing of the water in the stream nearby; the leaves rustled in the wind. The colors of autumn danced around me as the leaves floated to the ground. I held my laptop on my knees and researched the Rizzoli Bookstore. I wondered why I kept dreaming about a bookstore all the way in New York. I skimmed the images. I was intrigued with the layout of the books and I was more fascinated about the number of diverse books in there. I loved reading but I definitely read almost everything in our community library that was interesting to me. I favorited the website on the Rizzoli Bookstore for safekeeping. I could try to convince my mom to take me for my birthday coming up.

I observed the children playing in the park with their parents nearby. They danced, they acted as warriors, they played tag and allowed the desire of life consume their souls. I felt a smile pull at the corners of my lips and I genuinely enjoyed the moment. The angelic breeze that pushed my hair slightly behind my shoulders warmed my soul. The signs of autumn made me excited for the holidays to come. Suddenly, I remembered the pain of my dead father. Another year that he wouldn't be here for the holidays. My stomach churned and I had the urge to cry but I quickly pushed my feelings away, digging them deep within my soul. I couldn't do this to myself again and again. I always felt sorry for me but nothing too drastic had ever happened in my life to torment my soul the way I felt on the inside.

Thoughts of Damion flooded my head once more and I furrowed my brows, concentrating on all of the information I already knew about him. I wondered why he tried to get me out of trouble in the fight with Becca. Why did he care about what I did? Why did he feel the need to pull me back? Why did he stand up for me against Mrs. Banks in a nonchalant way? I was confused on his motives. Maybe he felt what I felt as well. Whatever that feeling was, it was very unnatural. I never felt something like that before. I also was curious to know if he had an impact in my life in some sort of way. Maybe I should ask my mother if she saw anything about him before.

I packed up my laptop and hopped on my bike. Even though I was sixteen, I still didn't have a car. I had my license but I definitely did not have enough money for a car. I began riding my bike up the hill in the park and over the tiny bridge of the stream. I pedaled fast, eager to get to my house to question my mother on her visions. I hoped desperately her aging wouldn't get in between this information I needed to know.

After about fifteen minutes of riding my bike on the side streets of Erin Springs, I made it to our trailer. I dropped my bike on the ground and ran inside.

"Mom?" I asked, glossing my eyes over the living room and the kitchen at the same time as I tried to find my mom.

The door to her bedroom off of living room opened slightly and she peeked her head out from behind it. "Yes, Esther?"

"Quick question, do you know anything about a Damion Storm?" I asked, watching her in anticipation.

She slammed her door open and it smashed against the side of the wall. "You stay away from that boy, Esther Green! He is trouble!" She shook her finger at me with her scolding eyes.

"Mom, you need to tell me what you saw." Fear rose up into my throat and I could barely swallow.

"Esther, you know this already. My visions aren't as clear as they used to be. I only see tiny bits and pieces now. But what I do know is something is coming. Something big… And I keep getting the initials 'D.S.' floating through my head… Damion Storm… He is going to lead you right into what this 'big' thing is… And I've been fearing for this moment my whole life. Ever since you were born, Esther. I regret using my abilities so much as a kid because now, in the moment I need them most, they're gone… Vanished like my wrinkly skin. Please, Esther. Please stay away from him."

Before I spoke, I listened to all of her words and allowed them to sink into my brain. My head was telling me to listen to her, but something was conspiring in my soul that I needed to disobey what she wanted me to do. It was almost as if my soul was whispering to me to pursue Damion… That whatever this 'big' thing was, I found myself drifting into no matter what course I decided to take in my life. I was also curious to know why I was feeling all these raging emotions and desires to pursue an unknown route in my life. "Mom… I can't stay away…" I meekly stated.

She clamped her jaw shut in disappointment. "Esther, please…"

I shook my head no as all of my feelings within myself was screaming at me to not listen to her. "I need to know what he is… I need to know if he is even a Clockwork. If he's human he cannot hurt me. But if I find out he's a Clockwork, I'll do my best to stay away from him. Just let me give him a chance. Let me figure him out. I *have* to know."

"I can't stop you from making your own decisions, Esther… But just know I am extremely disappointed in you that you will not listen to me, your mother that is also a Boundary." And with that she went back to her room, slamming the door shut.

I stood in the living room, my heart clenching because I hurt my mother. But I knew I couldn't give up on what my soul was telling me. I had to know Damion. I had to study him. And I especially had to know if he was even a Clockwork… or worse, a Creator.

Chapter 2: Who is He?

Today was the Autumn Annual Fair and it being my father's tradition to take us every year. After losing my father, we couldn't bare ourselves to go without him last year. But my mom wanted to bring herself and I closer again after my father's death by attending the fair. I didn't want to admit to her it wasn't really cool to go to a fair with my mom, but I was going to go anyways to make her feel better.

"Esther? Are you almost done getting ready?" she yelled from down the hall.

I stood in the mirror but I was invisible. I adored being invisible because it felt like I was almost in a different world, viewing my own self from a different perspective. I always struggled with the way I looked. It wasn't like I thought I was ugly. I almost felt as if after viewing the world in my eyes for so long, it was almost strange to get a glimpse of myself in the mirror. It was obscure to see my dark hazel eyes staring back at me as if I couldn't even recognize who I was. I suppose that was the truth about me, I didn't know who I was. I didn't know how to adjust to the world I lived in. I didn't know how to be a Clockwork that was forced to hide who I truly was for the fear of exposing ourselves to the humans. I wanted the world to know who I was and maybe then, I would know who I was too.

"Come on, Esther!" my mom screamed impatiently.

In annoyance, I threw on a cardigan over my tank top and whipped open my door, allowing it to slam against the side of the hallway. My mom stood in the kitchen with her arms crossed.

"Now, is that a way to treat the door?" she taunted.

"What the hell, Mom. Can't you see I was still getting ready?" I asked, making myself visible again so she could see me.

"I don't appreciate your tone with me, young lady. You better bite that attitude in the ass before I give you a reason to truly be angry."

I rolled my eyes, grabbing my crochet satchel from the dining chair. "And you need to bite that impatience in the ass as well."

"Esther. Get in the car. Way to make a big deal about me just trying to take you somewhere your dad would love to see us at…together."

I bit my lip, trying to fight the tears that began to well in my eyes. I slammed the trailer door open and stepped down onto the soft grass. I walked over to my mom's rusty car, opening up the door with a loud squeak. I got in and slammed the door shut. I let the tears stream down my face. I couldn't believe my mom was being such an asshole. Literally, all of this happened because I didn't get ready fast enough. I knew I shouldn't have said a couple things but it slipped out in annoyance. That was the thing about us. We always bumped heads. No matter how stupid, we always fought. My dad and I never fought. He was always so patient with me. I felt the anger rising up into my chest again, realizing dad should be here. Out of rage, I brought up my fist and collided it into the glovebox. I felt the little bite of pain surge in my veins from hitting a solid object.

"Esther," my mom said after opening the door of the car. "I'm sorry." She made her way into the car while trying to embrace me at the same time. I scooted away, trying to get away from her reach.

"I honestly just want to be left alone."

"Esther, I never like fighting with you over stupid things."

"Then why do we still do it? My birthday is coming up. I'm almost seventeen. We've done this for just about that much of time and we've never stopped."

"Here, honey. I'll try harder, I promise. It's been rough on me without your father. He almost kept me together in a weird way… He just knew how to deal with me losing myself. Who I am over the years… You know, because my abilities are fading. It makes me feel like I'm fading away too." Tears began to stream down her wrinkled, rosy cheeks. "I just only have feelings now. I can't even see the future anymore… And that hurts me. It tears me apart."

I frowned, staring into my mother's green eyes. "I love you, Mom. Nothing will ever change that." I leaned over, finally accepting the hug she has been eagerly trying to receive from me.

My mom was lucky. Her ability was more internal. She was able to accept her abilities and not risk anyone finding out about them. Unlike me, humans could possibly see me become invisible or create a force field. There were risks to me, but my mother never had those risks. Because of that thought, she would never be able to cope with the fact that apart of herself was gone, fading away each day her skin wrinkled and her bones became brittle.

"Enough of this sadness," my mom said, wiping her tears, "what did you want for your birthday?" She started to back the car out of the driveway and down our vacant street.

I stared into her fading green eyes. "Funny you ask, actually. Since I read almost like every book in our community library, I've been wanting to check out the Rizzoli Bookstore in New York."

"Esther, I don't have a good feeling... That's very far away. I feel like that just leads you into something bad."

I sighed. "I mean, I really don't want anything else for my birthday. I already have everything I need."

"Ugh, okay sweetie. I'll think about it, okay?"

"Okay, Mom. Thank you though, you know, for trying to make things better." I stared out the window of our old, rusty car. I watched the colored leaves fall gracefully around our vehicle as we drove down the back roads of Erin Springs.

"Esther, I love you. Everything I do is for you. To make sure your life is as amazing and pain-free as possible. I wish I could've seen Raymond's death so I could've prevented this tear in the core of our relationship."

"Mom, don't sweat it. It's fine. Life can't be perfect. I've already accepted that."

As she was driving, she reached over and squeezed my knee in reassurance. "I love you. I always will."

"I love you too, Mom." I gave her a small smile.

We arrived at the Annual Autumn Fair. The whole parking lot was already filled and there were groups of people walking into the gates of the fair.

"Honey, I'll go find a parking spot somewhere in this mess. Go ahead and get out and see if you can hop on a couple rides while I go park near the church. Here's a ten-dollar bill to help you get in. Be careful sweetie."

I hopped out of the car in front of the ticket stands as my mom quickly whipped the car around the corner. I slung my bag over my shoulder and proceeded to the ticket stands. Massive crowds of people began to flock in to where their shoulders would ever so slightly brush against my own. There was a slight breeze that brushed my wavy, long auburn hair gently over my shoulders. The people around me spoke to their families and laughed with their children. Some of the humans groaned due to the long line and others enjoyed the moment, patiently waiting to receive their tickets.

Suddenly, I felt the same familiar set of eyes on me from a distance. I glanced over, quickly noticing those electric eyes. "Damion," I whispered underneath my breath while furrowing my brows. He was staring at me but not in a way that had me fear if he was mentally stable, but in a way that he was almost admiring me the way his eyes glazed over all of my features from ten feet away. I shook my head, breaking my contact. There was no way he would be admiring me. I instantly became annoyed with the fact he always kept staring at me and I had no idea why. I shouldn't flatter myself and think it was because he was infatuated with me. That was impossible and absurd. I didn't ever do anything that would infatuate a man. I never did my hair; I never did my makeup and I certainly never dressed to impress.

I bit my lip, rationalizing the situation. Maybe I was mistaken about what men enjoyed about a woman. All I knew about relationships was from my own parents. My father admired my mother's strength, her abilities and most importantly her youthful beauty. Maybe men have been infatuated with me before, maybe they never confessed whatever secret feelings they had for me that dwelled in their soul. All I knew was that I never was infatuated with anyone before. No matter how hard I tried to possess feelings for another individual, it was just never there. I always told myself that it was simply because I haven't found the one that was constructed to mend between the core of my heart and my soul. But Damion was different. I already knew that. One thing about me was I was never blind to what desires my soul whispered to me.

It was my turn to receive my ticket. I handed the money to a lady with bright blue eyeshadow and rosy lips. She cashed in the ten dollars and immediately handed me my ticket. She never broke her stride and she continued to chew a piece of gum rapidly in the process.

"Thanks," I murmured. I immediately pushed open the rolling gate and walked into the fair. Instantly I could smell the familiar scents of cotton candy and popcorn. My stomach growled slightly and I rolled my eyes. I figured I should wait before my mom arrived but I was definitely hungry and I would be using my own money to buy myself a snack. That did not seem like a bad idea.

I walked up to a corn dog stand and waited patiently in line. After the people in front of me received their food items, it was finally my turn. I handed the cash to the concession stand assistant. As I was handing him the change, I felt an estranged vibe bring shivers down my spine. I quickly snapped my head to the side and in the distance amongst the crowds of humans, my eyes landed on a man with a hood over his eyes. That was definitely not Damion... This was something else. "I'm sorry, Sir. But I need to go."

I immediately dropped the change on the counter and began running in the direction of the hooded figure. Something did not feel right to me and with the way he was gesturing his hand toward a ride proved me to be right. Within seconds, I could see the barrel ride beginning to pull apart as it spun around rapidly. The expressions of the people on the ride went from excitement to pure terror.

"No!" I yelled.

Instantaneously, I threw forward seven invisible forcefields that enclosed each human safely inside the ride as the barrels became shaky. The operators immediately shut the ride down. When I noticed the humans were safe, I put all of my attention on the hooded figure that was running through the crowds of people. I released my concentration on the forcefields and ran after the figure.

"Move," I yelled as I pushed a couple people aside. The crowds of people became denser and I had no vision of the figure. As I was running, I tripped over a stick and collided right into a strong built individual. Knocking us both down, my hands landed on the man's chest and they were immediately engulfed in electric vibes. I looked down at his face, instantly recognizing his deep, blue eyes and strong jawlines.

"Hey," he said with a small grin.

"I'm so sorry." I quickly picked myself off of him and searched the crowds for the hooded figure. I couldn't find him.

"What were you chasing after?" He got up as well, searching my eyes intently.

"Nothing."

"Was it that man?"

"You saw him?" I asked.

"Yeah… I mean you two were the only ones running after they stopped the ride."

Shit. He did have a point. "I just wanted to see why he was running, you know, kinda weird am I right?" I added in a guilty chuckle.

He chuckled slightly. "Yeah. I suppose so. Since they only closed that ride down, did you maybe want to ride the Ferris Wheel with me? I'll reimburse you for that corn dog you left behind at the concession stand as well."

"Oh, you saw that?" My cheeks became rosy with embarrassment.

"Yeah, I literally received my ticket after you did and I wanted to say hi so I was making my way to the stand and then that whole ordeal went down."

"You were going to say hi to me?" Holy shit. He was going to say hi to me.

He laughed while smiling, showing his perfect row of pearly white teeth. "Yes, Esther. You're literally the only person I care to know in Erin Springs. Well, the only person I've talked to here." He quickly corrected himself.

"Yeah, I see." I dusted my shoe on the pavement, avoiding his stare.

"Come on, let's go on the Ferris Wheel."

"My mom might be looking for me though," I said quickly, remembering my mother.

"It's fine. We'll get the corn dog and the ride only lasts for what, a couple minutes?"

"I guess you're right."

The wind was blowing slightly, allowing my auburn hair to whip around as the Ferris Wheel climbed to the highest point of the park. Across from me sat Damion. I could feel his eyes on me as I scanned the park for my mother just in case she was looking for me.

"So, tell me a little bit about yourself. What are your parents like?" Damion asked, staring into my eyes as if the answers were hidden within them.

"I, uh… My dad is dead."

"I'm sorry," Damion said quickly before I could finish.

"It's fine. I'm over it. My mom and I are complicated. We love each other but we fight about a lot of stupid shit." I plucked at the frayed edges of the red seat I sat on. "How about you?"

"My parents and I don't get along at all. They keep moving me across the country. They say it's because of my dad's job but I'm not sure… I don't believe them, honestly. They always hide things from me. My dad and I never talk but my mother and I never seem to quit arguing. She calls me a nuisance. Tells me she hates me. Anything you could think of. But I've grown accustomed to the hate. The loneliness."

"Yeah… I can understand you on the loneliness." I thought back to school and how alone I felt constantly because I was so different from them.

"Enough of the sad… Tell me more about yourself. Your passions. Inspirations. Who do you want to be in this world, Esther?"

I thought about the questions carefully. "I love to read. I'm inspired by the stories I've read. But honestly, that's it. There's nothing else to me."

He threw his head back, laughing to himself. "Oh, Esther." He stared me directly in the eyes with a small grin plastered on his face. "I already know that's a lie. There's so much more to you. I know that. I can see that. I notice how you admire the weather, how you pay attention to close details that even I couldn't notice and how you look up the sky as if you long for more… You long to be something… But you already *are*."

"No." I laughed, shaking my head. "I'm not anything. Just a person that likes to read."

"Esther," he said gently. "You don't have to *lie* to me. We're friends. I am your friend; you can share who you really are with me and not coat yourself in a toxic form of existence that you are not."

I looked down, taking a deep breath. Maybe he was right. Maybe he was my friend and maybe I shouldn't hide who I am in front of him. But how do I even know if he too, was a Clockwork? If he wasn't, I would've shared my secret of the Provinces to someone that wasn't worthy. I couldn't risk that. Not even for this handsome boy that sat in front of me, eager for me to spill all of my secrets.

"You have beautiful eyes," he said, his eyes glossing over my features again.

I furrowed my brows. "What?"

"Nothing… Sorry, I shouldn't have said that if it made you uncomfortable."

I squinted my eyes. "I'm starting to think—" Suddenly, a loud cracking sound filled my ears. I looked beside me at the roller coaster track that was about twenty yards away. The coaster wasn't there yet, but from the distance, I could see a small crack in the track.

"Damion!" I yelled. "Look!" I pointed at the crack.

Damion stood up in our cart, squinting his eyes so he could see. "Oh no."

"Esther! Esther!" I heard someone from below scream my name. Our cart stopped right next to the track. I looked over the side to see my mom.

"Something bad is going to—" Suddenly, the roller coaster started making its way near the crack.

I looked at Damion with fearful eyes. If it came off the track, we were both going to die with many other people. He looked fearful too, thinking the same thing I was thinking.

I watched as the roller coaster zoomed down the track and cheerful yells erupted from the carts full of passengers. Suddenly, the roller coaster hit the crack, breaking the track instantly and the coaster flew in the sky towards our cart.

"Esther!" Damion yelled, running over towards me. He grabbed my hand and we simultaneously held out our other hands at the coaster hurdling our way. I quickly created an invisible force field that was the whole size of the track, repelling the coaster from colliding into us. Damion quickly ran to the side, pushing his hand out as if he would be able to grab the falling coaster and the people in it. Everyone was screaming. It was the only thing I heard. After a while, everyone started cheering. I was on the ground of the cart, trying to maintain my breathing. I couldn't remember how I got there. My body felt numb and I began to see stars.

Damion, in a hurry, sat by me, worry plastered on his face. "Esther."

Everything went black.

I felt a warm, wet rag on my forehead and heard rustling in my room.

"Esther? Honey?" my mother's voice filtered throughout the room like an echoing blow horn.

My eyes fluttered open. I looked around. I glanced at my body to make sure everything was there. "What happened?" my voice quavered.

"You don't remember?" my mother asked, slightly worried.

I tried to recall what happened by shutting my eyes and concentrating. Flashbacks of the events with the rusted bolts, the hooded figure, the talk with Damion, the roller coaster coming straight in our direction, the huge force field I created to prevent the coaster from harming people on the Ferris wheel, how Damion tried to catch the coaster which is likely impossible for him, the cheering crowd, Damion's blue eyes filled with worry and then darkness. I opened my eyes, looking at my mom. "The roller coaster."

My mom nodded her head. "Before the roller coaster incident, I saw the vision... The roller coaster came off the track, hitting the Ferris wheel, killing you and Damion instantly with a lot of other people. The Ferris wheel fell, killing more people on the ground and on the surrounding rides."

"What was the cheering at the end before I... I guess blacked out?"

"I guess another Clockwork was there at the time and had the coaster land perfectly without any harm done to anyone."

I thought back to the hooded figure. "There was a hooded figure there... I don't understand why a Clockwork would want to be hidden like that though. I'm also pretty sure he is the one responsible for the barrel ride attack."

My mother sighed. "I don't know either."

"Wait. What happened to Damion? Where is he?" I asked.

"He was here for a little while when you were... Sleeping. He got a call from his parents and then he left. He's a sweet kid. I can tell he has a heart for you." My mother stared at me with daggers.

I felt my cheeks burning. "Well, I'm sure he doesn't. It's likely impossible."

"I thought I told you to stay away from him, Esther. He's trouble. See what already happened in his presence. He could've been the Creator that destroyed the rides, Esther."

I rolled my eyes. "Whatever. I don't care. I barely know him." Even though I said that aloud, I didn't feel it. I felt like somehow, I did know Damion. There had to be a reason why we had an electric shock. It was like a spark trying to form into something.

"You should get some rest."

"I've been resting," I said. "I'm going to the park so I can focus." I got up out of bed, grabbing my sweater and I wrapped it around me.

"You sure you'll be up for that?"

"Yeah. I'll be fine."

Before I started to walk away, my mom rested her hand on my shoulder. "What you did earlier today was very brave. I am so proud to have a daughter as powerful as you. Be careful though. I'm sensing a weakness within your abilities after you created that enormous forcefield. Unfortunately, we are limited, Esther."

"Okay, Mom." I grabbed my book bag and walked out of my room. I walked through the kitchen and out the door, over to the bike rack. I unchained my bike and got on it. I pushed on the pedals and started pedaling down our driveway and then down the long, winding road to the park. Leaves fell everywhere as the sky started to get darker.

I parked my bike next to a blue one. I sighed, wishing I was there alone. I closed my eyes, turning myself invisible so I didn't have to socialize. I walked down the hill towards the creek, the wind pushing my hair back and the cold wrapped around my body. I took in the refreshing breeze and the beautiful atmosphere around me. Suddenly, I stopped in my tracks, noticing someone sitting near the creek. I was just about to turn around until I heard the sound of someone crying. I looked back at the figure as I started to walk closer to the creek. The crying got louder as I approached.

"I'll never be good enough..." I heard the familiar voice yell through his sobs. He held his legs close to his chest and underneath his frayed t-shirt, I could see his slender body expanding during each inhale. Suddenly, the waves in the creek grew more rapid and rocks levitated around Damion.

I sat next to him even though he couldn't see me. I looked at the rocks around him, furrowing my brows as I tried to understand how they were floating. His cries became louder and the waves crashed even more. Suddenly, all of the rocks flew into the water violently with a splash. I wanted to say something or just anything to make him feel better but I knew I couldn't.

"I should just be a..." He sobbed more, clenching his fist to the point where his veins were noticeable. "Creator... Start a new life..."

I gasped, getting up quickly. I stepped back and as I did, I tripped over a stick. I fell to the ground, making the leaves around me crunch. I looked at Damion. He was looking around, tears falling down his cheeks. Suddenly, he made eye contact with me. His eyes were never this blue before. They were almost the color of an electric tide.

"I know you're there... Show yourself."

My eyes widened. I got up quickly and ran, not caring if I was making noise. I ran up the hill towards my bike. I touched it, using all of my power to make it invisible too. It took so much energy to make another object invisible. Once my bike turned, I got on it and pedaled away.

I slammed the house door open, walking into the kitchen, passed my mom and into my room, slamming the door behind me.

"Esther? Honey?" I heard my mother ask.

I locked my door, leaning my back against the door as tears started to pour down my cheeks. I slid down onto the floor, pulling my knees up to my face. He couldn't be a Clockwork. He just couldn't. I didn't want anything bad to happen to him. No wonder he was so different from everyone else. The electrical charge? Maybe it happens frequently? He was the one that saved the people on the roller coaster. But what powers did he have? He must have a unique set.

How would I talk to him about it? How would I tell him I was the same way? What if I was mistaken? I cried even more, unable to figure out what to do.

"Mom!" I yelled, trying to unlock the door.

My mom rushed in, immediately noticing I was crying and she pulled me into a tight hug. "What's wrong, honey?"

I wiped the tears from my cheeks. "He's a Clockwork!" I yelled, trying to stop myself from crying. Whenever my emotions were acting up, there was never a way to control them.

My mom sighed, looking at the floor. "What is making you upset about this situation? I'm being a mom now… I want to help you through this, sweetie."

I looked into her bright, green eyes. "I'm scared. I'm just scared for us. A part of me wished he was human so you wouldn't care if I was friends with him. But you're telling me he is dangerous but I honestly don't believe you, Mom. Whenever we touch, electricity thrives in my skin."

"He's gonna make a big impact on your life, Esther."

"I understand that. But *how*?" I yearned.

"I don't know, Esther. Sadly, I don't exactly know what his abilities are, but I'm sure you'll figure that out soon. And that electrical shock... It happens when another Clockwork or Creator touches one another."

"Why didn't I know about the shock?"

"Most people dismiss that factor."

"Why didn't you just tell me this before?" I scoffed, quickly standing up.

"I'm not an open book, Esther! I can't tell you everything. You have to figure your life out on your own." My mother stood up.

"Whatever. Get out of my room."

My mom sighed, walking slowly and calmly out of my room. She stopped at my door, turning to look at me. "I do it for you, Esther." And with that, she walked away.

I bit my lip, sucking in immense amounts of air. My heart yearned for the simple fact I once again made my mother upset. I knew I would keep disappointing my mother but I couldn't help it. I wanted to pursue Damion. I wanted to confront him to see who he was. He mentioned becoming a Creator and the curiosity that surged through my blood-rushing veins wanted to learn more. He wanted to be a Creator, but why? What hurt him in his life for him to wish that upon himself? I was always saddened by living in seclusion and of my father's passing, but not once did I ever think about becoming a Creator. I didn't know much about the Creators but it is almost like façade to label oneself as a Creator. The main goal is to essentially create a better life for themselves but at what cost? From what I witnessed today with that hooded Creator tinkering with rides, I grew to understand more of what it meant to be a Creator. If they truly believed harming human civilization would fix their crushed souls, they were terribly mistaken.

After that thought, I received a pulsating sensation on my wrist that slowly moved its way up to my shoulder and then it began to coat itself throughout the entire surface of my skin. I could not see what was happening, nor could I register what any of it meant. I stood up, running to my mirror in a panic. I gasped for air as the tingling sensation moved its way up to my throat and then it burned at my eyes. Once the agitating furor reached my eyes, I immediately vanished in front of my mirror.

"What the hell?" I whispered, analyzing my empty reflection. I became invisible but this time it wasn't because I was overwhelmed with emotions, it wasn't because I was hurt or passionate about anything… This happened for a reason unknown to me. I usually cannot control my invisibility if I was raging with intense emotions but these emotions that submerged my invisibility were not mine… I could feel the power coming from an unknown source, controlling my invisibility as if I was nothing, only a mere puppet. I closed my eyes, trying to focus on becoming invisible but I felt resistance. I have never in my life felt a resistance such as this one. I kept concentrating, gritting my teeth to become visible once again. I opened my eyes, hoping maybe I would have gotten lucky but to no avail, I was still disappeared from the regular reality of the common, everyday life. I glanced around my room, noticing several purple forcefields illuminating in every corner of my room.

"Purple?" I whispered. The regular color of my forcefields were like a shimmery golden glow, but now they are illuminating in violet.

"Mom, can you come here for a second!" I yelled loud enough for her to hear. As soon as those words escaped my lips, all of the forcefields in my room disappeared and I was once again visible in my mirror. I could see my thick, scrabbly brows furrowed in the mirror in confusion. The sensation that surfaced over my skin was also gone and I felt normal again but that did not explain what happened to me and why it happened.

"Yes honey?" my mom said, opening my door. She peeked around the door to stare at me and she noticed my expression. "What happened?"

"I… I don't know." I stared in the mirror with my head tilted to the side. "Something odd happened to me…I felt like I was being controlled. Like, I had no control over my own abilities." I turned to stare at my mother in confusion.

"Wha—what did it feel like?" she asked.

"Something strong… Something that is unknown to me."

"I don't understand, Esther. Are you sure that it may be because your abilities are weakening after illuminating that large forcefield back at the fair?" She stared at me intently, studying my facial expressions. "That happens, you know. Using your abilities too much can weaken them. The amount of power that you had to derive from your soul to create that large, invisible forcefield was enough to send a ripple of confusion within you. Clockworks haven't had a true reason to use their abilities against demented forces such as you did at the fair today. The world today has its flaws, but the humans have their own forces to prevent crime. We aren't really needed so when we are born, we probably aren't born with the amount of abilities we needed to have in the past."

"So, I'm not powerful?" I said, trying to ignore the sharp pain that jolted in my heart when she said that. I wanted to be powerful. I wanted to be spectacular.

"Maybe Esther…You were born from me. And I'm sorry to say this, but me as a Boundary and only being able to see the future when my soul wants me to know the future, I'm considered weak. I don't have those ongoing abilities that the Fixers have, the Militants, and much more labels. You being born from me may have some weird impact on the strength of your abilities than the Clockworks that are born from powerful parents."

I inhaled a large breath of air, trying to comprehend what my mother was trying to tell me. "Why didn't we know about this until now?"

She shrugged her shoulders. "You only played around with your abilities when you were a child, Esther. What you did today was remarkable and required a great deal of strength. You need time to rest after something like that." She walked over to me, cupping my face in her warm, soft hands. She stared into my eyes with her forest-green eyes and smiled at me with large, pink lips. "You saved those people today without hesitation, my daughter. You found the good in your heart, your natural birth right as a Clockwork, and saved them. I'm proud of you, Sweetie. Unfortunately, nowadays, some Clockworks would've turned a blind eye to the attack and saved themselves. But you, you did more. I love you, darling."

I smiled, gingerly resting my head in my mother's hands. "I love you too, Mom. I'm so sorry about every reckless, terrible thing I've said to you today. I need to understand that you know, we may come from weaker blood, but that's fine. I can't be angry at you for not being able to control when you can see the future. I know Damion may look bad in your eyes, but he's shown me nothing but kindness as well. He cares to know me. He also has been like… my only friend. I truly believe in my soul he isn't a Creator. He wasn't the one that broke the rides on purpose today. In fact, I have an itching feeling he was the one that saved the rollercoaster from killing the people on the ground. If he did what I did, and helped

39

save those innocent people today, then there is no way he could be a selfish Creator."

She nodded her head slowly. "Whatever you feel like is right in your life, Esther... Follow it. I have to trust you to make decisions on your own."

"I do want to confront him at school, though. I need to know what is making him upset. Maybe if I expose myself, he'll come out to me as well."

"Just be careful that no one sees you two, or overhears you. The last thing we need is a problem with the Exols."

"I know, Mom. You can *trust* me. I'll do the right thing."

I was standing in a large, vast meadow. Ahead of me was a pedestal with a large, frayed novel sitting upon it. I furrowed my brows, trudging my way through the large sunflowers and violet roses. The sun cascaded its majestic glow, coruscating the vast meadow with spectacular beauty. I looked down, realizing I was wearing a lavender gown that dragged across the scattered flowers that brought kind tranquility to the ground I walked upon. I heard the overturning of tides in the far distant, knowing I was near an ocean. The smell of sea salt burned at my nose, but in mere happiness I breathed in more because for the first time in my life, I was near an ocean.

I finally made my way to the pedestal. I put my hand on the brown, leather-banded novel. As soon as my hand touched the cover, scenes of life flickered before my eyes. I saw the growth of roses with dew seeping out of its green stems. I saw large, 100-foot trees growing rapidly as if I was viewing a short documentary about the growth of life. I smiled giddily, eager to view more of the magnificent scenes. I saw the tides of the ocean, moving consecutively with the moon's rays. The scene changed to beneath the surface as if I were swimming in the ocean. I could view a humongous marbled palace that was covered with seaweed and ocean-life swam wickedly around it. Everything was so fast-moving that it was hard for me to keep up with the voluptuousness scenes. It was an intoxicating invite to a world unknown by the mere eye. I was being drawn in to beauty that I could not stray from.

Suddenly, the scene stopped all at once and I was now standing in the same meadow, but this time it was completely dried out. It was dawn. The book in front of me was nothing but ash. A gust of wind blew my hair back and the remnants of the novel flew away. I tried to grab the pieces in a hurry, but I was too late. I wanted to see the beauty once more, but now I could never see them again.

In the distance, hooded figures lurched out of the shadows of the trees. They surrounded the whole perimeter of the field.

"Esther Green," a hooded figure in red stepped in front of the rest of them. The voice was familiar. "Nice to see you again. I see clearly the curiosity in your eyes. I know that it's protecting you."

"Protecting me from *what?*" I asked.

He laughed, throwing his head back as he did so. I still couldn't view his face from where I was standing. "From *me*, obviously. Brilliance showed me its beauty once, but never again. It knows what I want. I didn't meet the cut… But you, Esther. It has shown you a multitude of times… Its glorious, monumental power. Every time you sleep, it keeps scurrying right back to you more than the rest. It's blocking my ability to reach your mind, Dear."

"I don't understand?" I meekly stated.

Once again, the ground began to rupture and the scene began to melt. The hooded figures instantly disappeared and once the scene corroded away, I shot up in my bed.

"Again?" I stated, scratching the back of my head. "Is this a sign or is this my mind playing tricks with me?"

I laid back down in my bed, pulling my covers over my shoulders. I snuggled my body into my bed, closing my eyes. Maybe it was one of those odd reoccurring dreams. Maybe I was eating something strange before bed. As each thought occurred, it still did not add up to what the strange dreams meant. I couldn't stay up all night trying to figure it out. I needed to sleep.

The next day at school, I sat in Mrs. Banks classroom. Damion wasn't here. I glanced back at his desk, studying the empty seat.

I thought it was very unusual that he wasn't here, since he hasn't been at my school for longer than a week. I thought maybe he could be sick. Or maybe he needed a personal day with how upset he sounded Saturday night. I was upset because I was eager to confront him about everything. But I couldn't.

"Esther, please pay attention to the board," Mrs. Banks said with an annoyed posture. I stared at the board, scribbling in my notes.

Maybe he would come tomorrow.
But he didn't.
Maybe he would come the next day.
But he didn't.
Maybe he would come next week.
But he didn't.
Maybe he would come the week after that.
But to no surprise, he didn't.

It was almost three weeks later and Damion still hasn't come to school. I felt alone and almost betrayed. Even though I knew him for a short amount of time, I felt like he should've given me a reason why he wasn't coming to school. I was scared if he did become a Creator and whatever happened next, it would be unknown to anyone what he may do as one.

My birthday was tomorrow and for once, I wasn't excited for it. It just felt like another pointless day in the year. My mother was excited, but I couldn't reciprocate the same feelings. I pretended I was excited for my birthday to make her happy, but in all reality, I was eager to get tomorrow started so it could end sooner and I wouldn't have to hear about my birthday again.

I sat in the lunchroom, gingerly picking at my salad with my crochet satchel attached to my hip. I watched as each student passed me without any acknowledging looks or anyone noticing that I was sitting all alone. Usually at my school, anyone who sits alone is made fun of vigorously. But I guess no one cared to pick on me today. The only person I feared that could potentially bother me today was Becca. There was no way I could be able to handle her constant, self-loathing annoyance.

I only felt like that simply because I felt alone. Again. Damion came in to my life, started a whirlwind only to leave without a word or a confirmation of what even happened that Saturday night. He didn't even know that I knew about him. He also didn't know that I do actually want to be his friend. We were like the same, but also different. Although, that was enough to draw me in to those ocean eyes. The same ones that seemed like rippling electricity when he cried. I wanted to know more about him, considering he was the first Clockwork that I ever encountered that weren't just distant relatives.

"Hey, Esther. Why the long face?" Becca's voiced echoed through my ears as she approached me from behind. She placed her hands on my shoulders and slowly brought in her face to whisper in my ear. "All alone, aren't you?"

"Becca, stop. I'm not in the mood for your immaturity today." I smacked her hands off my shoulders. I got up, leaving my lunch on the table. My crochet bag slung at my hips at the rapid movement. I stared into her menacing green eyes as she smiled wickedly at me. "Seriously, I've had enough. I'm so sick of you blaming me for something you'll never be able to understand. It's been a long time. Get over it." I snapped, bumping her shoulder as I walked passed her.

"Where you going, Esther?" she asked, laughing with her friends. "Can't take the attention I'm actually giving you?"

I turned back to look at her. "It's not the attention I want." I busted open the doors of the cafeteria and hurried to the girls' restroom. I felt tears welling in my eyes. I couldn't handle her. I couldn't handle school right now. I couldn't handle the fact my birthday was tomorrow and it's another year my father couldn't celebrate it with me. I couldn't handle the fact that I lost a potential friend that I actually could relate to. All of the emotions that consumed me were drastically overwhelming.

I kicked open a bathroom stall, slamming the door shut and locking it behind me. I plopped down on the toilet seat and cupped my face in my hands and cried. I continued crying until my eyes were burning with what seemed like the sensation of pepper spray.

I heard the door of the girls' restroom open and Becca's laughter with her friends bounced off the walls.

"Did you see her face?" I heard Becca say to her friends. "She looked like she was about to cry!"

The girls laughed.

I gritted my teeth. My sadness quickly turned into a boiling volcano, readying to burst.

"I mean, like come on... Who does she even think she is? Right? She thinks she's the only one that's ever been sad... or alone before... It's because she's so spoiled. Her mother, I swear, spoils her so much it's ridiculous." The more she rambled, the more I wanted to punch her in the throat. "When we use to have playdates, her mom would always watch us and never leave poor little Esther out of her sight... It was sad. Truly. I can't even imagine how her mom is like now with her husband being dead. She is probably always on her back." Her friends chuckled and continued to make fun of me.

At this point, I had enough. I didn't care about the Exols finding out that I used my abilities in front of them. And I certainly didn't care about the pain I was about to cause Becca.

As all the anger coursed through my veins, I stood up from the toilet and kicked the stall open. Her and her friends quickly stopped talking. I stood in front of them, daggers reflecting in my eyes.

"What was that?" I asked, my voice quavering with absolute rage.

Becca crossed her arms with an eyebrow raised. "Only the truth, baby Esther. Oh, so perfect Esther..."

I gritted my teeth and walked up to Becca. I simultaneously smacked her across the face and my hand stung with prickly sensations. She looked at me, stunned that I would even do something like that.

"I've had *enough*, Becca. I'm done fighting with you."

She bit her lip and brought up her fist, colliding it into my jaw. I doubled back, clutching my jaw as it began to swell with soreness.

"Yeah, get her Becca!" one of her friends said, cheering her on.

I grabbed Becca's hair and yanked it, pulling her head down to me. I brought up my fist and sent it spiraling through the air, rocketing my fist straight into her nose. She collapsed to the ground, blood oozing from her nostrils. She pinched her nose quickly, allowing the stinging to subside. Once I could tell she got her pain level under control, she pounced up and sent her fist straight into my cheekbone. My face swelled with more pulsating sensations, but I ignored it. I focused on creating a clear forcefield around the surface of my body. I brought up my leg, kicking her in the hip. She also didn't let that stop her from trying to send more swings my way.

Suddenly, a teacher opened the door of the girls' restroom and quickly noticed the scene in front of her. I quickly released my focus on the forcefield.

"Girls, office. NOW." She grabbed both of mine and Becca's arms violently, and walked us straight out of the bathroom and down the hall to the principal's office.

Once we arrived to the principal's office, Becca and I were forced to sit apart from each other.

"Now, can anyone tell me what actually happened in there?" Principal Foster snapped.

"She smacked me, Mr. Foster… She smacked me first and I *had* to defend myself!" Becca said, playing the victim card like she had never bullied me before.

"And I was simply sick of her shit," I said, rolling my eyes.

Principal Foster clasped his hands on the desk and leaned back in his office chair. "Well, Esther. Did you hit Becca first?"

"Yes."

"And did Becca hit you after that?"

"Yes."

"No, I didn't!" Becca yelled.

Principal Foster brought up his hand to silence Becca. "Becca, please. We need to make this as painless of a process as possible. I can clearly see a red mark and a slight scrape on Esther's cheekbone and jawbone. You defended yourself, admit to that."

I furrowed my brows, quickly retaliating. "*Defended* herself? What about the fact that I *defended* myself because I'm sick of her treating me like I'm nothing!"

"Esther, please. I'm trying to get to the bottom of this. I am very well aware of what is going on here. I know you two were friends awhile back before Becca's parents passed away. And to my understanding, Esther, you weren't too nice to her after that."

I shook my head, sliding back in the chair. "No, Mr. Foster. She was mean to me because I didn't go to her parents' funeral."

"And why didn't you, Esther?"

"Because she's a *shitty* person," Becca added.

"Becca, no more swearing or answering first. Please, and thank you. Now, Esther... Continue," Mr. Foster said.

"My mom didn't want me to go. She was too hurt about losing her friend... Becca's mother. And she also didn't want to expose me to death at a young age. She was just trying to protect me. She thought I wasn't ready yet." I stared at my lacey shirt, tugging at the frayed edges to avoid eye contact with Becca and Mr. Foster.

"Well, that's because your mom baby's you, Esther... You lost your best friend because your mom controls everything you do... You ever looked at it like that?" Becca snapped.

"Becca, you don't understand. My mom has her reasons to be scared and protective over me. Although it's really annoying, I can't help it. I love my mother. You're judging me for a point in my life that I frankly didn't have any say in. I'm sorry I hurt you and I wasn't there for you when you needed me the most." I felt the tears starting to sting at my eyes.

Becca stared at me intently. For a second, I thought she was capable of forgiving me. "Whatever," she said. I spoke too soon.

"Girls, I hope you know that none of you are leaving this room until this is settled. Becca, Esther is trying to reach out to you right now. Listen to understand, not to respond."

46

"Becca, I still care about you even after all of the suffering you put me through. I can't imagine what it is like losing both of your parents in a horrific accident without ever getting a second chance to say goodbye to them... Especially at a young age. I'm sorry, Becca. I really am." I started sobbing. I tried so hard to keep a badass image but it seemed pointless at this point. I wanted this to be over.

"Esther..." Her voice croaked. To my surprise, she reached over to gently touch my shoulder. "I'm sorry."

I stared at her through my blurry vision. I was shocked. "Becca, I don't want to keep fighting like this anymore. I miss having you as a friend." That was true. I did secretly miss having her as a friend. She was probably the only human that I could tolerate when I was younger.

"I won't bother you anymore, Esther. It's pointless. It's stupid." Becca stated.

"Well..." Mr. Foster stood up in his chair, stretching. "Now that this is somewhat reassuring you two won't brawl again... I still have to issue you both an out of school suspension for promoting violence on school property. I'll need to call each of your parents in the other room and inform them of your suspensions." He left the room and closed the door behind him.

I turned to look at Becca. "Do you really mean what you said?"

"Yes, Esther. After Mr. Foster told me to listen to understand, not to respond... I actually listened to what you had to say for once. Yeah, it sucks that your mom didn't let you come to my parents' funeral, but I shouldn't have made it this big of a deal. It was fun at first... To make you feel how I felt during that time. I only planned to treat you like shit for a little bit but then it ended up escalating and then it turned into this." She gestured to the air.

"I know my mom can be a little overwhelming sometimes... But she's still my mom. I do wish I could've been there though. I really do."

Becca smiled, making more blood ooze out of her nose. "Friends?"

I laughed. "Friends."

Chapter 3: He Returned

Mr. Foster was not able to get ahold of my mother and inform her that I was suspended. I figured she was just busy at her desk job in the neighboring city of Erin Springs. After my father passed away, my mother had to take up more hours at her job to support us.

I walked down the sidewalk as the first snowflakes trickled down, resting on the bridge of my nose. I blew cold air in and out, watching the steam manifest in front of me. A gust of harsh wind bit at my cheeks and my exposed chest. I snuggled my coat tighter around me and pulled my crochet bag closer to my hip. Although it was frigidly cold, I wanted head to the park and allow my mind to be at ease. I needed to reflect on the events from today and contemplate how to explain to my mother that me getting suspended and fighting Becca was almost like a positive occurrence for the day rather than a negative one.

As I began to enter the sidewalk that led to the bridge of the park, I noticed the familiar bicycle chained to the silver bars. My heart skipped a thousand beats, realizing that Damion was here. And now, I may have my chance to speak to him. I ran across the bridge covering a tiny stream and at the corner of the park, I saw the familiar shaggy black hair sitting under the willow tree.

"Damion!" I yelled as I was running, getting closer to him with each stride.

He looked up from his fetal position and flashed me a set of white teeth. "Esther," he murmured.

I was finally standing in front of him, unsure how to respond or what questions to ask first. I noticed he was studying me, his eyes starting at my feet all the way up to my face. It was almost as if he had questions for me as well. "I... I..." I stammered. "Where were you?" I finally was able to release the words from my mouth.

He chuckled softly, patting down on the lightly snow-covered grass beside him. "Sit down, Esther. Rest yourself."

I tugged at my coat, pulling it closer to my face as if I could hide my excitement and confusion. I sat down beside him. "Are you going to answer my question?" I stared into his ocean-tide eyes.

"I only had to rest my head for a while. I contemplated moving again with my family also. My mother told me it wasn't good for me to be here."

I furrowed my brows. "Why would she say something like that?"

Damion shook his head in anguish. "You wouldn't be able to understand, Esther. I wish you could understand and I wish we could..." His voice trailed off.

"Damion, I know what you are and what you're a part of. You don't need to invite me to your pity party." I stood up quickly. "If you won't tell me yourself, I'll show you what I can do." Instantaneously, I created a vibrant, violet-colored forcefield and I illuminated the forcefield over us and the willow tree. The snow that fell from the sky rested itself gently over my forcefield, blocking us from the snow that touched our skin. I studied his facial expressions and a small smile pulled at the corner of his lips.

"Beautiful," he whispered in bewilderment.

"They use to be golden. But now they range from a dark violet to a light lavender. My mother says it's because I'm a half-blood, so I'm weaker than the rest of the Beings within the Provinces."

"It's fine that you're a half-blood. Your forcefields are remarkable, Esther. What's your other ability?" He questioned as he leaned in, eager to see more.

I smiled. "Let me know if you can see me." I closed my eyes, concentrating on the sumptuous sensation of becoming invisible. I focused on my body and imagined it slowly sinking away out of view. I did it. I was invisible.

"I don't see you anymore," I heard Damion say.

I laughed, dissipating my focus on being invisible and I allowed myself to reappear. "Invisibility and forcefields is my specialty. The Exols label my set of abilities as a Protector. My mother is a Boundary, she can see the future and know what anyone is hiding from her. Like, feeling emotions and whatnot. She's aging though, so unfortunately her abilities aren't as vibrant as they were before. She can barely see anything until it's the very last second now. It's sad, truly. Watching her wither away from who she truly is…" I didn't mean to become emotional but as I spoke, tears began to trickle down my cheeks. I was finally able to release my emotions to someone who would understand.

"It's okay, Esther." Damion stood up and wrapped his arms around me, holding me tightly in a genuinely warm embrace. "I wish abilities were forever, too. It's terrible what we have to go through."

I sniffled and began to pull away from his embrace while wiping my eyes with the sleeve of my coat. "I'm sorry. I didn't mean to cry in front of you." I released my hold on the forcefield around us.

He laughed softly, staring into my hazel eyes. "Don't apologize for the way you feel. Bottling up emotions inside for too long can lead to someone's demise. Don't be that person. Don't bottle things up where every breath, you end up sucking in your tears. It's okay to *feel*."

Awkwardly, I shook my head and wrapped my arms around my body, eager to change the subject. "So, what are yours?"

He grinned. "What makes you think I'm a Clockwork?"

I laughed. "Maybe the fact that I never mentioned I was one. So, if you weren't a Clockwork, how would you know a Clockwork is a part of the Provinces?"

"Ahh, I see. You're clever, Esther. I should've known." He smirked. "So, you're ready to see what I can do?"

I laughed. "Um, yeah. That's why I'm standing here, isn't it? I showed you mine, now you need to show me yours."

"Okay, get behind me." He shoved me gently behind him and walked out near a park bench that was placed in front of a stream. There was no one in the park. He looked back at me, standing next to the bench. "You ready?" he called out.

"Yeah!" I yelled so he could hear me.

Simultaneously, he grabbed the handlebar of the bench and gritted his teeth, extending his arm further into the air. Sounds of crackling metal bounced off the trees of the park and his hidden muscles began to bulge from the sleeve of his sweatshirt. Finally, the park bench was ripped from its screwed position and he held it high in the air. He threw the bench down and clapped his hands together. "So, how was that?" He asked with a goofy grin.

"Intimidating," I said with a small smile. "Show me what else you can do."

He whipped his body around, staring back at the broken bench. Instantly, the park bench began to raise off the ground. He jolted his body forward, still standing in the same spot as the bench whipped ten yards away from him, breaking upon impact. "What about that?" he said, turning to me with a goofy smile plastered across his face.

"Um…" I began, trying to playfully embarrass him. "Beating up a park bench is all you can achieve?" I crossed my arms.

After I said that, suddenly I felt the ground beneath me begin to vibrate rapidly. I glanced up, watching all of the snow holt itself in midair. The trees in the park violently shook and I could hear branches breaking and the roots of the trees swayed underneath the rumbling ground. The water from the stream began to lift itself in the air and swirled violently around like a tornado. Leaves from the trees began to break off and flew quickly in the air. The whole park was moving. Suddenly, it all stopped abruptly and the snow fell quickly to the ground. The water violently crashed itself back into the rocks of the stream. The park was motionless and quiet again other than the intricate snowflakes gracefully falling to the ground.

"Damion, you're *powerful*," I whispered in awe.

He smiled, walking over to me and sat down on the ground next to the willow tree. I sat down also. "I wouldn't have shown off so much if you didn't tempt me," he said.

"That was amazing," I said, bewildered. "What can your parents do?" I was eager to know.

He shrugged his shoulders, resting himself against the bark of the tree. "That's the thing… My parents aren't apart of the Provinces. They don't have any abilities."

I furrowed my brows in confusion. "That's impossible… I never heard of that happening before."

"Esther, there's a lot you don't know about who you and I are. Everything we can do. What we can achieve. I don't know how I have the information I do, since my parents can't help me with being a Clockwork. I learned everything on my own. Without them." He looked down at the grass, plucking a strand from the ground. He gingerly brushed off the snow of the singular strand. "That's why we fight a lot… That's why there's a lot of misunderstandings… And that's why I lack the eagerness to hope for a better future."

I bit my lip, trying to concentrate on everything he was saying. "I was there that day… When you said you wanted to be a Creator."

He nodded his head in reluctance. "Yeah… That wasn't a good night for me. They were mad at me for saving the people on the rollercoaster. They said that it was dangerous for me to expose myself like that. They said the Creator that was labeled as a Fixer there, that broke the rides could've alerted the Exols about me for a larger prize. They told me most Militants with telekinesis couldn't perform something powerful like that. I don't know what they meant by that but I know I do things… differently than other Clockworks. I feel like an outcast, to be honest. I feel dangerous sometimes. Like, I have no control." His voice became hoarse and he sucked back tears that brimmed at the corners of his eyes. "I've hurt my parents before, Esther. I've hurt kids at all the schools I've been too. I've destroyed plenty of things out of rage." His voice was shaky now. "I'm destructive."

I stared at him intently. Gingerly, I picked up my hand and rested it on his shoulders. "I don't believe that one bit, Damion."

He exhaled a large breath of air. "Maybe this will be good for me." He turned to look me in the eyes. "That I met you… I have someone who understands what it means to be a Clockwork, gears that are stationed in time. You're extraordinary, Esther. I want to be friends with you. I want to be in your life. I have an attraction towards you that I never had with anyone before." He grabbed my hand and I felt the same electrifying spark. "And now I know that this spark has a greater meaning than just two Clockworks meeting. I felt a light spark with other Clockworks my parents introduced to me. But this, this is different. I want to know why it's different. I don't think we met by mistake, Esther. I am no Boundary, but I have a feeling we will both be impactful on one another."

"If you knew about the spark, why didn't you stop to think that I was a Clockwork when you touched me before?" I asked.

"I wanted to be sure before I accused you of being something you weren't and risk exposing myself to a regular human."

"So, what does this mean now?" I asked.

He chuckled softly, resting his head on the bark. "We should meet here every day. Tell each other events about the day, talk about the way we feel, our dreams and aspirations. The world is our oyster now, Esther. We don't have to hide from each other. I want to show you more about us and what Clockworks can do. I want to share my knowledge with you. I have all of this information bottled up in my head from an unknown source that I need to share with you."

"Well, I'm excited to learn more, Damion," I said. "I know my mom keeps a lot about us a secret."

"Yeah, I could pick up on that when I was at your house after the rollercoaster accident. When you were unconscious, she kept on glaring at me. I don't know if she knows that I'll expose the real world to you or not, but you deserve to know everything. Even I may not know everything, but we can find that out together."

"Yeah, I'm trying to get her on the Damion fan parade. I'm working on her but we'll see how that goes. Somehow I have to muster of the courage and let her know that I'm suspended if she hasn't already heard the voicemail."

"You're *suspended*, how?" Damion asked.

"Becca and I got into a fight. We beat each other up pretty bad. But on a positive note, I think Becca and I are sort of friends now."

"Well, that's good. I thought your guys' hatred towards one another was pretty stupid."

I tried to ignore the fact that stung a little bit when he said that. "Yeah, same. But I think it's over now. But my mom may not be that hard on me since tomorrow's my birthday."

"Your birthday is tomorrow?"

"Yeah."

"Well, thanks for letting me know. I might get you something." Damion chuckled.

"No, please don't." I pleaded. "Birthdays just aren't the same to me anymore. I wish we could stop celebrating them to be honest."

"Please, Esther." Damion scoffed. "Be happy tomorrow. Let the day take you. Don't control it."

"I mean, I guess you're right." I began to stand up. "Well, I need to get home before my mom gets home."

"Same time tomorrow?" Damion asked, gesturing to the willow tree.

I smiled. "Same time tomorrow."

I got home quickly, realizing my mom's rusty car was parked in the driveway of our trailer. I sighed as I trudged up the hill towards the front door. My hands were a little shaky and I was nervous to see my mother. I didn't receive any texts or phone calls from her about my suspension. But even though to some people that may be a good sign, it was a terrible sign from my mother. She was probably too angry to talk to me through an electronic device and she wants to save the ridicule for in person.

I opened up the squeaky screen door and then I propped open the main door. "Hello?" I whispered quietly. No answer.

I quietly tiptoed through the kitchen and down the hallway that only had two doors: my room and the bathroom. My mother's room was connected to the living room on the other side of the trailer. I finally reached my door and I gently opened it up so my mother wouldn't hear me. As I finally opened my door, my heart dropped straight into my stomach. She was sitting on my bed.

"Hello, Esther," my mother said with an annoyed look plastered on her face.

"Er... Um... Hello," I said, rubbing the back of my head. "How was your day at work?"

"Fantastic. Just fantastic." I could hear her sarcasm.

"Well, that's good." My legs were shaking.

"So, do you wanna tell me what happened at school today?" she asked.

"Oh, funny you asked... I actually had a great day at school... Becca and I became friends again."

"Oh yeah, is that so?"

"Yup."

"So why did I receive a call from the school that you're suspended for getting into a fight with Becca?"

"Oh, that's odd." I sat my satchel down on my dresser, avoiding eye contact with her.

"I don't need to be a Clockwork right now to know you're lying to me, Esther. Did you use your abilities to fight her?"

56

"I only used them to block some of her punches."

She shook her head in disappointment. "Do you understand the consequences of your decisions? Do you understand that the Exols could get involved if they knew you could've risked exposing the Provinces?"

"Yes."

"NO, YOU DON'T UNDERSTAND!" my mother screamed, barring her teeth at me. "If you continue to do things like this, Esther... I will personally lead the Exols here to punish you."

"Punish me? Aren't the Exols supposed to be peaceful? I mean, that's what you told me about them."

"Exols are labeled as being peaceful. But don't let their god-like complexions fool you. I got a lot of shit for falling in love with your father. Sometimes I wonder if they have a reason for your father dying of failed lungs and me losing my abilities so quickly."

"Mom, how would they even be able to do that?" I said in disbelief. "This stuff just happens sometimes. You can't stop it." I never met an Exol before but it was definitely a dream of mine to be able to meet one. When I was a child, I always wanted to be an Exol. Their power was intoxicating and riveting. I always wanted to be as beautiful as them as well.

"I don't know, Esther. But that's beside the point. You need to watch your back and not draw too much attention to yourself."

"Okay, I understand. Can you like, leave me alone now?" I asked.

"Whatever, Esther." My mom stood up from my bed and left the room shaking her head at me. She closed my door behind her.

I sighed, plopping onto my bed and I stared up at my ceiling. "It'll get better." I promised myself. I replayed the events of today back through my head and I remembered Damion's eyes and his little grin. I was excited to see him again tomorrow.

I ignored my mother for the rest of the night and relaxed in my bedroom. Tomorrow was my birthday and my attitude towards it was beginning to change. Even though my mother and I were in the midst of fighting at the moment, I was curious to know if she was still going to get me a gift. I was also curious to know how Damion would react to my birthday as well.

As the shadows of the night began to dance in my room and the day quickly passed me by, I turned off the lamp in my bedroom. I pulled my covers close to my chest and closed my eyes. Before I knew it, I went into a deep slumber.

Everything around me was dark. I felt extremely weary, my eyes struggling to stay open. I looked around, trying to find a way out. Suddenly, something glowed in the distance. I ran to it, my bare feet slapping against the ground. I came to a stop, holding up my hand as I shielded the light from my eyes. Once the light calmed down, I realized in front of me was a mirror. I walked towards it, fear rising in my chest. My reflection was watching me, sending a shiver down my spine. Suddenly, my left arm moved in the mirror, but not outside of the mirror. A flame emerged from my hand and sent small heatwaves throughout my body. In seconds, my reflection snapped its fingers and the fire disappeared. My hand flipped around in the mirror as if it were possessed. Suddenly water rushed out of my palms. I looked down, realizing I was standing in a river... A river I created.

In the reflection, my head twisted back and forth, sending pain throughout my body. Suddenly, lightning strikes circled around me and the sound of thunder echoed throughout my ears. A small twister came my way, trees spun around everywhere and I looked as if I were the most powerful person in the world. Suddenly my reflection started to age, adding wrinkles on my body and face. My eyes became hollow, not holding their true beauty anymore. My teeth fell out one by one into the water, blood pouring out of my mouth. It was a gruesome sight. I looked around, my frail body aching. I found a rock floating in midair and I grabbed it in a hurry. I threw the rock with all of my might, breaking the glass.

"Esther," I heard the same familiar voice from all of my pervious dreams. "Don't be afraid of the power... Embrace it." In the remaining shards of glass, I could see the familiar man standing behind me, his arms placed gingerly on my shoulders.

"I don't want that," I stated dryly.

He let out a laugh. "Yes, you do. I'm always here, Esther. In your dreams. I know what you want... I know what you dream about... I know there's a boy you think about. I can't ever see his face or hear his name, though. It drives me insane." He crept his hands up to my neck and back down to my shoulders. He traced his hands down to my spine, feeling the texture of my soft skin. "You want to be loved. You want to be powerful. You want to be a hero. All things Brilliance desires. I think you can help me find it."

"Don't touch me," I said, fear rising in my voice.

"Esther, is there any reason why it's so damn easy to get in your head? I haven't been able to ever get in the mind of the Exol Child. I tried countless times but he tricks me. He shows me darkness and I thought it was just the way his mind works... But I soon came to realize it was a defense mechanism and that he is completely unaware of my existence." Dante let out a laugh. "And he is also unaware of Brilliance. He knows of a power greater than we all know, but he cannot seem to surmise what it is. Same with the Spiritual-Human. I was able to get in his dreams a couple of times until he realized who I was. He knows about Brilliance and he's looking for It. But because he's looking, Brilliance is hiding from him. But you, Brilliance seems to be whispering to you. As soon as Brilliance knows I'm watching, It shuts me out like I'm a virus."

I backed away from him and turned to stare at him. "Have you ever considered the fact that you may be a virus?"

"Yes, that's what my mother called me before I exploded her head into little tiny pieces."

I scoffed in disbelief, trying to hide my fear. "You killed your own mother?"

He grabbed my arm as I tried to step away from him. He pulled me into his body and he stared at me with daggers. "Yes, and I'll do it again and again and again. She thought I was a nuisance because I was a mass-manipulator."

"You're sick," I said through gritted teeth.

"You don't understand what I want, now do you, Esther?" He gripped my shoulders painfully. "I want to know everything. All of the knowledge about not only Earth, but the cosmos. Space. Creation. Death. Life. Decay. Hope. Loss. Everything. Although I'm the Wise, I still need resources. And you can help me find that... So, if you tell me your location... We can find Brilliance together."

I laughed, moving away from him. "I don't even know if you're real. Or if Brilliance is real. You could just be the monster under my bed, giving me ridiculous nightmares to scare my existence. You may give me the chills, but I don't believe what my dreams tell me. They're weird. They're crooked. They can mean anything and they can mean nothing. I'm not a Boundary, so I can't be a psychic. So, as far as I know, this means nothing to me."

"Just ask your mother then." His body vanished instantly.

I woke up in a pool of my own sweat. "These nightmares are getting wack," I said, scratching the back of my head. I rolled over to glance at my clock and I realized it was 8 am. Might as well start my day now.

I whipped the covers off me and hung my legs off the side of my bed. I cupped my forehead into my hands. My head was throbbing from my nightmare but I knew I shouldn't pay too much attention towards it. I hopped off my bed and made my way to my closet.

I grabbed a rose-colored blouse and a pair of jeans. I undressed and dressed again and threw on some combat boots. I sifted my comb through my hair, untangling my waves. It was my birthday so I felt inspired to dress nicely. I left my room and was immediately greeted to the smell of eggs and bacon cooking on my mother's frying pan. I walked further down the hallway and into the kitchen. My mom was standing over the stove.

"Hi honey," my mother said gently and she flipped the bacon over. "Happy birthday, sweetie."

"Thanks, Mom." I sat down at the kitchen table and organized my utensils. "Are those Dad's special rosemary eggs, you're making?" I asked.

She turned to look back at me with a small smile plastered on her face. "Yes. I'm sure he would be thrilled that we're using his recipe. I know he wishes that he was able to say happy birthday to you, honey."

I nodded my head, annoying the tiny surge of pain that engulfed my heart at the memory of my father. "I know he wishes he could be here."

My mom dished the eggs and bacon onto two plates. She brought the plates over to the wooden kitchen table and sat down across from me, setting my plate in front of me. "Eat up, honey."

"Thanks, Mom." I began picking at my eggs with my fork. "I have something to ask you," I said, while taking a couple of bites.

"Yes?" she asked, raising an eyebrow.

"So, I've been having these weird dreams lately. And they probably mean nothing but I just want to know your input."

"Go on," my mom said, her face turning pale.

"So, there's a man that's visiting my dreams and claiming he's a part of some Prophecy called the Wise. And he says things like there's a thing called Brilliance and he's like eager to find it."

My mom wiped her lips with a napkin before responding. "Just a dream, Esther. Don't think too hard about it."

I nodded my head, dropping the subject. "Yeah, I thought it was too farfetched, also." I did notice how my mother was so quick on changing the subject and avoiding my eyes. She knew something and she wasn't telling me what she knew.

"Do you want your birthday present now or later, Esther?" she asked, avoiding my eyes again.

"Now is fine," I said. "Later I might be heading to the park." I avoided telling her that I was going to see Damion.

"Okay," she said, jolting from her seat with unexpected excitement. She walked to the shoe closet and pulled out a little pink birthday bag. "I didn't have enough time to put tissue paper in it." She placed the bag in front of me.

I looked at her and gave her a small smile. "Thanks." I dug my hand down in the bag, pulling out three tickets. I looked down at them and realized they were airline tickets. I furrowed my brows, reading further. The destination was to New York City.

"They're so you can see the Rizzoli Bookstore," she clarified, noticing my confusion.

"Three tickets?" I asked.

She shrugged her shoulders. "I want you to pick two friends. You're seventeen now so I want to give you some freedom."

I laughed. "Or you're trying to get rid of me. There's no way you would let me go to New York for a bookstore, Mom. What's going on?" It was strange. I know I asked her if I could visit the Rizzoli Bookstore but to have a two-day vacation seems a little off to me.

"Alright. The Exols are coming here to Erin Springs to do an investigation."

"Investigation?" I asked, puzzled.

"Yes. They believe we may have an infestation of demented Creators. I just don't want you to be here and witness them hunting Creators down."

"I think there's more to it, Mom. You're afraid they're going to know about me using my abilities, aren't you?"

She sighed. "It's complicated, Esther. I just have to do some business with them."

"Business?" I asked.

"Esther, please leave it alone. It's nothing you have to worry about, please. Just take Damion and Becca. Have fun, enjoy yourself. That's all you have to do."

"Is this about the attack on the Fair?" I asked.

She shook her head slowly. "They heard about it and I guess some humans are talking about the events that happened there and how they should've been killed. It sent a ripple of effect to the Exols that are now going to conduct an investigation. I don't want you or Damion to be here when that happens because you two are the ones that saved the people on the rollercoaster."

"Oh my god," I whispered. "So, they wanted all of those people to die?"

My mom shrugged her shoulders. "They believe in natural selection. The Creators would be punished for harming the humans but Clockworks aren't supposed to intervene like that. The world isn't ready to know about us. The police and the fire department could easily handle that situation and accept the fact thirty or more people died that day."

"I never remember Exols acting like this when I was younger. If we're made to fight and protect, I don't see why it is wrong for us to do that."

"You can. Just not in the public eye like that. We also don't have a Clockwork that can wipe their memories. If we did, then there wouldn't be an issue. The issue here is the humans are still talking about the event. They're not letting it go and that's what makes it dangerous."

"So, the Exols are coming here to find more corrupted Creators and they're also essentially going to wipe the minds of those that were there that day?"

"Yes. I don't want you and Damion to be questioned about the event and the Exols knowing about you guys. I never told the Exols about your abilities and if you're not around, they won't think to ask about you. Go ahead and take Becca too, I don't really want you and Damion being alone together like that. You're grown up, but not that grown up."

I couldn't help but let out a chuckle. "Wow, Mom." My cheeks grew rosy with embarrassment. "That's going a little bit too far."

"So, are you happy with your gift? Besides everything about the Exols coming here, I think you're gonna enjoy this getaway."

I shrugged my shoulders nonchalantly. "I mean, I guess so. It's a nice gesture but the meaning behind it still has me a little shaken."

"I understand. And last night, when I said I would purposely lead the Exols to you... I want you to know I would never do that. My job as a mother is to always protect you. It's just frustrating when you make it hard for me to do so."

I bit into a piece of bacon, avoiding her eyes on me. "It's just what kids do sometimes."

My mom laughed. "Oh yeah, because seventeen is classified as being a child." She gave me a small smile.

"I don't know. I haven't been seventeen for a full day yet, so I'll let you know after this year." I stood up from my chair and grabbed my empty plate. I dropped it in the sink to wash it later and picked up my crochet bag.

"Where are you going this early?" my mom asked.

"I just want to head to the park before it starts snowing today."

"Oh, okay. Will I at least get to see you sometime on your birthday?"

"Yeah, later tonight Mom. I got some stuff to do."

"Like what? Aren't you suspended?"

"Yes, but I can see if Becca will send me some notes that her friends send to her."

"Have you guys talked yet since yesterday?"

"She texted me a little bit last night, asking to grab a coffee and stuff. Maybe go shopping. She heard from the grapevine that some rich people that moved in are going to host a ball to celebrate."

My mom furrowed her brows, giving me another smile. "Oh really? I haven't heard anything yet."

"Yeah, I only heard from her so we'll see."

"Are you excited that you guys might be best friends again?"

I slung my jacket around my shoulders and pondered the question for a small moment. "Yes. I think it would be good for us."

I chained my bike to the rack at the entrance of the park. Damion's bike wasn't here yet but I knew he was going to be here soon. He sent me a quick text that he was running a little bit late.

I trudged through the wet grass, making my way to the frozen willow tree. I smiled slightly, thinking about Damion. This was our spot now, not just mine. Willow trees are the symbolization of peace, and the feeling I receive whenever I am around Damion is as calming as a cascading waterfall.

I sat down on the grass next to the willow tree, ignoring my pants becoming wet. I propped open my laptop and searched the Rizzoli Bookstore again. As I searched the webpage, I slowly warmed up to the thought that I was going to be able to visit. I needed more novels to my collection at home and this was the perfect opportunity to do so.

My heart started to throb and the regret of not being as thankful to my mother for the gift began to sink in. I felt selfish. The more I thought about it, I realized that I was selfish in my past. Even when my father was alive, I seemed to always pity the most minor inconveniences. That was probably why Becca despised me so much.

I heard the wet grass slosh from across the park. I glanced up and immediately smiled, noticing Damion make his way towards me.

"Hey," he said. He flashed me a grin, realizing I was staring at him. "Happy birthday, Esther."

I grinned. "Thanks, Damion."

He sat down beside me. "Sorry, I didn't get you anything. But honestly, I don't really know what you like."

I stared into his blue tidal-wave eyes. "I love reading. I guess that's all there is to me, to be honest."

He threw his head back and let out a chuckle. "Yeah, okay Esther. We've been down this before. You're more than just someone who likes books."

"Oh yeah?" I said, scooting a little closer to him. "Who am I, then? If you know me so well?" I playfully taunted him.

He reached up, tapping his chin with his index finger. "Someone that stops to observe everything. Someone who believes in forgiveness. Someone who knows how to diminish their sorrows. Someone that should be happy a little bit more."

"Someone who is selfish," I stated meekly.

He abruptly stopped and narrowed his eyes at me. "Where did that come from?"

I shrugged my shoulders. "I don't know, honestly. Just been reflecting lately."

"Sounds like you were negatively reflecting. That's never good."

"Well, sometimes you have to notice the bad in order to become the better version of yourself." I plucked a strand of grass from the ground and rubbed off the tiny dirt particles that clung to it.

"If that's what you believe, then what are you going to do to fix that?"

"I don't know... I guess be more grateful for everything I have rather than looking at what I don't have."

"Tell me what you have and tell me what you don't have," Damion said, staring at me intensely.

"I have a mom, a home, two friends, all five senses, all body parts..." I stopped, struggling to find more that I have.

"You're not focusing enough, Esther. Think about it. Truly think about it... What gift do you have that other people don't?"

"I am Clockwork... I can become invisible whenever I want and create forcefields. I am a part of a Province which, like I said, is being a Clockwork. I was created by something unknown to us to be a gear that sets time in my own image. The image of a Clockwork is to maintain tranquility on Earth... At least, that's what we're meant to do. But the Exols lose their shit whenever a Clockwork tries."

"Well, that's unfortunately correct but some rules are meant to be broken." He smirked at me.

I stared at him, a small smile pulling at the corner of my lips. "I bet you like using your abilities whenever."

"Yeah... Because if I don't, I feel like I'm locked up in my own body. It's like a personal relief. You should try it, to be honest, it may help with some of the negative thoughts you have."

"Yeah, I would use my abilities more if my mom wouldn't yell at me every time I use them."

"Well, look around you, Esther. Look at this park. What do you see?"

I scanned the park, looking at the empty playground, the empty benches near the stream and the trees that shook gently in the cold wind. "It's empty."

"Yeah, so your mom shouldn't be giving you any issues if you use them here... With me... We're alone, no one can see us."

"I guess you're right."

"I can teach you things that you never knew about yourself as a Clockwork, Esther. If you trust me to do so."

"I trust you, Damion."

"Since you brought up being selfish with no true idea on how to solve your issue, I think you should volunteer at the elderly home."

"*Volunteer?*" I said with disgust.

Damion grinned. "Yes, volunteer. The thing selfish people do to make themselves feel better. Who knows, you may like it."

I threw my head back, allowing it to rest on the bark of the willow tree and I let out an obnoxious groan. "Sure. Why the hell not. At least my mother would *maybe* be proud of me for once."

"See, it won't be that hard. Also, I was meaning to ask you something, Esther. My parents are having a huge formal party this weekend and inviting like, all of the citizens in Erin Springs. I was wondering if you would come?"

I instantly remembered when Becca asked if I wanted to go dress shopping with her. I had no idea that Damion correlated with the invitation. "Of course," I said with no hesitation. "I would love to come." Well, shit. That meant I had to get my dress very quickly.

"Well, I'm glad you're coming." He nudged me with his shoulder. "Maybe you'll smile more there."

I let out an uncomfortable laugh, staring at the ground as I tried to desperately avoid his eyes. "Yeah, I guess that's another problem I have."

"Don't beat yourself up about it, Esther. You just didn't have a reason to smile before."

I finally glanced up at him. "And what's that reason?"

He smirked. "I think you know what I mean, Esther."

I shook my head playfully. "Nope, I have no clue what you mean."

He rolled his eyes in pretend annoyance. "I guess if you can't see it now, you'll see it later."

"Well," I said, changing the subject as I put my laptop away. "I guess we will have to discuss this later. Ya know, I have to buy a dress soon."

"I suppose this is goodbye for now?" Damion asked.

"Yeah, until tomorrow at the nursing home... since you're dragging me into that."

Damion laughed. "Oh, get over it, Esther. You'll be fine."

"Mmmm, I'm not sure about that." I stood up, placing my bag over my shoulder. He stood up as well, inches away from my face. I raised an eyebrow at him.

"Oh, relax. I'm not going to kiss you."

I quickly furrowed my brows. "I'm surprised. Most boys would have kissed the girl by now."

"I think we both established the fact I'm not liking other 'boys'." He used his fingers as quotations.

I laughed. "Um, I'm pretty sure that's something that any guy would say."

He rolled his eyes. "Don't worry, I will but when I discover everything that goes on in that complex, charming mind of yours."

I rolled my eyes, mocking him. "Oh sure, because I'm such a complex creature."

"Oh, you are Miss. Green."

"Hey, at least I'll keep you on your toes though."

"I guess... Or frankly, on my nerves."

"Oh, slow down," I said jokingly, putting up my hands. "We're not on that level yet."

He laughed. "It's fine. If you got on my nerves already then we have an issue."

"A toxic one, at that... If we're ignoring my annoyance that you disappeared for a couple weeks."

"Oh, and when I got annoyed at all of your obnoxious fights with Becca."

"Like a match made in heaven, Damion," I said, sarcastically making fun of all the annoying romantic movies. "But I'm surprised you didn't think my kickass moments were not appealing to you?"

He shrugged his shoulders, trying to refrain from grinning. "My thoughts about that should remain unheard."

I smiled, ignoring the giddy feeling in my stomach. "I'll see you tomorrow, Damion." I began to walk across the park and up the tiny hill.

"Goodbye, Esther. Happy Birthday. Stay safe."

I continued smiling as I made my way across the bridge and towards my bike. He really knew how to charm me. But he was right, it was too soon to make anything exclusive. I believe friendship is best for us right now.

I finally got home, walking into our trailer. I still had a huge smile plastered across my face.

My mom rose a curious eyebrow at me. "Something happen at the park that makes you smile like that?"

I shrugged my shoulders, trying to shake my own smile. "Oh, nothing."

"Hmm... I don't even need to use my abilities to know you're lying to me right now."

"Yeah, well... To summarize it for you, I've been invited to a formal event this weekend."

"Oh yeah?" My mom furrowed her eyebrows at me, continuing to scrub dishes.

"Yeah. I need a dress."

"Oh, you need *money* for a dress, right?" she asked sarcastically.

"Yes."

"And when do you plan on getting a job?"

"Um, when I graduate?"

"Oh, right. Since it's so hard for you to work in school."

"I mean, feels stupid that I need to have a human job and hide who I really am all the damn time but oh well, am I right?"

My mom rolled my eyes. "You have the same fire as I did when I was your age."

"And what happened to that?"

My mom shrugged. "I became a mom."

"Look, I'm sorry I was hard on you earlier. I appreciate the tickets you gave me and I'm excited I'll be able to go. You were just doing something for me that you knew I wanted to do for a while now and I thank you for that."

"It's okay, Esther. I know it's hard for you to process some of the things that happen in an adult, Clockwork-like world."

"Yeah, but at some point, I am going to have to know. I have a couple years until I'm thrown into that."

"I know sweetie. Here, I'll give you money for the dress but I want to be able to come to."

"You want to go to Damion's house?" I asked.

"Yes. I want to see if I can get more of a feel of him and his parents."

"Technically he's adopted."

"Well, regardless… His adopted parents are equivalent to having real parents."

"I suppose you have a point."

"Yup." My mom handed me the money. "Now, take Becca and have fun on your birthday. Just get home on time, okay?"

I smiled. "Thanks, Mom."

Chapter 4: Returns with Ash

Becca picked me up in her green Kia Soul and whipped down the back roads, nearing the closest mall near our tiny town. She was eager to go shopping with me for a dress and ready to establish our friendship once more.

"Are you still getting a dress?" I asked.

"Actually, about that... My grandmother is getting sick again so I'm gonna take some time with her."

"I'm sorry, Becca." She always has to deal with terrible situations and I admire her strength in the worst times.

She smiled at me, her blonde hair swaying in the wind because she had the window cracked. "It's okay, Esther. My grandma is a tough cookie, always has been."

"And same with you," I added.

"Yeah, I guess. But me taking all my pain out on you wasn't the best idea. Not a tough cookie there."

"Yeah, but no hard feelings. Shit happens."

She laughed. "Yeah. Shit happens."

Becca turned up her music louder and began speeding towards the mall. We finally got there and she parked her car, whipping in the empty spot. We got out of the car and made our way silently into the mall.

"Wanna get a coffee really quick before we start shopping?" she asked.

"Yeah, that's fine." I wasn't really a coffee drinker but I haven't had one in a while either so hopefully it didn't bother me too much.

We made our way to a tiny coffee shop within the mall. The mall was packed with people and there were countless long lines of people in stores. I ordered a mocha Frappuccino and Becca ordered an Americano. We sat in a tiny, closed off section in the shop.

"So, how do you like those frappes?" Becca asked.

I shrugged my shoulders. "They're okay. I can handle cold coffee, not hot."

She laughed. "Yeah, I like hot espresso. I don't like sweeteners or anything."

I nodded my head, watching her sip slowly on her beverage.

"Esther, you know you can like, enjoy yourself here, right?" Becca said with a hint of annoyance.

"I'm sorry. I'm just taking in the moment, ya know?"

"Well, changing the subject. Let's catch up. Any guys you into? Since that's always the best icebreaker." She paused. "I know you've been hanging out with that Damion kid. How is he, by the way? Is he nice to you? You guys dating are or something?" She never stopped sipping on her coffee.

"Um, yeah he is pretty nice. We are not dating, we're just friends. And I'm not really into any guys right now."

"Other than Damion, right?" she asked with a smirk.

I rolled my eyes, blushing. "No, Becca."

"Hmm, I know I haven't been buddy buddy with ya in a while, but you've always been terrible at lying."

"Well, I guess you caught me in the act, then. And how about you?"

"About what?"

"Are you into any guys?"

She shrugged her shoulders again. "Eh, not really. I've been putting a lot of time into my grams lately. But that never stops me from looking." All of a sudden, she began to wave flirtatiously at someone behind me. I turned in my chair and it was a boy with chestnut hair and eyes. He smiled back at Becca but never approached us.

"I'm just too busy to care for someone else. I have to care about myself and my grams. That's honestly all I ever need. I feel like a man would complicate things but who am I to say anything. I still window shop but I don't have the time to buy."

"I guess that makes sense though."

We sat silently, sipping on our coffees.

"Oh, by the way, Becca. My mom bought tickets to go to the Rizzoli bookstore. She wants you to come with Damion and me."

"Damion and you?" Becca asked, raising an eyebrow. "I won't be third-wheeling, right?"

"I don't think that'll be the case, Becca."

"Well, if you stick to that, I'm perfectly fine. And if you and Damion want some alone time, I'll try to hit up one of those clubs. Hopefully I can get passed security though. I've been in desperate need of a drink."

I laughed. "Sometimes I wonder the same thing."

"Alright," Becca said, clasping her hands together. "Let's get shopping for you, Esther."

We went to countless different dress stores, but none of them caught my eyes. Until I saw a beautiful, forest green dress with elegant ruffles at the edges in a display window.

"Wanna try it on?" Becca asked, noticing my immediate reaction.

I smiled. "Yes."

After a long day of shopping, I ended up buying the forest green dress. I also had a great day with Becca as well. Soon enough, it won't feel weird being around her anymore. As of now, I was reading old memories in my journal. It was a tradition I did every birthday to remember times with my father, special moments as a child and past birthdays.

I laid down, staring out my window. I looked at the large clouds forming, indicating a large storm was coming. I rolled over, grabbing my journal. I didn't write in it now, but I use to when I was a child. Good or bad, it still enlightened me.

February 13, Friday

6 years old

Dear The Great,

I don't know what happened today. Some kid threw a paper airplane at me. I brought up my hand and quickly, the paper airplane flew back. I haven't told my mommy yet for the fear of her yelling at me, saying I'm a foolish child.

Love the Only,

Esther

I continued reading, finding every page remarkable. I didn't know who The Great was, but I think it might be the slight connection every Clockwork has with the Exols. Even though I didn't know who they were at the time.

February 18, Wednesday

6 years old

Dear The Great,

I wonder why I have a larger vocabulary than other students in the First Grade. I feel like I don't belong with these people... Like I'm a misfit. Maybe I am one, I'm not sure. Help me get passed this feeling. I'm trying to make myself stronger.

Love the Only,

Esther

~

February 20, Friday

6 years old

Dear The Great,

Today my class thought I disappeared, but I was there the whole time. I was arguing with the teacher and then all of a sudden, everyone began to panic. I think it's time to confront my mommy and daddy about this. I'm so afraid though. I don't want to get brought down by my family. Wish me luck. I'll write as soon as possible, The Great.

Love the Only,

Esther

~

February 23, Monday

6 years old

Dear The Great,

I told them and my mom said I was special—and I'm not a mortal. I'm a Clockwork. No, we don't live forever. She said in our child years we grow faster than mortals physically and mentally. That explains why I'm more accelerated than other students. But our age slows down once we hit the age of fourteen or fifteen. We relive that age for two years, eventually allowing the mortals to catch up to us physically, but mentally we are more intelligent. My mom says she is also a Clockwork with the abilities to see the future and see beyond people so she told me I cannot lie without being caught. She said I have the power to make force fields... and guess what? I can become invisible.

She said I have to learn how to use my powers correctly so the mortals won't find out about us. She also says there are beautiful creatures called Exols--

Suddenly, there was a roar of thunder and soon after a flash of lightning that made me drop my journal in fear. In a hurry, I got up out of bed and went to my window. I watched the lightning light up the sky and I heard the deep roar of thunder that shook the whole house.

In the darkness, there was nothing, but when the lightning struck, I saw a figure standing in our driveway.

"Mom!" I yelled.

Simultaneously, a flash of lightning struck a tree in our yard and instantaneously the tree caught on fire, the flames destroying the tree slowly. I watched as the tree burned and after it was singed completely, the fire started moving slowly towards our house. Lightning struck again, lighting up our yard and once again, the figure was visible but closer.

"Esther!" my mother yelled, running into my room.

"Did you see this? Did you see this before it happened?" I yelled at my mom, trying to see if she's keeping things from me.

"I had a dream but I thought it was nothing!" my mom yelled out of panic.

"*Nothing*? You can see things before it happens, Mom! Use your power!" I yelled.

"It doesn't always work like that, Esther!" she yelled back.

I looked outside at where the figure was standing. "There was someone out there," I said.

"Figure? Where?" my mom asked as she walked to the window. She looked out and as she did, another flash of lightning lit up the man's face in the window. My mom screamed as lightning hit the glass, shattering the window. Before the glass could penetrate one of us, I created a force field. The pieces of glass fell to the ground.

"Back away! Get out!" I yelled at the man.

He laughed, running his fingers through his Mohawk. His features were intense and almost demonic. He brought up his hand and, in the palm, sparks of lightning began to form.

"Esther!" my mom yelled. "Get out of the way!"

The lightning flew out of his hand and all both of us leaped to the other side of the room near my door. I watched as the lightning caught my bed on fire. In a hurry, I created a force field over my bed, hoping the fire will burn itself out.

"Esther! Run!" my mother yelled. I looked up to see her trying to get up in a hurry.

I looked back at the man and he was forming another bolt of lightning. I saw the flash coming my way and in a quick amount of time, I blocked the flash with a force field. I got up, running out of my room and across the tile floor. I slipped across the hardwood but still managed not to fall. I could feel the electrifying static in the air, knowing he was creating another bolt. I closed my eyes, simultaneously turning myself invisible and forming a strong, powerful field around me.

I heard the bolt coming my way, completely passing me and hitting the couch. "Mom!" I yelled, looking around frantically.

"Invisibility, very intriguing, Clockwork."

I turned around, watching the young man look around for

me. He was too close to the door and eventually, he would know where I was. I leaped onto the sofa, using my fist to punch out the window. The glass shattered everywhere but luckily my force field saved me. I used my foot to help myself up and before I could get out of the window, I felt static consume my body with an electric charge. I turned around to see the bolt tearing away at my force field. I heard a slight crack and I yelped. My force field was breaking! I jumped down, landing on my back in the grass. I glanced up at the window and the man was crouched in the sill, ready to jump. I got up in a hurry, looking for my mom. And then I realized it. A wall of fire making its way to our home.

With the best of my ability, I tried creating a force field made out of water but there was way too much ash in the air.

"Esther!" I heard the familiar voice embrace my body. I looked up to see Damion running towards our house. I looked back at the man, noticing he was creating another bolt of lightning but it wasn't for me. It was for Damion.

"Damion!" I screamed at the top of my lungs. In a drastic move, I created a shield around him before the lightning could penetrate him. Suddenly, there was a sharp pain in my head that made me fall to the ground. I was focusing too hard to keep the force fields strong.

I looked up at Damion, watching his fearful reaction to the man. I stood up slowly, trying to focus on the fields around me. I was right next to Damion when I decided to make myself visible.

"Esther," Damion said with a faint smile at my appearance.

"I'll put a force field around both of us. But you have to use your abilities to stop him."

"Who is he?"

"I don't know."

I lost my focus, breaking the fields to protect us. In an instant, lightning shot in our direction. Damion pushed me to the ground just before the bolt hit us. I closed my eyes, focusing on the force field. I opened my eyes to see a blue tinted one embracing us from the danger the man was causing. I wondered for a moment why my force field was blue and not golden once more.

"We have to stop him and save my house before it burns," I told Damion.

"Okay." Quickly, he pushed his palm out, making the man

fall down. I watched as the tree next to us lifted off the ground, breaking the roots that formed underground. Suddenly, the tree was forced at the man, smashing into him. "That should keep him busy."

"Esther!" I heard my mom yell. I looked ahead, noticing she was next to a set of trees with five large buckets.

"You can move water with your mind, right?"

"Yes. Hold onto me."

I wasn't sure why he said that, but I grabbed his waist anyway. In seconds, we were floating a few feet off the ground. We drifted across the yard to where she was standing. We touched the ground and I let go of him. Focusing, I extended the force field around my mom. Damion stood in front of us and I watched as he closed his fists. The wind blew his hair back and forth, the fire was closer to our house than before. Suddenly, the buckets of water tipped over, but instead of the water pouring over, it levitated in the air around us. The water was forced at the fire. A loud crack came from it, indicating it was slowly fading. Damion forced more water at the fire, putting it out slowly. It was such a remarkable event.

There were only a few flames left of it, nothing too serious to worry about. I glanced at the man, listening to his groans from the weight of the tree.

"What do we do?" I asked.

"I don't know," Damion said.

"Mom," I said, turning to look at her.

"Damion, take Esther to your house. I'll contact the Exols to take care of this man."

"Why can't I stay?" I asked.

"Our house isn't in the condition to live in at the moment. Esther, just listen to me."

I nodded my head. "Okay."

"Damion," my mom said, "Don't levitate, mortals might see you. Do you know how to drive?"

He shrugged his shoulders, smiling, "Depends."

Damion was driving down the backroads so no one would know there were kids driving a pickup truck. The truck quavered a few times into the other lane.

I replayed the events in my head, watching the man become so cold. He *wanted* to kill us. And the way Damion was so brave and so magnificent made everything so comforting.

"How did you know to come?" I asked.

"I saw the fire from my window and flashes of light. I knew it wasn't good."

"Do you think the man was a Creator?" I asked.

"Had to be. It was a storm with no rain. His two abilities were lightning and thunder."

"That's so weird."

"Not really," he said, keeping his eyes on the road, driving slowly. "But the man had a very interesting power. It appeared as if his thunder wasn't working as well as it had when he was young."

"But the man was young?"

"I think he's supposed to be a Nurturer and an Element. You know, works for Mother Nature and stuff."

I furrowed my brows. "Mother Nature exists?"

"Yes! Wake up and smell the roses, Esther! The world you think you know becomes the world you thought was just in those vague stories."

"I'm sorry my mom doesn't tell me anything!" I yelled, annoyed with him.

"Stop yelling, it hurts my ears."

I rolled my eyes. "Whatever."

"Anyways, whoever works for Mother Nature stops aging after twenty, I think."

"Wait. Since Mother Nature has been here ever since the birth of Earth, does that mean her abilities are gone?" I asked.

Damion chuckled. "She's like the Exols. They never lose their power and they never age."

"Well that's unfair. What about the Clockworks? How can we keep the world inline if we can't even keep our abilities?"

"I don't know. That's how life is."

I rolled my eyes, looking out the window. *I'll have to put that on my to-do list.* Damion calmly pulled into his driveway.

"It's really big even though there's one floor. My parents are on the west wing and I'm on the east."

"Wings? What the h—"

"No swearing at the Storm Manor," Damion said with a sly smile.

"You're such an idiot," I said, opening up the rusted car door.

I jumped down onto the perfectly paved driveway.

"An idiot I shall be called, my majesty," Damion said as he made his way to the little sidewalk next to the house. "My parents don't know that you're here and it's best that way... So, be a little mouse, kay?" He mocked.

I laughed. "Why is it best that way?"

"Well, they might bombard us with pictures and they'll make you lavish meals and whatnot."

I laughed again. "Why?"

He grabbed the doorknob, opening up the door. "Because I never brought a girl home before."

I laughed. "Cute."

I looked inside the house, slowly walking in. It was pure astonishing. The lights were beautiful. There were huge chandeliers and the walls were painted a soft, lavender mist. The walls weren't just walls. It was like huge squares with smaller squares on each.

"You can stay in the guest room for tonight," Damion said with a smile on his face.

I smiled slightly. "Oh, thanks." Breaking the small silence, my stomach rumbled. I looked at Damion, waiting for an embarrassing reaction.

He grinned. "I'll get you some food."

I laughed, "Its fine. I forgot to eat dinner."

"If your stomach is rumbling, then you're not fine. Let me get you something to eat."

"No, please, it's okay. All I'm going to do is fall asleep. If I eat then I can't sleep."

Damion sighed. "Okay."

"Alright."

We walked down the long, narrow hall. As I walked, I peered at all of the pictures on the walls and the antiques. Damion stopped at a plain, white door. He opened the door and gestured for me to walk in. I gazed at the room in total awe. Two walls were nothing but glass windows and that part of the house faced the woods. I glanced on the right side of the room at the king-sized canopy bed. The room was decorated in a white and mahogany wood theme. I continued looking at the bed, trying to fight the urge to jump onto it. I couldn't help myself and ran to the bed, leaping into the soft, silky sheets.

"Paradise," I said as I closed my eyes to soak in the soft bed and the beautiful atmosphere.

"It's not much, but you know, it's home."

I opened my eyes to look at him. "Did you just say 'not much'? Oh, shut up."

He laughed. "Goodnight, Esther. I'll leave you be."

I smiled. "Goodnight, Damion."

He turned off the lights and shut the door.

Chapter 5: Tears of the Strong

"Esther, wake up."

I woke up instantly to Damion sitting on my bed. "What? It's early in the morning." I groaned, putting the plush pillow on my face.

I heard him laugh. "You mean noon? Anyways, remember when you wanted to help people today?"

I threw the pillow at him. "We're still doing that after the fact we almost died last night?"

Damion shrugged. "Why not? And ow." He rubbed his face.

"Grow up, Princess. It was just a pillow."

"And we have to go before my parents come to this wing of the house."

I rolled my eyes. "What about a shower or some clothes?"

Damion sighed. "It doesn't matter, Esther. You're already beautiful."

I groaned, getting up. "Do you have a hair tie at least?"

He stood back, thinking. "Yeah. Let me go get some." He walked out of the room and down the hall. I sat calmly on the bed, waiting for him. After ten minutes of waiting, he came into the room with a shopping bag. He tossed the bag at me and I caught it.

"What is this?" I asked.

"I found some clothes in my mom's 'younger version' wardrobe. I grabbed a few that might fit you and there's some hair stuff in there. You know, like a flat iron I think it's called?"

"Oh thanks, but I don't flatten my hair. It could damage it."

"Let me guess, you like your waves?" he said with a smirk.

"Yes," I said grabbing my waves. "Why? Do you have something against them?"

He laughed. "Of course not."

"Okay. Get out so I can get dressed before your parents wake up."

"Alright, I'll just be patiently waiting out there." He pointed at the hallway.

I got up and shut the door and sat back down next to the bag.

I looked through the clothes, trying to find something worth wearing. I found a plain white blouse with a pair of blue jeans to go with it. I undressed quickly so I could put on the new clothes. They fit me perfectly, raising my happiness. I grabbed a hair tie, twisting my hair into a braid. I opened up the door, meeting Damion in the hallway.

"Ready?" he asked.

"Yup," I said as he opened up the door.

Simultaneously, we walked out of the house. We were instantly greeted with a small gust of wind and the rays of sunshine. I smiled up at Damion as we walked down the sidewalk. He glanced down at me with a soft smile plastered on his lips.

I sat across from a kind man in a wheelchair. I helped him get up when he needed me to take him somewhere.

"You are a very kind, young lady, Esther Green," Mr. Clark said with a smile.

"And you are a very generous man, Mr. Clark," I said with a smile on my face.

"Sorry to ask, but how old are you, darling? I always want to know my helpers' ages so I can think back to the time I was that age."

"Don't worry, its fine and I'm seventeen."

He leaned back, baffled. "I may be old and crippled but that, my dear, has to be a lie. You are intelligent and mature-looking."

I shook my head. "Lie or not, think what you want."

"Hmm, wise words, darling." He looked around for a second, then looked back at me. "Who is that boy you brought with you? Don't tell me he's also younger than the age he looks."

I nodded my head. "That's Damion. He's seventeen as well, but turning eighteen in May."

The old man nodded his head, examining Damion. "He looks like he's in his twenties and you look...hmmm." He cocked his head to the side. "I guess I can see seventeen. Very strange, very strange indeed." He looked at me. "And when is your birthday?"

"November 15th."

He nodded his head calmly. "Taurus and Scorpio, just like my wife and me."

I leaned in, confused. "Pardon me?"

"Horoscopes. Are you not familiar with them?" Mr. Clark

asked, his faded green eyes staring into mine.

"No, sorry. I haven't heard of them."

"It's a very touchy subject. Do you have a heart for the boy?"

I was caught off guard by the question. I care deeply about Damion, but I knew I didn't love him. I only knew him for a couple months. "I don't know. I'm just a kid."

The man smiled into my eyes. "I know he cares for you, it's obvious."

I turned around, watching Damion talk to an older woman. They were both laughing very loud. He looked at me with a goofy grin plastered on his face. I smiled back, turning my head to look at Mr. Clark.

"I noticed the way he looks at you, Esther. His eyes hold so much compassion for you."

I looked down at my palms, trying to ignore the fact I was having a strange, intimate conversation with the man.

"He's talking to my wife right now. We both noticed it. But anyways, do you want to know why they're getting along so easily right now?

I looked at him, narrowing my brows. "Why?"

"They have the same horoscope."

"If they have the same horoscope... Then that means—"

"We are both Scorpios. We are deep with emotions, Esther. And yes, Taurus and Scorpios do get along well when they love each other."

"What do these horoscopes have to do with?" I asked, curious.

"Birth months, basically to describe it in a simpler way. We are a water sign and they are an earth sign."

I nodded my head. "Intriguing. I'm just not sure if I could follow a horoscope to know who I am."

He smiled warmly at me. "Very clever, Esther. Some of us aren't that easy to see our own shadow, so we look to a different source to learn who we should be."

"I guess I could see where the confusion comes from though. I have issues of knowing my purpose and maybe checking that horoscope could give me some insight."

He shook his head and began wagging his crooked finger at me. "Esther, I already know you don't need the sign of a Scorpio to trust in yourself to know who you are. You may not see it yet, but you have a will in your soul that shines through your eyes. I've seen many things and people in my time. I know when I see a heart of gold and the eagerness of positive determination. You are determined, but you do not know what you are determined for, essentially."

"I guess I just need to wait and live to know who I'm supposed to be."

"Well," Mr. Clark clapped his hands together, "You came here to simply improve your attitude, so instead of talking deep, do you mind if you go get me a glass of milk from the kitchen. It's down the hall."

I smiled. "Yes. Of course." I got up calmly, turning on my heels as I began to walk across the room. I glanced at Damion to see he was already looking at me with a smile on his face. I returned the smile and I watched something in his eyes glimmer.

I was truly curious about what Mr. Clark said. Damion caring about me? I knew Clockworks were incredibly fast when it came to maturity. If Damion actually did care for me, then there was no denying it because it was not impossible.

I walked into the kitchen where pots and pans were clacking and a few seniors were sitting down to eat whatever the chefs were cooking for them. I walked up to the bar, looking for anybody to help me.

"Um. Excuse me?" I asked politely.

A young man came around a stove with a smile. "I apologize. What can I do for you?"

"Oh, I would like a glass of milk."

"Who for?"

"Oh, um... Mr. Clark." I smiled.

"Okay. I'll be right back."

"Okay, thanks." I got tired and decided to sit on a bar stool. I watched the seniors around me, imagining myself being older and happy. Suddenly, something caught my attention amongst the elderly. I looked closely at a man and a woman. The woman was creating a floral with her fingers. But not with material, only her bare fingers. The man laughed and mumbled a few words. He moved his hand up, creating a spark that made the lights flicker. I got off my stool and walked over to them. The man looked up at me like he was about to hurt me.

I jumped back, trying to keep some distance between us. "I couldn't help but notice what you were displaying."

"You didn't see anything," the man said, glaring at me. I looked into his dark, coal eyes, watching my own dark reflection. I stepped back, confused why I even walked up to these people.

"Oh, sorry to disturb you." I walked back to the bar, wondering where the milk was. "Wait a minute," I said as a realization swept over me. I walked up to those people because I saw them using their abilities. I got off the stool and walked over to them.

"Didn't I tell you, child? You have no right to be next to us."

"Oh, yes, you're right." I started to turn around until I stopped myself, turning to look back at them. "I have no idea what you are doing to me, but I saw you two using your abilities."

"Pan," the man whispered. "How is she resisting?"

I furrowed my brows. "Resisting?"

"What are you?" the man asked.

"No. What are *you*?" I asked.

"We are special people. But your mortal mind won't comprehend it."

I laughed like I was insulted. "Clockwork? Yeah, me too."

The woman and man laughed. "Oh," he said, "I wasn't entirely certain you are one."

"Oh."

"How did you escape my husband's ability?" the woman asked.

"What was that?" I asked.

"I have the ability to manipulate people. Also, to control the electricity around us."

"Oh, well I'm not sure. And interesting abilities."

"What are yours?" he asked.

"Invisibility and force fields," I said, my abilities sounding useless compared to the man in front of me.

"Ahh," the woman said, "Sometimes manipulation cannot reach the brain to those who have force fields."

I smiled. "That's cool." I thought about Pan's power— something involving flowers, nature or life. "So, are you with Mother Nature?"

Pan smiled radiantly; her dull eyes gleaming. "One time I was."

"Well, what happened?" I asked, concern rising in my voice.

"He was aging," she said, gesturing at her husband, "And I was young and extremely beautiful. Mortals were growing curious, asking why I was in love with an old man." Her husband chuckled. "Being a Nurturer is very hard, losing your powers slowly, becoming weak but then feeling young and radiant. It was difficult."

"Um, your milk is ready? I've been standing here for a while now." I turned around, noticing the man that took my order for Mr. Clark.

"Um, it's probably no good now. Can you get me another please?" I asked with a faint, embarrassed smile.

He sighed. "Okay. But last one."

I turned back to Pan and her powerful husband. "So, what did you do?"

Pan smiled. "Well, I took the long journey to the Exols. It took me months to plan the trip. I had to make sure I was ready."

I furrowed my brows. "Why does it take so long to plan?" I asked curiously.

"There are these gems called Halcyons. They are the most beautiful gems to crowd this earth, darling. Halcyon means carefree-happiness, or light. But the way to find them is the darkest, mind-manipulating adventure ever.

"There are fifty gems in very dangerous places. You need three gems to get to the Exols. Sometimes the Halcyons are underwater where there's a great chance you have to fight some hideous beast or simply be in the most beautiful place on Earth. To some mortals, that's Hawaii. There are very few Clockworks that take the risk to go see the Exols. Some are afraid of the journey and the death it brings. They could also be afraid the Exols will know they use their abilities simply for fun."

"Where were your gems located?" I asked Pan.

"The first one I found was on a deserted island. Well, not entirely deserted. There were strange beasts called Himphlyns. I don't have much of a fighting ability considering I was born to be a Nurturer. Fighting them off and managing to stay alive was very difficult. The second Halcyon I found was in a jungle with not only exotic animals, but with an offspring of Himphlyns that take the shape of a large snake called Slithneens."

"I never knew there were creatures involved," I merely stated, thinking back to what Damion told me. It was the real world, but with material I could find in fictional stories.

Pan laughed. "Of course. Earth is not a peaceful place, honey. We, Clockworks, were put on this planet to protect the helpless from ravaged beasts and possibly ourselves if the Creators become too out-of-control."

"Why haven't these creatures you've encountered actually made their presence known?" I asked, wondering why we're not even fighting off the ratchet beasts.

"Centuries ago, we did fight off the creatures. But we didn't kill them, we trapped them in variously strange locations."

"Why not just kill them instead of worrying if they'll ever escape?" I asked.

"The Exols wanted it to be as clean as it can."

"That's strange," I said underneath my breath.

"Anyways, the third one I found was on the edge of a cliff. It wasn't dangerous, but it was extremely intense. The gem was on the edge of the cliff, but the key was to be as gentle as you could when walking towards the gem. The plateau was very sensitive, every hard step, the more the gem leaned towards the edge of the cliff. If it falls, it breaks. If it breaks, you have to look for another place you could find a gem."

"How did you manage to receive the gem without failing?" I asked.

Her husband smiled. "This is my favorite part of the story."

Pan grinned. "You already witnessed me creating a floral, but what I can also do is move rocks any which way I want as long as I focus." She took a sip of her drink. "I moved the rock as carefully as I could without touching it. I brought it to me, making sure the gem wouldn't fall and break. And it worked." She said as she smiled. "I realized that I shouldn't let my fears break me and basically control me. The purpose of the dangerous expeditions is so the Exols can teach you very important life lessons. Some are too eager or afraid to continue on and that is why they die while trying."

I smiled. "Intriguing."

"When I was greeted by the magnificent scenery the Exols created was one of the most amazing sights I'll never forget. The waterfall was such a beautiful blue, flowing gently into the river in the Land of the Exols. I remember looking up to see such a marvelous palace that took my breath away. I couldn't help but watch these exotic, large birds fly around in such an elegant manner. It was extraordinary. But I couldn't forget why I came there in the first place.

"I told them I wanted to age like my husband and at least keep my abilities as long as him. They questioned me, searched me to see if I was guilty with any broken rules and whatnot. They knew I was worthy from the journey I took. I got what I greatly desired and they sent me home safely."

I smiled. "That's one of the most amazing stories I ever heard in my life. You're a true inspiration Pan."

Her husband smiled. "Yes, she is. And that is why I love her. She risked her life for a long, happy relationship with me."

"You two are very sweet," Pan said smiling. "You should probably get your milk. The young man is getting very inpatient."

I chuckled awkwardly. "Yeah. Well thank you for the lovely story." I walked away without another word and grabbed the milk on the counter.

I walked out of the kitchen to see Damion standing next to Mr. Clark with a curious expression. "Sorry," I said, "I got lost in a story by a sweet couple in there."

"I figured," Damion chuckled. "I wanted to check on you, but Mr. Clark insisted me to stay."

"That's okay. Um, what happened to Mrs. Clark?"

"She wasn't feeling well so she decided to take a nap," Damion said.

"Oh," I said as I gave Mr. Clark the milk. "I hope she feels better, but I think it's time for Damion and I to go."

Mr. Clark nodded. "I understand. Thank you for keeping us company."

Damion gave him a friendly smile. "You're welcome."

I walked across the room of elders and out the door. Damion hurried quickly behind me.

"What's wrong?" he asked.

"Did you know there's creatures on some strange foreign island? Or islands?" I asked, stopping dead in my tracks.

He looked confused, furrowing his brows. "I usually know a

lot, but no. And why haven't the Exols told us to do something about it?"

I shrugged my shoulders. "I don't know. I guess hundreds of years ago we did fight them off, but the Exols wanted it to be clean. So, we trapped them on some strange islands in the middle of nowhere."

"How do you know this?"

"I met some older Clockworks in the kitchen. One was basically someone who is meant for war and the lady was a Nurturer. Mortals were starting to become very curious why she was with an older man and her abilities would slowly fade faster than her husband's. So, she decided to go to the Exols and present what she greatly desires. I guess she had to go on some long journey to show she was worthy to the Exols."

"Yeah. I know about the expedition details, but the only thing I didn't know about was the creatures." Damion looked down for a moment, trying to comprehend something. "Why haven't they lost their powers yet?"

I shrugged. "I guess some are lucky and they get to keep their abilities a little longer."

Damion scoffed. "That's not fair to the others who are losing them at young ages."

I nodded my head. "I know. We should probably check on my Mom."

"Yeah."

We started walking at a slight pace down the sidewalk.

We reached my house in twenty minutes. I walked across my yard, looking at the fried grass and the burn marks on our home.

"That doesn't look good," Damion said.

I nodded my head, walking up the porch steps. I opened up the door to see my mom sitting at the kitchen table. "Mom?"

She got up instantly, giving me a warm hug. "Esther. Glad you're okay."

I hugged her back. "I'm glad you're okay too. What are you doing?"

"Trying to look for some new furniture." She laughed. "Our house looks like crap."

I smiled. "It does."

"Police and firemen came. They were very confused about what happened. The neighbors were also very curious."

I nodded my head, dismissing what she said. "What were the Exols like?" I asked, excited.

"Well, like how they're described. They're not that fascinating."

"Oh." I looked down at my shoes.

Damion smiled. "Okay. Well, I should get home."

"Oh, does your mom want her clothes back?" I asked.

"No, keep them," he said, laughing. "See you at the party." With that, he left.

I woke up late the next morning, trying to remember my dreams from the night before. I rolled out of bed, walking towards my calendar. Damion's party. I picked up a marker and crossed off yesterday's date.

"Esther, darling! Are you awake?" my mom asked.

"Yeah, I just woke up," I yelled, trying to project my voice through the walls.

"I want you to get your dress on, but do nothing else, okay?"

"Alright." I walked across my room, heading towards my closet. I opened up the doors and pulled out my dress. I quickly undressed. I unzipped the back of the silky material and slowly pulled it up. I put my right arm through the one-strap dress, adjusting the strap to fit my shoulder perfectly. I looked in my mirror, admiring how the beautiful green silk fit my body perfectly. It hugged my chest, making me look more like a woman. Below my chest was a belt, making the dress look puffy and ruffled. I smiled at my reflection. But I guess I wasn't ready yet. "Mom, I'm ready."

Seconds after I said that, my mom came into the room with a curling iron and a few boxes. "I love your waves the way they are but I think they deserve to be more exaggerated."

I nodded my head. "It's okay, Mom. I want to *seem* beautiful."

My mom frowned, kneeling down next to me. She reached up, placing her warm hand on my cheek. "You are the most beautiful girl I ever laid my eyes on."

I smiled. "Thank you." I looked over at the boxes. "What's in the boxes?"

"Jewelry. Eye shadows. Blushes. Some other stuff. It's good to wear a few enhancers at parties, honey."

I shrugged. "Sounds cool to me."

My mom smiled, plugging in the curling iron and setting it on my dresser, allowing me to watch my reflection in my mirror by having me sit down. "Now. You have to sit like a lady, Esther. Cross your left leg over your right whenever you sit down. Don't spread them. It makes you look... strange."

I laughed. "I know, don't worry."

My mom got on her knees in her white, cut-off dress, rummaging through one of the boxes. She pulled out sparkly silver nail polish, shook it and then opened it up. She glanced at my hands, stopping for a moment. "Wow. I never realized you have perfect hands."

I laughed. "Oh wow... Thanks, Mom."

She started painting my nails with the liquid, evenly stroking each part of my nail. When she was done with my left hand, she switched to my right, giving it the same professional finish. She closed up the polish, setting it back down in the box of other polishes. "I think the iron is ready. Want me to start curling your hair?"

"Yes, please."

She grabbed my brush that was sitting on my dresser and started combing through my matted bed hair. I sat calmly, allowing my nails to dry without getting chipped. She pulled parts of my hair back, twisting it into a clip. She picked up the cylinder object, gently putting a clump of my hair in the hot device and rolled up. She waited patiently, then released, allowing my hair to lay perfectly passed my shoulders, curling up near the lower part of my chest. I smiled, admiring the silky curl.

After an hour of curling my hair, my mom was done. She didn't let me see my hair perfectly curled though.

"It's a surprise. I want you to admire your beauty when we're done with all of it."

"Okay," I said.

"Close your eyes." I closed them, feeling the soft strokes of golden eye shadow coat my eyelids. She did the other side the exact same way. "Gold looks good with hazel eyes, honey. Today your eyes are more of a soft green than caramel." She finished that side and I opened my eyes gently to see her smiling at me. "Your eyelashes are already long enough; you don't need mascara. The last thing is blush and lip gloss." My mom picked up a palette, wiping a small brush in the powdery substance. She applied the blush a little below my cheekbones. "When you smile, it makes your smile more radiant." She set the palette down, picking up a tube of bright pink lip gloss. She opened it up, dipping it into the tube and out. She applied the wet substance onto my lips, smiling as she took a step back. "Done."

I stood in the mirror, admiring myself. "I feel beautiful."

"Oh, Esther. You've always been beautiful. I love the little specks of freckles you get from your father and I remember him saying how much he loves your auburn hair. If only you had my bright, red hair though." She playfully winked at me.

I smiled, feeling the warmth of happiness in my heart. "I miss Dad. I know he would be proud to see me right now."

"He would be proud to see you every day, sweetie."

"I know. I love and miss him."

"Me too, honey. I want you to have fun today. Damion does seem like a pretty good kid and I can tell he cares for you. I think I judged him too harshly in the beginning and I'm sorry for that, sweetie. I truly am."

We arrived at Damion's house, struggling to drive my dad's old broken-down pickup truck in the grass as we tried to park.

Suddenly, my mom hit something, making the truck shake awkwardly. I gasped, starting to laugh at the friendly scare.

"What the hell was that?" my mom questioned, looking in the rear-view mirror.

"No swearing at the Storm Manor," I said with a faint smile.

My mom looked at me with her eyebrows raised. "Where did you come up with that rule?"

"I didn't. Damion did."

She laughed. "Oh."

I opened up the door and jumped down onto the soft grass with my flats, closing the truck door.

"Go ahead in. I need to find a bathroom," my mom said.

"Okay." I walked towards Damion's house, stepping down cautiously. I couldn't help but smile. It seemed like this was going to be the best night of my life. And possibly everyone else thought the same thing.

I walked up the porch steps, listening to the quiet antique waterfall rush in his mother's beautiful garden with dozens of colorful flowers. I knocked on the door. Someone opened it up instantly with a smile on her face. She was incredibly beautiful. Black, long hair laid perfectly passed her shoulders and her eyes shined a bright, beautiful blue. She smiled a radiant smile and her eyes gleamed. "Esther. Welcome home." She gestured for me to follow her inside.

I picked up my dress, walking in next to her. Everything about the people here seemed warm and comfortable.

"I'm Damion's mother, Ella Storm. Damion has told us many things about you." She looked down at me. "Don't worry, the people in the purple ties here know about Clockworks. They're a part of our family. Even though they may not have abilities, they still support Damion. By the way, he is outside on the dance floor. Last I heard he was dancing with his cousin, Grace. I believe he still is."

I smiled. "Okay. Thanks." I walked down the hall, loud music pumping throughout the house along with everyone talking almost at once. I walked calmly to the back of the house, nearly exhausted at how long the walk was. I opened up the sliding glass door and walked out to see everyone dancing along to the pop music. Some danced crazy and some danced quite graceful, but in all, everyone was smiling and enjoying themselves.

Suddenly, arms embraced me, making me startled. "Esther, I'm glad you came." I recognized the calming voice. Damion pulled away with a smile on his face. I looked at his attire, noticing how much of a gentleman he looked. I glanced up, realizing he was looking at me, his mouth nearly open and his eyes were wide. I blushed, looking down.

"You clean up nice, Miss Green," he said, smiling a lopsided grin.

"As do you, Mr. Storm." A calm song came on that reminded me of resting swans.

"May I have this dance?" Damion asked, holding out his hand.

I smiled, taking his hand. "You may."

He brought me out to the dance floor, wrapping his arm

around my waist. I placed my arm on his back and simultaneously, we lifted our hands, locking them together.

"I don't know how to dance," I whispered, making sure no one near us would hear.

"Step on my feet."

"What?"

"Step on my feet, I'll guide you."

Carefully, I stepped on his feet and then he moved one step to another. In seconds, we glided around the dance floor in pattern with everyone. He moved with such grace and confidence; it made my heart warm. We moved with everyone else in such a passionate, lovely way. Suddenly, Damion broke our hands apart, grabbing my waist. He lifted me up and spun me in the air. I looked down at him as he set me gently back on his feet. I laughed, smiling. He smiled too, grabbing my hand again. We spun quickly, slightly making me dizzy. Following the others, we spun again but the opposite way. We moved quickly, one step after the other.

I stepped off of his feet, feeling as if I could actually dance. I gave him a reassuring smile and he returned it. The music changed, but making the melody a little darker, but slower than the other. The base hardened, making me step down slowly, we waited, paused in our position, and then the base hardened again, making me step down once more. The music changed to a softer, more relaxing melody. Damion moved me across the dance floor. Once we reached the edge, he twirled me making me smile and laugh. He held me closer to him, but a lot tighter than before. We stepped over, following everyone else, the melody becoming more inspirational. We stopped and he lifted me, smiling up at me. I smiled back as he sat me down and gently dipped me in such a graceful way. He lifted me up, the music more focused on the beat instead of the melody. I moved my leg across the ground as he lowered me to the floor. He held me closer to him again, moving us so elegantly across the ground. The music changed quickly into an epic beat. He lifted me off the ground, moving to the left, he set me down and dipped me to the right. I spun around, rolling back into his arms and he lifted me up again, following the same routine we did before, making me spin right back into his arms. Once I came back to him, the epic music stopped and slowed down.

As we danced, I hugged him, stepping on his feet as he

guided us across the floor.

"You're not bad at dancing for someone who can't dance."

I looked at him, smiling. "You're really good. How do you do it?"

He shrugged, grinning. "I just follow the music."

"Ah, I wouldn't have thought of that," I said, joking with him.

He laughed. "I'm surprised you're not wearing your favorite color," he said, moving us to the right. "Yellow."

I shrugged. "I don't look that good in it. I look better in green. Looks like I have to change my favorite color."

He smiled. "Your beautiful no matter the color you wear. But I do have to agree... You look absolutely striking in green."

I laughed, looking down at the floor, both my hands resting on his shoulders. "I guess green is my favorite color now." I paused, thinking. "You never told me your favorite color, Damion. What is it?"

He chuckled a deep laugh. "Green."

"Why?" I mumbled, still looking down.

"I don't know. It was blue before I met you."

My heart fluttered. I looked up at him, smiling. "You're so very sweet."

"As are you, darling." He laughed. "The feast is coming up soon. Want to take a break?"

"Yeah." I got off his feet, walking towards the brightly designed bench that faces the woods. I sat down, Damion sitting down next to me.

He looked at me, the only thing lighting up his face were lights. "I know we are young now, but promise me you'll never leave me."

I smiled, grabbing his hand in the dark. "I promise you I won't leave you."

He grinned. "Instead of joining their feast, want to have our own in the woods?"

I smiled. "Yes."

We both sat in the woods, sitting across from each other. The only thing lighting up our faces were little lights. We danced all day and now it was a brisk night. We were lucky the high was 60 degrees with it being winter. I took a bite of the peanut butter and jelly sandwich.

"Why eat fancy food when you can simply feel satisfied with toast and jelly sandwiches?" Damion asked, taking a bite of his toast.

"Exactly what I was thinking." I grabbed my juice and drank out of it.

"I finally feel like a kid again. Everything feels peaceful, Esther. I love the feeling."

I smiled. "Is that because we're feasting like children?"

He laughed. "Yes, and the fact that I'm happy to be here with you."

"I'm happy to be here with you too." I laid down on the small blanket. "This is the best day ever. I'll never forget it." I looked up at the moon shining behind the trees, casting shadows against the pines.

"Same." Damion laid down next to me, looking up at the sky. "Hey, look. The stars formed a cow." He pointed up at the sky. I tried to find a cow, but I couldn't. I turned my head, looking at him.

"Your mom looks like she could be an Exol."

"Yeah. I know. If only her soul was as beautiful as she looked."

"I'm sorry, Damion."

"It's okay. I'll be out of there soon enough."

"Yeah. You just have to have hope that it will get better."

I realized Damion wasn't at school today which made me truly curious because we were both supposed to return today. I thought about every possibility why he wasn't here, but none of them seemed truly reasonable.

Willingly, I left school. Snowflakes were sticking to the ground. I opened my book bag, pulling out a button-down sweater. I walked towards my bike and unchained it.

I pedaled down the road to the park, wondering if he was there. I rode quickly, panic burning in my throat. In minutes I got there, throwing my bike to the ground and I began running down the large hill to see Damion sitting by the rushing creek. Huge rocks levitated in the air around him, reminding me of the scene a while ago. I turned invisible, not wanting to be seen.

"Hiding from your curiosity will get you nowhere," Damion stated dryly.

I made myself visible, walking closer to him. "Damion, what's wrong? Why weren't you at school today?"

He looked back at me, tears streaming down his cheeks. "Why do you care to know?"

"What do you mean? I always care about you. Every month. Every week. Every day. Of course, I'm going to be worried when there's definitely something wrong."

He looked back at the rushing creek. "Look around you, Esther. Tell me what you see."

I looked at the trees swaying violently in the harsh wind. My eyes scanned the rushing water again as each small wave seemed like a huge tsunami to insects. I felt the bitter prick of cold on my cheeks as the wind smashed into me.

"Everything in this park, I'm moving. The nature around us is what's happening inside my head."

I sat next to Damion, pushing a rock out of my face and into the water. "Why?"

He looked at me, his blue eyes mysterious and his black hair matted on his head. "I hurt my mom today." He closed his eyes tightly as if he was replaying back the painful event. "I told my mom I didn't want to go to school today because I just didn't feel right... I felt like I just didn't belong at that school. We fought. She yelled and screamed at me and I yelled back. We both said very hurtful words but she didn't understand how I was feeling and..." He stopped, wiping his nose on his sleeve. "I told her I wished she was never my mother and I actually ended up with parents that are just like me. She picked up the hot skillet and threw it at me. I fell to the ground, trying to fight the urge to strike back. She got on her knees and punched me in the nose and yelled at me." He looked me in the eyes as the treacherous regret began to sink in even more. "I couldn't control myself... The skillet was sitting on a flame before she threw it at me... I pushed her into the stove and the flame eventually caught her shirt on fire and then a section of her body... I ran to the sink, using my telekinesis to put out the fire with water. It worked, yes... But my mother was slightly charred on her stomach. She screamed at me to get out of the house. I didn't hesitate."

I scooted closer to Damion. "Don't worry, everything will work itself out."

He stood up quickly. "No, it won't! It never will!" he

screamed, staring at me with venomous eyes.

I stood up, inches away from his face. "Let me help you, stop putting up a barrier around you."

He turned his back towards me. "You have it so good, Esther."

I shook my head. "No one has it good. Everyone faces bumps in the road, Damion. Everyone. Not just you."

He turned violently my way. "Not you. The only thing you've faced was a few dangers and your dad. Nothing that I experience on a daily basis! You go around acting like everything is bad for you when it's *not!*"

I stepped back, shocked. "Is that really what you think?" I snapped. "I haven't told you nothing about me! How do you even think you have the right to judge me?" I yelled.

"LIES!" he screamed, making an unexplainable force throw me to the other side of the park. I pushed my hands out in front of me, quickly creating a force field so I didn't collide into the park bench. I fell to the ground, landing on my back. My breath escaped my lips, making me gasp for air.

"Esther!" Damion yelled. I felt the ground vibrate, indicating he was running my way. He knelt down beside me, picking up my head with his cold hands and setting me gently in his lap. "I'm so sorry," he said, pushing hair out of my face. "I didn't mean to hurt you. I care about you so much... I can't lose you... Please don't leave me."

I caught my breath, looking up at him. I wasn't sure how I was supposed to react until I noticed his bright, blue eyes softening and guilt reflected in them like a broken mirror. I reached up, placing my hand on his face. "I will never leave you... No matter death or negativity. I will always be with you."

He picked me up, holding me closer to him as he embraced me. "I can't explain to you how sorry I am. I just have so much anger... so much power... brewing inside of me." His voice cracked. "I'm scared, Esther. I'm scared of my abilities."

I lifted my arms up, embracing him. "Why did you ask me not to leave you? I wasn't going to die from such a small impact."

Damion smiled. "I didn't mean it like that. I didn't want you to hate me."

I laughed. "I'll never hate you, Damion. Ever. I promise."

He smiled, the snow was now sleeting, making his hair look wet and longer than it really was. "You complete me, Esther Green. Without you, I will be broken."

The joy of being a Clockwork was not only the abilities you desire, but also the feelings you build stronger than any mortal could ever imagine. The most important feeling to us was not only the joy of feeling special, but the feeling of love. With love comes anger, and with anger comes sorrow, but in all, love overpowers them all.

A couple more months passed and the New York trip was right around the corner. It was now officially February and it was still frigid, but not as bad as it has been. Becca and I have been building our friendship up and now I feel more comfortable being around her. Damion and I hung out almost every weekend. We would hangout under our willow tree in our large, winter coats and talk about our day. We would occasionally sit at our local diner and enjoy the moment. My mom is coming around even more to the thought of having Damion around more. I finally felt better. I could tell I was happier. I didn't feel lost anymore.

"The thing about sadness, Esther Green, is that it's everlasting. It will always be there—almost like fear, but you have to overcome it." Damion paced back in forth in the park. His large, black sweatshirt took up most of his body, making him look as if he were in Alaska.

I took off my blue sweatshirt, wrapping it around our willow tree. "But how?" I asked as I tied double knots.

"You overcome it by doing the opposite."

"Doing the opposite?" I questioned.

"Hence, you're angry, what do you do?"

"Break something."

He smiled. "Besides that, how would you overcome it?"

I furrowed my brows. "Being calm. I don't know."

"You're right. But sometimes pushing away your emotions doesn't help. You either release your emotions by crying or like you said, 'breaking stuff.'"

"So, what are we doing today?" I asked.

"I'm going to teach you some stress relievers." He took off his sweatshirt, throwing it on the ground. I watched as he took off his undershirt too, revealing his abs I never thought he had before. I was baffled to think he was intensely muscular from his soft, but hard expressions. He caught me staring, a grin spreading across his lips. I blushed, looking down.

"Aren't we going to get frost bite?"

"No, Esther. You can alleviate thoughts on body temperature with the technique I'm going to show you. Do you have something else underneath your shirt?" He asked. "It takes a lot of mental force and physical movements.

I took off my shirt, revealing a tank top. I smiled.

"Okay, the first thing I like to do is think about what's bothering me," Damion stated, walking closer to me. Once we were face to face, he said, "Close your eyes." I closed them. "Think."

I thought about my dad resting in the hospital bed, his lungs throbbing in pain. I imagined life without him and the love he had for my mom and me.

"Now," he said, putting his warm hands on my shoulders, "Think about something you wish you could do right now at this exact second."

I thought about how amazing it would be to feel weightless. Suddenly, I felt myself overturning. I wanted to open my eyes but I was afraid I would ruin it.

I heard Damion chuckle. "Open your eyes." I opened my eyes, realizing I was upside down in the air, parallel to the tip of the willow tree.

I laughed in awe. "How is this even possible!"

Damion looked up at me, smiling. "Every Clockwork possesses a simple Spiritual ability. Most people are too focused on the abilities they have instead of their Spiritual-Human side."

"How come you know all of this stuff when your parents aren't Clockworks?" I asked, still levitating in the air.

He shrugged. "I guess I'm not as oblivious like the rest of you. Now close your eyes and think about walking on the ground where I'm standing."

I did as he told me and quickly, I felt myself flip and my feet landing on the ground gently. I opened my eyes, looking at Damion with a smile. "Am I supposed to feel better yet?"

He laughed. "There's still more I want to teach you." He looked around, making sure no one was around. "It doesn't matter what kind of powers you have. Anyone can do this if you believe you can." He closed his eyes, sighing. He inhaled the air, suddenly but slowly he flipped, his hands on the ground and his legs in the air. One leg moved and the other moved slowly after until he landed back onto the ground. He looked at me, laughing at my expression. "Don't worry, it's easier than you think."

"You picked up your whole body though."

"Humans can do it if they practice. We can do it if we breathe."

I sighed, closing my eyes. "What do I think about?"

"Peace."

I thought about sitting next to a calm waterfall without a worry in the world. There was no war, no violence, no people. It was only Nirvana. I felt myself overturning in the air. My hands were pressed against the ground and my legs were stretched high. My first leg moved and then my second and calmly, I found myself back onto the ground. I opened my eyes, staring at him in pure astonishment.

"Let's try together but with our eyes open this time."

I thought about a bird soaring through the clouds, enjoying the journey of being free. Simultaneously, Damion and I began to move gently, our hands pressing against the ground. Slowly and calmly, we did our flip, landing at the same time.

"Do it again," Damion said, "Until we both feel satisfied."

We did it again and again, basically dancing in the air. I moved calmly and gracefully, thinking peacefully. I felt my lingering sadness slowly decaying. It was beautiful to feel almost liberated from the dark areas of my mind.

"Now, I'll teach you another one. It's about being weightless." He walked towards the park bench, sitting on backboard. "Once you become more experienced, you can do this on the highest peak of any mountain without falling."

"Is our Spiritual Side almost like martial arts?" I asked.

He nodded his head. "Yes. Some Clockworks were only born with their Spiritual Side. They're professionals at anything involving their Spiritual Side because it's the only thing they know."

I furrowed my brows. "Interesting."

He smiled. "I know right." He rolled his body across the park bench, using his hand to slowly lift him up. He closed his eyes, frozen in that position. A breeze of wind suddenly embraced him and his hair flopped back and forth. The air came my way, circling around me and suddenly disappearing.

After several minutes in that position, he slowly flipped to the ground. "Since I wasn't only born with Spiritual, I can't do it for very long."

I smiled. "It was still pretty long."

"Some can do it for weeks without breaking concentration."

I nodded my head. "Wow."

He grinned. "Would you like to try?"

I shrugged, walking towards the park bench. "Sure." I got onto the backboard, slowly maneuvering so my hand could be lifting up my whole body. Suddenly, I felt heavy but then I remembered to think peacefully. I thought about soft music soaring throughout the air, violins streaming and the sounds of flutes moving gracefully to the melody. Suddenly, I broke concentration, falling over onto the ground. I looked around, confused.

Damion smiled. "Ten minutes."

"Ten minutes?" I gasped. "Felt like two seconds."

"Now, let's do everything I taught you today together."

I closed my eyes, thinking about being weightless.

"Hold my hand," I heard Damion whisper. Quickly, I grabbed his hand. We both overturned, swiftly levitating into the air. "Open your eyes."

I opened my eyes, looking at him, both of us were upside down. We laughed. He pulled me up so we weren't upside down anymore.

"Ever heard of dancing in the sky?" He asked.

"No," I whispered.

He pulled me closer to him. I wrapped my arms around his neck and he wrapped his tightly around my waist.

"Think about a ballroom. Think about grace."

I thought about large, puffy dresses and how they moved swiftly across the ballroom in steady steps. Suddenly, we both began to move in the air. Damion gave me a little twirl and I rolled back into his arms. We both laughed as we fell into each other.

"Dancing in the air is hard," Damion said.

Instead of dancing elegantly, we danced playfully. He would twirl me every now and then but we mostly swayed back and forth.

I glanced at our willow tree, admiring it. "Our tree is

beautiful."

He laughed. "I agree."

"Think we should call it a day before kids head to the park?"

"Yeah. Sounds like a good idea." We shifted over to our willow tree. Simultaneously, we landed gently on a few branches. Damion went down slowly to the next branch, extending his hand out to help me down. I took it and he gently brought me down to him. We continued this process until he landed on the ground. Damion held out his arms, wanting me to jump into them. I fell into his arms and he swung me around twice as we both laughed. He sat me down gracefully, staring into my eyes.

"You're so beautiful."

I felt my cheeks get warm. "So are your abs."

We both burst into laughter. Once we calmed ourselves, he brushed the hair out of my eyes, staring into my eyes. We both were smiling, unsure of what we should do next.

I decided to sit down and he did the same, our bodies touching. We wrapped our sweatshirts around us in the cold. He grabbed my hand and held it. "Damion," I said, taking my other hand and placing it gently on his face. I looked into his deep blue eyes, admiring how they always glowed. "Thank you for being here."

"Of course." Damion smiled slightly.

I felt my cheeks get warm. "I adore you, Damion."

He furrowed his eyebrows. It looked like he was in deep thought. "Do you ever think we should use a deeper word?"

"Like what?" I asked curiously.

"Um...." Damion shifted softly. "Like, you know, the 'L' word."

"Love?" I asked.

He nodded his head sheepishly.

I thought about it for a moment, realizing that would be the best word to describe my feelings for Damion. But I wasn't sure if I could tell him that yet. "I have a good idea."

"What's that?"

"I know we do feel that way about each other. But wouldn't you think it would be cool to make a game out of it?"

"What do you mean?"

"Whoever says 'I love you' in any situation loses... But wins.

You know what I mean?"

Damion smiled. "That actually seems like a good idea. I think you'll be the first to say it."

I laughed. "Psh... I think it'll be you." I punched him softly in the arm as I said it and we both laughed.

I laid back on the grass, looking up at the white, fluffy clouds as the trees around us slowly shook. With Damion beside me, it was like I could enjoy life to the fullest. Nothing worried me. Damion slowly laid down next to me. In seconds, the snow lifted up into the air, levitating as the flakes moved swiftly around Damion and me. I smiled, fascinated once more with Damion's abilities.

"Tomorrow is when we fly out to New York," I stated.

Damion sat up, staring at our Willow tree. "I'm quite excited. I'm sure Becca is as excited."

"Oh yeah, she can't stop talking about it. She's mostly excited to get into a club down there."

"She's crazy."

"Yeah, but hilarious." I rested my head on his shoulder, excited for our trip tomorrow.

"Let me guess, we aren't going to be sleeping in the same bed, right?" Damion asked.

I shook my head, giving him a huge grin. "No, we are going to be old-fashioned about this."

Damion flashed me a set of white teeth. "Alright, Esther. Deal."

I laid in my bed, excited for our trip tomorrow. I was thinking about buying a new bookshelf for all the books I was going to buy tomorrow.

My eyelids became heavy and I finally drifted to sleep.

I awoke in the same field with the pedestal from the same dream a couple months ago. This time, I was aware it was a dream. The field was illuminating in violet rays of light. The novel was floating above the pedestal and it gingerly made it ways towards me. I stepped back slightly and then I fell rapidly to the ground, tripping on a stick. The novel finally made its way to me, disappearing into my chest. I glanced down at my body, realizing I was now illuminating violet out of my pores. I felt light and dark within my soul and I screamed, not knowing how to cope with the feelings. I saw flashing images of everything beautiful and everything tragic. From birth to death, growth to decay and peace to destruction.

I finally awoke in my bed and it was time for the flight. I had to meet Becca and Damion at the airport. Quickly, I grabbed my suitcase and my drove me to the airport.

"I want you to stay safe, Esther. Please promise me you will." She drove Dad's old pickup truck down the backroads.

"Of course, Mom. We will. Everyone's excited for it."

"I hired a taxi driver to help you guys out so I don't have to worry about you guys getting in so many taxis that could risk your safety."

"Oh geez, Mom. Really going all out here."

She shrugged her shoulders. "I'm just worried sweetie. I have a weird feeling but it's probably just me being a mom, you know?"

I nodded my head, thinking back to my dream that gave me the creeps. "Yes, I understand."

"I love you, Esther."

"I love you too, Mom."

I was allowed to sit by the window on the plane. After almost an hour of arguing, we finally came to that conclusion. Damion sat in the middle and Becca sat by the aisle.

"It feels strange to fly, doesn't it?" Damion asked no one in particular.

"I don't like the feeling when we lifted," Becca said, making a disgusted face as if she was about to barf.

"Not on me," Damion laughed, gently shoving her face away as we all laughed.

"Flight 507 will be landing shortly." A woman's voice came on the special announcement system.

"Finally." Becca groaned after two hours of being on a plane.

We received our luggage and the three of us stood outside the airport. The city of New York was in front of our eyes. Large, incredibly beautiful skyscrapers seemed to touch the sky and the cold, chilly weather reminded me of home. It was definitely a fascinating sight.

Our taxi, 233, pulled sharply against the curb. The driver's door opened and a man in his late teens got out of the car. He had a

Brilliance by J.G. Lynn

bit of facial hair and his eyes were slightly yellow, almost like a honey-brown. He looked at us, flashing a set of white teeth as he opened the backseat door. "Welcome to the wonderful city of New York, I am Draculus, your taxi driver. I'll take you anywhere you want to go during your trip here. Just call me." He handed Becca his business card and he looked at me with a smile and winked. "Well, just don't stand there children, get in the car!" Draculus laughed.

Damion, in a hurry, got in the car, I followed him and Becca followed me. The seats were quite uncomfortable and the taxi cab smelled like someone lived in it.

"So, how's your mom, Esther?" Draculus asked.

I was caught off guard on how he knew not only my name, but my mom too. "Pardon?"

"She's the one that called our taxi cab and she spoke to me personally on the phone. Mrs. Green described she was worried that it's your first trip without her and whatnot. I told her I would protect you guys, make sure your safe and stuff and she gave me your names and a description of each of you so I knew who I was picking up. That boy is Damion with the cool eyes, your Esther and the one with blonde hair is Becca. I think your hair may be dyed or it's natural... Not sure, Beckly."

"Oh, hell no, don't call me 'Beckly'." Damion and I laughed. Becca looked at us like she was going to attack, but she sat back in the seat.

"So, Draculus, why did you choose a job involving transportation?" I asked. Someone as bulky as him should be a football player.

He shrugged, starting to drive forward. "Felt good. I ain't about that business tux life where you print papers and whatnot."

I looked up at Damion, noticing he was staring at all of the buildings and the people walking on the streets.

"Move your large ass out of the way! Damn it, I hate New York!" Draculus yelled, slamming on his breaks. Becca slapped my leg gently and I looked at her. She had a concerned look on her face mixed with the urge to laugh.

He looked back at us, smiling. "I forgot to ask, where do you wanna go first?"

"The hotel," Damion said, glaring at the man.

"Oh, you're wanna those give-me-what-I-want-when-I-want-it type of people, aren't you?"

"Focus on the road. You're driving children, remember?"

"Oh, so you don't like it when I do this?" He swerved the car into the other side of the road and dozens of cars honked as he swerved back into the original lane.

"You asshole!" Damion yelled. "You could've hurt not only us, but other people!"

Draculus shrugged. "I have the license kid, so I know what I'm doing."

I looked at Damion and he was clenching his jaw, avoiding my eye contact. Why was he acting like that? We drove the rest of the way in silence. Draculus attempted jokes but Becca and I faked laugh. Damion stared out the window the whole time.

"Well, here we are," Draculus said.

I edged closer to the window, feeling Damion's breath on me. The hotel looked like a stone palace with edges of gold to set it off. "It's astonishing," I said underneath my breath.

Draculus got out of the car and made his way over to Damion's side of the door and gently opened it. He held out his right hand, gesturing to the building. "Your luxury awaits you."

Damion got out of the taxi and he walked around the car, grabbing our luggage from the back. I got out of the car, a slight, calm wind pushing my hair behind my shoulders. Draculus grabbed my hand and I felt a small shock go through me. I glanced up but he gave me a warm smile that made me forget my worries. He helped me get onto the platform and I smiled up at him. I glanced at the beautiful building before me.

"Beautiful, isn't it?" I felt his breath on the back of my neck.

"Definitely."

He helped Becca out of the car, kissing her palm as he did so. Becca's cheeks turned a rosy color and she sheepishly walked towards me. I looked back at Draculus and he was grinning. Damion was glaring at him as he set our luggage down.

"Oh, you need help with that, boy?" Draculus asked.

He gritted his teeth. "No. I can carry these quite fine."

"You sure?"

Damion smirked. "On second thought, here." He picked up all three of the bags with no problem and threw it at Draculus.

He struggled with the bags but he smiled reassuringly at

Becca and me. "Just call me when you guys need a lift, okay? Your bags should be up in your room shortly."

"Alright, let's get registered." Damion walked passed us and up the stairs of the large, magnificent hotel.

"Is he alright?" Becca whispered in my ear.

"I don't know," I said.

Draculus appeared at my side. "If you girls ever need a lift without that buzz kill, feel free to get a hold of me."

I looked up at him and his caramel eyes smiled at me. I felt myself blush. "We sure will."

Becca chimed in. "Got any good places where you wanna take us?"

I looked away from his eyes, looking at Becca. I was about to protest, but I began to think it was a good idea.

"Meet me tonight when the boy is asleep," Draculus said, smiling at us.

"Are you guys coming?" Damion yelled across the platform.

"Come on, let's go." Becca and I walked across the platform and proceeded up the marble stairs to the glass doors.

Damion looked passed me once we met him at the doors. I turned around, noticing Draculus was staring at me. I looked up at Damion only to find him walking away with a harsh wind.

I followed after him, admiring the marble floor and the stone walls around us. The lobby of the hotel was huge and slightly memorizing. Stone fireplaces warmed the air and plants filled the area giving the scenery a homey-type of feeling. Ahead of us was a wide staircase that led to the elevators.

"We're already registered," Damion said dryly. "We're on the 20th floor." He began jogging up the steps.

"Damion, are you alright?" I asked, setting my hand on the golden railing of the staircase.

He stopped on the landing. "Oh, yeah, of course. Why wouldn't I be?"

"Are you sure because that sounded quite sarcastic."

"Can we just get up to our room?"

I shrugged my shoulders. "Yeah. Sure. Whatever." I walked up the stairs, turning to look at Becca. She sighed, rolling her eyes. She mouthed the words, 'buzz kill'.

We got to the elevators and Damion chose one. We waited

alongside with another family.

Once we go to our level, Damion gave me the keys to unlock the door. I gently stuck the key in the slot and turned. Simultaneously the door unlocked and I opened it. I heard Becca gasp as we walked inside the room. There was an elegant staircase leading to the bedrooms and the downstairs consisted of a living area and a kitchen. One whole side of the room was nothing but glass windows that showed us the scenery of New York.

"Wow," I heard Damion whisper underneath his breath. It was the first time he was pleased since the start of the trip.

"I call the bedroom near the windows!" Becca yelled.

"No, I do!" I yelled.

We both took off running through the kitchen and up the spiral staircase. Quickly, I created a force field, blocking Becca from passing me.

"Why can't I get passed you!" she yelled.

I laughed. She still didn't know about my abilities. I ran into the room, jumping onto the bed. "Hah! I won!"

"Bitch," Becca mumbled, walking into the other room. "Oh, this one has windows too!"

I laughed at Becca silently. I lay back, resting my head on the plush pillow. *How did my mom have money for all of this?* I asked myself. Suddenly, I heard slamming in the kitchen and then the sound of pages rustling. My heart started to race. I got up from the bed, walking down the spiral staircase. Damion was sitting on the leather couch with a phone book on his lap and a phone in his hands.

"What are you doing?" I asked.

"Getting us a new taxi driver," he stated dryly.

"What? Why?"

"So you can stop kissing up to him."

"I'm not kissing up to him!" I yelled. "You just don't like him naturally!"

"Oh really?" He raised his eyebrows. "He obviously likes you and Becca. He helps you out of the car... The way he looks at you and smiles... And you smile back! Yeah, it's *not* just me."

I shrugged. "So what if he likes me... I'm pretty sure he's just protecting us. And Mom requested him too."

"Whatever," Damion said, throwing the book and phone across the room. "I don't trust him." He folded his arms across his chest, staring at me with an eyebrow raised. Noticing I didn't have a response, he got up, walking towards the door and with that, he left.

Becca walked down the stairs and stopped halfway. "What was that about?"

I looked up at her, confused about the situation. "He's jealous of Draculus. He's accusing me that I like him."

Becca looked at me confused. "Wait, but don't you like Draculus?"

"No, of course not. Why would you think that?"

"He asked us out... and you agreed to it."

"What?" I asked. "When did that happen?"

"Just outside. You know, Damion went to register and we both stayed outside to talk to Draculus."

I looked down, trying to recall the event. After Damion threw the luggage at him, I walked in with Damion and Becca stayed outside for a few more minutes. Damion walked out to go get her and they both came back in. "Becca, I don't remember being there with you. Are you sure I was?"

"Yes. Of course, I'm sure!"

Damion opened the door with our luggage in his hands. He gave me a small smile and I knew he was trying to be as cordial as he could. "Do you guys want to see the bookstore today and do sight-seeing tomorrow?"

I smiled at him and he smiled back. "Yes, let's go to the bookstore today. I think it'll be a good idea."

"Becca?" Damion asked.

"Oh. Yeah. It'll be cool." She looked like she was still as confused as I was about the situation.

"Alright. Call Draculus, Becca." Damion looked at me but I avoided his eye contact.

Becca pulled out her phone and called the number. "Hey, we want to go to the Rizzoli Bookstore—okay—in five minutes—kay—thanks." She hung up. "He said he'll be here in five minutes."

"Okay, let's go." Damion held out his hand for me to take. "I haven't been nice to you lately, and I'm sorry for that. I truly am."

I took his hand, smiling. "I'm sorry too." He embraced me and I wrapped my arms around his neck. It felt good to have his warm body pressed against mine. I still had to figure out the situation with Draculus.

"Kay. Guys. You know I don't have a love life, why do you guys have to torture me?" Becca said.

We laughed, breaking apart.

"You know, Damion, you should smile a lot more. You have a beautiful girl that likes you... She likes those smiles." Draculus looked at me and winked with a grin.

I saw Damion clench his fists but he continued looking out the window of the taxi. I sighed, knowing I should stand up for him. "Draculus, he does smile a lot. Just leave him alone."

Draculus turned in his chair, looking at me. His honey eyes caught me by surprise and I could instantly smell the warmth of caramel calming me, allowing me to feel intoxicated for him. "Whatever you desire, honey."

"Hey, guys... Look." Becca pointed her finger out the other window closest to her. A huge building connected to other buildings stood before us. Cars continued driving passed us. Even though the bookstore was very basic, it was still an intriguing sight.

"I'll let you guys get out now. Cross the street, alright?"

Becca opened her door and we walked simultaneously with other people. Damion grabbed my hand once we reached the sidewalk and I could feel his warmth radiating around my fingers. Gently, he pulled my hand next to him, turning me towards him.

"Thank you, Esther, for helping me," he said, his lip pulling up into a line of happiness. His usual blue eyes gleamed.

I smiled warmly. "I would do anything for you."

The three of us walked into the bookstore. We were greeted by the smell of old and new pages and the scenery around us had an old type of feel to it. Wooden pillars decorated the structure and there was a staircase leading to the second floor.

"This is incredible," I said.

"Let's walk around. Split up and see if we find something truly remarkable," Damion said, turning on his heels, walking towards the Fiction section.

"I'll catch you later, Esther," Becca said, walking towards the Italian History section.

I smiled, *finally alone.* I continued to walk ahead, passing through a few New Yorkers. I was surprised to see women in high heels with thick blotches of makeup that smothered their round faces. It was strange because I never saw women dress up in Erin Springs every day for no particular reason.

I walked up the small staircase to the second floor, gently sliding my hand across the dusty, smooth surface. I reached the second floor and the smell of books grew stronger. All around me were shelves of books.

I calmly made my way to a large section that many people gathered around. I reached over a woman, picking up a brown book with an interesting cover. I scanned over the book, trying to get a feel for what kind of book it was. Not very intrigued after reading the storyline, I set the book down and went to the center of the room so I could find any sections that I desired.

Suddenly, I felt a powerful shock surge through me. My body trembled and the hair on the back of my neck stood up. A peculiar sensation swept across my legs and willingly, I walked through the slight maze of stories, making my way behind an abandoned set of books. Why wasn't anyone around this section? Without hesitation, my hand picked up a small, blue book. My eyes lingered on the novel, realizing there wasn't anything written on the cover. I opened up the middle of the book; there was only a phrase on the page.

Lift the red book. Easy to find. It's the only book that's red.

I looked up at the wooden bookshelf with a confused expression. Red book? I skimmed the bookshelf, quickly finding the red book. I picked it up, looking at the cover. Blank. I flipped through the pages, suddenly hearing something fall to the ground. Another electrifying surge went through me and I looked down, noticing it was a small, golden key.

"What?" I whispered in bewilderment. I bent down to pick up the key. There was an inscription on it. In beautiful italics it read, *"Clockwork."*

But what did it belong to? I turned around to find only a wooden wall behind me. There's not a door anywhere. I sighed, skimming through the pages of the red book again. Suddenly, something caught my eye... Another phrase.

Find the black book. Put it up against the wooden wall.

Instantly I found the black book. I opened the pages, spontaneously putting it on the wall. It felt like my body had no control of its actions. In seconds, there was a rumble and the ground below me started to shake. The wooden wall began to morph: the wood cracking and splitting open, slowly moving apart. In front of me was a black door.

I put back all of the books on the shelf. I peeked my head around the corner to see if anyone heard the noises. Nobody seemed to notice because they continued with their conversations. I sighed, wiping my forehead as I turned around. A small sign above the door read, "Restricted."

I felt butterflies swarm in my stomach as I anxiously walked through the door. Not wanting to be seen, I made myself invisible. The room was incredibly dark. A loud noise behind me made me jump, instantaneously turning around quickly with a blue tinted force field around me. Calming my nerves, I realized the door was disappearing. My force field faded.

"Wait," I said aloud, coming to the conclusion there was no other way out. Instantly at the sound of my voice, the room lit up. I turned around to find out it was not a room—but a chamber.

The chamber was filled with old antiques with dust and cobwebs surfaced over them. The chamber would've appeared beautiful if it wasn't dirty. Slowly, I walked across the hardwood floor, my footsteps were the only sound I could hear along with my heavy breathing. I squinted my eyes in the dim lighting, noticing a book on a stand across the room. My heart started racing, remembering my dreams. *Was it real?* I proceeded towards the stand, hesitantly walking up a few steps of stairs before I reached it.

I set my hand calmly on the book. It was opened to a section called, "Spiritual Humans." I took a deep breath, feeling uncomfortable about being trapped in a room with old antiques and a strange book. Gently, I lifted the book, looking at the cover.

The Book of Brilliance

Powerful Beings of Earth

"Oh my god," I whispered to myself. Intrigued, I flipped the old, worn pages to the Contents, reading ever so carefully. Quickly, I noticed the three beings; Exols, Clockworks and Creators. "Oh my god," I whispered to myself. "This is a book about our world."

Breaking the silence, my phone rang from the pocket of my hoodie. I pulled it out, noticing it was my mom. I hit decline, putting it back into my jacket.

"I heard that's a good book," a voice said, echoing throughout the chamber. I looked up, frightened. How did they know I was here? "Don't fret, it's fine... Honestly." An older woman appeared out of the darkest shadows of the room with a warm smile plastered on her face. Her skin was a dark shade, making her brown eyes seem more open. "I'm too old to understand that thing... It's always been a trouble to read."

Making myself visible I said, "How is it difficult?"

"Only the Souls can read the novel, dear. The book knows you and who you are as a person. It could choose only a few sections for you to read, the whole book or nothing at all."

"Why?"

"I can't describe anything to you, sorry. I am one of the unlucky ones. The book didn't trust me... I wasn't a good person."

I furrowed my brows. "Is it always about trust?"

"No. It's about the right timing too. You can't know something unless you're ready for it. Also, humans can't even read the book. There's another side of the book that allows humans to read a small novel about fantasies."

"Are you a human?"

"No. I'm a Creator. I was never a fan of life. I hate it. I'm just waiting to get rid of my soul, stuck in this chamber for what seems an eternity."

"Why are you stuck in here?" I asked, feeling uncomfortable.

"I went to the Exols when I was a kid, asking for a new life. New people. New beginnings. But they brought up my history of stealing, killing for money and using my powers for violence... Instead of killing me, they trapped me in here to protect the book. I've been here for almost a century and no one had ever come in here. I can feel myself dying."

"So, I'm the first one?" I questioned.

"Yes. How did you come in; may I ask?"

"I read the instructions in those books outside of the door... you know, in the library."

The old lady chuckled coldly. "Wow. No one even sees instructions in those books."

I looked at her firmly. "They just don't look hard enough."

She shrugged. "Possibly. But let me tell you." She started

walking closer to me, shaking her finger. "No Clockwork or Creator knows where this book is... They search frantically all over the world for it... To grasp the power hidden inside. But somehow you found it... Were you even looking for this book?"

I shook my head. "No. I think I just followed the little taste of adventure."

She smiled, showing me her yellow, decayed teeth. "The book Chose you."

I stepped back, almost knocking into the stand. "What do you mean the book *Chose* me?"

"People want to use that book for harm, Miss... They search everywhere for it... But you were completely unaware that the Book of Brilliance even existed... But you followed your instinct." She paused, looking down. "It believes you are wise enough to carry its responsibility, Clockwork. You must protect that thing with your life. Brilliance knows you're a Soul."

"Ma'am, no need to seem rude... But I'm *just* a kid that screws up a lot... There's no way in hell I can keep that book safe."

She shrugged. "Brilliance differs, honey. It believes you can. What is your name?"

I paused, unsure if I could trust her with my name. "Esther Green." My name instantly flew out of mouth.

She grabbed my wrists, looking me straight in the eyes. "Esther, you are one of a kind. You must protect this book and only show it to the people you trust. Soon, in time, the three Beings will all know the book has Chosen someone." She looked down, pausing. She looked back up at me, her eyes grave. "The world will indeed become dark because the Creators want it... We'll all have to fight, Esther. People you love will *die* before your eyes. You will have to learn how to control your suffering and remain strong... Brilliance is your life now. Everything you do is to protect your existence. If it gets in the wrong hands... To a Creator whom is the Wise... Better best your hell you're all gonna go up in flames."

"How come I never knew about this book if it's so important?" I asked, trying to comprehend everything.

The woman shrugged. "Maybe the people who care about you didn't want you to necessarily know about it. For protection basically."

"You know... All of the Creator sightings causing chaos... Is it because of Brilliance?" I asked.

"I haven't seen what the world is like, honey, but I assume so."

I nodded my head, glancing at the book and its shiny-gold tone. "How do I protect it?"

"Keep it by you. Never let it out of your sight. You'll learn more about it from others. Also, in an odd way, Brilliance protects you too."

I sighed, reaching over to pick up the book. The moment my fingers touched the book, electricity engulfed my body as I held the book in my hands. I dropped down onto my knees, crying out in pain.

"It's Choosing you, honey, the pain will be over soon... Don't worry." Her voice soothed me, calming my screams. Suddenly, the pain started up again, washing over my body with the feeling of dozens of needles penetrating me. I fell to the ground, laying on my back and looking up at the ceiling. Tears poured from my eyes and all I could hear were my screams burning my ears. I felt my body trembling wildly with pain.

Suddenly, the atmosphere changed and I was behind the same bookshelf, standing upright. I held The Book of Brilliance in my hands as I looked around the shelf. Everyone was carrying on with their own conversations, looking at books and enjoying the calming atmosphere. I took deep breaths, trying to comprehend what just happened. Suddenly, a sharp shooting pain penetrated my wrist. I set the book down on a nearby table, simultaneously pulling up my sleeve. Circles after circles were engraved in my wrist with unique designs between each. Roses and stems entwined itself between each circle. I shook my head, knowing this was real... Not just a dream. But the thing was, this couldn't be real. This wasn't real. Why was it me? Out of all people, I had to find it? I had to be the one to suffer? I wasn't sure how to feel or how to comprehend everything. I didn't even know how to tell Damion.

"Esther!" I heard Damion yell. "Esther!" I grabbed the book and walked around the bookshelf, looking over the balcony. Damion was standing, looking around. In a hurry, I ran down the stairs, my heart thumping wildly and without stopping, I accidentally collided into him. Damion fell down, looking up at me with a smile on his face. Suddenly, the smile shifted into a frown once he noticed my sickening expression. "Esther... What's wrong?"

I swallowed, biting my lip. I couldn't even find the right words to express what I truly wanted to say so instead I showed him the book. Instantly, he read it, his mouth dropping and his eyes were wide. "What the hell?"

"Why didn't you tell me, Damion? Suddenly I just walk into a library and nearly die because of this!" I yelled. I looked around, noticing everyone was staring at us.

Softer, almost in a whisper, Damion replied. "I heard about it in stories my aunt used to tell me... But I didn't know it was real since you know, she's mortal."

I bent down next to him, whispering in his ear. "It Chose me. Brilliance Chose me to protect it."

Damion backed away, looking at me with fearful eyes. "You're shitting with me."

Spontaneously, I rolled up my sleeve, showing him the circles on my wrist. "It's real, Damion. We need to go somewhere so I can tell you about it in private."

"We can't just leave Becca."

I looked around, pulling down my sleeve. "Where is she anyways?"

"Becca!" Damion yelled.

Suddenly, Becca came out of the Italian section, carrying five books in her hands with a smile plastered on her face.

"She's human, she won't understand what we're talking about," Damion stated. He handed me his sports bag. "Put the book in here."

I put the book in the bag, slinging it around my shoulders. "Humans can't see anything written in the book either. All they see is a different book."

"Yeah, I know. My aunt told me." Damion looked at Becca. "Check those books out. We'll be outside."

Damion grabbed my hand and we both walked out into the chilly air. The sky was a dark gray but the New York lights kept the night awake.

He looked me straight in the eyes. "Tell me everything, Esther."

I explained to him everything that happened. How there was a lady trapped in there and she told me that no one had ever been wise enough to find the hiding place. I described the pain I felt when Brilliance Marked me and how I had to protect the book with my life.

Damion looked at me sympathetically. "I'll be the one that protects you... What did she mean by the world will become dark?"

"The Creators will find out that the book has Chosen someone and they'll do everything they can to find that Clockwork and who knows what will happen next."

Becca came out with her books. "I found some really good books, guys. I called Draculus to let him know we're done. Wow, we sure did spend a century in there. Right?" She chuckled. Suddenly she stopped laughing, noticing we were being serious. "What's the matter? You guys act like you've seen a ghost or something."

I laughed, trying to act as if nothing was wrong when, in the inside, I felt like there was a hurricane going on inside my head. "No. We're just tired."

Becca smiled pleasantly. "We'll be at the hotel soon."

The taxi cab pulled up viciously against the curb. Instinctively, Damion jumped in front of me. "You meant it when you said you'll protect me," I whispered in his ear. His shaggy black hair flew back and forth in the wind and I caught the warming aroma of him.

"Hey, y'all!" Draculus said, smiling with a bottle in his hand. He was about to fall but he caught himself with the hood of his car.

"Hi!" Becca said cheerfully, unaware of what was going on and how uncomfortable both Damion and I felt. She opened up the door, getting in the car. Damion and I followed. We sat down in the red seats, feeling quite awkward.

"I don't know how to act anymore," I said quietly.

"Me too... It feels different now."

Draculus got into the driver's seat, pulling the car off the sidewalk and continuing to drive down the road. "So how was the library?"

Becca explained her whole story about how she tried to find her favorite books and how long it took. I looked at my hand, slowly rolling up my sleeve to see if the Mark was still there. It was. The Mark held the creation of curlicues. The largest circle held all of the other circles that slowly became smaller. Suddenly, Damion rolled my sleeve down, making me look up at Draculus. He was staring at me directly in the eyes in his rear-view mirror. He grinned. Awkwardly, I smiled back.

"So, Esther, what books did you get?" he asked.

I shrugged. "None. It wasn't that interesting." I lied.

"No. Esther. You got a book, remember? It's in your book bag." Becca grabbed my back, using her other hand to open up the bag. She pulled out the book, looking at it. I was about to grab it, but she moved her hands away from me in time. "A book about mermaids? You gotta' be shitting me, right?"

I smiled faintly. "What can you say? I like mermaids." I looked at Damion and he smiled faintly.

"That's a very interesting book, Esther," Draculus said, turning to look at me. Suddenly, I noticed his eyes weren't his usual honey color, they were gold.

"Please," Damion said, venom in his voice, "Look at the road when you drive. You're *drunk*."

Draculus smiled, suddenly sending a strange sensation into my body. "Did you tell Damion about our plans tonight?"

"Excuse me?" Damion said with a hiss and he sat up in the seat.

I looked at him. "I don't know what he's talking about." I felt another sensation spontaneously making me say, "Actually, I do. Becca and I are going tonight."

He looked at Damion with a grin. "Sometimes being spoiled makes you lose the things you love." Draculus touched my knee, still continuing to drive perfectly. I felt electricity surge through me and I smiled, a small giggle rising in the back of my throat.

"Esther, what is he talking about?"

"Nothing, I don't know what he—actually we always had something for each other, Draculus and me."

Suddenly Damion opened up his door and Draculus slammed on the brakes, stopping the car. "I obviously overstayed my welcome. Thanks for acting like you cared about me, Esther. I thought I had someone who actually understood me." He got out of the car, looking at me. "Good luck with your damn book. You're on your own." He slammed the door and Draculus sped off. I turned around in my seat, watching Damion walk into an ally. I felt a sudden rush of loss. What just happened?

"Don't worry, beautiful, we got rid of the negativity in your life." I looked up at Draculus, believing in his words. "Show me the book again, Becca." Becca smiled, showing him the book. "That's a special book."

I grabbed Brilliance, putting it back in the bag. "Mermaids are cool."

"So, guys, meet me outside of your hotel at 3 am."

"What should we bring?" Becca asked.

"Dress fancy... I'm taking you guys to one of the many greatest clubs right here in New York."

"What about our age?" Becca asked, edging towards him, smiling.

"To be honest, Esther looks twenty and you look hmm... twenty-five, they won't second guess. A few of my buddies work there, they'll make an exception." Draculus looked back at me, grinning. "Bring your beautiful, mysterious wonder too, Esther... And don't feel bad about that kid. He doesn't deserve an angel like you."

I blushed, melting into every word he said. He was intoxicating and I couldn't keep my head above his chemical. I glanced out the window, noticing we were at our lavish hotel. Draculus got out of his car, opening the door where Damion used to sit. He took my hand, helping me out of the car. Slowly and tenderly, he kissed my hand. He looked up at me slowly, his intricate golden eyes locked on mine. Instantaneously I felt an unexplained passion course through my body. Everything I remembered about the people I love vanished and Draculus was the only primary thought rummaging in my head.

"That seemed to work perfectly." He laughed calmly. "Everything about you is perfect, Esther... Your eyes, your hair..." He gently touched my hair. "Your soft, angel-like skin... Those sexy freckles..." With the back of his hand, he slowly caressed my face.

"Don't forget about me," Becca said with a flirty smile.

"Don't worry. I have a friend who is *dying* to meet you tonight."

"Oh," she chuckled. "Can't wait to meet him."

"Remember girls, I'll be here at three. Sleep well... It's good to be robust."

I sat in bed, declining every voicemail my mother sent me. I tried really hard to remember what happened to Damion and where he went but my mind was strangely foggy. I tried to think about my mom, but memories never resurfaced. I couldn't remember anything. The only thought going through my mind was Draculus. Draculus. Draculus.

I laid back in my bed, sighing. I looked at the sports bag Brilliance was in, tempted to read it... But for some odd reason I couldn't even remember where I received the book but underneath, I felt like it was important. I yawned, deciding I should go to sleep because Draculus said we had to be healthy. I rolled onto my side, shifting into a deep sleep.

I walked around the old, wooden house. Each step I took sounded like thunder beneath my feet.

"Esther," my mother shouted, "come quickly." I ran across the hardwood floor, entering the Victorian bedroom. My father was laying on the ragged, canopy bed. I couldn't see his face because everything was dimmed to the point where I couldn't see much in front of me.

"Do you remember?" Mother walked up to me, examining my face.

"No."

"Do you remember Damion?"

"No."

"Do you remember Brilliance?"

"No."

She sighed, sitting down on an object that I couldn't physically see. "Do you know the story about vampires?"

"Yes. You told me them as a child."

"Vampires are not real, am I correct?"

"Yes."

"Do you know other Boundaries besides me?"

"I don't believe so."

"A passage in a book states something about a witch. What is her name?"

I looked at the green wallpaper in the room, suddenly seeing a name plastered on the ripped paper. "Ava Blacksmith."

"Correct. Did you know she used her powers for evil despite the fact she was a happy Clockwork?"

"No."

"She morphed other Clockworks into beasts unimaginable. What are they?"

"Bloodsuckers." The words escaped my cold lips. Air vaporized out of my mouth in the cold air.

"Correct."

"What does that have to do with memories?"

"You'll figure out when the time is correct. As for now, Becca's grandmother is dying."

"Okay," I said with no emotion.

Suddenly, I sat up in the hotel bed, looking around my room. I glanced at the bag Brilliance was in. I slowly got up, making sure it was still there. It was. I took a deep breath, contemplating what my dream was really about.

"Esther," Becca whispered in the dark. "You alright?"

"Yeah. Just a dream."

"We should start getting ready."

"Yeah. We should." I cleared my throat. "Can I borrow one of your dresses? I didn't pack any."

"Yes, you may. Just not the dark blue mini dress though. I'm wearing that." I walked into her room, turning on the light. My eyes were sandy and I felt groggy from the lack of sleep. Becca searched her bag, pulling out a ruby red dress. "Here." She tossed it at me and I caught it. "That'll look good on you."

"Thanks." I went into my bedroom, undressing and dressing again. In the corner of my room was an elegant floor mirror. The dress was short, middle-length on my thighs and the dress hugged my chest, nearly exposing something that it shouldn't. I sighed, trying my best to pull it down further. I walked away, grabbing eye shadow from my bag. I put a gold color on my eyelids and I felt radiant. I brushed through my wavy hair, realizing my hair actually looked stunning in the early morning.

"You ready, Becca?" I asked.

"Most definitely."

Chapter 6: Stupidity Gets the Best of Us

The music around us was dub step and almost everyone was dancing like crazy animals. Others were sitting down, enjoying a drink. Girls would wear ridiculous costumes that seemed strangely exotic or short dresses that exposed too much.

"So," Draculus said, looking at me with pure red eyes. "You look absolutely stunning in that dress."

"I still can't get over your contacts. Where do you get them?" I asked, memorized with his eyes.

He shrugged. "Places. People. You know, the usual."

I smiled. "The usual."

"She sure is liking Darius... Isn't she?"

I looked behind me, watching Becca dance with a muscle man named Darius. He had the same red eyes like Draculus. Almost all of the men here did.

He took my hand, staring me directly in the eyes. "Let's dance." We slowly walked out onto the dance floor, the lights shining on us and everyone else. He took my hand, gently placing me in front of him.

"I can't dance."

"Just walk back and forth. Be sexy."

I did as he told, stepping out and placing my high heel firmly on the ground. I realized he imitated what I did like he was my shadow. I stepped out with my other high heel, following the same routine. I stepped back with one foot and then the other. We continued this process, becoming fiercer as we did so.

Draculus grabbed my waist, turning me towards him. "You're boring... Follow me." He put both of his hands on my hips. "Move them." Sighing, I moved them the best way I could. I continued moving them, wishing this could be ballroom instead of this. Draculus pushed me away, flipping backwards, standing up instantly. He began moving like a robot and all of his friends with the red eyes joined him. Slowly, I moved off the dance floor, watching.

Women lined up, choosing each man they desired. Suddenly, all of the men began dancing in sync like robots. The women danced around them, trying to act sexual. Draculus walked up, exiting the circle of dancers. He flipped five times up in the air, landing onto the ground perfectly only to begin dancing again. He walked back into the circle. The men picked up each of their ladies, dancing with them in a provocative way.

I turned my back, disgusted. I walked up to the bar, sitting with my back towards them.

"Wanna drink?" the bartender asked me.

"No thanks."

"No. Take one." He pushed the drink towards me, his red eyes glaring at me mysteriously.

I took it, not wanting to start any trouble. The instant he turned around I poured the drink onto the ground. Relieved with myself, I smiled slightly.

"Did you see me dancing out there?" Becca asked, her eyes glassy. I could tell she was drinking.

"You went up there?" I exclaimed, disgusted.

"Yeah it was fun." Suddenly, Darius walked up to Becca, grabbing her waist.

"Hey, baby."

Becca laughed. "I'll see you later." She gave me a small smile and I caught Darius staring at me with a twisted grin. Before I could question anything, they walked away, moving towards the dance floor.

Draculus walked up to me, smiling. "I was good, wasn't I?"

"And disgusting," I said, rolling my eyes.

"Excuse me?" Draculus pulled up a bar stool next to me.

"The way you all danced... It wasn't normal."

"Oh. You're one of those ballroom types of people? Sorry I didn't know." He glared at me.

I rolled my eyes. "And you're rude too... You threw me away to dance with some girl up there!"

"Umm... That girl was your friend."

Instantly, I could feel a headache coming on. "She's drunk and she's only, like, a few months older than me?"

Draculus looked at me, his eyes becoming a gold color.

"You're so beautiful... I'm sorry I was stupid. I'll never do it again."
He grabbed my hand, making me feel intoxicated. "I'm sorry."

Buying into it, I said, "It's okay."

"I'll just have to teach you how to dance." He whispered in
my ear, inhaling my scent. I looked at him, smiling. He lifted up my
chin with his finger. "I can't tell you enough how glad I am that
you're in my life." He leaned forward, his lips puckering. I closed
my eyes, feeling the same sensation.

Suddenly, a sharp shooting pain engulfed my wrist where the
Mark was. Instantly, I thought back to my dream where my mom
was describing Bloodsuckers and Ava Blacksmith: the Dark Witch.
Simultaneously, I came to the conclusion that Ava, using her
Boundary ability to create dark magic, turned Clockworks into
Bloodsuckers. Generations passed and the Bloodsuckers became
their own ability. Therefore, they have the powers of a Bloodsucker
and a Clockwork combined.

Images of every touch with Draculus came to my mind. I felt
the same electric shock with him just like I did with Damion. That
means that Draculus was a Clockwork. The transformation of colors
within his eyes was definitely a sign that he was a Bloodsucker too.
And that's why he wanted Becca and I so badly because they only
feast on women.

I thought back to not remembering anything and how much
of a struggle it was to keep Damion at my side. Draculus's power
was manipulation. That was why I fell under his spell so easily. And
everyone else in this room were Bloodsuckers too. Well, the one's
with the red eyes.

I opened my eyes, noticing fangs growing out of Draculus's
mouth. Instantaneously, I picked up a glass on the counter and threw
it into his face. The glass smashed against my fingers but I ignored
the pain. I looked over at Becca, realizing Darius was about to bite
her.

"Becca!" I screamed, running across the floor. I picked up a
chair, crashing it down on Darius. Becca fell to the ground, laughing
and smiling. She was drunk and totally out of it. "Get up!" I yelled.
"Get up!"

I looked up, noticing all of the men with red eyes were
coming my way. I created a force field, picking up Becca and
hanging her on my side because I couldn't fully pick her up. I tried

my best to run out of the club, but women blocked off the entrance. I realized the Bloodsuckers with manipulation were controlling them, making it to where Becca and I couldn't escape.

"Where's the book, huh, Esther?" Draculus shouted, his nose completely covered in blood.

"Shit," I said to myself. I had to go to the hotel and get it.

"So, you're the Protector, huh?" Darius said.

I dismissed the force field around Becca and me. I quickly created one to push the girls out of the doorway. I tried my best to run but it was hard with an intoxicated Becca on me.

Suddenly, someone grabbed my leg, making me fall. My skin slapped against the floor and I dropped Becca on the ground. I looked up to see it was Draculus. I yelped, trying to back away from him on the floor.

"You aren't going anywhere!" He reached his hand out, grabbing my thigh roughly.

I kicked him in the crotch, hurrying to get up. I made myself invisible, trying to find where I dropped Becca. I looked ahead to find men around Becca as she screamed out in pain. My heart sunk, realizing they were eating her.

"No!" I yelled, creating a field made out of fire that burned most of them. They fell to the ground, cowering. I ran over to Becca, blocking the combination of abilities trying to kill me. Fire and electricity were thrown at me and mixtures of water. More abilities came and I couldn't make sense of what they were, but I continued blocking them. They didn't know where I was, but they had an idea. I touched Becca, using all of my might to make her invisible too. I picked her up, trying to run across the floor and focus only on the door.

"Block the door! We can't see her but we know that's where she's heading!"

I put a force field around us, running out the door in time. I found myself in the streets of New York, the sun nearly awake. I made myself visible, calling for a taxi. The taxi pulled up against the curb. I ran to the door, opening it. I put Becca's invisible body on the car seat, getting in next to her.

I told the driver my destination. I looked at the club, realizing Draculus and his men were looking around for me. They found me in the cab instantly, running towards it. "Go! Go!" I screamed.

The taxi cab driver stepped on the gas, passing other cars. I looked behind me, watching the Bloodsuckers pulling people out of vehicles, biting them and throwing their lifeless bodies on the ground. In seconds, they got in the cars, driving our way.

"Do you want me to call the cops?" the cab driver asked frantically, driving through the streets of the city as fast as he could.

"No! Just drive!" I yelled.

"Fair enough!" He stepped on the gas harder, passing cars and yelling at people to move out of the way.

In minutes we arrived at the hotel and Draculus's men were out of sight. "Watch her," I stated.

"Watch who?"

"Stay here. I need to get something." I got out of the car, taking off my heels and continuing to run across the platform. I pushed open the double doors, running up the stairs. I ran into an elevator with a few other people. I hit floor 20 repeatedly so we could be taken there first.

"Whoa, lady, chill!" A guy yelled.

"Come on! Come on!" I yelled at the elevator.

"Level 20 pursuing," the elevator speaker said.

"Yes! Yes!" I said with excitement. The people in the elevator groaned, but I ignored them.

In a minute, the elevator opened on the 20th floor. I ran down the hallway, stopping at my door. Dammit, I forgot the key card inside. With all my might, I kicked down the door, shattering it into many wooden pieces. I ran into the suite, running up the spiral staircase. I grabbed the sports bag and felt the weight of the book inside. Quickly, I pulled off the dress, putting on jeans and a hoodie. I grabbed my phone and tried to call Damion. I looked out the windows, seeing Draculus's cars by the taxi. "Shit." I hit end, throwing the phone in the bag.

I ran down the stairs and across the room to the door. My heart was pounding and I could barely breathe. Once I reached the door, Draculus was standing in front of me, a smirk on his face.

"Hello, Esther."

Fear embraced my body and I backed up in a hurry, trying to get out of the way. Draculus smiled, picking me up by the shirt to only throw me across the room. I landed on the wooden table, feeling it collapse instantly.

"We only want Brilliance... No harm done to you."

"Never!" I yelled, getting up off the broken table with a struggle.

"Suit yourself."

Darius walked in front of Draculus, his eyes a flaming red color. Suddenly, fire formed from his hands. He threw the fire bolt at me and instantly, I created a force field, blocking the flame. I closed my eyes, turning myself invisible. I opened them, slowly walking underneath the staircase, sliding my hands around the cold metal while crouching. I circled around the living room: my destination the doorway.

"Can't run from all of your problems, Esther," Draculus said. He turned to his men. "Give this place everything you got. If there's any sign of resistance, you know where she is."

Simultaneously, the men used all of their abilities together, completely destroying the place. Some could mimic water, create fire, use telekinesis and much more. Furniture overturned and electricity surged throughout the hotel room. The counter tops disintegrated and acid penetrated the walls, making the bathroom visible.

Suddenly, someone splashed water where I was hiding. My force field blocked it of course, but they saw the resistance.

"I found her," a buff man stated.

Draculus turned around, smiling at me. "Block the doorway, gentlemen."

I sighed. There was nothing else I could do.

"Jeremy, touch her and bid her from her ability."

A man with blond hair and red eyes walked in my direction. I stepped back a few feet, tripping over a small sofa. Jeremy smiled, putting his hand over me. The moment he touched my force field, I lost all ability. I was visible again. I looked at him, shocked. What kind of ability was that?

He grabbed both of my arms, putting me in a headlock. I was useless against him. He was bulky and I was frail. I could smell blood in his mouth, fearing for the worst.

"Get the bag, Darius."

Darius walked over to me, grabbing the bag. I tried moving away but it was useless and he took it easily from me. He pulled out Brilliance, tossing it at Draculus. He caught it and opened it up. I struggled against Jeremy's grip.

"No!" I yelled, trying to get away.

"Wait," Draculus said. He flipped through more pages. "There's nothing in it... It's a fraud!"

"No, did you see that?" A guy next to him asked.

"See what?"

"A phrase... See?" He pointed at the book.

Draculus looked down, reading aloud. "The only way you could ever know what's truly inside this book and read its beholding magic... Is if you kill the Protector or you must be Chosen personally by Brilliance itself. You must be a Soul."

Darius smiled, walking up to me. "That's easy. I could be the Wise Soul."

I shifted in Jeremy's arms, trying to get away. Darius put his hand on my face, gently touching me.

"Shame..." He sighed. "Someone as beautiful as you has to die so horrific." My body shook with fear and I could feel the tears coming. Darius noticed it. "Ohh, tsk tsk, we'll try to make it quick... Won't we?" He turned to look at Draculus and he smiled at Darius. "What should we do first? Use our abilities or bite her first?"

"Abilities," Jeremy said.

"Alright. I'll burn her first... How about that?" Darius created a flame, grinning evilly. He turned and flipped quickly, fire coming straight at me. I held up my arms, trying to protect my face. The fire never came. I looked up, realizing Darius was in a thinking position. "I lied. We'll do it slow."

All of the men laughed.

"Jeremy, put her on that sofa. Mallek, paralyze her for this particular occasion."

"Sir," a younger kid about my age spoke up. "The ability only lasts for a few minutes."

"Then paralyze her again. Think before you speak. Now get your ass over here."

The boy walked over to me; a magnetic look held in between his two hands. Quickly, he threw the magnetic force down on me and instantly my body was thrown into pain. I screamed as I fell to the ground, trying to move. But I couldn't. I felt the pain but I couldn't move.

"Perfect, thank you, Mallek."

"Yes, sir."

Jeremy picked me up, throwing me onto the sofa. "The pleasure is yours, Darius."

"Thank you." He knelt down beside me, grinning. I could feel fear but it was the worst fear you could ever imagine... The fear of dying. Leaving everyone you care about to fend for themselves. "Oh, honey." He stroked my hair. "It will only hurt for a few minutes." He created a small flame, slowly moving his hand towards me. I looked at his sickening grin, realizing he was enjoying what he was doing. He put his hand on my arm, instantly making me scream out in pain. I continued screaming, trying to move but knowing I couldn't. I could feel the tears rolling down my cheeks as he continued burning me.

"Stop!" I yelled. "Please stop!"

"The more you scream, the more I'm going to do it." He created another flame, placing it on my other arm. I wanted to scream but if I wanted it to stop, I couldn't scream. I felt the pain and I could feel the tears flowing out of my eyes. I never knew this was how I was going to die... Slowly and painfully, getting tortured and there was nothing I could do. Darius got up, backing away from me.

"Electrocution, anybody? Minimum of volts so you don't kill her."

A large guy took off his shirt for no reason and began walking towards me. He had blonde hair and a small beard. He created electricity, throwing the bolt at me. Instantaneously I screamed out in pain.

Suddenly, the man was thrown across the room, his feet flying up in the air and he was knocked into the staircase. He hit his head, blood pouring out of his broken skull and electricity filled the room. The Bloodsuckers looked at their friend, their red eyes bewildered.

"Who the hell just did that!" Darius yelled.

Suddenly, another unexplained force pushed Jeremy into the windows, shattering the glass and making him fall 20 stories.

"The kid... The kid that loves her," Draculus said.

"The girl?"

"No, god no. The boy. *Damion Storm.*"

I knew it was Damion. I felt happiness surge through me.

He appeared at the doorway. "Hell, yeah it was me." Damion

used his hands, pushing more men out the windows.

"Don't just stand there! Get him!"

Damion ran across the floor, jumping over the broken table and he ran up the white spiral staircase before anyone could catch him. He appeared over the balcony, my bed in his hands. Damion had a small smile on his face, amused that he could carry the bed. He dropped it on a few men, killing them instantly. He jumped over the balcony, landing on the other sofa. He glanced at me, his eyes showing sorrow and regret. It was like time had stopped, reminding me of the time we had first looked at each other. But something else was inside his eyes: despair. Suddenly, a fireball was thrown in his direction. He ran behind the staircase quickly as Darius continued throwing fireballs at him.

"Draculus! Do something!" Darius yelled.

"I don't have any powers like yours... I can only manipulate."

"Manipulate him then!"

"No!" I screamed. Damion had an easier chance at being manipulated because he couldn't block his mind like I could.

"Shh." Mallek came up behind the couch. He touched me, giving me my feeling back. I looked at him, bewildered. His red eyes were fading into gold. "He's dead so you have your powers back."

I stood up, quickly creating a force field around Damion. I fell back down, feeling powerless and exhausted.

"I'm sorry," Mallek whispered.

I watched as Damion continued running, simultaneously fighting the men back.

"Dammit! It's not working!" Draculus yelled.

"The girl." Darius turned around, looking at me. "She's protecting him. Mallek! Paralyze her again!"

"No!" Mallek shouted.

"Excuse me?"

"I don't want to live this way anymore! I'm done with your games! You're hurting the people who are balancing this world! You promised!"

"I never liked you in the first place." Spontaneously, Darius created a fireball, burning Mallek. He continued shooting more, burning him alive. Mallek stood there, watching Darius burn him with dead eyes. Mallek knew he was dying, but he was strong and confident in why he was being killed, for the good inside him. He crumbled to the ground in ash, completely destroyed.

"No!" I yelled, tears coming to my eyes. I looked at Darius. "You killed him!"

"And you're next." He walked towards me. I couldn't protect myself. I was too broken and hurt physically and mentally. I was too tired protecting Damion anyways. Darius snapped his hand, fire illuminating. "Brilliance will be ours."

"No!" Damion yelled, looking at me. His blue eyes were dark and alarmed. He reached out his hands, slowly picking Darius up mentally. Suddenly, Draculus attacked Damion. I lost my concentration protecting Damion and he lost his concentration trying to protect me.

I knew I had to fight. I just couldn't lay here in pain. I had to move or I would end up like Mallek and the whole world would go up in flames too. Darius looked at me, grinning. "He can't save you now."

My eyes were dead as I watched him walk towards me. Slowly, I moved off the couch, falling onto the ground. *Good start*, I told myself. *Now just try to stand up.* I grabbed a hold of an end table, using it to lift myself up. I looked around, realizing Darius, Draculus and another powerful guy were the only Bloodsuckers left.

I finally stood up, staring at Darius with a smile. I could move despite the pain I felt. *I can do this because I need to survive.*

"Oh, how heroic..." Darius stated. He lifted his hand, throwing a fireball at me. I created a force field, blocking the flame. He walked closer to me, throwing one after the other. I backed up, making sure my field was healthy enough to protect me. With my other hand, I created another force field, pushing it at him. He fell to the ground instantly, swearing. I created another one with that hand, keeping him on the ground. Mentally, I made the field wrap around him so he could stay on the ground.

Quickly, I attempted running over to Damion to do the same thing to his attackers. The guy I didn't know mimics water. Damion was trying his best to fight the both of them off. He was fighting with not only his abilities, but knives from the kitchen as well. He threw a knife, penetrating the water guy in his shoulder. The guy looked down, staring at the knife in total shock. He used his telekinesis to throw the guy out the window. Damion looked at Draculus, smiling.

"You can't protect her forever, Damion... Soon, in time, she will leave you... She'll move on, loving someone else... Going through life again and the new guy will protect her..." Draculus walked towards him, knowing he was hurting Damion. "And you'll be *forgotten*.... Not even memories will save your absence." He struck Damion in the nerve. Damion looked down, dropping onto his knees. He clenched his fists, tensing his jaw. I saw the pain wash over him and my heart sunk.

"Damion! Don't listen to him! He's trying to destroy you!" I yelled.

Damion looked up, getting back on his feet. He glared at Draculus menacingly. "Liars are assholes." He brought up his fist, punching Draculus in the nose, sending him into the wall. The wall crumbled onto him. "That's for Esther you bastard. Never play with her mind again."

"We need to kill Darius. If any of the Bloodsuckers are left alive, they'll get the word out that I was Chosen. Then we'll have to fight again."

Damion walked passed me, picking up a knife that was stabbed into an end table. He walked towards Darius, bending down next to him. "Didn't your parents ever tell you *not* to play with fire?"

I quickly released the force field, Damion simultaneously plowing the knife into Darius's back.

I looked around for the book, finding it on the ground. It was slightly burned and wet at the same time. I grabbed the sports bag, putting the book inside. I slung the bag around my shoulders, looking at Damion. He was crying. I didn't have time to ask him what was wrong but I had a feeling he was guilty that he left me.

"We need to go. The cops should be here any moment. I bet a lot of people are curious on why there's people falling out of a skyscraper," I told Damion. He nodded his head and we both walked out the door. The hallways were vacant. Suddenly, police officers started walking around the corner.

"Go," I whispered. We both walked out the opposite exit, running down the stairs. My body throbbed from the movement.

"Where's Becca?" Damion asked.

I could feel my chest burn with sorrow. "They bit her."

Damion stopped running, turning to look at me. "Where is she?"

"She's in the backseat of a cab. We need to get her."

"How? There're cops trying to find us at the moment. There's no way we can even get out of here without being questioned."

I sighed, thinking. "We can't just leave her."

"She's probably dead anyways."

I shook my head. "That's not true. It can't be."

Damion sighed, starting to run down the stairs. "We'll get her."

"Let me make us invisible. Stop." Damion walked up the stairs towards me. He looked at me with uncertainty.

"Are you sure you can handle it?" He wiped his face. I realized more tears were coming.

"Yes. Give me your hand. I know you're sad now Damion, but we need to keep moving." I grabbed his hand, closing my eyes. I thought about cloaking us and how important it was. I felt the rush, sensational and vibrant. I opened my eyes, realizing I couldn't see Damion.

We continued holding hands as we walked down the staircase together. Slowly, quietly, we opened the door, entering the lobby. We were both extremely exhausted from the stairs, but we ignored it, knowing we had to pursue our rescue. The lobby was empty and the doors of the hotel were open. Police dogs were by the door, waiting.

"Just go slowly," I whispered. "They'll think the dogs are delusional."

We slowly walked out the doors, the dogs barking and jumping. Civilians were gathered, looking up at the building.

"She's in that taxi over there," I whispered. We walked through people slowly, reaching the taxi in a few minutes. I looked in the taxi window, realizing no one was in there. "I made her invisible, but a guy took my abilities away. I got them back but I didn't focus on Becca anymore."

"She has to be around here somewhere."

In the distance, I could see her blonde hair flowing in the wind. She was talking to news reporters.

"Yeah, it's weird... Everyone heard screaming and noise coming from that room... But nothing's there." A civilian said, looking up at the hotel.

"Damion, did you hear that?"

"Yeah. I guess the bodies disappear after a while once they die."

"That's good. I think."

"But they have our images on surveillance. Sure enough they'll find us."

"Becca's over there. Just whisper in her ear," I said.

We pushed through people, trying to get to Becca. In seconds, I was steps away from her.

"Yeah. I don't know what happened... Who I was with... Or where I got these bite marks... It's strange," Becca said to the reporters.

"Becca," I whispered in her ear. "Walk away from them and keep walking down the sidewalk until you hear me say stop."

She turned around to only find no one there. "I have to go. My family must be worried sick."

"Ma'am, we didn't get your name!" The lady yelled. Becca was already walking away and Damion and I followed.

"That was easy," Damion said.

"She listens to those kinds of things." Once we reached a quiet place, I yelled at her to stop. I looked around, no one was watching. We appeared suddenly in front of her.

"Oh, hell no!" she yelled, backing away from us in the small alley.

"I thought you didn't remember who we were?" I asked.

"Of course, I do. I lied to protect the both of you! I had a feeling to."

"Okay, but how are you feeling?" Damion asked, referring to the bites.

"Pretty damn freaked out that's for sure. I was bitten by vampires. My best friend turns out to be some weird ass alien. We were being followed. I was losing my blood and passed out. The taxi driver starts freaking out and wondering why I'm in the backseat of his car. I guess he couldn't see me until then. I heard glass break and there's people falling out of the window from our room and they suddenly disappear. Police show up because they don't know what's going on and they evacuate the flippin' building. I get interviewed and here the both of you are... Appearing out of nowhere."

Damion sighed, looking at me. "Tell her what we are and what happened and why it happened... I'm too tired to," I said. I sat on the ground, my injuries starting to really affect my body.

"Becca, the world is different. You know what you see in movies? On some cases those things may be true. There are three powerful Beings known as Clockworks, Exols and Creators. Exols are our Gods basically and we're Clockworks." He continued explaining the whole process of the world and what it actually is. I stepped in describing they weren't vampires, but Bloodsuckers and how I was Chosen and now I have to protect Brilliance. I explained that the only reason why we were allowed in a club was because Bloodsuckers owned the place and Darius manipulated her to drink.

Becca shook her head, confused. "So, this is all real?"

"Yes," Damion said.

She slumped down against the brick building in the alley and whispered, "I can't believe this."

"I know it's hard to understand," I said. "Even being Chosen still confuses me." I looked down, realizing the imprints were conspicuous along with my charred skin.

"Did those things hurt you?" Becca asked, finally realizing the marks all over my body.

I bit my lip, remembering the pain I felt. I was burned and electrocuted repeatedly. I could still feel the pain that washed over my body again and again.

"Thank you for... um, saving me, Esther... From those Bloodsuckers."

I looked at her, remembering she was bitten. I was still unsure what would happen to her. "How do you feel?"

Becca shrugged. "I mean, I feel groggy since I lost a lot of blood. I get lightheaded easily too."

I looked at Damion, wondering what we should do next. "Are there Healers?"

"I think so. I'm pretty sure there are if there's Bloodsuckers." He gave a little chuckle then suddenly regretted it. "It's almost noon too."

Suddenly, my phone rang in my book bag. I pulled it out, realizing I had 24 missed calls from my mother. Quickly, I hit answer. "Hello?"

"Esther Green!" My mom screamed into the phone. "Do you know I have been trying to get a hold of you THIS WHOLE TIME. YOU ARE VERY IRRESPONSIBLE."

"Mom, please, I can explain." She didn't know what happened to us.

"Becca's grandmother is on her deathbed and you are out there ignoring life and everyone who loves you!"

"Deathbed?" I whispered into the phone.

"You better get home quickly, Esther. You're grounded... Forever basically." And with that, she hung up.

I pulled the phone away from my face hesitantly, realizing Becca and Damion were staring at me with anxious eyes. "We need to get home... Becca, it's your Grandma. She's sick. She's not doing good."

"How do we go home?" Becca asked quietly. "Everything seems different now."

I took a deep breath, thinking about Brilliance. I could feel the tears starting to come and my throat was hoarse. Damion, quickly noticing my teary eyes, wrapped his arms around me gently. Sadly, I had to pull away because of the burn marks.

"We can't get on a plane," I said, "We're too beat up."

Damion sighed. "I don't know any other way to get home."

"I can make our injuries invisible. I am getting stronger at that. But we all need to hold hands."

"Are you sure you can handle all of that power?" Becca asked.

I shrugged. "I'm going to have to."

"Well, let's get to the airport. Just make sure no one sits on us."

The three of us stood in front of my house in the gravel driveway. Burn marks were still conspicuous on the worn-down roof of my home. I took a deep breath; Brilliance was still in the book bag on my back.

"This is going to be the worst beast we had to face so far," Becca said reluctantly.

"Ready?" Damion asked, looking at me.

I nodded my head.

We trudged forward, walking up the driveway. I dragged my feet as I walked, extremely weary. Damion walked up the wooden steps first, opening the screen door. Simultaneously we walked into the house to find my mother sitting at the kitchen table. Quickly noticing our injuries, she shot up in her chair, running towards me. Surprisingly, she embraced me but I jumped away in pain.

"What the hell happened!" she yelled, worry rising in her soft voice.

I wasn't entirely sure how to present the subject so I showed her the circles engraved in my wrist along with the burn marks from Darius. She quickly realized what they were and what they meant.

"No." She shook her head in disbelief, backing up, quickly falling into the table. She grabbed it for support. Damion ran to her, helping her stand up perfectly. "This can't be happening." She stared into my eyes, searching for answers. "Not my daughter."

"I'm sorry, Mom... But why didn't you tell me this was going on?" I stated dryly, referring to the search of Brilliance.

"I didn't want you to know about the violence... I wanted to keep you away... To protect you from this sickening world."

"Good job protecting," I stated. "Now I'm in the middle of it."

"Is Brilliance safe?" she asked.

"It's in the bag. No one can read the book unless they're Chosen or you kill the Chosen one." I looked down at my feet. "And they already tried to kill me."

"Honey," she said, rushing towards me again. She wanted to hug me but she knew she couldn't. "I'm sorry this had to happen to you... I can't even..."

"They were Bloodsuckers. We killed all of them. So, no one knows someone has been Chosen."

"You mean the things Ava Blacksmith created?" my mother asked.

I nodded my head. "I didn't know about her until I dreamed it."

"I believe that's the book telling you things. Or, for any cause, protecting you."

"Yeah, I know. Is Ava still alive?"

My mom nodded her head slowly. "There was a time where all Boundaries joined together in a group, testing the waters to see if we could all work together to create something beautiful. But instead, Ava created something hideous. We broke apart, not wanting to speak of Ava's creation. Eventually, she became a powerful witch, becoming something like Mother Nature... But uglier. Don't get me wrong, she is beautiful, but what she created isn't. She gave Boundaries a bad reputation and we were considered evil witches. But none of us are witches. It's Ava Blacksmith who's a witch."

Changing the subject, I asked, "Where's Becca's grandma?"

"Did you not hear me on the phone? She's dying, Esther. It's her time."

Becca instantly broke down crying, her whole world crumbling. It felt like my heart was brutally ripped out of my chest, watching her go through this and the world was stopped. "We need to go see her!" I said, quickly moving towards the door, but then my whole body engulfed in flames, reminding me I couldn't move fast.

"All of you need to be healed first," my mother said. "You can't go to a hospital looking like that."

"Why don't we just get healed at a hospital?" Becca asked.

My mom, quickly noticing Becca's bite marks on her body, sighed quietly. "They would want to know a story on your injuries but we can't give them any ideas."

"Where do we find a Healer?" Damion asked, his arms crossed.

"I know one that has a shop not too far from here in town. Keep the book locked up somewhere, Esther. Tell him that your Mark is a fake tattoo, k?"

I took the sports bag off my back, walking down the hallway into my room. Tears still fell from my cheeks and the only thing I could think about was Becca crying in the other room. I opened up my closet, finding a safe. I put the book in it, shutting the door and locking it. I put a sheet over it.

I proceeded to my mirror and I looked inside it. I was absolutely horrendous; a huge gash started at my eye down to my chin. My clothes were bloody and full of dirt, mixed with ash.

My mom's car was parked in front of an old building that was only one floor. Black curtains covered the windows and the small door, making it to where the inside was unnoticeable.

"I don't want to ask about your injuries," my mother said, "or it'll make me cringe."

"Why are we at a Tikki God shop?" Becca asked.

Damion turned around in the front passenger seat to look at

Becca. "It's not a Tikki God shop, it's what it says to mortals."

Becca crossed her arms over her chest, rolling her eyes. "Let's not do this name calling thing or I'll start calling you an alien."

I looked up at the inscription engraved in the bricks, realizing it read, 'Alvaro's Supernatural Vision'. "Mom, what is he?"

She shrugged her shoulders, gathering strange coins from her purse. "No one knows. We know he has the power of a Boundary, but he's mixed with something else. He is the Light Witch."

"What do you mean?" I asked.

"His eyes aren't normal human eyes. They're like cat eyes. Ava was the same way. He isn't an Exol because they have normal human eyes with a gold circle around the iris."

"He must be half-cat," Damion said with a small grin.

"Alright," my mom said, "I'm ready."

"What are those coins?" I asked, getting out of the car.

"Coins we use."

"We're not the only ones, are we?" I asked, getting on the sidewalk.

"We are. It's just we mixed with other Beings too. Alvaro is a Clockwork, but he's something else too."

"Does he know what he is?" Damion said as he knocked on the door.

"Yes. But he doesn't tell anybody."

Suddenly, the door slowly opened. Inside I could see there was very little lighting, giving an eerie feel to the place. Becca gently pushed Damion inside, considering he was hesitant. I followed them, my mom coming in after me. The door shut behind us with a harsh wind.

"I don't like this," Damion stated cautiously.

The place was lit up only of candles. The flames flickered and danced in the air and the sound of soft, dark Celtic music played. In the corner of the room, I could see dark, green cat eyes staring at us. I couldn't see his body, only his slanted eyes glowed.

"Visitors, intriguing," a dark, enchanting voice rumbled. Instantly, I felt Becca's warm hand grab mine out of fear.

"Why did you come?" the voice asked. Suddenly, the slanted green eyes moved swiftly in the air, edging closer to us. "I smell fear, interesting." I felt a cold presence pass me, making me turn around. One by one, the candles were blown out. Suddenly, the lights were turned on. It was still dim, but it was enough to see everything. The room consisted of liquids in jars, weapons hung on the walls and much more.

"We came for healing," my mother finally said.

Someone clapped their hands together, making us look the other direction. A man that seemed to look thirty stood in another corner of the room. He had shaggy hair that was combed perfectly, making him slightly attractive. He was frail, but underneath there could possibly be fighting muscle. "What kind of healing? Mental, physical?" Suddenly, he noticed the three of us and our injuries. "Hmm... Physical I presume." His eyes looked at the each of us, stopping to look at me. "This one was most damaged."

"Yes," my mother said. "I have coins to pay for the expenses."

He grinned, looking quite appealing in a strange way. "Good. Good. My name is Alvaro, I would be happy to take care of each of you. But one at a time unfortunately."

"Damion, go first." My mom pushed Damion closer to Alvaro and he grinned.

"Hello, boy. I see a very interesting conflict in your life. Well, conflicts to be more precise." Alvaro stared into Damion, grinning more as he read about Damion. "Intriguing... Sadly, I cannot tell you what I see or it'll ruin the surprise. But trust me, your life will make more sense on why you belong." He gestured his hands to the red curtains that had golden spirals around them. "Now, shall we?" Damion nodded his head, following Alvaro into the curtains.

"He's creepy," Becca said.

"That's only because he's different," I said, watching the red curtain sway back and forth.

After moments of waiting, it was finally my turn. Becca already went after Damion.

"I'm very curious to know what happened to the three of you. Very different injuries," Alvaro said as he led me into the room behind the curtains. In the room were candles that lit up the whole room. There were potions sprawled across a table next to a small bed. "What is your name, Clockwork?"

"Esther Green."

"Interesting. Please proceed to the bed. And unfortunately, I have to ask you to take off your clothes and change into these." He handed me a set of undergarments.

"Is there a room I can change into?" I asked.

"No, sorry, but I'll have my back towards you. I need to prepare my potions." He smiled, his slanted cat eyes looking at me. "You can trust me. I do not lie."

He turned his back to me, grabbing a jar filled with red liquid. He picked up a jar of purple liquid, spilling it into the red. "Please do not watch me, for I will not watch you."

I turned around, pulling off my sweatshirt gently and then my undershirt. I grabbed the white undergarment, realizing it was to cover only my chest. I wrapped it around me, hooking the soft material from the back. I took off my pants, grabbing the other undergarment. It looked like a short skirt with no design or ruffle. I pulled it up, turning around to look at Alvaro. His back was still towards me and he was mixing the liquids together.

"Good. You're done. Get on the bed for me. Preferably lay on your back."

I walked over to the bed, getting on it carefully. I slowly laid on my back, looking up at the wooden ceiling. The sheets were cold and I felt slightly uncomfortable.

Alvaro walked over to me, staring into my eyes. "Hmm... Interesting. You're a Half-Blood. Born from one Being that mated with a mortal." His eyes widened and he looked down at my wrist, looking at the Mark. "May I?" he asked, gesturing to my hand. I nodded my head, watching him. He gently reached over, picking up my hand, examining the Mark.

"It's a tattoo," I lied quickly.

"You don't have to lie to me, Esther," he said, continuing to look at my wrist, "Your secret is safe with me."

I believed every word he said. It wasn't like Draculus's manipulation, it was truly believing in Alvaro's compassion without any magic or spells.

"Is that how you and your friends were injured?" he asked, setting my hand down gently at my side. I nodded my head. "I wish I could explain to you that everything will be okay and that you have nothing to worry about, but sadly I can't."

"Will I be killed?" I asked softly.

Alvaro smiled a reassuring smile. "Don't think about it,

Esther."

I looked up at the ceiling, taking deep breaths. "Why couldn't the book Choose someone like you? Wise. Different. Kind. But I'm none of those things."

He looked at me with a frown. "Do not have doubt in yourself, Child. You *are* all of those things. And most importantly, you are brave. You rescued your mortal friend, protected the book and that nearly destroyed your life. You protected Damion as he protected you." He paused, searching me with his cat-like eyes. "I see everything you have seen. I know your life. I know you as a person. Brilliance Chose you for a *reason*. Everything has a reason, but as individuals we do not understand them."

"It feels like I can't talk about my feelings to anyone... But it's like you understand." I furrowed my brows.

He smiled calmly. "That's because I have seen your life as I mentioned before. I know what you feel." He stopped, taking the potion out of the bottle, rubbing it gently across my waist with soft hands. "I also understand your father is dead. I understand the pain, Esther, losing someone you love."

I looked up at him, staring into his slanted, green eyes. "What happened?"

"Well, unfortunately, I can't remember my parents. I don't think I had any... But I still have the memories of a woman taking care of me. But that wasn't what I was going to tell you." He sighed. "You know, like any other person in the world, we fall in love. I fell in love with a beautiful woman named Calypso. She didn't know who I was and it saddened me. She was mortal. I couldn't present myself to her because of my eyes. She would know about the world that we keep hidden... And I couldn't risk that. Every day, I would watch her, wishing she could love me. But I knew she couldn't love a monster like me.

"Calypso eventually fell in love with another man. It burned my heart, honestly. But she was happy and I appreciated that. I started to distance myself from her. I would wait a few weeks until I went back to her house or her work to watch and make sure she was okay. After standing outside her house for hours in the cold, I realized she would never know that I care so much..." Alvaro closed his eyes, replaying the events. He opened his eyes, rubbing the potion onto my wrists. "After a year of being together, Calypso married him. After three years, they had a child named Raho. From watching, he was an interesting child that understood life at a young age.

"I waited years until I saw her again." He gave me a small smile as he smeared the potion over my wounds. "I knew I had to give her space. I felt bad watching her... So I left, basically. But that was the worst mistake I had ever made.

"One night, I was walking along the depths of an alley. Thoughts consumed my body and I had to think about everything that was going on at that time in my life. But the sound of someone screaming alarmed me. It was a woman. I ran down the alley, water slapping against my bare feet. I came to a small clearing, realizing there was Calypso and her husband, along with many other men. They were throwing her around, treating her like she was nothing." He clenched his jaw, his soft features fading. "I always carry around a weapon, whether a sword or a dagger. At that time, I had five daggers stored away in sheaths that wrapped down my leg and a sword on the other side of my waist in a sheath. I thought of myself as a Protector at that time, that's why I carried the weapons. I stepped out of the shadows, everyone stared at me, quickly noticing my eyes. At first, they were frightened and I told them to give Calypso to me and that's when they laughed. They pushed Calypso to the ground, smashing her head into the cement, her blonde hair coated with blood. I screamed, pulling out each dagger and throwing them at each man, killing most of them instantly. Four men remained including her husband. I pulled out my sword and they pulled out guns. They shot at me but I blocked the bullets with my sword. I ran at them, slashing the other three men, killing them. I left her husband last on purpose. Once I killed all of his men, he was frightened. He smelt of alcohol.

"'What are you?' he had whispered, grabbing a metal rod on the ground, using it as his sword.

"'She loved you and you betrayed her!' I yelled at him, slashing him with my sword. Back and forth combat continued for a few minutes until I killed him out of hatred."

"What happened to Calypso?" I asked.

"I picked her up in my arms, carried her to this building nearly 70 years ago. She was dying; I knew I had to do something. I wasn't skilled with healing so I quickly experimented with each potion. I remember the sweat running down my back from nervousness. I didn't want her to die. I finally found the right potion, rubbing it on her head. I believed she had a concussion and it quickly faded with that potion. I remembered her eyes fluttering open and she looked up at my eyes, a small smile spread across her lips. She wasn't afraid of me.

"'I always knew you would come,' she had said. She knew that I was watching her; she saw me. But she thought I was her guardian angel, not her lover. But it made me proud anyways. Suddenly, she had started to cough uncontrollably. I couldn't make sense of what was going on. I then came to the conclusion she was stabbed underneath her ribcage and she was dying once more. She was breathing her last breaths and I didn't have time to make the same potion again. I bent down to kiss her so I could feel her for the first and last time... And with that, she died before my eyes." Alvaro held the potion bottle, tightening his grip. "It was painful."

I looked up into his eyes. "She wasn't afraid," I whispered.

"I still feel like a *monster*," he said, venom growing inside of his mouth.

"You're not a monster," I said, "If you are, then you're the kindest monster I ever met."

Alvaro smiled, looking down at me, setting the potion down on the table. "Her son eventually moved on into a foster home. I wanted to take care of him but he was another painful memory created by an angel and a demon."

I looked up at the ceiling. "Don't let your eyes control your life, Alvaro."

"Easy to say but hard to do. The Exols kept me here. Trapped here. For my actions." He grabbed two liquid potions, opening up the bottles. "This is the last part of the healing." He threw both of the potions up in the air, the liquid stopping midair. He reached up his hands, his left hand close to the blue potion and his right hand close to the green. Slowly, he moved his hands together, the liquid following his motion in the air. The potion turned a strange color and the room lit up with various colors. Suddenly, he moved his hands down, the potion following his movement, splashing onto my body. Quickly, a wave of relief washed over me and the uncomfortable pain was gone.

"You're done," Alvaro said, helping me up gently. "Take it

easy though."

I sat up in the bed, my legs hanging over the side. "Thank you." I looked at my wrists, realizing the burn marks were completely gone. "And I'm sorry about Calypso."

Alvaro grinned. "That was nearly a century ago, so don't be sorry." He looked at his shoes, thinking. "I know a lot about Brilliance. I wish I could tell you everything I know but we'll be here for days. So, if you ever have a strange question, come to me and I'll answer it. Also, if you're ever in pain, I'll be glad to change that."

I hopped off the table, picking up my bloody clothes. "I will."

"You might want new clothes, Esther. Don't wear those to a hospital."

I nodded my head, tossing the clothes back onto the ground. "You're right. I think I left all of them at New York though."

"All of your clothes for a two-day trip?" Alvaro questioned.

I shrugged my shoulders. "I don't plan my clothes. That's weird. I'm kidding, I have some at home."

Alvaro laughed, walking across the room. He grabbed a white robe off the rack. He walked towards me, giving me the robe. "It's so you don't feel naked as you walk out. There's a boutique down the street for you and your friends."

"Thank you." I wrapped the warm fluff around me. He gestured me out of the room and I walked ahead, exiting the room from the red curtain. My mother and my friends were standing there, waiting for me in their robes.

"Ready to go, Esther?" my mother asked patiently.

I nodded my head, walking towards Damion. I wrapped one arm around him and he wrapped one of his arms around my waist. I could feel his warmth against my body and that was all I needed because I felt extremely weary.

"Thank you for allowing me to heal them," Alvaro stated. "And do not worry. Nothing will happen to Becca. She only lost blood and that's the only thing Bloodsuckers can do. They can't turn a human into one."

My mother nodded, gesturing us to walk outside. She walked up to Alvaro, giving him the golden coins. Damion continued holding me as we walked outside into the chilly weather.

We sat in the white hospital room, waiting for our signal that we were allowed to come into Becca's grandma's room. I looked down at the clothes I was wearing. I chose a pair of tight-fitting jeans, along with a white shirt and a jean jacket to pull over and hide the imprints. Becca chose really tight skinny jeans and a really tight long-sleeved shirt. Damion, on the other hand, chose a pair of pants and a white t-shirt with a blue hoodie.

"We're ready for you," the nurse said.

We all stood up, walking towards the lady. She gave us a fake smile, guiding the four of us down the long, winding hallway. There was a woman sitting in a wheelchair, hunched over as she coughed repeatedly. I looked away, glancing up at Damion. His blue eyes scanned the sick patients in the hallway.

"Here's her room," the lady said cheerfully.

I walked into a bright, radiant room as Becca and her grandma laid comfortably in the hospital bed. There were dark circles underneath her brown eyes and her face was hallowed out. It didn't even look like her from what I could remember.

"Oh, Becca. I'm so sorry," she said with a smile.

Becca wrapped her arms around her.

Becca stared into her grandma's dark eyes, watching as the felicity in them began to fade. Suddenly, the beeping stopped on the machine. I glanced at my mom frantically, quickly looking down at her grandma. She was still smiling but she was frozen in that position.

"Move," the nurse pushed me aside, making me fall into Becca. "We need some voltage!"

"Voltage?" Becca asked frantically, looking at my mom. But she wasn't there. She left the room.

"Becca," Damion said, tugging me and her out of the room, "Let's go."

"No!" she said, trying to break free from his grasp. He lifted Becca up in the air, taking her out of the room. I turned my head and the doctor was using electrical pads to shock her grandmother back to life. Every time they placed the pads on my her, her body would jump up in the air in a spasm. I felt the tears streaming down my cheeks and my Mark throbbed as if it felt the same pain that coursed through my body.

After a few minutes of anxiously tapping our feet, the doctor strode up to us. He looked at Becca with a frown. In slow motion, I watched Becca break down crying. She was screaming hysterically and all of us got up quickly, embracing her. Her grandmother passed away.

My mother placed her head against Becca's face. "Don't worry, sweetheart. Everything will be okay. She's in better place now, sweetie. It's okay. It'll all be okay. We'll be here for you. You're still a part of the family, don't worry."

Becca pulled away from our hugs, wiping her tears. "I knew it was coming. I mentally prepared myself for this moment, but it still didn't help. I need to go call my Aunt. She has all the funeral arrangements set up." After Becca said that, she collapsed to the ground in tears. We all bent down, hugging her.

"Esther," Damion said, his hand on my knee, "I know this is a lot for you to process. I know Becca's grandmother just passed away but you were still Chosen by Brilliance."

"No shit," I said bitterly, watching the kids play in the park, the cold embracing everyone. Damion and I sat underneath our willow tree, excluding ourselves away from the people. I felt the wind prickle my exposed skin and gingerly, I pulled up my jacket.

"I still can't tell you how sorry I am that I left you... When you needed me the most. When I was gone, I stayed on park benches. I felt every core of my being telling me something was wrong."

Flashbacks of the events reoccurred. Images of Darius burning me continued to haunt me, giving me nightmares almost every night. "I can't believe Mallek died." I remembered his kind features and his extraordinary ability. Despite the fact he was a Bloodsucker, he still had compassion.

"He died for what he believed in." Damion looked down at his shoes.

"When I was laying on that sofa—helpless and afraid that I would die, I thought that was how I was going to die. I wouldn't get to see..." I paused, looking around as tears blinded my eyes and my voice became hoarse.

"Don't say it," Damion stated, "You know I would've come."

"And you did. But how did you know to come?"

"Just like Becca said, I had a feeling to. I got your call but I thought it was strange for you to be calling me... Because you usually don't." He stopped speaking to think. "Maybe it was Brilliance. I had the feeling to come and Becca had the feeling to lie."

I nodded my head. "Brilliance was the one who reminded me of my dream about Ava Blacksmith and the Bloodsuckers before Draculus could kiss me... And bite me."

Damion looked at me, tears forming in his blue irises. "When I saw you laying there... Nearly dead... It felt like my whole world stopped." He looked down, pulling a piece of grass out of the ground. "I thought you were going to die."

"I didn't," I stated eagerly. I grabbed his sweatshirt as I stared into his eyes.

"I care about you, Esther... And I *never* want to lose you."

"I never want to lose you either," I said, leaning into him. He wrapped his arms around me and I did the same. We sat there, paused in that position.

Unfortunately, I still had to go back to school even though I was carrying a deadly secret and Becca's grandma passed away. Becca was managing but she still preferred to be alone. Her aunt is lettering her live with them in Alabama. Somehow, I had to try and keep a low profile and not draw too much attention to myself. Like that was going to work.

I sat in the classroom, listening to my teacher explain the theory of atoms. Material I already knew. I rolled my eyes, tapping my pencil repeatedly against the desk. My eyes began to slowly droop as exhaustion took over my body.

Everyone around me quietly whispered about Spring Break, describing how amazing or boring it was to be with their families. I felt my stomach overturn, remembering Becca's seemingly lifeless body after she was bitten. I thought back to Draculus's color-changing eyes and his manipulative charm. Images of fire and lightning flashed before my eyes, sending shivers down my spine. I thought of the healing process Alvaro did, the liquids floating slowly in the air, combining together and then falling onto me, healing me instantly.

I looked down at my wrist. My long-sleeved blouse covered

the Mark and a wash of sadness came over me. I didn't want this life... *I don't want to walk outside and fear for my life.*

The bell rang, indicating it was time for our next class. I shoved my books in my book bag, walking out of the classroom. Everyone walked ahead of me, acting as if I didn't exist.

"Hey, beautiful," a voice said behind me. I turned around, realizing it was a boy with short brown hair and dark eyes.

"I'm not interested," I said, turning around while adjusting my book bag strap.

"No, its fine, honey," he said, quickly grabbing my arm. I turned around, shoving him away. "Don't be like that." He pulled me closer to him.

"Let go of me or I'll knock you on your ass," I said through gritted teeth.

"Feisty, I like that." He nodded his head with a grin. Spontaneously, I pulled my hand away and he fell into me. I brought up my knee, hitting him in the nose. I grabbed the back of his shirt and lifted him off the ground with difficulty. I threw him across the ground and his head smashed into the lockers, blood was dripping from his nose. I turned around, walking away from him with a slight pain in my heart. It was starting to affect me when I would hurt mortals. I was supposed to be hurting other Beings, not the ones I was protecting.

I looked down, realizing my Mark was conspicuous. I rolled down my sleeve, walking down the hallway with a slight pace. I licked my lips and slowly jogged down the hallway so no one knew I knocked the kid on his ass.

I nearly ran into my classroom with all eyes on me. I felt my stomach drop down into my stomach.

"Miss Green, is everything all right?" Mr. Koker asked me with intense eyes.

I swallowed, nodding my head. "Yeah. Just thought I would be late," I lied with a small smile. I walked along the desks, taking my seat carefully.

"We all have those moments." He turned his back to us, beginning to write on the chalk board.

I tried to calm my breathing as I thought about the poor boy knocked unconscious in the hallway. I wished Damion could be here, sitting right next to me, making me feel comfortable and telling me not to worry.

Well, the boy was the one who put his hands on me first. I couldn't get judged about that.

Mr. Koker presented America's History the whole class period without stopping. I could barely stop thinking about what happened before the class started. I didn't understand why it was affecting me so badly. The bell rang and the school day was over. I picked up my book bag, slamming my books inside and I nearly ran out of the classroom. I ran down the hallway, passing through people, trying to get back to the area I hurt the kid. He was gone but there were a few drops of blood on the floor.

If anyone found him, they would've cleaned up the blood. But they didn't, so he must've gotten up and walked away himself. I took a deep breath, running my fingers through my hair. *I'm taking everything too seriously*, I told myself.

I adjusted my book bag on my shoulder, gathering up my pride as I walked down the hallway with all of the other kids. After a while of walking down the hallways of the school, I stepped outside into the cloudy weather, the cold embracing me. I breathed in the chilly air, my lips becoming numb.

Suddenly, a cold hand touched my exposed shoulder, making me turn around instantly. It was the kid.

"You're pretty hot, beating me like that."

I looked at him with furrowed brows, deciding if I should hit him again or not. "Shut up and go away."

"I saw that tattoo on your wrist... Never thought the great Esther Green would get a tattoo."

"I don't have a tattoo," I said, walking away from him.

"Yes, you do." He grabbed my arm viciously, turning me around and lifting up my sleeve. He placed his thumb on the Mark. Suddenly, my vision became clouded with words and phrases. *The Prophecy of the Exol Family.* Suddenly, words and phrases moved so fast that I could barely read a thing. *The Prophecy of the Spiritual Human. He has of course, lost everything beholding to him. His family to be more precise. He will learn to stand up and fight out of anger, protecting the Prophecy of the Half-Blood with delicately intricate forces.*

"Get away from her!" I heard Damion yell. Underneath the phrases, I could see Damion standing in front of me, his jaw

152

clenched. Suddenly, he picked the kid up by his shirt, throwing him into a tree that stood next to a bench a few feet away. The phrases quickly disappeared and my vision was back to normal. Becca clung to my shirt, looking at the kid worryingly. She looked at me, her eyes petrified with fear.

"Are you okay?" Damion asked, turning around to look at me, his eyes bulging as they scanned me.

My breathing increased as my chest heaved up and down. I stared at the ground, trying to make sense of what happened. I looked up, making my decision. "I need to see Alvaro."

Alvaro's head was cocked to the side as he stared into my eyes, making sense of what happened. "The boy was mortal—not a threat." He looked down at the Mark. "May I?" he asked. I nodded my head. He picked up my wrist and gently examined it. He pressed down on the Mark, phrases simultaneously appearing.

"Do you see it?" Alvaro asked.

"Yes. What are they?" I asked, looking at an illustration of a man sitting on the highest peak of a mountain, meditating inside my head.

"Intriguing." Alvaro released my hand gently. He walked to his desk, picking up a piece of paper. "It seems to me that the book is inside you. You don't physically need the book to read. You can press the Mark and it reappears."

"So, I don't need the book of Brilliance. I can use my mind?" I asked.

Alvaro nodded his head slowly, setting down the piece of paper after writing on it. "Besides, Brilliance in its book form does become a struggle."

"To keep the Brilliance book safe—should we burn it?" I asked.

Alvaro grinned. "I don't see why not. Book form doesn't matter much at all. It only makes the process of protecting it more difficult."

I nodded my head, getting off of the table. A question swarmed through my head as I was overwhelmed with a curious feeling. "Will this kill me?"

Alvaro looked at me with his cat eyes, searching mine. He sighed. "Esther, it would be wrong for me to tell you such a horrendous thing."

I looked down at my shoes, sighing. "Yeah. Okay."

Alvaro came around the table quickly, moving closer to me. "Esther, dear. Do not be upset with me." He looked at me intensely. "I just don't want you to dwell on the day."

I shook my head. "I understand." I rubbed my arm, staring at him. "The lady in the chamber: you know, the place Brilliance was in. She did tell me that the people I care about will die before my eyes."

Alvaro smiled faintly. "I think she referred to the War."

"So, there is going to be a War?"

Alvaro's smile faded. "My largemouth can't keep shut since I keep telling you your Prophecy."

"Prophecy?"

He rolled his eyes, disgusted with himself. "The Half-Blood Prophecy."

"Is it in Brilliance?" I asked curiously.

"Yes. But there is a good chance it will not show you, Esther. It doesn't want you to know anything until it happens. They're called the Soul Prophecies."

"Why? I want you to tell me what the Soul Prophecies are."

"Sometimes you may not find your future likable."

"Well, it would help to *prepare* for it."

Alvaro smiled. "Yes. It would help indeed." He paused, changing the subject quickly. "If you want to know your upcoming future, you and your friends will be suspended from school because of that boy who didn't understand boundaries."

"That figures."

The three of us stood outside in my backyard. The book laid on the ground a few feet away from us as the wind tore at our bodies. Fire was lit in the fire pit on the other side of the yard.

"Are you ready?" Damion asked, his black hair flapping violently in the wind.

"Yes," I stated. I stared at the book, watching the pages flap around in the binding from the thick wind. I looked over at Becca and she was staring at the fire, fear in her eyes. I could tell she wasn't taking this all too well.

Damion used his telekinesis to mentally move the fire across the lawn near Brilliance. He pushed the fire into the book, watching the book burn instantly. The pages slowly overturned into black balls of ash. I could smell the smoke tickle my nose.

I felt a burning sensation on my arm that alarmed me. I quickly rolled up my sleeve, examining the imprint. I pressed my thumb into my skin, the phrases appearing. *It worked. Brilliance is only inside my mind.*

"It worked!" I said with excitement.

Damion grinned, showing his white teeth. He ran over to me, picking me up and swinging me around in the air. We laughed as he set me back down. We stared into each other's eyes, watching our own reflections.

"No one knows the secret about the book. It'll make everything easier."

I nodded my head, smiling. "Less to worry about."

"Wow," Becca said, staring at me, "I never knew you lived this type of life... I never would've thought, when we hated each other, you had a war going on inside of you."

I looked at Becca as a small smile spread across my lips. "We all face a battle, Becca. It's the way life is."

"I'm a mortal. I won't face any battle. I mean, other than my aunt in Alabama."

I shrugged my shoulders. "You never know."

"You guys wanna order a pizza?" Damion asked. "Since we're all suspended."

"Pizza wouldn't hurt a bit," Becca said, starting towards the house in a jog.

Damion's eyes locked on mine, smiling. He held out his hand and I took it. "Now all you have to do is protect yourself and Brilliance will be fine."

I smiled, holding onto his arm as we walked together up the small hill towards my house. "You must help with that."

"Oh, you know I will." He chuckled, swooping me up off the ground, carrying me bridal style.

"I noticed you've been using your super strength lately."

He laughed. "Of course. Only professionals use their super strength."

I laughed as we got in the front yard of my house. Damion walked up the porch stairs, continuing to carry me inside.

"Esther," Becca said, coming up to me with worry-filled eyes. "Your mother wants you."

"Now?" I asked, wanting to sink my teeth into pizza.

Damion set me down gently. "Go to her. We'll save you a piece when it comes."

I walked into the living room, going behind the wall that lead into my parents' room. My mother was sitting on the half-made bed, holding a photograph in her hands. A piece of paper was rolled up scroll-like next her. I walked further in, noticing tears were streaming down her cheeks. My heart dropped into my chest, fearing for the worst. Gingerly, she handed me the photograph. I took it carefully, looking down at it. My parents stood close to each other. My mother was young and vibrant. Her green eyes shined into the camera with happiness and her dark auburn hair was healthy and alive. My father, on the other hand, had a full set of dark hair that covered his eyes. His brown eyes were a golden color instead of their usual dark brown. In between them was a child at the age of six. I looked the same in the photograph, but much older now.

"I want you to keep it," my mom said quietly.

"Is..." I stopped myself, inhaling my breath. I couldn't say the words.

"Yes. Everything is fine."

"Okay."

"But Esther, you've been Chosen. I don't think you understand what this means. Everything is going to change. Evil people are looking for that damn thing. I wish your father was here... Helping me understand what I need to do now to keep you safe."

I could feel my lip beginning to quaver and I fell onto the bed next to my mom. She held me in her arms, rocking me back and forth. My tears streamed down my cheeks, wetting my mother's burgundy shirt. Images of my father pushing me on the swing when I was a child passed throughout my mind. His smile flashed through my head and more memories came. The way he would spin me around in the air, making me feel weightless and free. When he would throw me up into the air, allowing me to soar in the sky and catch me. The thing was, he always caught me. Whenever I was down, he would be there to lift me back up.

He was a mortal. But he taught me a valuable lesson about

them. No matter their ignorance, they still love and the right ones would always care. If they don't, then they're obviously not the right one. Mortals are young and carefree—but they teach you to be alive. We, Clockworks, we're serious mystical Beings, but they look at the world differently; some positive and some negative.

The thought of my father gave me faith in the world. I had to do what was right. *I will protect them from our world. I will save them. Because I can do anything and nothing can stop me.*

Chapter 7: Losing the People You Love the Most Can

Hurt

I laid in my bed, looking up at the ceiling. Tears stained my cheeks as I thought about Brilliance. I wish my father was here. Flashbacks of all of the wonderful times we had together resurfaced painfully. I haven't contacted my friends in a week. I was sure they understood that I needed time alone. I wish I could see Damion's bright blue eyes and his bright, radiant smile.

The funeral was tomorrow but I couldn't gather myself to go. My mother insisted I should since it was for Becca. I knew it was going to remind me of my father's funeral.

"Esther," my mother said, knocking on my door. She opened it, slowly walking towards my bed. Tears streamed down her cheeks. "I noticed when you burn this up. I decided to salvage it for you. I think it'll help you during your new journey."

I slowly reached over, grabbing the piece of paper from her hand. It was the scroll I saw sitting next to her a week ago.

"Are you hungry?" my mom asked.

I shook my head no, opening up the paper. I laid back on my bed, admiring my father's intricate handwriting.

"I'll leave you alone. Love you, Esther." My mom turned her back towards me. She walked out of my room, closing the door behind her.

I found it funny how I always wished of having a purpose in the world, and now that I have it, I don't want it. I'm scared. I'm utterly terrified. I keep seeing the same phrases from Brilliance flash in my head. I felt like my brain was going to explode.

I took deep breaths, trying to stop my emotions from becoming too unbearable. Tears dripped onto the letter as I crumbled it up, moving slowly to put it in my drawer. I got off my bed, walking towards my window. I looked up at the full moon that hid behind the trees across the street. *As brave as you are, you will succeed.*

158

I inhaled, slowly exhaling, knowing that this wasn't a game anymore. This was real life coming to attack me. But I wouldn't be alone. I wouldn't do this alone.

When the time comes, I will fight back. And I will be ready. I will kill with no hesitation.

I stood in front of the mirror in a black dress with fishnet ruffles going down to my knees. I had black leggings on to keep my legs warm and fishnet gloves to keep my hands warm. My wavy hair laid perfectly down my back.

"Hey," Damion said, appearing in the doorway. I looked at him, trying to fight the urge to cry in front of him. He moved swiftly towards me, embracing me with strong, comfortable arms. I put my hand on his shoulder, my fishnet gloves sticking to his black tuxedo. I moved my head, staring at the mirror. I saw Damion's black hair spiked for the occasion and my hair laid down my back, his chin resting on my shoulder. We looked older than the first time we met. Our features were more intense and broader now that we knew what was coming our way.

I pulled away to look at his blue eyes, my hands still resting on his shoulders. "Damion, when the time is up and they know who was Chosen, promise me we'll be ready."

Damion gingerly lifted his hand, resting his warm palm on my cheek. "I promise. I will do *anything* to protect you." He paused; his jaw slightly clenching. "You know what Draculus said? About you leaving me?"

I shook my head slowly, watching a fire illuminate in Damion's eyes. "You know I will *never* leave you, Damion."

He grinned, flashing a set of white teeth. He brought me back into his arms, hugging me tightly. "Now you just have to get through today."

"Yeah," I mumbled into his chest.

During Becca's grandmother's funeral, I kept on replaying the events during my father's funeral. I blocked out Becca's sobs, remembering my father.

"Reymond Green was a very interesting individual as we all know." One of my father's workmates I never met before stood on the platform next to the podium, delicately dabbing his teary eyes.

"He was a quiet man; he didn't say much. But we didn't need words to hear him."

I felt the cold wind wrap around me, slowly moving up my legs like a ghost, creating uncomfortable goose bumps. Chills swam down my spine as the first few snowflakes began to fall. I looked up at Damion and he was staring down at me with thoughtful eyes.

"Are you cold?" he asked with a whisper.

I shook my head, trying to hide my goose bumps. "No."

He took of his black tuxedo jacket, wrapping it around my shoulders gently. "It's not okay to lie... Or in this case—be modest."

I looked up at him, smiling slightly. "Thanks."
I thought back to my father's funeral. I remember looking at my mom whom was now standing at the podium, shielding her crying eyes with lose sections of hair from her bun.

"I love Reymond. He was my other half. He knew every little quirk about me; simply as what toothpaste I like, my insecurities and so on. But he embraced all of that, loving me for who I was.

"Don't get me wrong. We did fight. But what is love without arguments? Everything can't be *perfect*. Especially if you have a mother who never wanted you to marry the love of your life... But you learn to fight for the things you want. They can't be given to you." My mother was referring to the time where my grandmother didn't want her to marry my father because he was a mortal. In our world, it was wrong to do, considering my father would have to eventually find out about my mother being a Clockwork. My mother didn't care—she loved him.

My mother continued on with how they had met, describing their love in great detail. She told the small crowd of people that I was born and that I was the greatest blessing of their lives. I felt the tears beginning to pour down my cheeks at the memory. Gingerly, I dried them with the handkerchief everyone was given before the funeral.

A huge gust of wind happened suddenly, snow blowing in all of our faces. I turned around in my chair, spontaneously noticing a figure standing close to a tree in the cemetery. He was wearing a white suit with a black cape that covered his clothes. He had black sunglasses on that shielded his eyes. *Alvaro*.

"Who is that?" Damion whispered, staring in the same direction as me.

"Alvaro."

"What's he doing here?"

"I don't know," I said, calmly and quietly standing up. "I think he might want to talk to me." I ducked down, trying to avoid everyone staring at me. I glanced at my mom but she was too lost in Becca's speech to notice me. I stepped down on the thin line of snow, edging closer to the woods where Alvaro was standing. The cemetery was surrounded by large, pine and maple trees, giving it an eerie feel.

I walked towards him, unable to see his eyes behind his sunglasses. He smiled at my approach, gingerly running his fingers along a single piece of grass he had plucked out of the ground.

"Esther," he said, grinning, "Nice to see you."

"What are you doing here?"

He moved swiftly towards me, reaching his hand up to dab my wet face. "You're crying."

"I know," I stated. "That's what funerals are for."

"Oh." He glanced at the ceremony behind me. "So that's what's going on."

I nodded my head. "Of course... Why else would I be here?"

He chuckled softly. "I was only kidding, Esther. Lighten up."

I grabbed my arm as if I were shielding myself from the tears that were beginning to unleash. "Why are you here? Why are you wearing the sunglasses?"

"I can still roam Erin Springs, but that's as far as I can go under the Exols." He stared at me. "To shield my demonic eyes," he stated, his bubbly persona fading.

"Your eyes are brilliant. Don't hide something that is you."

He looked down at my wrist, staring at my fishnet glove that hid the Mark. "I would say the same thing to you." He sighed, looking into my eyes. I could see his narrow eyes faintly behind the sunglasses. "I hope you do know that when you leave, I can no longer protect you."

I looked at him with shock, trying to comprehend what he was saying. "What do you mean?"

He looked at me, his face contorting with surprise. "She hasn't told you yet, has she?"

"What do you mean?" I asked again, furrowing my brows.

"Your mother has been preparing for quite a long time." He

161

looked at me intently, his jaw slightly tightening.

"She knew this was going to happen?" I asked, my anger slowly rising.

"Yes. She didn't know about Brilliance though. But after it came, she has been seeing *things* more clearly."

"So, I'm leaving? And why can't you protect me?" I asked, my body beginning to shake with rage.

He licked his chapped lips. "That is further information your mother will explain to you. But as for me not being able to protect you—" He paused, looking down at the snow. "Remember the story I told you? About my lover?"

"Yes."

"Yeah. Well the men I killed were human. Unfortunately, I was trialed by the Exols for killing the people we are to protect. By punishment, they forced me to stay in Erin Springs until the end of time, as you should remember. So don't question why I can't be there for you." He continued staring at me, his eyes intense behind his Ray Bans. "When you go, you'll be on your own."

"I'll still have Damion and my mother," I stated.

He turned his back towards me, taking deep breaths. "That's what you think."

"What?" I asked, simultaneously hearing another voice.

"Esther," my mother said. I turned around, staring at her smeared makeup. "People are beginning to line up to see Becca's grandma's body. We'll be last." She took a deep breath, wiping her smeared makeup with her handkerchief. "I need to talk to you about something."

I glared at her. "I think I know what it is."

She looked up, finally noticing Alvaro standing behind me. "Keep yourself away from her. She needs to figure things out on her own."

Alvaro stepped beside me, looking down at my mother. "You're only upset because she knows you've been lying to her. Besides, I haven't told her anything. I don't plan to because like you said, it's for her to figure out." He stepped closer to my mother. "But she does deserve to know what's going to happen... You need to *prepare* her." That was the first time I ever saw Alvaro lose his gentle persona.

"I shouldn't have gone to you for help. I knew you couldn't

keep it inside of you forever, you little *monster*." My mom raised her hand as if to slap Alvaro but quickly, I jumped in front of him, spontaneously slapping me in the face. I felt the penetrating sting that welled my eyes with tears.

My mom recoiled her hand, looking at me in horror. "Esther, I'm so so—"

"*Enough*," I said, venom coating my voice. "I want to know what's going on right now. You can't keep hiding things from me."

Alvaro sat down on a small bench I didn't notice before. He flicked his hand up as if he had been defeated. "Just tell her already, Carie."

My mother sighed, looking around to make sure everyone was standing by the casket. "We're moving to Pennsylvania tomorrow night. We need to get home soon to start packing."

I looked at her, furrowing my brows. "Why can't we just stay here?"

"*Esther*," she hissed, "we can't stay here. Who knows if the Bloodsuckers didn't tell someone that you've been Chosen."

Alvaro looked at me, taking off his Ray Bans. "It's not safe for you here *anymore*." His cat eyes stared me down.

I shifted on my feet, feeling uncomfortable. "So this is how it's going to be now? I can't have a normal life?"

My mother looked at me, her eyes blazing. "Didn't you always want the adventure? Didn't you always want a *meaning*?"

I leaned in, glaring at her. "I didn't want to leave everything behind!"

Alvaro stood up, coming towards me. He embraced me with strong arms, his warm body thawing mine. "I know it's going to be hard... But it's for your protection."

"What about Damion?" I asked, pulling away to look at my mom. Alvaro stepped away from me, looking at my mom as well. He calmly put his sunglasses back on.

"You're going to have to leave him behind," she said solemnly. "Love doesn't last forever. Make it easier on yourself."

"No!" I yelled, my face inches away from my mother's. "I will never leave him behind!"

Alvaro moved in front of my mother, guarding me from hitting her just like how I guarded him. He rested his hand on my shoulder, staring at me with compassionate eyes. "It's only temporary. The both of you will reunite again."

I looked down, tears beginning to fall out of the corners of my eyes. "That's if he takes it well."

"Tell him after the funeral," my mother said.

I looked up, glaring at her. "Now that you lost the love of your life, you want me to lose mine now." I moved away from Alvaro, shoving my shoulder into my mother. She fell onto her butt, staring up at me with anger. I rolled my eyes, walking away from her. I proceeded towards the funeral, listening to everyone talking about Becca's grandma or generally catching up with each other. I saw Damion socializing with a couple people. He turned around, simultaneously staring at me. He grinned. "Hey."

I wiped away my tears, managing to smile. "Hey. When I get done looking at Becca's grandma and talking to her, you want to go to our tree?"

"Yes. It's been some time."

I walked passed them, edging closer to the coffin. I looked down, realizing her grandmother didn't even look like herself. She seemed like a plastic manikin, showing absolutely no emotion. Her eyes were closed and her lips were sealed together. Her hands were clasped together at her waist. I turned away, trying to fight the tears. I remembered my father's funeral and how he looked like a plastic mannequin. Phrases from his letter played throughout my head. Images of him pushing me on the swing as a child resurfaced as well as the time, he and I had made a mess baking my mother a birthday cake.

"Esther," Damion said, staring at me with solemn eyes. He came towards me, wrapping his arms around my waist, keeping me close to him.

"It hurts." I cried into his shoulder, remembering everything my father had ever told me. *"See look, I throw you up in the air… and you fly like a hero."* He told me that before my parents even knew I was a Clockwork. *"Sometimes things aren't just given to us, Esther... Sometimes we have to fight for them."* *"Love is strange, huh? I gave up everything for your mother and she did the same for me."* *"Sometimes, when skies become darker than before, tell yourself the sun will always shine behind the clouds."* *"You've always been beautiful, Esther. You've just never noticed it before."* *"I believe in you. And I know, as brave as you are, you will*

164

succeed." I felt the agonizing pain in my stomach as the phrases continued and the Mark on my wrist burned as if it felt sadness itself.

Damion and I sat underneath the willow tree, snow gently grazing our faces with the prickly cold. I still had Damion's coat around my shoulders, keeping me slightly warm. I glanced at him, noticing his body was moving unevenly, indicating he was shaking tremendously. There was no one in the park in the cold weather.

"Are you cold?" I asked him.

He shook his head.

"It's not good to lie." I quickly created a heating force field around us and the tree, blocking out the cold.

He looked at me, grinning. "Nice."

I smiled, looking down at the snow-covered ground. "Now we just have to do the same thing to the ground."

Damion laughed, throwing his head slightly back. He stopped suddenly, staring at me with blue eyes. I watched as he extended his hand towards me, resting it on my shoulder. He leaned into me and I did the same. He used his other hand, gingerly placing his trembling palm on my cold cheek. Simultaneously we closed our eyes. Images of Alvaro and my mother at the cemetery flashed throughout my head, slightly making me feel guilty being here with Damion. *I need to tell him.* Before our lips could touch, I jerked away. He opened his eyes in bewilderment then I could see the hurt setting in.

He looked down, ashamed. "I know. I shouldn't have done that."

"No, Damion, it wasn't that at all... I just need to tell you something." By the tone of my voice, he quickly sensed it wasn't good. He continued staring at me, his eyes seemingly opaque. "Alvaro and my mother both agree that staying here in Erin Springs would increase my danger level. They think Draculus had time to inform others that someone has been Chosen." I paused, staring into Damion's eyes, trying to find signs of emotion but there were none. I bit my lip, continuing. "I'm moving to Pennsylvania tomorrow night. It was so sudden—my mother told me at the funeral. Alvaro seemed to be rambling about something... But my mother has been lying to me—"

"You *promised*," Damion hissed, staring at me with boiling eyes. "You said we would never leave each other!" He screamed in my face, beginning to stand up. He grabbed a hold of the willow tree as if he were using it to support him. Tears began flying down his cheeks. "Do you know that you're the *only one I have left?*" His words penetrated my heart.

"Damion," I said, standing up. I looked at him and my heart welled up. "You have a family who loves *you*."

He turned his back towards me, his hand gripped onto the tree. "They *don't love* me..."

"Don't be ridiculous, Damion," I said, taking a step closer to him.

He turned around abruptly, his eyes staring at me like daggers. He never looked at me like that before. I felt the fear slowly tearing at my body. "If they loved me don't you think they would understand me? Or don't you think my father wouldn't work away his life so he doesn't have to see me! *Is that what love is?*"

I looked at him, knowing he was right. "Damion, I lo—"

"No." He held up his hands. "If you loved me you wouldn't be *leaving* me."

"Damion, please. I don't have a choice."

"There's always a choice, Esther!" He yelled, spit flying in to my face. He moved closer to me, grabbing my hands. He stared into my eyes intently as the soft Damion started to come back. "We could run away together... You wouldn't have to leave... I would be the one protecting you—not your mother."

I moved away from Damion, looking at the white, sparkling snow. "Damion, you know I can't just leave my mother. She not only lost the love of her life, but her daughter as well if I did that." I looked up at him, noticing his face was slowly crumbling in defeat. I felt the pain in my heart become more intoxicating. I wasn't only hurting him, but myself too.

"You *lied* to me... You said we would always be together... And you can't just give up everything for me?"

"Damion, that's not true."

"And you know that game you came up with? About whoever said 'I love you first' loses but also feels the satisfaction of expressing their opinion? Yeah, that's damn well stupid. You *can't* make a *game* out of love." He paused, grabbing hold of the tree. "Well, you know what, I think you could. Cause you've done it already."

I looked at him, horrified. I stepped towards him, grabbing a hold of his body, using all of my strength to pull him towards me. I leaned in, trying to kiss him so he could know that I do love him. He pushed me away violently, staring at me with demon-like eyes.

"Don't you dare try something like that on me again. I hope you have fun protecting Brilliance. You're on your own this time. And I *mean* it." He brought up his fist, smashing it down onto our willow tree. The tree split down the middle, cracking the bark with a horrendous sound. He stared at me, his eyes blazing. "That's our love breaking apart." He walked into my force field, knocking him on his butt. Quickly, in shock, I stopped concentrating on the force field. He got up clumsily, looking at me. "*I hate you,*" he said through gritted teeth. I looked up at everything in the park, noticing every tree swaying violently, the large creek overflowing with water and objects moved viciously in the air. I felt vertigo coming on and I fell onto the tree in slow motion, simultaneously cracking my head on the solid bark. I looked up at the sky, feeling blood pouring into my eyes. Snow danced in the air, intricate designs inches away from my face.

"Esther," I heard Alvaro's voice filter throughout the air. I couldn't see him because my eyes began to slowly darken. I felt his strong, but frail arms pick me up. After that, everything became black.

I heard movement around me, footsteps moving around on hardwood floor, another set of feet tapping nervously on the ground. Voices filtered the air, making me want to suffocate myself with a pillow so I didn't have to hear the noise.

Slowly and gingerly, my eyes fluttered open. At first, I couldn't see anything but darkness. My eyes began to work slowly, showing me the dim-lighted room and the wooden ceiling above me.

"If she goes, I can't be able to heal her and you know that Carie."

"It's your fault you got yourself in trouble with the Exols, Alvaro."

Alvaro sighed. "We can't let the Prophecy of the Half-Blood be true. If I'm away from her, she has a greater chance of being killed and you *know* that."

"We've both seen the future, Alvaro. If this is her destiny

then so be it. We shouldn't change something that can't be tampered with. Esther is in charge of her own life and she is the only one who can change the Prophecy."

"Don't you think this is too much for a child to handle?" Alvaro asked, his voice sympathetic.

"I am aware of that. She is my daughter, you know."

"Shhh," Alvaro hissed. "She's waking up."

My mother's face was suddenly over me, staring down at me with worry-filled eyes. "Honey, how do you feel?"

I got up quickly, looking around for Damion. Suddenly a rush of vertigo came over me, making me fall quickly back down. Alvaro rushed over towards me, catching my head before I could fall back onto the bed.

"Careful," he said. "Don't strain yourself."

"Damion?" I whispered; my voice barely audible. I turned my head, trying to find him.

"Honey," my mother said gently, "Damion is okay. He went back to his house and he accepts the fact that you're leaving."

I got up again, balling my fists together while clenching my jaw. "You're lying!"

"Esther, darling, I'm n—"

"He said he *hates* me, Mom!" I screamed, watching my spit spray out. "When can you *stop lying*? How can I know to trust you!"

"I do it for your own good! I don't want you moping around, Esther!"

I looked up at her, my eyes squinting from the newly profound tears resurfacing around my irises. "He did everything for me, Mom! When it was *his life,* he chose to protect me! He was there for me ever since I met him! Huh? Who did he drop everything for?"

My mom stared down at me, her eyes blazing with anger. "That's *nothing.* He should understand what you have to do to keep Brilliance safe!"

Alvaro stepped in, looking at my mother with soft eyes despite his clenched jaw. "*She's only a child.*"

She looked at him as if she were slapped in the face. "I thought you were with me on *this*?"

"She just lost a father who loved her a year ago and now you're taking away the only thing that ever made her *happy*? You need to think about what you're doing, Carie."

168

"She needs to know that she will be killed if she stays here Alvaro, and you know that."

"Stop!" I screamed. "Stop acting like I'm not here when I *am.*" I looked at my mother, glaring at her with daggers. "How can I possibly understand if you won't tell me *anything?*"

"I don't want to frighten you."

"I'm already scared! The both of you keep saying I'm going to die!"

Alvaro stared at me with his cat eyes. Sympathy slowly seeped out of them. "We both had the same vision... If you stay here, you will be slaughtered."

I took deep breaths, trying to comprehend everything. "So, you both think I won't be killed if I leave?"

Alvaro nodded his head, smiling slightly. "It won't be hard— starting a new school, making new friends... You'll fit in perfectly."

I laughed coldly. "Yeah. I'll definitely fit in... It's not like there's going to be a war happening because of me."

"Esther, please stay positive," my mother said.

I looked up, glaring at her. "It's pretty hard to do that now."

She sighed, turning her back towards me so she didn't have to see my face. "You need to make sacrifices... There's so much more going on than just a little boyfriend."

In anger, I jumped off the bed, pushing my mom violently into the wall. "He's not just a *little boyfriend*. He's so much more than that!" I paused, looking at her lay on the ground helplessly, trickles of blood ran from her scalp down to her face. "If it weren't for him, I would be dead!"

Alvaro moved gracefully, standing in front of me. He rested one hand calmly on my shoulder. "That is true, Esther. But there is more at stake than your relationship with the boy. We need to get you out of the state and hide you in the wilderness. Once the secret is out, Creators will rise up against everyone, creating their own army to retrieve Brilliance. They will do harm to this world with the knowledge of Brilliance. If you haven't seen it yet, there is a large section on how to *destroy everything*. That's what they want. Creators want the knowledge to become the most powerful group— even more powerful than the Exols. Clockworks will either join you or betray you and if they do side against you, they'll then be labeled as a Creator."

"What about the Exols?" I asked innocently. "Where will they be when there's a deadly war going on?"

He shrugged his shoulders impatiently. "They don't interfere in these cases. They may help a little, but they expect the Clockworks to keep the world peaceful by fighting."

I looked down at the ground, the fear inside my chest painfully eating my insides. "I don't think I can do this..." I glanced up at him, tears flowing down my dirty cheeks.

He wiped my tears away, smiling at me. "It's hard to comprehend, Esther. But Brilliance Chose you for a *reason*."

"The book made a mistake."

He laughed, showing a set of teeth. "It never makes a mistake."

I wrapped my arms around him for reassurance. He smelt of vanilla and graham crackers. "Why do you smell like graham crackers?"

I felt his body shake, indicating he was laughing. "I had them for lunch."

I pulled away from him, slightly confused. "Lunch?"

My mom was starting to get on her feet, staring at me with opaque eyes. "You were out the whole night. That means we have to leave soon."

"How would we have time to pack up all of our furniture?"

"Your father and I have been saving up money ever since we met each other. It was for emergencies."

"How much money is there?" I asked curiously, pulling further away from Alvaro.

"Over millions," she stated dryly.

"So that's how you were able to pay for all of that stuff... But still, how can we pack quickly?"

"The house has already been chosen. Over these years I've been putting furniture in the house. Now, it's completely finished with new clothes for you... A nice room..."

"How'd you know to do this?" I asked, trying not to let the poison escape my lips.

"I always knew something awful was going to happen and I had this really strong intuition to follow through with it."

"So, you've been lying to me all of this time? Pretending your abilities were weak when they weren't?" My anger started to boil out of my mouth, stinging her with my words of poison.

"I am losing them, Esther. Just not fully yet... I came to Alvaro for reassurance."

I looked over at him. He was standing quietly in a thoughtful position. "The difference between your mother and I is that I *don't* lie."

"Shut up, you pathetic demon," my mother said.

"I'm not a demon. I'm just someone with a birth defect," he said reluctantly, giving me a wink. I smiled slightly.

"Esther, we should probably get going."

"Can I at least try to see Damion?" I asked. "So I don't leave on a bad note? What about Becca too?"

"Call them," she stated.

"Now?" I asked.

"No. Of course not. In the car ride to Pennsylvania."

Alvaro embraced me with strong, confident arms. He rested his chin on my head like Damion use to do. "Be strong, Esther."

I stood inside my old bedroom, not able to comprehend it was no longer mine. I remembered waking up from a nightmare to only have my parents sitting there, at my bedside, telling me everything was alright and it would never come true. But so far, all of my nightmares were becoming true. Images of me sitting at my desk, writing in my diary as a child coursed through my mind. I remembered the Creator who had once came in to attack my family for the fun of it and while doing so, my diary was destroyed.

I walked into the family room, remembering running through the house naked when I was three years old and I had just gotten out of the shower. I grew up in this house... And to leave all of it behind was unbearable.

I sucked down the lump that was forming in my throat, knowing I had to stop crying and remain strong. But it was hard to remain strong when everything I love was staying in one place while I was going to another.

"Esther," my mom's voice yelled calmly. "I don't have all day. Come out here with your favorite belongings now."

I sighed, looking at the small suitcase I had in my hand. "I guess this is all I need."

Part Two;

Everything Has Changed

Chapter 8: New Beginnings

My mother was driving up a long, winding road, undergrowth and large trees completely surrounding us. Her small car used all of its momentum to get up the steep hill. I watched as she pressed down on the gas, gritting her teeth as she sped up the hill. I could feel the car wobble as if it were going to tip over and fall.

"You weren't kidding when you said you're going to hide me," I stated dryly.

"It's for your protection, Esther and you know that." She continued driving deeper into the woods, her car finally staying balanced.

I sighed angrily, curling my feet up on the seat. I looked out my window, trying to find the sun through the excessive tree growth. I saw its small rays trying to peek out and find me, but it couldn't. I laid my head against the window, trying to suck in the tears. I had to stop crying. Suddenly, I could feel the sun's warmth on me and gingerly, I looked up in amazement.

There was an opening and the sun was shining on my face. I got up from my lousy position, sitting straight up in bewilderment, staring ahead.

There was a large, white mansion that sat on top of the hill with satisfaction. There was an exterior part that was like any other ordinary house with two stories. It broke off into parts with cylinder rooms on each side of the mansion and behind it stood large blocks of the mansion smashed together. I gasped.

"Mother? How did you even pay for this?"

"Like I said before... We had extras."

In front of the house was a large platform that took the shape of a large, circular gazebo. It was a place for my mother to park. We were driving around a large, beautifully cascading waterfall fountain. It was unbelievable.

"I didn't want you to live in a wreck and be unhappy at the same time."

"Money can't buy my happiness," I whispered reluctantly.

.

She parked underneath the gazebo, getting out of the car.

"Get the bags," she said quietly.

I sighed, getting out of the car. I stepped down on the platform, the slight wind chilling me to the bone. It was early March. I walked towards the back of the car, opening up my mom's trunk. I grabbed the two bags, slinging them over my shoulder as the weight of the bags brought me down.

"Get in here when you're done," my mom called out to me, walking inside the luxurious house.

I gritted my teeth, wanting to scream. *This isn't home and it never will be.* Images of Damion flashed throughout my head, remembering his never-ending smile that seemed to last forever. In anger, I threw the luggage onto the ground. I ran away from the platform, edging closer to the backyard. I wasn't entirely sure what I was doing but it was enough to calm my feelings.

I stopped in my tracks, gazing out at the large yard that led to the trees in the back. Right behind the house was a nicely decorated patio along with a Jacuzzi and a pool next to it. Unfortunately, they were covered for the winter. Another gust of wind hit me, making me wrap my coat around me tightly. I continued walking around the house, my feet hitting the patio. There was a smaller gazebo made for people instead of cars near the forest. Right next to the gazebo was a golf cart.

"Why?" I asked to myself aloud. I felt the Mark burning. I rolled up my sleeve, watching my arm pulse as if Brilliance was alive. I took deep breaths, shutting my eyes. I had to remember why I was here. Alvaro said I was going to be killed if I stayed. He and my mother were just trying to protect me. But why couldn't Damion understand? Breaking my thoughts, my phone rang. I pulled it out, realizing it was Becca.

"*Hey,*" she said into the receiver.

"Hey."

"*What happened to you?*"

I sighed, pulling my phone closer to my ear. "I moved to Pennsylvania because Alvaro and my mother believe people know I was Chosen."

There was a long pause. "*How'd Damion take it?*"

I laughed into my phone coldly. "He didn't take it well at all. I tried calling him but he never answers."

"I could try to run by his house when they let me go back to school?"

"Do whatever you think is right." I paused. "And try and visit me once summer comes... I hope this transition will be good for me. Keep me updated on the move to Alabama." Just saying the words, I couldn't feel anything good about the move. I hung up, not wanting to talk anymore. I walked around the mansion to the front, grabbing the luggage I had dropped. I walked slowly towards the front entrance and I walked up the marble steps, opening up the huge, polished door. I walked in, quickly inhaling at the interior. In front of me was a large, grand staircase with a gold railing and next to it was a large dining room that was filled with different furniture with no purpose of being in the room in the first place.

"How do you like it?" my mother asked cheerfully as she descended the staircase.

"It's a little big for two people." I sat down the luggage, crossing my hands over my chest.

"God dammit, Esther... Just be happy," my mother said, walking passed the dining room and into another.

I glared at her as she walked out of the foyer. "It's kind of hard to be happy."

"Don't sass me, honey... Now go upstairs and find your bedroom. You'll like it."

I rolled my eyes, beginning to walk up the stairs. I never had to walk up a grand staircase in my old house. My legs thumbed against each carpeted step, making my hair bounce up and down. After nearly forty steps, I was finally at the top, breathing heavily. The upstairs had the same vintage style as the downstairs. Furniture was misplaced in the large corridor and a huge, glass chandelier hung above my head, extending near the foyer downstairs. I leaned over the golden railing, looking down below at the red and gold carpet that acted as the theme in the house. I liked Damion's house better—it was white with brown wood, not making the house pop out too much like how this one did. Our old house didn't have a theme to be honest, so this absolutely doesn't feel like my mother's taste.

I released the railing, wiping my sweaty hands surreptitiously on my jeans. I walked down the large hallway, trying each polished door to see if it was locked. Almost all of them were.

175

Finally, I grasped the golden handle, opening it slowly. Before me was a decent sized room with a canopy bed. I never had a canopy bed before. The curtains around the bed were a sea-foam green sort of color. The bed posts were made of cherry wood too. The room was painted a soft yellow, making it to where the yellow was barely noticeable. The windows were pushed out on the right side of the room and they were filled with blankets and pillows. *Good place to look out at the moonlight and be depressed*, I said silently to myself.

I walked towards the left side of the room, noticing a large closet took up most of the wall. Gingerly and hesitantly, I proceeded forward, opening up the two decorated glass doors. I gasped surprisingly, looking at the rows of clothes hanging on racks. The clothes were color-coated along with shoes that lined up the wall. There was a section for high heels, boots and sneakers.

"None of this feels like me," I whispered to myself, feeling the lacy material on a stray shirt. I bent down on my knees, picking up a single black combat boot. This sort of felt like me... But hardly. I sat the boot gently back down near its partner. I stood up, looking for the jean jacket and blouse section. Almost instantly, I found the section I was looking for. Rows of colorful blouses sat patiently before me, some short or no sleeved, some long sleeved, lacy or silky and more. I saw the different styles of jean jackets and instantly fell in love. Maybe this wouldn't be too bad.

"Now that you've warmed up to the place... You should start school tomorrow."

I stabbed my fork into the potatoes, avoiding my mother's intense stare. I picked up the utensil, shoving the potatoes in my mouth. I hadn't eaten since I got to the mansion. "Okay."

My mom reached her hand towards me, grabbing mine reluctantly while squeezing it hard. "You may meet someone different... Maybe someone quirky and human."

I looked up at her, trying to avoid my anger. "No one could ever replace Damion."

She sighed, her happiness slowly decaying. "It's going to be hard—I know. But you can't let something so *small* affect you. You need to stay strong for Brilliance and all of the people who are counting on you."

I stared at her with opaque eyes. "This isn't something small. The whole world is at risk."

"I meant your relationship with Damion."

I gritted my teeth, trying to control myself. "My feelings for Damion are the same percentage as Brilliance."

My mom took deep breaths, avoiding my daggers. "Let's just not talk about this."

"Do you even care that Dad is dead?" I spurted out.

"*Of course, I care,*" she hissed, glaring at me. "He understands that I need to focus on your safety, Esther."

I swallowed the lump in my throat, wanting to change the subject. "So, what is this new school like?"

She looked caught off guard. "Oh... Um... It's a private school."

I stood up in my chair, nearly knocking it over. "A private school? What the hell, Mom?"

She sighed, resting her back on the comforting chair. "Before you freak out—it's an intelligence academy. You'll be with people your own IQ level."

"Am I going to have to wear a ridiculous uniform?"

"Only on Tuesdays. That's when their football team plays a game. You're free to wear what you please any other day of the week."

"Are there any dress rules?"

"Not that I know of. The Principal told me personally that she doesn't care what her students wear."

I nodded my head. "Okay."

A smile began to appear on her lips as she stared at me. "I want to pick out your outfit."

"Oh lord."

I stood at the edge of the driveway, the wind nearly knocking me to the ground. The trees violently swayed back and forth as well as my hair. The cold air prickled my cheeks, turning them a rosy color. I looked down at my attire, feeling ridiculous. My mother picked out a short, black skirt along with a really tight white shirt, making me feel too exposed.

I turned around, looking up the hill. The trees covered the house, making it to where no one could see it. It was a drastically

177

long and exhausting walk down the hill too.

I wrapped my coat around me tighter as the wind picked up. I held my book bag on one of my shoulders as the bus came to a screeching stop. I saw white faces peering at me along the windows, staring me down. Nausea swept over me and instantly I knew I was going to be an outcast again.

Gingerly, I proceeded forward, walking up the hard, metal stairs of the yellow bus. The smell of smoke suffocated me as I walked past the driver. I bit my lip, noticing there was no seats available for me. I walked down the aisle reluctantly. I glanced frantically around for a seat as annoyed eyes stared up at me.

I saw a seat, beginning to sit down next to a robust girl with black pigtails. She noticed my arrival, instantaneously setting her book bag down next to her so I couldn't sit down. "Can you please move your bag?" I asked, trying to avoid my annoyance.

She grinned up at me. "I'm good, bitch."

I clenched my fist, readying to pounce on her. *They're just testing you. Don't give in.* I sighed dramatically. "Please."

"Come on!" the bus driver yelled. "I don't have all day!" The laughter of children flooded my ears, making me feel sick to my stomach.

"Come on, just make her sit down!" I heard a girl yell with annoyance.

"No!" the girl with the pigtails yelled, avoiding my glare. I lunged at the girl; my teeth clenched as I felt a set of strong, boney fingers pulling me back. I turned around frantically with my fist soaring through the air. I almost collided my fist into the figure until I noticed soft, brown eyes staring at me. He had an expression as if he were saying, *come on, do it. But I'll like it.* I dropped my fist to my side.

"You can sit with me," he said, his voice deep but it had a childish side to it. He led me down the aisle, allowing me to get in the seat first. I sat down, setting my book bag on my knees. I stared out the window as I felt his body collapse onto the green seat next to me. I could feel his dark eyes peering at me, making me shift uncomfortably. "Where did you come from?"

"A place far away from here," I mumbled, continuing to stare out the window. The bus pushed forward, speeding down the winding road.

"Wow. Must be really far. I guess you're not in Kansas anymore," the boy said softly. I looked up from the window, smiling slightly as I stared at him. He was grinning with pursed lips. I glanced up at his hair, noticing it was the same color as Becca's. "Good. You smiled." He extended his hand. "I'm Mason Knight, the one and only."

I grabbed his hand gently and he shook our hands up and down while grinning. "I'm Esther Green."

"The one and only," he said, staring into my eyes. I didn't feel an electrical shock so he wasn't a Clockwork.

I grinned, taking my hand away from him. "I guess you could say that."

"So how do you feel about moving?" he asked curiously, rubbing his fingers on his pants.

"I—uh—don't know," I stuttered, not wanting to tell him anything.

He smiled as he stared at me. "Let me guess... You didn't want to move."

"How'd you know?" I asked.

He shrugged his shoulders. "I just assumed from your body language and socially awkward presence."

"That's rude."

"So is punching someone in the face," he said, his smile not leaving his face.

I crossed my arms across my chest. "I didn't punch anyone." I paused, turning to stare out the window. "Not yet at least."

He laughed. "You amuse me slightly, Kansas."

"My name's not Kansas."

"Wrong. It's your nickname."

"I came from Oklahoma. Not Kansas."

He clapped his hands together, smiling. "I finally made you say where you're from." He paused, his face contorting in curiosity. "Why don't you have a country accent?"

I thought back to Clockworks and how we usually speak properly. "I prefer speaking the correct way." Damion always spoke the correct way too. Becca had a slight accent—but it was nothing that became annoying.

"Yeah. Almost everyone in this school enjoys speaking correctly too. There are some people who speak way too correctly that you can't even understand them."

"Interesting."

"Hey, we're here," Mason said, staring out the window. I glanced out the window; the bus moved slowly around the parking lot with many other buses. The school was large and most of it was built with bricks and glass. "We have a lot of greenhouses," Mason explained, "That's why we enjoy glass."

"Do you know where the West Wing is?" I asked.

"Oh. I don't know. Maybe it's on the west side of the school," he said sarcastically, laughing to himself.

"Can you show me where it is?" I asked, my annoyance slowly coming back.

His laughing slowed down. "Yes. Of course." I picked up my book bag, slinging it around my shoulder. Mason picked up his bag, standing up in the aisle.

"Hey, Mason!" A guy yelled at him from behind. "I see you like picking up the new girls!" I looked down, my cheeks flushing with embarrassment.

"Oh, shut up, Matthew," Mason said, his tone slightly serious. "It's good to be nice once in a while."

"Once in a while? How about be nice all the time?" I asked as the anger swept over me. I pushed passed them, walking down the aisle of people quickly.

"That's not what I meant!" I heard Mason call out to me.

I stepped down off the bus, the cold embracing me once more. I walked with the crowds of students that edged closer to the entrance of the school. Suddenly, I felt a hand clamp down on my wrist, making images of Brilliance course through my eyes. I pulled away viciously, staring at the person in disgust. It was a girl with dirty blonde, curly hair and she had a large mole over one of her gray eyes. She wore a short skirt and a tight shirt and behind her was more girls that were almost wearing the same attire.

She looked alarmed and annoyed, but she smiled with perfect teeth anyways. "You're the new girl, aren't you?" I nodded my head slowly, my hand protecting my wrist. She didn't have an electric shock. "My name is Leila and these are my friends. You should hang with us."

"I'm Esther," I said, not taking my eyes off of the girls. The principal wasn't kidding when she said the students were allowed to wear whatever they wanted. All of their skirts were shorter than mine and their shirts were tighter, exposing most of their body.

"You shouldn't hang out with losers... Just to let you know." She glanced at Mason and a group of his friends. "Like them." She whipped her head around, staring at more groups of people. "And them... Well, you get the gist."

I nodded my head slowly, forcing a smile at the fake people. "I will make a consideration, but I do deserve to make my own friends."

"Like us," Leila said, smiling. "You should really be friends with us."

Suddenly, a white bus pulled up to the curb next to the girls and me. Large, bulky teenagers piled out of the bus. The first one had blond hair that spiked up and intense green eyes. He walked over to Leila, picking her up off the ground bridal style like how Damion used to pick me up. I watched uncomfortably as they kissed passionately, forgetting the world around them. Gingerly, I placed a finger on my lips, wishing Damion could be standing next to me.

I remembered why I had to leave my home and angrily, I adjusted my book bag, walking away from the 'popular people'. I walked into the school building as the first bell rang. The inside was incredibly remarkable. Three chandeliers hung from the ceiling, lighting up the entrance. A glass elevator stood a distance away from me along with a set of marble stairs. The entrance was crowded with laughing students as they got ready for their school day. My old school was nothing compared to this school. A sign labeled "West Wing" hung above a large hallway on my right side. I walked across the ground, my gray boots slapping against the slushy floor. The hallway was filled with long, green lockers that matched the seats on the school bus. Classroom doors were glass, making it easier to see what was happening inside each one.

After a few minutes walking down the hallway, I found my locker; 346. I began rolling my combination, stopping at each number; 6, 16, 6. I opened it up, the smell of cinnamon wafting around me. There was an air refresher plugged against a wall inside. *Wow. This locker has outlets.* I unpacked my book bag, setting my five spirals and textbooks inside. I put three binders inside, keeping two for my first few classes.

181

I sat in Physical Science, listening to the teacher demonstrate a computer program on the enlargement board. I tapped my pencil against the desk, trying to avoid thinking about Damion. It's been a few days since I had last saw him and I already felt vulnerable.

Images of him shattering our willow tree flooded back to me; his poisonous eyes staring at me in disgust as if I had ripped his heart out. *It's hard for me too... Try being Chosen. We both have to relive our lives away from other Clockworks.*

I bit my dry lips, looking around the classroom. Students expressed themselves in either positive or negative ways. It felt like there were also people who were left out of the society of students though. *So, I won't be the only one.*

The bell rang, indicating it was lunch time. I got up from the metal chair, watching as everyone piled out of the classroom, laughing and smiling. I frowned, wishing I could have Damion and Becca circling around me as we talked about the stupidity of teachers.

"Hey," a girl with chestnut hair said with a smile, "Your friends with Leila, right?"

I shrugged my shoulders as I picked up my binders. "I guess so."

"Well, I suppose she wants you to eat with us."

"Okay. Sounds good. I'll just head to my locker, okay? You can come if you want?"

She held up her hands. "No, thank you." She turned on her heels, exiting the door with her head held up high. I followed after her but I turned the opposite direction, heading towards my locker. The students walked passed me as if I wasn't even there.

I did my combination quickly, opening my locker. I picked up my bag and searched it for money. "I forgot it," I whispered to myself, my stomach rumbling for food. I sighed, tossing my book bag into the rectangular shape and I closed the metal locker. Almost instantly, I felt a shiver run up my spine. I looked behind me, realizing a girl with white hair and another girl with black. The white-haired girl had gray eyes and the girl with black hair had dark, nearly black eyes.

"Hey, you're the new girl, right?"

I turned around, noticing it was Leila's boyfriend. He stared down at me with his dark, green eyes. "I'd appreciate it if people

182

could stop calling me 'the new girl'," I said bitterly.

He chuckled softly, raking his dirty blonde hair back. "I'm sorry. What *is* your name?"

"Esther."

"Esther what?" he asked, his opaque eyes showing a hint of amusement.

"Green."

"Ah, so you're green?" he asked with a small smile.

"Sure."

"You don't talk much, do you?"

"Well, considering I don't trust you; I'm not going to say a lot."

He laughed again, leaning his body against my locker. I could smell his minty breath. I grabbed my hand as if I was protecting myself. "I'm Ace Winter."

I nodded my head, extending my hand. I wanted to see if he had an electric shock. He took it and I felt nothing. "Nice to meet you."

"So, we should probably head to lunch? We'll get a detention if we're late."

I nodded my head. "Yeah."

I sat on my bed, looking up at the abnormal ceiling that had way too much decoration. I thought about my first day and I knew it wasn't as bad as I thought it would be. It seems like the "popular" people really like me. I should probably take that into consideration. Mason and Ace seemed friendly but they were nothing compared to Damion. I hadn't talked to Mason since I yelled at him but that didn't matter too much.

I looked down at my wrist, staring at the Mark. A strong, powerful sensation swept over me. I never tried reading Brilliance... And right now, seemed like the perfect time. I pressed my thumb into the Mark, phrases appearing.

Prophecy of The Exol Child

For Exols it's forbidden to have a child. The power the child possesses will become too strong to manage and the Exol Beings wouldn't know how to control the child.

But one family didn't think that through. They were simpleminded... But sometimes love is too strong and you *have* to do stupid things.

Their love was so powerful it lit up the Exol Palace, sending emotional and sensational vibes to everyone.

Eventually, they had to conceal their love because it was affecting others. To do so, they had a child.

They loved their child senselessly and unconditionally. They knew they had to protect him... If the other Exols discovered their secret, they would kill their child.

The family knew what they had to do.... They had to send their child away to someone who could protect the boy from being killed.

The father knew a young mortal who could take care of him. Willingly, the father sent the child away to live with the mortal family, hoping the boy wouldn't discover his own abilities that could destroy the world with one flick of the wrist.

After the boy was taken to safety, the other Exols knew what had happened. But it was already too late.

For punishment, the Exols killed the Mother peacefully so the Father would have to live alone without a wife and a son to love.

The Exols could never find the child, but they continued looking.

As of now, they are still unsuccessful.

But this child and the Spiritual Human will fight together to help protect the Half-Blood.

One of these three will unfortunately die a very painful death during the War for Brilliance.

"One will be at the gates and the other will regenerate with such beholding power."

Spiritual Side

Something that intrigues me, the writer of Brilliance, is the fact that Spiritual Humans are usually part of the Asian race. I find it remarkable that somehow and someway, Humans gained the ability to also have a spiritual side. It's nothing compared to the Clockworks that were born with it though. But I do believe mortals learned how to do martial arts, meditating etc. by watching us performing the arts.

Classical Routines;

Stress Reliever; stand on two feet, your hands outstretched and clasped gently together. Slowly move, lifting one of your legs up while simultaneously circling one hand in formation. Continue breathing while focusing on peaceful events.

Continue the routine until you feel fully satisfied.

I pulled my hand away from the Mark, staring down at my wrist in pure astonishment. So, a Spiritual Human was someone who was only born with their Spiritual Side and the Exol Child was born from two Exols.

So, leaving me one question; *how the hell am I going to find them?*

"Esther?" my mother said, knocking on my door. "Can I come in?"

"Yeah. You can come in," I said, watching as she opened my door and began walking across my room towards me. "How are you?"

"How are *you*? Your first day and all."

I shrugged my shoulders reluctantly. "It's bearable."

"Did you make any new friends?"

"I guess... Kinda. But it's still too early to know," I said. I watched as she swayed back and forth in her nightgown, watching me with eyes filled with curiosity.

"I applied for a few jobs today... I'm pretty excited."

"Oh, that's cool." I played with the lacy ribbon on my pajamas, avoiding her eye contact.

"Do you like your new clothes?" she asked.

"Yeah. I'm not into the whole wearing skirts thing though. A pair of jeans would be fine."

She laughed. "Okay, I just wanted you to feel presentable on your first day."

"Like I said, jeans are fine."

"So," she said, her voice quavered as she awkwardly stood by my bed. "What are you going to do this weekend?"

I shrugged my shoulders, pulling up my sheets. "I'm probably going to take the golf cart into the woods and relax."

I watched as my mother nodded her head slowly. "Just be careful. I won't be home at all tomorrow because of my job interviews. Make sure you take care of yourself and don't let anyone come into the house. Alright?"

I nodded my head, smiling slightly. "Alright."

She bent down to kiss my forehead. "Goodnight, Esther. Sweet dreams."

"Sweet dreams," I said as she turned off my light. I rolled over in my bed, staring at the large windows on the other side of the room.

Chapter 9: Don't Forget What You Have, Not What You Lost

I sat at the dining room table as the sun shined through the large, glass windows. I picked at my eggs, listening to the wind smash into the house. The only one in the house was me and I had to admit, I didn't like mansions. Noises were always everywhere, making you feel like it was haunted. But I knew nothing like that existed, so I kept quiet about my childish fears.

I picked up my plate, kicking open the kitchen door. Sunlight lit the whole room despite the cold temperatures outside. I sat the plate down in the sink while washing off the egg yolk. I grabbed an apple off the island and I sunk my teeth into it. I walked out of the kitchen, yanking my coat off the hanger and wrapping it around me. I opened one of the double doors, the cold air instantly smashing into me. I pulled my hood up and walked down the steps. I proceeded across the platform, my boots clacking against the ground. I made my way to the backyard, continuing to walk down a narrow path. I had a plan.

After a few minutes I was standing by the gazebo. I climbed up into the golf cart, strapping the small seat belt across my waist. I pulled the keys out of my pocket and jammed them into the golf cart. I stepped slowly on the gas as the cart came to life.

I drove into the thick underbrush, the cart making a path as it moved quickly through the forest. The trees around me smelt like pine and maple as they swayed gingerly back and forth in the chilly wind. I looked up, finding the sun trying to peak through the trees. I could feel the crunching of twigs underneath the cart as it plowed through leaves and broken twigs.

The wind howled as it smashed into the pines as I came to a small clearing. There was melted snow on the ground and faint flowers were dying in the small meadow. The sun lit up the clearing, shining heavily in my eyes. I pulled out the key and the cart slowly died down. I grabbed a hold of the handlebar as I jumped down onto the melted patch of snow. I grabbed the duffel bag that I had placed there the night before from the back of the cart. I swung it over my shoulders, proceeding towards the center of the meadow.

In defeat of the weight, I dropped the bag onto the ground, zipping it open. Overflowed contents spilled out around my feet.

"This is going to be a struggle," I whispered to myself as I picked up a hammer and a piece of wood. I grabbed a small box of nails that I found in a spare bedroom in the mansion. I ripped open the box, taking out a few nails and I placed them in my mouth, holding them between my teeth. I grabbed another set of nails, simultaneously placing them on the ground.

I jammed the nail into the wood with my hammer. I continued pounding, grabbing another piece of wood that collided with the one I already had in my hand. I continued this process until I had a stable six-foot-tall structure in front of me. I bent down, picking up a piece of scrap metal that I found in the garage last night. I smashed the piece of metal into the wood, giving it a swooping motion. After the first structure was built, I lit a match, giving the flame to the bowl inside the structure. I built more structures with different elements because that was all I could work with.

I stood in the middle of the meadow, all of my structures surrounding me. I was quite impressed with myself for building so quickly and effectively. The reason I built was to prepare myself physically for the War that everyone keeps on talking about. If I didn't have Damion to help me with preparation, I had to do it myself.

I closed my eyes, trying to follow through with my senses. At my left I could hear the structure turning quickly, indicating something was coming my way. In a fury, I created a thick force field, blocking out the boiling water. A hot sensation collided into my right side, burning my skin. I yelped in panic, creating another field to block the right side. I heard the combining clank of metal in front of me, knowing a boulder was coming my way. I dropped my two force fields, trying to get enough energy to block the huge rock that was hurtling my way. I created a large force field while opening my eyes, simultaneously seeing the rock shatter to pieces a few inches away from my face.

Behind me I could hear the structure moving. I created another field, blocking my back side. Suddenly, more structures were combining metal, indicating the material was going to hit me all at once. I panicked, my blood rising to my throat. I knew I had to be powerful in order to block out all of the elements that were hurled my way.

I focused on protecting my whole body from the blazing fire, boiling water, large boulders and small, penetrating rocks. I could feel the small expansion of the force field growing stronger but it was already too late.

Combination of pain and burning sensations collided into my body, completely breaking the weak force field that didn't expand fast enough. I fell to the ground as my body throbbed and the smell of burnt skin wafted throughout the air.

I screamed out in pain, feeling trickles of blood pour down my arms. I heard the combining metal again, one last time, knowing I had to get back up and fight what was left of the elements. I gripped the ground as I gritted my teeth, trying to ignore the flashing pain. If I was in a battle now, I would die if I didn't get back up. *You have to teach yourself to be strong, Esther. Be immune to pain.*

The tears wanted to come, but I sucked them in. I put my foot on the ground, standing up slowly. I saw the fire coming at me from most of the structures. I held my hands out in front of me, turning them in a circular motion. I could see the blue tinted force field growing larger, expanding at a quicker rate than before as my hands moved rapidly.

I saw the fire combine into the force field, slowly trying to burn it. The fire didn't succeed and it slowly burned itself out. A small smile came upon my lips. I had remained strong despite the pain I felt. I looked around sharply, noticing I had used up all of the elements in the structures.

I continued smiling as I fell slowly to the ground. The last thing I saw was the sun shining down on me.

"What the hell did you do to yourself?" I heard my mother's voice. "What was going through your head?" I felt a shattering pain in my arms as someone tugged on them furiously. My eyes fluttered open and I watched as my mother was rubbing my burnt skin angrily.

I pulled away quickly, staring up at her in shock. "What are you doing?" I shrieked.

"Healing your wounds!" she snapped. "Now lay back down!" I laid back down, staring up at her curiously.

"You can't heal," I stated.

"Alvaro sent me some potions just in case shit like this was going to happen."

"Don't swear," I stated meekly, staring up at the large ceiling. I guess I was in the living room.

"What did you *do?*" she asked.

"Preparing myself for when—you know—when the time comes. I need to teach myself to be powerful. I'm *weak*. My force fields aren't strong enough and I noticed the color of them changed. Something terrible is happening to me."

"You don't just hit yourself all at once!" she yelled. "You have to do it gradually unless you want to kill yourself! *Is that what you want?*"

I stared up at her, gritting my teeth. "No. But do you want to know what I want?"

"Tell me."

"I want to go back *home*," I said, trying to keep the whine out of my voice.

"This is home," my mother said dryly as she rubbed my wounds.

"No, it's not!" I yelled. "Damion is home. Father is home. Oklahoma was our home."

"Exactly. *Was*."

"Do you even care how much pressure this is on me?" I yelled, sitting up. "Do you even care that the love of your life is *dead?*"

"How many times do I have to tell you, Esther? Of course, I care. I just can't have you *die* next." I watched as the tears began to form around her green irises. "I love you and I don't want to *lose* you."

I sucked down the tears that wanted to form. "I know you do... But I don't want to lose Damion either."

"He wants you to be safe, Esther. And safety is here."

I bit my lip, tasting blood in my mouth. "I want him to be safe too. You said it yourself, Creators are going there to try and find the Chosen one. What if they destroy the whole town?"

My mother paused. "There's enough Clockworks there to wipe them out."

"Whatever."

My mom sighed, wiping her teary eyes. "You have school tomorrow. I suggest you get in the shower."

"School tomorrow?" I furrowed my brows. "It's Saturday."

"No. It's Sunday night. Because of your stupidity you were knocked out for a while."

I sighed, getting up. "When's the healing going to kick in?"

"Since I'm not Alvaro and I can't do it on the spot—probably overnight? Hopefully."

I laughed coldly. "Yeah. Hopefully."

I stood in front of the large mirror that hung next to my door, watching my reflection as I brushed through my dark waves. I thought of Damion and his intriguing eyes—all of the times he had looked at me.

I sighed, trying to get him out of my head. I also thought of my dad and how he always brought a little bit of light in my personality. But without him, I felt darker than ever. His memory felt so far away now.

"Esther," my mother said, appearing in my doorway, "Hurry up. Your bus is going to be here soon."

I nodded my head. "Alright. Just give me a few more minutes." I continued looking in the mirror as I brushed my long hair.

"Honey." I glanced up at my mom, watching her as she stood properly in the doorway. "I just want to say I'm very proud of you."

"For what?" I asked curiously.

"For staying sewed together all the time." She walked calmly towards my canopy bed, sitting down on the plush comfort. "It's strange for me to say this, considering I'm your mother but... I look up to you. *You're* the one who helps me stay all in one piece. You're so *strong* and *brave*." She paused, staring down at her palms. "Without you, I would be broken."

I looked away from her, continuing to stare into the mirror. I watched my mother's reflection, studying her mirrored face in my peripheral vision. "That's hard to believe," I whispered, my words barely audible.

"You may not see it but everyone else does. It's like you keep your thoughts invisible from believing what you really are." She stared at my back intently. "Like your beauty. Everyone sees it *but you.*"

Gingerly, watching my reflection, I raised my hand, resting my palm on my cold cheek. I didn't feel beautiful. I only felt confident. "I'll take your word for it."

I walked onto the bus while being greeted with many voices carrying on their conversations. Some kids threw paper balls back and forth and while doing so, one hit me in my cheek.

A boy laughed. "You hit her! Nice!" I gritted my teeth as I continued walking down the narrow aisle. They continued throwing balls back and forth so I decided to make a small force field around me.

A small shiver went up my spine. I moved uncomfortably, looking on the right side of the bus. The girls that were staring at me a few days ago were once again watching me with intense and eager eyes. I plopped down next to Mason who was striking up a conversation with one of his friends.

"Hey Esther," Mason said with a grin. "What's up with you?"

"Uh... I don't know."

He laughed. "No. You're too grammatically correct. It's 'I dunno' not 'I don't know.' You gotta' lighten up a little bit more and stop being so laconic."

"Laconic is a large word. I'm surprised you know it."

Mason smiled. "You do have a sense of humor—I'll give you that."

"As do you, Mason."

His smile became larger. "Why of course."

I looked up from his face, staring forward. The girl with the black hair was staring at me from her seat on the bus. Noticing I was staring back at her, she looked away from me. "Hey, Mason, who are those girls over there?"

"You mean the Windchester twins? Black and blonde hair? Well, the blonde could have white hair." I nodded my head. "Not to be rude but they're literally the freaks of the school. Every new kid that comes here they check them out and watch them constantly until they touch them. It's really weird."

"So, it's common for them to stare at me?" I asked.

He nodded his head. "Yes. If it makes you uncomfortable, I could stand in front of you."

I blushed, looking down at the ground. "That's very generous of you, Mason. But I'm fine."

"Okay." He leaned into me slightly while laughing. "But their stares are poisonous."

"Okay," I said while laughing.

The bus lurched to a stop and everyone stood up, book bags around their shoulders. In a cordial order, we all exited the bus. My feet smacked against the pavement as I stepped down.

"I'm going to meet up with some of my friends. I'll see you later, alligator," Mason said, brushing my shoulder as he walked away.

"Esther!" Leila screamed as she collided into me with a hug. "It's been forever since I've seen you!"

I pulled away from her while grasping my arm for protection. "It was only two days."

She let out a fake laugh, clutching onto Ace's arm. "Esther is so funny, isn't she?"

Ace was staring at me with amused eyes. "Yes. She is."

"Umm... I'm just going to get ready for class now. Nice seeing you guys."

Leila grabbed my arm, pulling me back. "It's free day, remember? No classes."

"What's free day?" I asked curiously.

"Just a day where you can hang out in the Auditorium or Gymnasium to eat and drink and do school work. After lunch we have a talent show and then a little theater skit a group of kids provide for us."

"It's really fun. You should hang out with us," Ace said.

"Okay. That's sounds great." I threw in an awkward laugh.

"Well, let's not keep waiting," Leila chimed in. She pulled away from Ace, turning her back towards me. "Where's my crew?"

"They already went inside, Babe," Ace said, staring at me despite the fact he was talking to Leila.

"Oh," she turned around giddily. "That must be why."

We began walking towards the school with crowds of

students following us. Ace and Leila had their hands clasped together, swinging them as they walked. I looked away, shutting my eyes hard as more images of Damion flashed around in my head.

"Hey, I'm going to meet up with you guys later. Okay?" I said, trying to avoid looking at them.

Leila smiled. "Okay. We'll be in the Auditorium."

I watched my reflection in the bathroom mirror. Gingerly, I turned on the faucet, swooping my hands into the water and simultaneously splashing my face with water. The extremely chilly water felt good on my skin. I grabbed a paper towel, wiping my face dry. I tried not to think about my dad and Damion.

But I couldn't help myself. I grabbed my phone out of my book bag and dialed Damion's number. I held the phone close to my ear, tapping my foot continuously. *No answer.* In anger, I threw my phone back into my book bag. I clutched the edges of the sink, staring into the mirror as I watched the anger illuminate in my eyes.

"Hello," a small, vibrant voice echoed throughout the bathroom. I turned on my heels, eyes narrowed. The girl with white hair was staring at me with opaque eyes.

"Uh, hi." I grabbed my book bag carefully, my eyes locked on her.

"I'm Luna Windchester and you're Esther Green? Correct?" she asked.

I nodded my head slowly, studying her expressionless face. "Yeah."

"My sister—black hair—is Rosa."

"Cool. Well, if you don't mind... I'll just be on my way." I moved closer to the door, back turned towards her.

"That's a nice tattoo," the girl said abruptly.

I looked down, realizing my sleeve was slightly raised. I pulled it down quickly, fear growing inside of me.

"Where'd you get it?"

"A tattoo shop," I said quietly.

"Interesting. Did they know you were under age?"

"No," I said, my eyes staring at her in my peripheral vision. "I passed surprisingly."

"Can I see it closer? What design is it?"

"I should really get to my locker... I need to put my book bag away... Get some books for fun day..." I rambled.

"Okay. Go ahead. Terribly sorry for being curious all the time. *I'm just trying to figure you out.*"

I turned to look at her, my eyes widening. "What did you say?"

"Just trying to see if you're nice or not." Her lips pursed into a thin smile.

I moved quickly out the door without another word. My heart raced slightly and I lost control of my feet. I was running down the hallway, trying to get as far away from the bathroom as possible. I noticed a bulky figure ahead that was walking in front of my mental path.

"Watch out!" I yelled, trying to stop on my feet. I fell forward, colliding into the large figure. We both slid across the ground, banging into a set of lockers.

"Oh," the figure groaned as it clumsily stood up. A face appeared over my slightly blurred vision. *Ace.* "Are you okay?"

I stood up, using the lockers to hold myself up. "Yeah. You?"

"Of course." He searched my face with an eager expression. "Why were you running?"

"She was scared of me," a quiet voice said in the distance. I looked in the direction of the voice, noticing Luna walking down the hallway with a grin.

"Well, I wouldn't be surprised," Ace said reluctantly, turning to look at her. "Everything you do and say is frightening."

Luna shrugged with a thin smile, her red lips tightening. "How rude." I stood behind Ace, watching the scene above his shoulder. He was larger than Damion, bulky and muscular. Damion had hidden muscle that was concealed by his large sweatshirts.

"Stay away from her, Windchester. You hear?" Ace's voice growled slightly.

"Alright." She twirled a long piece of hair around her finger. "Whatever you say."

"Now go. Stay far away from *us*, Freak." He stayed in his position as Luna continued to stare at me with a smile and gracefully, she turned on her heels and proceeded down the long hallway. "I'm sorry she frightened you. She does that a lot."

I shrugged my shoulders as he turned around. "She didn't scare me," I lied, "she only bothered me."

Ace grinned. "Same thing."

"Sure." I bent down and began to collect the books that had fallen out of my book bag. Ace bent down next to me; cologne wafted the air. "What are you doing?" I watched as he stared at the ground, shuffling my books around.

"Helping you. Why?" He glanced up. "Is there something wrong with that?"

I thought back to Damion, reminding me of the times when he had picked up my fallen books whenever I had dropped them. He was the only one who had helped me. I swallowed hard, shaking the thoughts away. "No. There's nothing wrong with that." I forced a small smile. A grin appeared and his minty green eyes stared at me in triumph.

"I finally broke down your barriers," he whispered.

More images of Damion flooded back. I had walls built around me and so did Damion. "They're still up."

His smile faded slightly and then it came back slowly. "Looks like I have a lot of work to do."

"Maybe," I said, grabbing my book bag so he could put my books into it. "But that would take *forever.*"

"I have time." He placed the books into my bag gingerly, grazing my hand softly. *Again, no electricity.* "Your hands, they're cold."

I smiled. "It's cold in here."

"Let me warm them." He stood up, slinging my bag around his shoulder. He held out his hand to me and I grabbed it, lifting me up off the ground carefully. He continued holding my hand as we walked down the hallway.

"There you guys are!" Leila said. Two of her friends were behind her. Ace dropped my hand quickly, giving me my book bag. I looked up at him, furrowing my brows. *It was just a friendly gesture to hold my hand? Why does he act like it's a law?*

"Sorry," he mumbled, "She could get mad about things like that."

"Then why'd you do it?" I pushed.

Leila ran to us quickly, simultaneously colliding into Ace. He kissed her passionately and she returned it carefully. I rolled my eyes as nausea swept over me. *Lovers.*

I stood in the middle of the meadow, moving my hands around to block the fire hurtling towards me. Even though I was preparing for the War—today's events crossed my mind a lot.

Ace reminded me of Damion way too much. It seemed like they had the same smile... But Damion's held something more as well as his blue eyes. Ace probably had more of a friendly gesture than Damion did? His green eyes held uncertainty in what he wanted while Damion was confident in his feelings for me.

Ace always looked at me... Even when Leila was talking to him repeatedly. It was all too strange and hard to put my finger on the right spot properly.

I gritted my teeth as a large boulder came my way. I held my hands up, creating a fiery force field that slowly charred at the rock. It didn't destroy it but it was enough for the boulder to crumble to the ground. More elements flew at me and I quickly created a strong, powerful force field that was five inches thick. The elements recoiled as my field expanded. It expanded to twelve inches and soon enough, the elements disintegrated besides the boiling water. The water sloshed up and into the ground, burning the grass instantaneously.

I smiled. "I'm becoming stronger," I whispered to no one in particular. The elements were finished so I decided to do something else. *Connect to my spiritual side.*

I closed my eyes. I thought of Damion's voice and how it lured me in positively. I thought of his icy blue eyes and how they stared at me with triumph—the way his body shifted as he would stride elegantly down the sidewalk—the way he would throw his head back while laughing.

I felt my feet lift off the ground and I could feel myself floating. I opened my eyes, picturing Damion floating next to me while he grinned. I pictured us talking about life—things we hate, things we love and so on. We would soak our bodies with the beams of the sun despite the harsh winter wind. We would enjoy everything together... If it weren't for the fact none of this was *real.*

I felt myself falling as I remembered the way he looked at me when I said I had to leave. I remember the harshness in his voice when he said, '*I hate you.*' I watched as the trees shifted violently in the air and the way the park turned to life. *He was extraordinarily powerful.*

I felt my body slam into the ground and I was awoken from my thoughts. I stared up at the dark sky as the confusion swarmed around me.

"How long was I thinking?" I asked myself. I stood up and my body throbbed. It didn't feel like I had any broken bones. The taste of blood in my mouth alarmed me that I probably bit my tongue. It was daylight when I began fighting the structures.

"My mom's gonna kill me." She must be worried sick. I grabbed the golf cart key out of my pocket and ran to the cart that was parked at the edge of the meadow. I stepped up, sitting down on the soft chair and I jammed the key into the hole. The cart hummed to life and I began driving down the path.

In five minutes, I made it to the entrance of the mansion. My mother's car wasn't anywhere in sight. I stepped down and began running across the platform and up the marble staircase. I opened the door and all of the lights were turned off—the way I left it. *So, she hasn't come home yet. Well, good. But where is she?*

Someone shook me awake violently. "Esther. Wake up." I awoke quickly, looking around furiously. I was on one of the couches in the living room. I guess I had fallen asleep.

"Why'd you come home late?" I asked sleepily.

"I had to take care of something."

"Of what exactly?" I asked, sitting up.

"Nothing you should be concerned of." I watched as something in her eyes flickered in the darkness.

"Tell me. We promised no secrets."

"I said it's nothing you should worry about," she said sternly.

"I'm going to figure out what it is." I stood up, walking away. "And in the meantime, I'm not going to talk to you."

"Okay. I'm fine with that," she called as I ran up the stairs at a fast pace. I walked down the hallway drowsily, wanting to get to my bed and fall asleep for school tomorrow.

I entered my bedroom, pulling off my clothes. I grabbed a nightgown and I wrapped it around my body as I yawned. I proceeded towards my bed, sitting down on the plush comforter. I grabbed a remote that sat on my night stand and simultaneously, I turned on the TV. I laid back in my bed, my muscles slowly relaxing.

"Breaking News," the news reporter said with a hint of distress, "Erin Springs, Oklahoma has gone up in flames." I sat up quickly, my eyes glued to the screen. My heart raced quickly as I thought about Damion, Becca and Alvaro. "We are unsure what happened. At the moment, there are many reports coming in from civilians saying they saw figures in dark cloaks roaming the small town. They destroyed half of the town. The FBI and Special Force Units are doing further investigations." She paused, listening to the cameraman. "There were new updates I was unaware of. New figures in *light cloaks* were seen fighting off the figures in dark cloaks. What exactly are we dealing with? No one knows for sure." She paused once more. "Firemen are trying to put out the fires. Many were killed during this unfortunate time. It will take months to rebuild this small town.

"We were also given feedback of another strange event. New York City, a few weeks ago, there were strange reports given to us about another strange occurrence. There were civilians reporting strange noises in one of the many New York hotels. The noises consisted of bloodcurdling screams and sounds of shattering glass. A room in the hotel was completely destroyed and it followed the description of broken glass. But somehow, the hotel's surveillance was knocked out the whole time these strange events were going on. People were taken in to be questioned but they reported not remembering anything. Are we facing the paranormal? Illuminati?"

My blood rose to my throat and I could feel myself swaying. Erin Springs... It was destroyed? I could feel my eyes welling up with tears. I let out a bloodcurdling scream because I had to let out all of the pain. I screamed again as my mind pictured Damion lying dead on the ground, blood pouring out of his mouth. I could see Becca running for her life as a Creator attempted to burn her alive before she could move safely to Alabama. I continued screaming as the images were flooding throughout my head.

"Esther!" I heard my mother scream. But I couldn't see her. I couldn't see anything but bodies piling up beside me. I could feel someone tearing at my arms with talons. I glanced up, screaming. It was my mother. Her eyes were blood red and her ears were pointed up. I rolled off the bed, falling to the ground clumsily. I tried to run out the doorway but Alvaro was standing in front of me. He grinned, showing a set of sharp teeth. I screamed again as I backed up into something.

"Esther!" I heard my mother yell. "Stop!" I whirled around, my hair slapping me in the face. My mother's eyes were glaring at me and she held a dagger in her hand. I fell to the ground as I continued to scream. Tears poured down my cheeks as all of the images clouded my eyes.

"Put a block on your mind!" I heard a faraway voice yell. It was barely recognizable. "A forcefield! Shield your mind!" Someone screamed. "Think peaceful thoughts."

Instead of Damion lying on the ground dead, I pictured him sitting by me, stroking my arm gently. I could feel the fear fading slowly.

"Put a force field around your mind now," my mother said gently.

I created a small force field around my mind. The happy and bad images faded and I could see my bedroom floor in front of me. "Wha—what hap—happened to me?" I whispered, my tears dropping onto the floor.

"Someone nearby tinkered with your mind. They showed you horrendous images you would never want to see in real life."

"I don't understand," I whispered, my words barely audible.

"There must be a Creator nearby. They purposely wanted you to suffer."

I looked up at my mom while tears streamed down my cheeks. "What was real and what was fake?"

"The broadcast was real," she said solemnly, her eyes opaque. "Whatever else you saw was fake."

I swallowed a lump in my throat. "Is Damion *safe? Please.* Tell me he is," I said with a whiny voice.

"I left this afternoon because Alvaro contacted me. He said there was a group of Creators in Erin Springs searching for you. What he understands is they have your name, not a description."

"It'll only be a matter of time before they do find me."

"Yes. I believe Draculus had time to inform them you have been Chosen. Alvaro and I are still unsure on all of the facts."

"Damion... Becca... Are they okay?" My mom shifted uncomfortably on her feet. "TELL ME!"

"Becca is fine. I checked on her. Alvaro swept the lands to see if Damion was alright." She paused. "But he wasn't found."

I got up off the ground in a simple movement. "I need to go to Erin Springs. I have to *find him*." I started to run out of my room until my mother grabbed my arm.

"Alvaro, me, and others didn't kill all of the Creators. Most escaped. They may be lurking around the town. I can't risk you going there."

"But Mom! Damion might be hurt!"

"Knowing him, he's fine."

I looked up at her. I could feel my face contorting in pain. "*Mom.*"

"His parents were at his house. They said he had a tantrum and left the day before. He probably made it out of the town before the Creators destroyed it."

"Why don't the Exols help?" I yelled. "They can punish Clockworks for breaking their laws but not punish the Creators?"

"It's just how they work. If they're Creators then most of them have a plan to kill. It's out of the Exols league because they're peaceful."

"They're not peaceful! They make *us* suffer the consequences! I always looked up to them as a child!"

"Things simply change."

"Why can't you ever just agree with me? You're my mother! You should care about what I'm going through!"

"I *do* care, Esther. I do. It's hard. I know. But there's more at stake than just your relationship with Damion!"

"Mom, I feel complete with him. If you haven't noticed... I'm unhappy without him. All of my childhood I was stubborn... Damion came along and I was happy and I understood everything more clearly. Then I left... And now my thoughts are jumbled up and I'm unhappy and stubborn *again.*"

"You need to learn how to act on your own. He doesn't have a control on your thoughts; *you do.*"

"Mom..."

"Keep a block on your mind until you fall asleep tonight. If those images ever reappear, you know what to do. As for now, I need to find who did that to you. Keep yourself protected until I come back." She grabbed a hold of something at her side. It was a sheath with a sword in it. I gasped surprisingly, my eyes lighting up in shock. I never knew she could fight? She exited the room without another word.

I collapsed onto the edge of my bed, breathing heavily. "I don't think she listens to anything I say." I looked down at the Mark. "You changed everything."

I sat at the lunch table at school, listening to Leila speak obnoxiously. My mother never found a Creator the night before but she doesn't think the mansion is safe enough for me to be alone. She encouraged me to invite people over when she wouldn't be home.

"Did you guys hear about the incident in Erin Springs, Oklahoma? I heard the government believes it was a terrorist attack," Leila said as she chomped down on her piece of pizza. I shifted uncomfortably next to her.

"But who were the people in the white cloaks?" Ace asked while finally staring at Leila.

She shrugged. "How am I supposed to know? Maybe this was all a top-secret social experiment conducted by the government."

Ace looked at me. His face contorted into worry. "Esther, my god, are you alright? Are you sick?"

Leila and her friends stared at me. "Yeah. Your face is pale white," Leila said.

I swallowed a lump in my throat. I didn't notice I was thinking back to the image of Damion lying dead on the ground until now. "I need to go to the bathroom." Ace looked up at me worriedly.

"I'll come with you," he said.

"Don't be ridiculous, Ace. You can't go into our bathroom."

I stopped listening to them as I got up and jogged out of the large cafeteria. I could feel all eyes on me but I ignored them. I pushed open the double doors and began running down the hallway. The hallway was empty due to class hours. I arrived at the nearest bathroom and I pushed open the door. I ran into a stall, lifting up the seat. I felt like I was going to be sick.

I waited patiently for anything to come up but nothing did. I got up off the sticky ground, ruffling my school uniform. It was Tuesday.

"I saw what happened," a soft voice said. "You alright?"

I unlocked the stall door, rubbing one of my eyes. Luna was watching my reflection in the mirror. "Why do you care?"

She turned around gracefully. "I'm just curious to know. Nothing wrong with curiosity, right?"

"Curiosity kills things."

"How was your night last night? What do you think of that Oklahoma thing?"

I shrugged my shoulders. "I don't know and I don't care."

She smiled. "Interesting. Well, hope you have a good one. Bye." She waved her hand up as she skipped happily out the door, her long white hair bouncing as she did so.

I rolled my eyes and began washing my hands in the sink. I finished, turning off the faucet and then I dried my hands. I walked out the door, nearly knocking into Ace. He caught me with a chuckle.

"You alright there? I saw Luna and..."

"I'm fine," I said quickly.

He searched my face. "What about lunch? Why were you...? Upset?" I bit my lip awkwardly. "You can tell me... Don't worry. *Everything is safe with me,*" he said softly. *He's not a Clockwork nor a Creator. I can trust him.*

"I moved away from Erin Springs," I said quietly despite the fact no one was in the hall.

"Esther," he said as his face fell with compassion, "I'm so sorry." Before I could react, he embraced me with soft arms. He held me close to him and I could hear his heavy breathing. "Are your friends okay?"

I shrugged my shoulders, pulling away. "I don't know."

"If you need anything... Just call me. I'll be there for you. Okay?"

I nodded my head. "Okay."

Chapter 10: I Hate it Here

At night, my mother patrolled the grounds, looking for any Creators for my protection. I believe she had a few Clockworks helping her but she never allowed me to meet them.

She was beginning to wear all black and she carried around her sword frequently. She was changing... Dark circles formed underneath her eyes, indicating she wasn't getting any sleep. She doesn't talk to me anymore; she locks herself up in her bedroom most of the time. At dinner she wouldn't talk because she would watch the news.

One day, when I wanted to call Becca, I couldn't find my phone. I had asked her and she said she took it away because Creators could track it. I had yelled at her but of course, none of it sunk in. I was worried about her but there was nothing I could do.

School was changing; I had been there for two months already. I hadn't heard from Damion at all... and I hadn't heard from Becca either but my mother said that Alvaro contacted her and Becca may be coming here. But who knows?

Mason was practically my best friend. We hang out almost every weekend but I wouldn't consider him a boyfriend at all. Ace was... different. Not in a bad way, but he was just... well, different. Leila was fake as always—nothing I could really do about that. Ace and Leila broke up a month ago also.

"Esther, can you please pay attention to the board? I don't tolerate daydreaming in my classroom," Mr. Sparks growled.

I looked up quickly. "Did you ever hear the story about the man who daydreamed and he saved his business because he came up with an idea?"

Mr. Sparks leaned into my desk, his eyes illuminating with anger. "Are you talking back to me?"

I shrugged my shoulders, tapping my pencil against the desk. "That's how talking works, now isn't it?"

"*Sometimes I wish I could just strangle you,*" he growled.

"Is that a threat, Mr. Sparks?" I asked, leaning against my desk, face inches away from his.

He growled, pounding his fists on the desk while walking away. "You're stupid."

"Not really," I countered.

"Esther," Mason hissed. I looked over at his desk, studying his worried expression. "Don't tempt him."

"You should listen to your friend, Esther." Mr. Sparks was writing on the board. At my angle, I could see a grin appearing across his lips in triumph.

"I wouldn't feel so satisfied yet, Sir," I whispered.

He dropped the chalk, his hands balling up into fists. Underneath his thin dress shirt I could see his muscles tightening. "Esther, leave my classroom."

"I'd be happy to," I said. The bell rang. Everyone got up while grabbing their textbooks. I walked out the door with the crowd of students, smiling in satisfaction. *Wait. I never talk back to teachers...The only time I did was when Damion didn't move to Erin Springs yet.* My face fell as the thought had hit me. I was changing... I was losing the light Damion had formed inside of me.

"Esther," I felt someone clutch my shoulder. "What was that back there?"

I turned around, noticing Mason staring at me with eager brown eyes. "I don't know."

"You've been acting strange lately... Are you okay?"

"Yeah," I said with too high of a voice. "Yes. I'm fine," I recovered.

"Esther!" Leila said as she appeared in front of me, blocking my view of Mason. "How are you?"

"I—uh—I'm good," I stuttered.

"Excuse me," Mason said, pushing Leila gently to the side. "I was talking to her."

Leila turned on her high heels, staring Mason down. "Did I give you permission to talk?"

His mouth opened wide, shocked that someone would ever say that. "Wow. I didn't know I was watching another episode of Gossip Girls." I chuckled slightly.

"Please... Can you like, leave? For now?" Leila asked with a tone.

"Yeah. Whatever." Mason looked at me with a slight smile. "I'll just see you later." He walked away without another word.

"Okay, now that he's gone," she said, turning to look back at me, "I can finally tell you something. You know Lina?"

"A friend of yours?"

"Yeah... But not anymore. She is wearing the same exact outfit as me today... Isn't that terrible?" Leila asked, her eyes nearly clouding with tears.

"Uh... sure."

"It's ruining my image... So... You wanna know what I did?" she said with excitement.

"What?"

"I put a sticky note on her back that read 'slut'." My mouth dropped open as she clapped her hands together happily.

"Leila... That's terrible..."

"Look! She's walking down the hallway now!"

I turned around, watching Lina walk down the hallway. She was totally unaware of all of the people laughing at her. She walked passed us with her head held up high. I felt sorry for her... She didn't even know. I glanced at Leila, realizing she was laughing while pointing at the poor victim. Something welled inside my chest and I had a feeling that I needed to do something.

My feet started moving forward and there was no going back now. I reached my hand out and pulled the sticky note off her back. I turned to Leila, tearing up the small piece of paper in front of her. "This is wrong."

"Esther... We're friends... Why would you do that?" Leila asked, her voice filled with venom.

"Well, guess what? We're not friends anymore. What you did to Lina was wrong and cruel." At this point everyone was staring at us including Lina.

"I'll make your life a living hell, Esther. Just you wait. Never act like you're better than me because, well, you're not." She stomped on the ground like a child and began walking down the hallway.

Lina glanced at me. "I didn't need your help." I continued staring at her, trying to keep my face emotionless. Why did I even help her?

A boy I never met before came up to me with a group of

friends. "Good way to ruin the fun."

"It wasn't that fun for me," Lina said bitterly.

"Yeah... Try keeping your disgusting nose out of everyone's business," a girl said, shoving me with her shoulder. The students rolled their eyes as the warning bell rang. My mouth fell open and I was utterly shocked.

"Tough crowd," Ace said, appearing at my side.

"You could say so."

I sat in my assigned seat in Study Hall, watching all of the students picking out books and talking surreptitiously. I glanced at the three other individuals that were sitting with me. Well, they had to.

"You know," a girl said with bright green eyes, leaning into the table, "You shouldn't have done that to Leila."

I glared at her, trying not to explode. "What she did was wrong."

"Well, now you're in trouble. Everyone here *wants* to be Leila's friend. She's the richest and prettiest girl in this school." The girl looked down at the table as if she were searching for something more to say. "Now you're a target. You stood against her power."

I leaned back in my chair. "This is a school. Not a dictatorship."

"Well if Leila's here... It's far more than just a school."

I looked around the Study Hall area and almost everyone was staring at me. Their eyes penetrated with anger. "You weren't kidding when you said I was a target."

"Yeah. Well. Consider yourself friendless from now on."

I chuckled with venom. "I'm not the only who stood up against Leila." I looked ahead and my eyes laid on Mason. He was standing by one of his friends and they were looking at books on the mini shelf. Next to them stood the substitute librarian. She was very old and cross eyed. She stumbled almost every time she walked. I watched as Mason noticed the lady standing over him, drool nearly pouring out of her mouth. He jabbed his elbow into his friend, trying to get his attention. Once he did, he pointed at the old lady and they both laughed quietly.

"What you kids doin'!" the lady yelled, staring in the opposite direction of the boys.

Mason burst into laughter. His laugh echoed quietly

throughout the silent hall.

"I will not tolerate this type of behavior!" Spit flew out of her mouth as the boys continued laughing.

I found myself laughing quietly at the situation. Suddenly, I felt a hard object hit me in the back of my head. I turned around in my chair, noticing Leila and a few of her friends laughing.

"Oh, I'm sorry. Did that hurt?" Leila taunted while laughing.

I picked up the book in a fury, readying myself to throw it. The Mark hummed underneath my sleeve and an overwhelming feeling had hit me. *Don't hurt the people you are to protect.* Knowing my thoughts were correct, I slammed the book down at my table. I grabbed my book bag and slung it over my shoulder violently.

"Awh, why give up so quickly?" Leila asked, frowning with no sympathy.

I wanted to pick up the book and throw it in her face so badly. But I had to control my anger. "You're lucky I did." Everyone was staring at me and some people began to stand up as if there was going to be a fight.

"Words don't hurt me, honey."

I bit down on my lip as I began to walk out of the Study Hall. I pushed students out of the way so I could get to the door quickly. I opened the doors in a fury as the sensation of wanting to fight back swept over me. The hallway was empty and dark—not a soul in sight. I slammed my book bag on the ground in anger as all of the thoughts of Damion came into my head.

"I want him *here*," I screamed as the tears began to pour out of my eyes, "with me." In distress, I created two sharp force fields to release my anger. One of the force fields hit a drinking fountain, completely cutting it into two. The water spewed out across the ground and air, soaking me from head to toe. The bell rang. *Shit, students are going to see what happened.* I grabbed my drenched book bag and ran down the hallway.

"Looks like I'm walking home today," I whispered to myself.

I gazed out the window, watching the moon sit perfectly in harmony as the stars danced around it. I cuddled up against the window, listening to the steady rainfall.

I closed my eyes, picturing Damion was sitting next to me as his strong arms wrapped around me.

"Have you ever wanted to see Space?" Damion asked quietly in my thoughts.

"I see it every night, remember?"

"No. Like actually go up there and see how it feels? Being weightless? Knowing there's nothing that could pull you down... Be free?"

"I've thought about it."

"Why not keep thinking about it?"

"I don't have to think about it more than once," I whispered, continuing to stare out the window.

"Why not?" he asked curiously, totally oblivious.

I looked at his face. The moon was lighting up his fair complexion; the moonlight shone through his inquisitive blue eyes and his lips were parted slightly. "You make me *feel* free. Like I am weightless. Like there's nothing holding me back."

His lips pulled back into a grin. "Since the first time I saw you I fell in love."

"Me too. I didn't know love at first sight even existed."

"It does now." He extended his hand and closed his eyes. He leaned in and the moment his hand touched my face, the image of him disappeared and I opened my eyes. I felt a tear streaming down my cheek, wishing it had been real.

"Esther," Mason said as I closed my locker, "you can't let people hurt you."

"That's easy for you to say," I said bitterly.

"I'm not your enemy so stop treating me like one."

"It's just so hard, you know?" I said loudly. "If only you could understand."

"Yeah. Okay. Maybe I don't understand... But I could try if you tell me *everything.*"

I turned my back to him, closing my eyes tightly. *Maybe I could tell him about Damion? Not about Clockworks and everything with it, but only Damion?* I turned around, staring him in the eyes. "I cared about someone back at my old home. I cared about him a lot. And, I only have one parent now."

"And?"

I shrugged my shoulders, wanting to give the shortest story

as possible. "I had to leave him. That's all."

Mason furrowed his brows. "So, you're having a hard time without this person? That's what I'm getting from this whole conversation. Yeah, losing a parent sucks too."

"Yes."

"Well, move on to someone different. It helps almost every girl who loses their boyfriend."

"Not a bad idea... Not a bad one at all."

"The first step you should take is asking that 'new' person out... You know what I mean?"

I nodded my head, looking down the hallway as my eyes were locked on someone else. "Yes. I know what you mean."

"Maybe ask them to dinner. Not too formal of a dinner. Maybe like seafood? Every guy likes seafood..."

"Yep... They sure do." I watched as Ace talked with his friends. They laughed together at an unknown joke.

"Esther! Watch out!" I heard Mason yell. Before I could react, I felt a hot, sticky substance splash all over me. I glanced around, my eyes growing with anger. Leila looked back at me as her and her friends laughed.

"Esther, I'm so sorry," Mason whispered. I looked down, realizing there was coffee stained on my white shirt. I bit my lip, trying to hold everything in.

"No. It's alright," I told myself more than I did Mason. I glanced in Ace's direction. He was running towards me with a shocked expression.

"Are you alright?" Ace said when he was a few feet away from me.

"Yeah. Didn't burn me too much." I turned around with my sticky books and began walking down the hallway to the closest bathroom.

"Hey, wait up!" Ace yelled, grabbing my arm. I looked back at him, studying his green eyes.

"What do you want?" I asked.

"I know a locker room near the gym on this Wing. It's always vacant since there was a new gym built on the other side of the school."

"And you're saying?" I asked.

"I'll help get that stuff cleaned off of you." Ace turned

211

around to look at Mason. "Tell our Study Hall teacher we're going to be late." From this distance I could see something flicker in Mason's eyes and his jaw tightened.

"I'll talk to you later, Mason."

"Okay. Have fun with your coffee," he managed a smile.

I smiled. "I will."

Ace and I walked away from the crowds of students trying to get to their classes on time. We continued walking down the fairly lighted hallway and we came around a small bend. The bend led us into a vacant hallway with old, rusty lockers.

"This would be a perfect scene for a horror movie," I said quietly.

Ace laughed. "I would have to agree with that."

Ace and I came to a set of doors. We both stood there awkwardly for a few moments until he pushed the doors open. We entered a large gym that was only lit by the light that shined through the large, glass windows on the ceiling.

"Wow. This is *old*," I said reluctantly.

"Yeah—the faded paint and all."

"So... Where's the locker room? I look like a mess."

"Right this way," he said with a grin. He led me further into the large gymnasium. We walked along the bleachers and into a small doorway. The locker room had a few lockers lined up against the wall and windows lighted the whole room dimly. Old, crumbled papers laid on the ground stiffly and everything was caked with dust.

"I come in here to think," Ace said, sitting down on a wooden bench. "It may be old but it's peaceful."

I smiled slightly, admiring his spirit. "I think a lot too."

"I can tell." He looked up at me. "You always lose yourself in your thoughts... The facial expressions you make when you think... It always makes me curious to know what you're *truly* thinking about."

"Oh," I said, leaning up against the lockers, "you wouldn't want to know."

He grinned. "I would actually. I wish I knew what everyone was thinking."

"Wouldn't that make things a little boring though?" I asked. "I mean... If you knew what everyone was thinking there would be no curiosity."

He shrugged his shoulders like how I would. "Sure. But it'll make life so much easier... You would know if someone truly cared about you."

"Or if someone truly hated you," I said quietly.

"Well, I certainly don't. So now you have one less person to be curious about."

A small grin appeared across my lips and my heart skipped a beat. "You have one less person to worry about also, Ace."

"Good. And hey, did you know my name isn't really Ace?" he said, cocking his head to the side a bit.

"What is it?" I asked, growing curious.

"It's Acea. Ace is the nickname Leila gave me."

I nodded my head thoughtfully. "I like Acea better."

"I guess you like me for who I am then."

"Well, of course. Who wouldn't?"

"Leila likes me for my appearance—not for who I am on the inside."

"Then she isn't a true person. Think about that instead of her appearance also."

Acea shrugged his shoulders. "I guess I dated her for the reputation. We're both very popular at this school and everyone adores us... So, I thought it would be a good idea."

"Sometimes the things you think are good turn out to be the worst thing ever imagined."

Acea stood up, coming closer to me. He continued staring into my eyes as he placed his two, large hands on each side of the lockers, trapping me into his body. He stood a few feet away as his green eyes illuminated with triumph. "I like your wisdom."

Nervously, I grabbed a strand of my hair, twisting it around my finger. "I admire your spirit."

"I believe I finally broke down your walls," he whispered. I could smell the coffee on my shirt wafting throughout the air.

I laughed softly, staring into his minty green eyes. "I think there's still another wall up," I whispered, my words barely audible.

"Let me break that one down too." He began leaning in while simultaneously closing his eyes. Instantaneously, I did the same. The Mark underneath my skin vibrated and images of Damion flooded throughout my head. I saw his radiant grin and his eyes smiled at me. The scene shifted and we were sitting underneath our willow tree, laughing and talking about life. *I couldn't do this.*

I pulled away from Acea in a hurry and I watched as his face slammed into the lockers. "I'm so sorry," I said as he looked at me with alarmed eyes. "I just can't." I turned on my heels, trying to run out the door in a hurry. Acea grabbed my arm, making phrases appear in front of my eyes. It was the same phrases of Brilliance I had already read. I jerked my hand away from him in a fury, the images simultaneously fading.

"What did I do wrong?" Acea said, his voice slightly whiny.

"You didn't do anything *wrong*," I said with the same whiny voice. "It—it's ju—st I can't do *this*."

"Why not? Those barriers around you shouldn't be that strong!" I noticed his whiny voice change into a hard, rude-sounding mimic.

"They are when you care about someone else!"

He stepped back a few feet like I had slapped him. "I—I don't understand."

"You're going too fast Acea. I don't even know your middle name."

"Acea Tyler Winter."

"I think I should get going. The bell is going to ring soon and I have to get home quickly." As I walked out of the locker room, I took off my sopping wet shirt, revealing another layer of coffee on my tank top. I groaned, disgusted with my appearance.

"Esther!" I heard Acea yell. I spun around on my heels, staring at him as he stood quite a distance away. "Let me go slow, then. It'll be worth the wait."

I scoffed. "You'll be waiting forever."

He grinned. "I can wait that long for you."

I couldn't help but smile. But the worse thing was, he was too much like Damion. But then again, Damion had something that Acea would never have. *Me.*

"There was another attack. It happened last night in Missouri." My mother slammed her battle gear on the dining room table, avoiding my eye contact. "Fifty civilians were killed by the Creators."

"They're coming closer." I stared at my mother, waiting for her to rush over to me and give me a large hug, telling me that everything would be okay. But she didn't. She stared at her battle gear; her eyes seemingly opaque. "Mom?"

She sighed. "I know that. I'm just trying to think where we could relocate."

"Mother... You spent millions on this house and you're willingly going to give it up? Just like that?"

In anger, she slammed her hand on the table, making me jump back in my chair. "Of course, I am! I'm willing to give up everything *for you*. I'm not going to let you get killed."

I stared at her, my face contorting in sorrow. "Stop doing so much for me. You haven't gotten any sleep, Mom. You're exhausted."

She sighed, collapsing onto a chair. "I can't rest, Esther. Brilliance can easily be taken away from you. You need to understand that *you* hold the key to Earth's survival."

I picked at my dinner with my fork, not knowing how to respond or how to react. "I do understand. I just don't understand why Brilliance Chose me."

"It's self-explanatory. It Chose you because it sees something in *you* that it hasn't seen in anyone else. Brilliance tinkered with all of our minds. It made you have a liking for the Rizzoli Bookstore and it allowed me to let you go."

"I still don't understand what it saw in me."

"That's because you don't have the confidence in yourself to know."

I leaned back in my chair, studying my mother's face. I could see her aging wrinkles and her sunken eyes. "If Brilliance Chooses people whom are wise... Then doesn't that mean the person who has to kill me is wise?" I thought back to the dreams of the man.

My mother nodded her head, avoiding my stare. "Yes. There are still people who are wise that weren't Chosen. I suppose those are what Souls are. I can't give you the full definition because I honestly don't know."

"Draculus wasn't wise. Darius wasn't wise. What would happen if they did kill me?"

My mother shrugged. "You wouldn't die I suppose."

"Is that why I didn't die when they were torturing me?"

"Yes, possibly."

"Have you heard from Damion?" I asked, changing the subject.

"No."

I groaned, picking at my food once more. Where was Damion? I started thinking about today's incident... with Acea. "Why isn't Brilliance showing me anything new?"

"I don't know. It just doesn't want to, I guess."

I stood up, slightly annoyed with my mother's laconic responses. I grabbed my plate that was filled with food and walked into the kitchen, kicking the door open with my leg. I walked around the island, edging closer to the trashcan. I dumped out my food and placed my plate in the sink for further washing.

"Is Becca still coming over?" I asked through the kitchen walls.

"No! I thought I told you that already," my mother called back.

"Oh. Guess I didn't hear." I looked out the kitchen window, staring at the falling sun. The sky was painted with shades of purple and pink that danced around the clouds with beauty. *Why do I feel so alone? I feel like Becca and I are so distant... And I can't even feel Damion anymore... I miss my dad too... It's like they all dropped off the face of the Earth.*

Without another painful thought, I walked out of the kitchen to find my mother standing over the TV in the living room. From the slight distance, I noticed a news reporter talking frantically with the sounds of explosions from a distance.

"We are sorry to inform our viewers of more attacks. This time the attacks ranged from California to Tennessee. Our Special Units of Reinforcements are sorry to conclude that they have no one in custody. The figures in the black capes are still unidentified and we do not know what they truly desire."

My mother turned around in a hurry and suddenly stopped when she noticed me standing in the kitchen doorway. Her eyes looked at me in alarm as if she didn't know I was listening. "I need to go take care of it."

"Mom, please let me come. I can help."

"No. They're doing this because of you. They'll kill you on the spot and you better hope your luck they're not the wise Soul." She paced towards me, grabbing her gear off the dining table. She pulled her sword out of her sheath, making the slicing noise known to happen in movies. My mother sighed, stabbing the sword back in her sheath. "A friend of mine, Caru, will be patrolling the grounds for you. Stay in the house, okay?"

"Okay," I said. She grabbed all of her gear and walked towards the foyer without another word. Before she grabbed the handle, I had the urge to do something. "I love you."

I watched as she stopped in her tracks, head hung low. She didn't look back at me, but I already knew there was a war going on inside her mind. "I love you too," she said. And with that, she opened the door forcefully, walking out into the sunset. She pulled the door shut without another word. I found myself smiling as I stood in the kitchen doorway. *She still has her mother qualities despite the fact everything has changed.*

"So, how'd the coffee thing go with Ace?" Mason asked as he stood by my locker. I stopped fumbling with my books, replaying the romantic scene in my head. He tried to kiss me but I never gave in.

"Oh. Good. We couldn't really clean up all of the coffee. It was like, impossible." I laughed awkwardly.

"Oh, I bet. So, is that why you two never came back to class?" Mason asked, his tone unreadable.

"Well, yeah. It was almost time to leave from school so..."

"So. you didn't come back to class to say goodbye to me. Kay, I got it."

I sighed. "Mason, I said goodbye before I left to clean up. I wanted to walk home yesterday anyway."

"Speak of the devil," Mason said, looking behind me. I turned around to notice Acea coming my way with a small smile on his face.

"Hey Esther," he said with a smile once he reached me.

"Hi."

"So, I was wondering... Do you want to hangout during Easter break? I'm free tomorrow."

"Oh good, looks like I don't have to buy you," I said sarcastically.

He laughed. "I love your humor."

"Um, well, I'm going to go now," I heard Mason say. Acea looked up like he just noticed Mason.

"Oh, hey squirt," Ace said, reaching his hand out to ruffle Mason's hair. Mason grabbed his hand, throwing it back at Acea angrily.

"Please don't touch me. I'm no smaller than you."

"Actually, you are. Do you even lift?" Acea asked with a sort of mockery.

"No. I don't need to lift. I actually play a sport rather than kill my body with steroids."

Acea laughed, flashing a set of white teeth. "What sport do you play then?"

"Soccer," Mason said.

"Oh, interesting... Is that why you're frail and spineless?"

Mason laughed, "Like I said, I don't need steroids."

"I actually don't use steroids. These are real." He held out his arm and flexed right in front of my face. I had to admit; they were impressive. But I would never be interested.

Mason rolled his eyes. "Okay. I'll be leaving now. Bye Esther."

"Bye Mason," I said quietly. I watched as Mason left. He shook his head every once in a while, indicating he was talking to himself mentally.

"He's a buzz kill, ain't he?" Acea said with a laugh.

"No. He's actually great company."

"Well, I need to show you some better company," he said with a laugh.

"Alright. Fine. We can hang out over break if you want to so badly."

"Yes!" Acea said with a hand gesture. "Finally. I told you I'm going to keep trying."

"Well, I admire your dedication."

"And I admire your attitude," Ace said with a smile.

The bell rang before I had a chance to say something. "Bye." I turned around while closing my locker and began walking down the crowded hallway. Up ahead I noticed Leila and her friends walking my way while laughing and giggling. My heart skipped a beat, realizing they might mess with me.

"Oh, look!" I heard Leila yell with a giggled voice. "It's Esther." All of her friends began laughing hysterically. I bowed my head, avoiding eye contact. Before I had time to notice what was going on, I felt my books slam into my face, busting my nose with pain. I fell onto my butt, staring up at the ceiling. I rolled onto my side as I prepared myself to fight back but then the Mark vibrated and I instantly knew I couldn't hurt the people I was to protect. I crouched on my fours, staring at Leila and her friends as they laughed while walking away from me.

In anger of refraining myself, I slapped my hand against the tiled ground while gritting my teeth. "I hate it here!" I couldn't help but yell at the passing students. I watched as they walked away from me, not even bothering to bend down and help me pick up my books. I looked down at the floor as I tried to suck in the tears. *I hate it here. I hate it here. I want Damion. I want Becca. I want to go back home... The people I love can protect me... not distance.* I watched a tear fall onto the white tile. One by one, tears dropped onto the ground as my anger consumed me slowly.

"You know," a voice said, their feet appearing by my face, "you shouldn't act like a coward... Stand up for yourself. Show some independence."

I looked up, wiping the tears on my sleeves. It was Luna. Her sister Rosa stood a few feet behind her. "I'm not hurting anyone."

"Here, let me help you up," Luna asked, extending her hand. I rejected it by standing up myself. "Suit yourself." I ignored her remark and grabbed my books.

"You shouldn't be a coward, Esther," Rosa said and her voice was surprisingly dark compared to Luna's sweet voice.

"I'm anything but a coward, alright?" I snapped.

Luna laughed, her voice sounding like chimes in the wind. "That's quite ironic, actually."

I rolled my eyes and started walking passed them down the hallway. Mr. Sparks's classroom wasn't that far away from my locker which was good. I arrived at his classroom, opening the door and taking my seat close to the board. I felt Mason's eyes on me.

"Hey, are you alright?" Mason asked, pointing to my eyes.

I nodded my head, wiping my eyes. "Just angry, that's all." The bell rang again and class began.

"Okay," Mr. Sparks said, clapping his hands together, "we're going to start off the day the right way. We're learning about the past, present and future! But first, I have a very important question to ask someone." He looked directly at me. "Got anything smart to say today?"

I laughed coldly, slightly shocked he wanted to pick on me.

"Well, actually, I do. It's not right for a teacher to choose a child and discriminate them in front of a classroom. Just saying."

Mr. Sparks mimicked my cold laughter. "Hilarious. And how long have you been teaching to know the rules?"

"I'm not a teacher, I'm a student. I've been a student for quite some years."

"Well, there it is!" Mr. Sparks yelled. "The answer! Who has more experience?"

"Me," I said to throw him off in a tangent.

"Obviously no. I am older than you, therefore I am smarter than you."

"Not likely."

"SHUT UP! WHEN WILL YOU LEARN TO KEEP YOUR MOUTH SHUT!"

I shrugged my shoulders. "Never, unless I want to die. I need to open my mouth to receive the nutrients I need to survive."

"That's unfortunate."

"Is that a death threat, Mr. Sparks?" He already got me in my argumentative zone.

"Maybe. Why? Do you have a problem with that?"

"Yes. It's very rude to treat your student like that. You should thank me more often because I am the very reason why you have a job. I am here to learn and you are here to teach me."

"Esther, just stop," Mason hissed beside me. "What has gotten into you?"

I looked at Mason. "He targeted me first! I'm not going to let him do that!"

"You let Leila push you to the ground," a student spoke up. I felt a dagger get stabbed into my heart. Why was everyone gaining up on me?

"Yeah. I saw that too. Why do you let her stomp on you but not a teacher? Do you have a problem with that?" another kid stated.

"Yeah," Mason said, "and why do you let your boyfriend stomp on your *best friend* without fighting back?"

I looked at Mason, horrified. "Acea isn't my boyfriend and he never will be. I didn't even know he was hurting your feelings! Why didn't you say anything?"

"Because I don't want to *hurt your feelings*, Esther," Mason said.

I felt the tears beginning to well up around my irises. "I hate it here," I whispered.

"Esther, you know the school policy. When you're in a classroom, do not mumble. Speak again, please," Mr. Sparks taunted.

"I HATE IT HERE! I WANT TO GO HOME!" I screamed.

"Please leave my classroom, Esther. I do not tolerate that kind of behavior."

"I'd be happy to." I got up and left in a hurry before anyone could see me cry. I pushed open the glass door, stopping in front of the empty hallway to take a deep breath. I couldn't hold it in any longer and all of my feelings erupted like a volcano. I stood, horrified with myself. *I'm actually breaking. It's finally happening...* I felt my body shatter, slowly showing the cracks engraved in my skin. I needed an escape—just in case someone might find me—the strongest person emotionally splitting into two. *The locker rooms.* Despite the fact it was old and dusty, I had to admit it was peaceful. In a hurry, I ran down the hallway before anyone decided to wander outside the classrooms to get a break. I turned the corner, coming to a set of double doors that led into the abandoned gymnasium. Hesitantly, I pushed the doors open and I was greeted by an old, musky smell. That was normal for the gymnasium.

Gingery, I continued walking on the dirt-crusted floor, wiping my tears as I did so. Lights from the high glass windows shone through the dust, making the place slightly eerie, but comforting at the same time. I walked into the locker room. I looked at the old, crumpled papers on the ground.

A small part of me actually wanted Acea to be in the locker room. I guess I just wanted someone to talk to... Someone to understand me. But I didn't think Acea could grant such a wish anyways. I collapsed onto a wooden bench as more tears began to stream down my cheeks. Why was it so hard? To just fit in? To be liked amongst people? Was that too much to ask for?

I only wanted to be accepted by these people. But that could never happen. Sometimes I desperately wished that they could know what was really happening with me. *I am saving their lives... I'm protecting them right now... I was Chosen to keep this world safe from harm.* But why couldn't they understand?

"I miss Damion," I said to myself as another pang of

221

emotions struck me, "he's the one who only accepted me for who I was." Because of him, I didn't feel alone. I felt safe. I was less arrogant. I actually understood what life really had to offer. He grabbed my hand and showed me the beauties of life even when I didn't notice it before.

Then I had to leave him after I finally felt alive again... Without him, I felt darker, more exposed to unhappiness. I missed his hugs, the way he throws back his head when he laughs, and the way he cared about me. I wish I had kissed him instead of being such a baby about emotions. The thing was, I was afraid of love... affection... feeling tenderly. It was all so new to me and I just couldn't understand the concept... *Is it possible I don't feel what I thought I did with him? Is that why I can't love? Or is it because I don't know how to love someone?*

No. No. I do *feel* something for Damion. When I first saw him, I instantly knew that there was something about him... Something worth fighting for. Maybe that was why our relationship happened so quickly. He felt the same thing I did. Maybe we felt that way because we were both alone, outcasts from the human world. Yes, I had my mother... But I didn't have friends. I believed having friends was a very important aspect of life and it still was. Without friends, what do you really have?

I pushed the painful thoughts away. I was quite sure in twenty minutes I would have to face the people of school again. Even if I didn't want to, I had to. I couldn't be cowardly. I was stronger than this. I could no longer cry because in time, I would have to fight my enemies back.

I stood in the middle of the meadow, knife in hand and my eyes fixed on the target. I gritted my teeth, focusing on how to throw the dagger precisely. Instantaneously, I threw the dagger and it spiraled through the air with a whipping sound, hitting the target directly in the middle. A grin spread across my face and triumphantly, I picked up another knife and threw it again, but this time it bounced off a tree trunk and landed motionless on the ground. My smile faded and I knew it was only luck for the first time.

Slightly angered, I grabbed another dagger and I focused on the target. In seconds, the knife was spiraling through the air, hitting the tree beside the target. I groaned. How was I supposed to fight if I didn't know how to use weapons? Invisibility and force fields wouldn't help me all the time.

"Hey," I heard the familiar voice.

I turned around, surreptitiously kicking the knives under the grass. "Hi, Acea."

"Your mother said I would find you here." He looked around, taking in the beautiful scenery, slowly admiring the luscious, purple flowers in the meadow. "She said you spend most of your time here."

"Yeah. I do actually. It calms me."

He grinned. I noticed the sunlight directly putting its rays on him. "Just like how the locker room calms me."

"Sorta. But the meadow is obviously more beautiful," I said with a laugh.

"It sure is... Guess what it reminds me of?"

"What?" I said, turning around to walk towards my target.

"You."

I smiled a little, knowing the pickup line was original. "Have you ever heard of originality?"

He shrugged. "Not quite. Maybe you could teach me it."

"What do you mean?" I asked, turning around.

"You're different," he said, staring me directly in the eyes, "and I like that about you."

"That's a first," I said under my breath.

He stepped closer to me with a smile on his face. "I mean, not any original girl has targets in a beautiful meadow and knives everywhere on the ground."

"Oh, I was hoping you wouldn't notice."

"You have a very good sense of humor, Green."

I shrugged, "I guess it comes naturally."

He laughed. "But anyways, why *do* you have targets and these cannonball structures everywhere? Planning to murder someone?"

"Depends," I stated. I pulled the knife out of the target, while grabbing the other knives off the ground as well. "I'm only kidding. I'm trying to learn how to be precise with weapons... You know, for self-defense purposes."

"And how is that going for you?" he asked.

"Terribly."

"Can I see one?" Acea asked.

"Yeah sure." I walked towards him, extending a knife and I watched as he grabbed it.

"Thanks." He gripped the knife tightly, his muscles pulsing through his shirt. He didn't look like the average eighteen-year-old. He was larger, bulkier with more muscles exposed than any other ordinary teenager. But Acea wasn't a Clockwork, making it all the stranger. Becca also looked slightly older than her age, but it didn't make much of a difference.

He took in a deep breath and whipped the dagger through the air. The knife whizzed through the air, slicing into the target. Right smack in the middle.

"Luck," I whispered. "It was only luck."

"Give me another one then and I'll prove you wrong," he said with a lopsided grin.

Willingly, I extended my hand, giving him another dagger. "I don't think you'll be able to."

"You can talk, Esther, but you can't act." He held his breath, his muscles bulging out of his V-neck once more. He whipped the dagger again. The sharp object hit the target with a loud crack; it hit the other dagger, breaking the metal in two.

"How?" I breathed.

"It's simple really, just focus."

"I *do* focus," I said, slightly annoyed.

"Here, let me show you." He gently took my arm, taking a few knives out of my hand so I only have one.

"You better teach me correctly or I'll kill you," I joked.

"Literally," he said with a laugh.

He grabbed my waist with soft hands, positioning me correctly. "Keep your arms in first," he whispered in my ear, tucking my arm into my body. "Move your right leg back since you're throwing with your left hand. But do this when you're about to throw." I nodded my head, listening to his instructions.

"Focus on only you're target... Think about the movements... The center... Then THROW."

I listened to his words, throwing the dagger through the air. I felt it escape my hands gently and I watched as it spiraled through the air, stabbing the center of the target.

"Think it was just luck, Green?" Acea said jokingly.

"Maybe. I might have to try again," I said. Acea placed a dagger in my palm, stepping back a few feet to give me my space to throw. I played out all of his instructions in my head, remembering to think about the target... the center. I threw, leaning forward slightly with my foot placed a few inches behind me. The knife released from my hand and began soaring through the air like a graceful bird. It smacked against the center of the target with a loud bang.

"Think its only luck now?" Acea asked with a smile.

"No. I believe it was me this time."

"And that's where the confidence comes from... In yourself." I looked up at Acea as a smile began to form across my lips. He definitely was a charmer. He knew what to say.

"I like your wisdom, child," I said, falling down into the flowers. I looked up at the puffy clouds and the forest tree tops. It was certainly a beautiful day.

"Child?" Acea asked with a chuckle. "You're actually the child, Green. I could crush you into a million pieces."

"Literally," I said, smiling at my joke.

"Is that a fat joke?"

"If only you intend it to be."

"Nice one." He fell onto his back, laying down next to me. "The sky is quite beautiful, isn't it?"

"It sure is."

"I like its color of blue..." Acea said, trailing off. "If you could paint the sky, what colors would you use?"

I shrugged my shoulders, taking the question into consideration. "You know those marshmallows in the flavor variety pack? With the light oranges, purples, blues, pinks, yellows and greens? Yeah, I'd paint the sky into a rainbow."

"Doesn't those colors already happen in sunsets?" he asked.

"Yeah. But you see the colors everyday... Not just before the darkest times of the night."

Acea looked at me, tucking his hands underneath his head. "My mother would sometimes tell me it's always darkest before the dawn."

I looked at him, watching the sunlight light up his minty green eyes, turning them slightly to the color of aqua blue. "Why do you say that?"

225

"Because... I think I finally found my dawn."

I felt my cheeks burn and I had a lump in my heart. "A friend of mine," I said, anonymously referring to Damion as a 'friend', "would tell me there's always happiness in the darkest of times... And I think I finally found mine."

"Let me touch you," Acea whispered.

"I have barriers," I stated.

"Then let me hold your hand... We'll start off small and work our way to the kiss." He gave me a pained look and reluctantly, I extended my hand to his. He grabbed my hand, his warmth invading my cold skin.

"We held hands before," I said.

"I know. It's better than nothing though."

I smiled slightly. "Maybe."

"You know," Acea said, propping himself on one of his elbows, "I want to know why you're so distant from this world... It's like you live in your mind."

I shifted uncomfortably in the grass, unsure if I could trust him with basic information about Damion and why I had to move. "I just do. Is there a problem with that?"

"No, not at all. I'm just curious."

"Why did you say your life was dark before you met me?"

"Well, it was the same thing every day... My parents are rich with their 'high-power' jobs that control their lives... Me hunting daily so I can get my mind off of life... Everyone looking up to me at school like I'm some Godly figure... Leila controlling me any second she has the chance to... But that all changed when I met you."

I shifted again at Leila's name. "Oh."

Acea sighed. "Is she bothering you again? I noticed how you got uncomfortable."

"It's fine."

"No, it's not." He sat up, looking down at me so he could see my face. "Has she been hurting you?"

"I'm fine," I said, shoving it off like it was no big deal.

"It's obviously not. Please, Esther, let me help you."

"I'm fine," I said again but more sternly. "I'll be fine. A small, sixty-pound girl can't hurt me."

"She can hurt your dignity," he stated dryly.

"I don't care about my reputation. I'm probably not going to

226

stay here any longer."

"Why?" he asked, continuing to stare at my face.

"Well, I moved from Oklahoma. I might continue to move."

"There's not much of a reason to..." Acea drifted.

"My mom switches her job a lot. It's only natural."

"You still haven't told me about your darkest times," Acea said, bringing up the subject again. I groaned, rolling onto my side, facing him.

"Will you leave me alone if I tell you?" I asked with a hint of distress.

"Yes!" Acea chimed. "I'm all ears."

"Well, back at home I really cared about someone."

"Were you two dating?"

"Yes," I said, "but anyways, we care about each other. We were together for about six months... We went to Hell and back. We've seen each other at our worst and... we still *loved* each other." I felt Acea shift on the grass, trying to act as if the words didn't affect him. "I had to move away and he didn't understand." I remembered the scene with Damion underneath our willow tree. He had told me he hated me and images of him splitting our tree painfully flashed throughout my mind. "I haven't heard from him since."

"Is that it?"

"No. My father died a year ago. I had to leave everything behind."

"Why didn't he understand? If I were him, I would've understood every word you said. I would enjoy my last minutes with you."

"Thanks, Acea, but people aren't all the same. Everyone thinks about a situation differently."

"True. I'll have to agree with you on that." He paused, looking up at the sky again. "Why do you always wear sleeves? It's kinda warm out, you know."

I looked down at my purple sweater, glancing in the direction of the Mark. "Because I want to. I'm cold."

"Esther, its sixty degrees out. You shouldn't be that cold."

"Well, I am that cold."

"No, you're not."

"Can you just drop it? You never give up, do you?"

"No. I don't give up unless I have a perfectly good reason

227

to."

"I like wearing long sleeves because it makes me feel safe." It wasn't a lie.

Acea nodded, smiling up at the sky. "Okay. I give up. I believe you."

"So... How do you like the break so far?"

"It's alright... I feel a bit lonely when I'm without you."

"You're with me right now," I stated.

"Yeah, I know... Hey, Esther?"

"Yeah?" I asked.

"Do you... think... maybe we could be official?"

"Official?" I asked.

"Yeah. Like we're actually boyfriend and girlfriend. It's what we do when you like someone, mystical creature." He laughed.

I felt my stomach lurch and at that exact moment, I missed Damion even more. I didn't want to move on... I didn't want to accept the fact that we were in two totally different places, separate from each other. Wherever he was... To be exact.

"Sure," I blurted. Maybe I need to learn how to accept it. Even if I didn't want to.

Acea smiled. At least he could accept everything with no problem. "I think I'm finally tearing down your walls."

Chapter 11: The Darkness is Near

It was finally May. The warm weather had come to stay and I had to admit, I was getting happier each day. Acea could really turn my frown upside down. My mother was still tensed, but I think she was beginning to notice how much she truly loved her daughter and how much she wanted to be there for her. Which is a good thing, I missed her.

I still received hate at school. Leila certainly enjoyed pushing me to my limits but I haven't cracked yet. Acea received hate too once the school discovered we were dating. He pushed it all away because he didn't care what everyone else thought. He cared about me instead of all of them. I tried to push away my life at Erin Springs. It wasn't working too well though, but I was trying hard to forget. And forgetting a memory was actually one of the hardest things to do.

"So, how are you doing today?" Acea asked as he helped me sort my books in my locker.

"Pretty good," I said with a flattered smile. "How about your day?"

He nodded his head. "I think people are starting to look at me in a good way now... I think they finally understand it's not about the person, but the way they act."

"Oh, we have an Aceacrates over here," I said jokingly.

"Aceacrates?" he asked with a laugh.

"You know... Socrates... Acea... Aceacrates."

"Oh!" he shouted. "I get it now!"

I laughed at his slight stupidity. "Well, I'm going to clean up before class. I'll see you later."

He grinned. "Bye." He wrapped his arms around me, embracing me softly despite his bulky figure.

I pulled away after a few seconds, waved to him and began walking away. I proceeded down the hallway, entering the girls' restroom only to find Leila and a bunch of her friends with her. I

229

began to turn around until I realized I shouldn't give them the satisfaction. I walked further into the bathroom, turning on the sink to wash my face. I ignored their obnoxious giggles, focusing only on the cold, refreshing water. I pulled my head out of the sink, turning off the water. I dried my face with a few paper towels, ignoring Leila's stares.

In the mirror, I watched as Leila looked at a student walk out of a stall. The student was tall with a darker shade of skin. Leila leaned over, attaching a sticky note on the girl's back.

"Um," Leila said to the girl, "there's a sticky note on your back... That girl right there put it on you. I watched her." Leila pointed at me. The girl slowly turned her head to look at me. She was twice my size and height. Her expression represented a very pissed off person, which was quite reasonable, I would be pissed too if someone put a sticky note on my back that had profound words written on it. But the thing was, I was not the one who put it on her.

"Think that's funny squirt?" the girl said, edging closer to me with a cocked head.

"I didn't put the sticky note on your back, I swear," I said compassionately.

"Yes, she did Marlene. I *watched* her," Leila said.

Marlene stared me down, coming closer to me. "I don't appreciate liars."

"Neither do I," I said, glaring at Leila with wide eyes.

"You wanna know what else I don't appreciate? Smart asses." I took a few steps back as she walked closer to me. I stared at her with wide eyes, trying to figure out what to do. I didn't want to fight anyone. Once she reaches for me, I could grab both of her arms, smash her head into the bathroom counter and then make my escape.

"I wouldn't consider myself a smart ass, just saying," I said with a hint of mockery.

That was when she blew. She reached her hands out quickly and before I could react, she grabbed a hold of my school uniform collar, pushing me into the wall while simultaneously lifting me up off my feet.

"So, are you afraid yet?" she said through gritted teeth.

I shrugged my shoulders, holding onto Marlene's hands. "Afraid of being two feet off the ground? Yeah, no. That doesn't frighten me at all."

She growled in anger, releasing one hand from my collar, raising it in the air, readying to punch me. Before her fist could collide into my face, I kicked her in the shin. I fell to the ground, landing perfectly on my feet. Marlene regained herself and kicked her leg out to trip me. I fell onto the hard tile, smacking my jaw against the hard floor. Ow. I heard Leila's laugh echo throughout the bathroom.

"Give Esther what she deserves."

I felt a heavy object land on my back and I could feel my hair being viciously pulled back. "Knocking off a few extra pounds would be marvelous, Marlene," I said through gritted teeth, trying to ignore the pain. I've been electrocuted and burned nearly to death; I can definitely win this fight. *But how do I move out of this position?* I noticed a trashcan in front of me. It was small in size and easy to knock over. I could probably find an old bar of soap in it. Carefully, I extended my hand while Marlene was too busy yanking on my hair and bouncing on my spine. I tipped the small trashcan over with no trouble.

"Quit squirming!" Marlene yelled.

I ignored her as she continued yanking at my hair. I felt blood pouring down my face because she was pulling on my scalp. I rummaged my hand through the contents of the trash can until I found an old wrapping of bar soap. It could work. I laid there with no motion for a few seconds, trying to regain the strength to move.

Spontaneously, I flipped on my side with all of my might, making it to where she was now on my stomach. With hope, I smashed the soapy wrapper into her eyes, shoving the contents on her face while gritting my teeth. She yelped out in pain while clutching her red eyes. In a hurry, she scrambled to get up. She placed one of her hands on my stomach, getting up and running to the sink. I got up slowly as my back engulfed with pain.

"Esther!" Leila screamed. "Why did you do that!"

"Oh my god! She burnt Marlene's eyes!" her friend yelled.

I turned on my heels to look at them, wiping streams of blood from my forehead. "I think it's time for you to tell her the truth. Who *really* did it."

Leila laughed. "Just because you shoved a wrapper full of soap into her eyes doesn't make me scared of you. You'll *never* be scary."

"I don't want you to be afraid of me," I said. "But I do want you to stop hurting everyone else because you hate me. They never did anything to hurt you."

Leila smiled. "It's the only way for revenge, Esther."

I laughed. "We're in middle school. This isn't a war. We're children."

"You don't look like a child. You look a few years older than you really are."

I shrugged my shoulders. "I age faster. Everyone is different."

"True. But if you treat me poorly, I'll make your life a living Hell."

"It's already a living Hell, you don't need to make it worse than it already is."

"I do actually."

"No, you don't. Plus, I stood up for something I thought was wrong. How is that treating you poorly?"

"You were my friend. I expect you to follow in my footsteps."

"I'm not a follower. I have my own sense of mind. I don't need to be directed."

The bell rang. I was late.

Suddenly, I felt a hard object hit me in the back. I turned around quickly, realizing it was Marlene. She lifted her fist, punching me in the jaw before I had time to react. I stumbled back a few feet. Leila and her friends were laughing.

"You think you can get away with this?" Marlene said through gritted teeth.

"It was only self-defense."

"Sure it was."

Before she had time to punch me again, I created a thin force field around my face. It wasn't circular, it was only large enough to coat all of my features. She lifted her hand again, gritting her crooked teeth. Her veins were showing in her eyes and they were filled with pure hatred. I watched in slow motion behind the surface in front of me. Slowly, her fist moved forward, colliding into my face. All I could feel was the vibration of the force field taking in the impact. I didn't move a muscle and I didn't even blink my eyes.

Marlene stared at me, her eyes filled with shock and her mouth dropped open in bewilderment.

"Impossible," she breathed.

"Anything is possible." I brought up my fist, colliding it into her jaw. She stumbled backwards from the impact and her eyes rolled back inside her head. Her legs gave out and she fell down, smacking her head into the granite counter. Leila screamed, running out of the bathroom. Her friends followed her and all I could hear were their high heels clacking against the ground.

Once the door shut, I stared at Marlene on the ground. I bit my lip, slightly worried if she was alright. I heard the door open and my heart dropped into my stomach. Luna walked around the corner, her eyes opening widely when she noticed Marlene on the ground.

"What a shame," Luna whispered.

"I swear, I didn't mean to do it—"

"It was an accident. I understand," Luna said quietly. I bit my lip, staring at Marlene on the ground. Luna walked over to her gracefully, bending down next to Marlene. With trembling fingers, she stroked Marlene's neck. "She's unconscious. She'll be alright."

"I was only protecting myself. Leila blamed me for something I didn't do... And Marlene wanted to hurt me. I only hurt people that want to hurt me."

"Go to class. I'll take the blame," Luna said, staring up at me with her gray eyes.

"Are you sure?" I asked in bewilderment.

"Yes. You didn't deserve this today."

I glanced in the mirror, making sure there was no blood on my face. There were only a few bruises. I cut off my force field as I began walking out of the bathroom. I focused on the bruises, slightly cursing them to go away. I felt the rush and instantly I knew they were gone. Only I could feel them because my invisibility forced them away from an individual's eyes. Now I had to face Mr. Sparks.

I reached his door, taking deep breaths. I knocked twice, waiting for someone to open the door. I heard the click of the handle and the door opened slowly. Mason was staring at me.

"Where have you been?" he hissed.

I moved passed him, avoiding all the eyes on me. Mr. Sparks turned around from the board to stare at me. I sat down, making the stupid desk squeak.

"Nice to finally have you join us, Esther. Now may I ask, where were you?"

"I was late," I said confidently.

"Well, yes, I know that." The class burst into laughter. "But why?"

"I was late to school." I watched as Mr. Sparks glared at me doubtfully. I felt my Mark vibrate and his expression suddenly became more relaxed.

"Well, okay. Don't be tardy again." He turned his back to the board and began with his lecture once more. I stared down at the Mark, a grin pulling at the corners of my mouth. *It does protect me.*

"Do you ever wonder why we had a connection when we first saw each other?" Damion asked.

I shrugged my shoulders, picking at the purple flowers in the meadow. "Sometimes I think our relationship went on too quickly."

"Why?" he asked. "I believe it was love at first sight."

"What if love at first sight isn't real?" I asked him.

He stared at me, the sun reflecting in his bright, blue eyes. "It is real," he whispered, "because we wouldn't be here right now if it wasn't."

I felt my lip quaver. "What brought us together anyways?"

"The stars," he said. "We were meant to be soul mates when the world was created."

"How was the world created?"

"I'll tell you the next time we see each other, okay?" he said with a faint smile.

I sighed. "You know I'm not very patient."

"I know you aren't. That's why I'm making it to where you learn to be patient."

"I have a lot of qualities I need to learn."

"Especially kindness," he said. "I don't agree that you used Brilliance to manipulate everyone who saw you do it. Now Luna is taking the fault."

"She volunteered. And what was I supposed to do? Let Marlene beat me up in front of the people who want to destroy my life?"

"You need to protect those people who want to destroy your life. That's what you were wired to do."

234

"You sound like my mother," I stated.

"I'm not your mother though. I just don't want you to jeopardize yourself... and everything you have left."

"I don't have much left," I said dryly. "I don't even have you left. You're *gone*."

"Not forever and you know that. If you and I were meant to be soul mates, we'll see each other again." He moved closer to me in the grass with a smile on his face. "We'll see each other again." He grabbed my hand, clasping it into his.

"It's been so long since I've seen you, Damion. I don't think I can stand the life here anymore."

"You have Acea now. He's there for you."

"I know. But he *isn't you*."

Damion's smile grew wider as he stared me in the eyes. His skin was nearly transparent which was very unlike him. "I wish I could be there when they come for you."

"Come for me?" I asked, slightly horrified.

"You won't be safe forever, Esther, and you know that."

I sighed. "Where are you? Why can't Alvaro find you?"

He lowered his head. "I'm ashamed to tell you where I am. You'll hate me."

"Damion, I wouldn't hate you... Where are you?"

Suddenly, before he could answer, there was loud movement coming from the woods. We both glanced up, noticing dark figures standing before the tree line. He turned to look at me with fearful eyes.

"They're coming for you." My heart dropped into my stomach and heat surfaced across my face.

I woke up, my heart racing. I looked around while my heart was still beating heavily against my chest. My room looked normal in the dark moonlight. Everything was how I left it.

Raising the hair on the back of my neck, I heard voices coming from the vents. I threw the covers off my body, slowly walking towards my window. Below the window curve, there was a vent. I got on my knees carefully, pressing my ear against the vent. I heard my mother talking slightly hushed but I couldn't hear the other voice.

"What do you mean?" she shrieked. "Why are they taking all of the Clockworks?" She said something more but the AC kicked on so I couldn't make out the words anymore. Maybe she was talking on the phone? With tiptoes, I walked silently to the other side of my room where the house phone was placed on my dresser. I wasn't allowed to use it and I would listen to my mother's remarks about not using the phone, but right now seemed like the perfect time. I picked up the phone, placing it ever so gently against my ear.

"How has she been?" I heard a familiar voice. Alvaro.

"She's been... Distant. Sad almost. She found another boy she likes, but I can tell it's only to forget about the boy. I'm worried about her. How long do you think she's going to last?" my mother asked.

"Well, if she lasted this long without killing herself... She'll last long enough before... you know..."

"Yes. I know. The War. Will she be strong enough to fight back?" my mother asked.

"Have you been training her?"

"No. I don't want her to use those techniques on the children that bully her at school." She paused. "But I think she's trying to learn."

"She gets bullied *too*?" Alvaro shrieks. "Hasn't she been through *enough*?"

"We can't do anything about her personal life at school. That's something she needs to deal with."

"And how has that been working out for her? I already see future fights with other students that may cause her to be at a terrible place at a terrible time. The more they bully her, the more the darkness is going to make itself known."

"How much time do we have left, Alvaro?"

"Not much. The Creators found a leader. That leader has the ability to be wise."

"Shit."

"Yeah. Now you see where I'm going with this."

"And how exactly are the Creators working together for power? Don't they all want it for themselves?" my mother asked.

"The leader, known as Dante Jett, promised the Creators something in return for their help to overthrow the humans."

"What are they receiving?"

"Immortality," Alvaro stated. I gasped into the receiver then quickly, noticing what I had done, covered my mouth. I bit my tongue, hoping they didn't hear me.

"Do you think Ava Blacksmith and Dante are working together?"

"Most certainly. Ava is probably one of the most powerful witches there is."

"Alvaro. You and her are the *only* witches. Other Boundaries aren't witches."

"Sorry, I just think you guys are according to Brilliance."

"Brilliance isn't always right."

"So far, it's right about the Prophecy."

"And, according to your vision, Alvaro, I'm not going to be with Esther any longer. Correct?"

"Correct. I also cannot be with Esther either. I'm glued to stay here. The Prophecy of the Spiritual Human will be with her along with the Exol Child."

"Have you been able to read Brilliance?" my mother asked with curiosity.

"Of course not. Only Esther and the Writer can read it as long as Esther isn't killed."

"Hopefully she'll be able to read her Prophecy before the time comes."

"That's what I'm hoping too."

"So, in our earlier conversation, Dante is capturing Clockworks with his army?" my mother asked. At this point, I was shoving my ear into the phone so I could hear better.

"Yes. There was a letter outside of my house from the Exols. They were describing that Dante was capturing all of the Clockworks and holding them captive in hidden camps. The Exols believe they already know where the Chosen one is, they're just 'playing with their food', if you know what I mean."

"Playing with their food?" I whispered, slightly shocked.

"Did you hear that?" Alvaro asked.

"Yes... I did. I'm going to go check on Esther. Bye." I heard the click of the phone on the other line, indicating the call was over.

In a hurry, I slammed the phone back down on my dresser. I paced across my room, jumping onto my bed. I could hear my mother's footsteps down the hall. With a racing heart, I flipped my covers over my body, nuzzling against my pillow. I opened my mouth slightly, allowing myself to look like I was in a deep sleep.

My mother barged open my door, quickly walking towards my dresser. I heard her pick up the phone and the sound of crumbling plastic echoed throughout my room. She broke the phone.

"It's not right to eavesdrop," my mother said harshly. I remained silent, closing my eyes tightly. *I know*, I wanted to say, but I couldn't find the words. I wanted to race out of this room, out of this house and further beyond so I could fight back. Clockworks were being imprisoned so the Creators could get to me faster. This wasn't child's play anymore—it was becoming real.

"And Esther, I hope you do know that I love you very much." And with that, she closed my door quietly.

"I love you too," I whispered, opening my eyes. I stared outside, watching the moon behind the treetops.

"Did you hear that Luna Windchester beat up Marlene Leetas?" Mason said excitedly on the bus the next day.

"Yes. I know."

"Marlene said she thought she saw you do it but then she and Leila's friends suddenly came to the conclusion that Luna did it." Mason stared at me widely like he didn't have any faith that I could do such a thing.

"That's strange. I don't know why she would accuse me of doing that."

"Yeah. But it's all cleared out now."

I nodded my head. "Yeah."

"How have you been? It's been awhile since we talked." He stared at me with his big bright eyes.

"I've been fine." I thought back to last night. Dante was capturing Clockworks so he could get closer to me. He was the Wise, therefore he could kill me easily and Brilliance would be transferred to him. He was the man that used to haunt my dreams before Brilliance protected me from him.

"You don't seem too convincing," Mason said, his face contorting into curiosity.

I shrugged my shoulders. "I just miss my home."

"Oklahoma, right?" Mason asked.

I nodded. "I miss the people there and I want to go back." I wanted to find Damion. I wanted to see Becca's smiling face. I wanted to hear Alvaro's laugh. And overall, I wanted to fight back. I didn't want to hide anymore. "I think it's stupid that I even have to go to school."

Mason laughed. "Don't we all think that?"

"I suppose so," I said as the school bus began circling around the parking lot of the school. Once the bus came to a stop, everyone got up in their seats, waiting patiently to get off. I stood in the aisle and watched everyone file out of the bus. Up ahead, I noticed Luna and Rosa talking in hushed voices. Simultaneously, they looked back at me. I looked down quickly, pretending I was fascinated with the gum wrappers on the floor. Hopefully Brilliance brainwashed Luna into thinking she did it also.

One by one, we exited the bus. I stepped down on the pavement while waiting patiently for Mason to step down also. I watched as he grabbed a hold of the metal railing and stepped down. It looked like he was afraid of falling even though the bus steps were two feet off the ground.

"Hey, I'll see you in History. Alright?" I said.

He nodded his head. "Yeah. You can go find Acea."

I watched as he clenched his soft features. I wasn't sure why he hated Acea. He never did anything wrong to Mason. I turned on my heels, adjusting my book bag strap on my shoulder and began walking with the other students. I walked inside the school, making my way down the hallway towards my locker. I walked for some time before I finally reached it. I did my combination quickly. I opened my locker and pulled out my morning books. I looked around, expecting Acea to come out of nowhere and hug me from behind. I waited patiently and I pretended that I was still fiddling with my books. But he never came.

Sighing, I closed my locker and began walking down the hallway towards Mr. Sparks's classroom. I started to think. Maybe I should go look for Acea? Maybe he wasn't feeling well? I glanced at the clock, checking to see how much time I had left. Eight fifteen. I had another fifteen minutes left before the final bell would ring. I turned around and started walking the other way down the hallway. I watched as students laughed and talked amongst each other. But in all of the faces I was looking at, none of them fitted Acea's portfolio.

I kept walking, passing one of the abandoned hallways. I caught two figures in my peripheral vision, making me turn my head. It was Acea and Leila. I walked quickly to the other side of the wall, turning my head as I hid behind the wall. Why were they together? I listened surreptitiously, trying to make out each word in their conversation.

"I still care about you, Leila, and you know that," I heard Acea say compassionately.

"What about Esther?" she pouted, crossing her arms.

"You know I only dated her to make her feel happy and we could know more about her."

"What have you found out?" she asked curiously.

"Well, I know why she wears long sleeves all of the time. My notion is that she's depressed. She's sad about a long-lost lover she had to leave behind. Because of her depression, I believe she cuts herself in order to get away from that pain." My mouth dropped open. That was not true at all!

"She's not so strong after all," Leila said.

"I guess not. But trust me, Leila. I want you and me to work out. You mean the world to me... I honestly love you."

I watched her smile from behind the wall. Acea wrapped his arms around her frail body and he lowered his head. Their lips connected and they kissed passionately. I turned away, noticing tears falling from my cheeks. I wiped them away while shaking my head. Should I say something? No. I should just go home. I'll tell the nurse I was sick.

I walked down the hallway; my head bowed. He played me. He only wanted to break down my walls because he was a spy for Leila. She knew how to break me down from the core. She knew my weakness. *Damion.*

I walked in to the nurse's office. The old lady was sitting at her desk, jotting down something onto paper.

"I'm sick," I said, trying to make it sound reasonable. She turned around to stare at me. I watched as she raised one eyebrow, staring me down from head to toe. I raised my hand and coughed into it to make it more convincing.

"Do you want to leave school?" she asked, pulling out a thermometer from the pouch strapped across her waist.

"Yes," I stated, "I do."

"Okay. Stick this underneath your tongue." She handed me a cylinder-like object. I took it willingly and stuck it underneath my tongue. I waited patiently for her to tell me to give it back to her.

"Stop and pull it out," she said, clicking off her timer. I gave the object back to her. "Normal temperature. But what are your symptoms?"

I shrugged my shoulders. "Upset stomach. Nerves."

"Test coming up?" she asked.

I shook my head no, thinking of Dante. "Worse than that."

She smiled slightly. "Okay. Since you never complained to me before, I'll let you off with a warning. Go home and get some rest." She turned in her chair. "Want me to call your mother?"

"No. I'm fine. I have two legs. I can walk."

"Suit yourself."

I watched my mother pace around the dining table. She poured each of our glasses with apple juice. Once she finished, she sat the pitcher firmly down on the table and sat down. She clasped her hands together, staring me down.

"Mother?" I asked. "Is there... Something wrong?"

"Oh. No. Nothing's wrong," she said.

"Are you mad that I left school early for no particular reason?"

"You had a reason. You were brokenhearted that a boy used you."

"No compassion whatsoever," I stated dryly, looking down at my soap.

"Maybe... I'm just anxious."

"For what?" I asked.

"I'm anxious to give you something." She stared at me, her pale green eyes looking into my soul. She was trying to use her abilities I assume. But obviously it wasn't working.

"What is it?" I asked

"Remember the photo I gave you? It had your father, you and me in it?"

I nodded my head. "Yes."

"Well, I got you this." She reached her hand underneath the table and slowly pulled something out of her pocket. She lifted her hand, allowing the gold object to dangle. It was a locket. "It has that same picture but smaller inside." She reached over the table to give it to me. I reached for it willingly. I looked at the intricate designs on the locket. It was the same design on my wrist. Inside the design, my initials were engraved. E. A. G. Esther Alexis Green. I flipped over the locket. On the back was Damion's initials. D. L. S. Damion Lee Storm. Why were his initials on it too?

I looked up at my mother for answers.

"He's family too," she said.

I nodded my head thoughtfully. I opened the locket, staring down at all of our smiling faces. We were happy then. Nothing could ever tear us down. But sadly, it could. I wrapped the necklace around my neck, staring at my mother with a smile on my face.

"Thank you." I got up from my chair and I walked over to her. I bent down, embracing my mother in my arms. She reached up, grabbing a hold of my head. She kissed my forehead and I could feel her smile.

"I love you, Esther. You're still my daughter."

I pulled away from her so I could look at her. "I love you too. And you're still my mother and nothing could *ever* change that."

She reached up, patting down my hair. "You're going to be brave; you hear me?"

I nodded my head. "I hear you."

"When the time comes, promise me I can count on you to keep Brilliance safe."

"You can count on me, Mom." I watched as her smile grew wide.

"Brilliance did the right thing. It Chose you."

"Now I have to make sure it keeps doing the right thing."

I slammed my locker shut the next day. I wanted to leave before Acea would find me. I held my books close to my chest as I walked the opposite way to Mr. Sparks' room. Mason had promised me that he would walk me to our classroom. He was very supportive.

Suddenly, I felt a strong, vigorous yank on my arm. I turned around, quickly noticing it was Acea. I pulled my arm away while glaring at him. "What do you want?"

"I was wondering why you left school so early yesterday... And you didn't wait for me today," Acea stated. He stared me down with eager eyes.

"Why do I always have to wait for you?" I said, trying to erase the venom from my voice. It didn't work.

"Why are you being this way?" he asked, sounding hurt.

I shook my head, moving away from him. "Don't play stupid. You know exactly what you did." I turned my back to him and I started to walk away. My heart was throbbing and my emotions felt like a tidal wave. I tried to fight the urge to cry.

"Esther! Wait!" I could hear his feet clacking against the ground. "I never meant to hurt you."

I turned around, my body shaking with anger. "You never meant to hurt me?" I yelled, making heads turn our way. "What exactly was going through your mind when you decided to play me? Did you think I would say, 'oh, go ahead and tear me down? Start from the core.' Did you *really* think I was like that?"

"I thought you were emotionless," he stated bleakly.

"Not according to what you told Leila! You said I was depressed! You told her that I cut myself because of Damion!"

"So that's his name?"

"Yes. It is. Do you have a problem with that?" I yelled. I fought back the tears. I couldn't give him the advantage.

"I was just wondering who the mighty strong Esther had a soft spot for."

"Just... get away from me." I turned on my heels, moving away from him quickly.

"Hey, listen, Esther... I'm sorry... I do care about you, okay?"

I ignored him, continuing to move down the hallway. I went along the wall, entering the way to the hidden staircase. Mason's locker was on the second floor. I continued walking up the stairs, carrying two of my textbooks for class. I rounded the small corner, entering an entirely different atmosphere. The second floor consisted of many glass walls, allowing in the morning sunlight. I walked along the wall, carrying my books underneath my armpit. In order to get to his locker, he said I had to cross down another abandoned hallway to get there quicker.

I moved along the wall, turning into a dark, narrow hallway. I always wondered why there were so many abandoned hallways in the school. It was quite a large school with newly built hallways and sections so I suppose that was why. I rounded the corner, entering another empty hallway.

I felt the hair on the back of my neck beginning to stand up. It felt like there was someone or something behind me. I stopped dead in my tracks, daring to turn around. I could hear clacking coming from behind. I knew who it was.

"Why'd you care to follow me?" I asked, my eyes locked on another dark hallway up ahead.

"I wanted to see what you were up to... I wanted to see if you were cutting yourself," she snickered. I heard more laughter after that. She had more people with her. I guess my thoughts were loud enough that I didn't hear them following me.

I turned around, glaring at Leila. "I don't cut myself and there's nothing wrong with the people that do it too. They need an escape so don't you *dare* judge anybody that need help." I glanced at all of the faces behind her. It wasn't her normal crew. It was Marlene, Ariena and Larisha. They're the most robust girls in this school. They were very capable of doing me harm.

"What about the boy? Why do you care about him *so much*?" Leila asked mockingly.

"Don't talk about him," I said through gritted teeth.

Leila laughed. "Ace was right. The boy is your soft spot." The three girls behind her laughed. "What about your daddy? Didn't he die from AIDS?"

"I don't have a soft spot," I said, venom oozing out of my mouth. "And no. Why the hell would you think that?"

"Oh really?" she perked her head up. "What would happen if I were to know this 'Damion' child?" She laughed. "And I thought your daddy did because you're such a *slut*."

"I'd say that's impossible for you to know him and I'm not a slut."

Leila gritted her teeth as she stared me down. "Did it hurt when you discovered that Acea didn't really care about you? That it was all a game?" I clenched my fists, trying not to attack. "He pitied you. You were just the sad, quiet girl that never said anything... And that's all you'll ever be." She paused, stepping forward. Our bodies were only two feet apart. "We pity you," she frowned. "You won't be anything in this world... Only hopeless space."

"You don't know me!" I screamed, throwing up my fist, spontaneously smashing her in the face. She stumbled backwards, falling onto her butt.

Marlene came after me first. I stayed low to the floor, barely crouching. Marlene attempted to lift up her leg but I grabbed it, standing up quickly and I twisted her leg to the side. I brought up my knee, kicking her in the stomach. She fell down while groaning in pain.

Ariena came after me next. She steadied herself, watching where I would shift my body. She was more intelligent in fights. She understood the opponent and their actions. But I didn't think she could out-smart me. I shifted my body to my left, extending my right hand. She reached out her hand to grab my right, but quickly, I punched her with my left hand. My fist collided into her nose and I could feel the cartilage shift underneath my fist. Disgusting.

Ariena still stood, wiping the blood off her nose. "Wise," she breathed, "but not enough." She lurched forward, grabbing me from the waist. We both hurtled to the ground, simultaneously crashing our skulls into the tile floor. I gritted my teeth, using my legs to lift her body off of me. She landed next to my head and I stood up quickly. This time Larisha was running towards me, extending her fist with no hesitation.

Using precise timing, I grabbed her extended arm, using all of my strength to throw her to the ground. She landed on top of Ariena. I could hear footsteps behind me and quickly, I turned, trying to avoid the use of my abilities. By touching each of them, I knew that none of them were Clockworks.

Marlene was running in my direction with her teeth barred. I watched as she shifted directions and she ran passed me. I looked behind me, slightly confused. Then I noticed what she was doing. She grabbed a hold of my long hair and pulled me viciously to the ground. I held onto my hair, trying to release her grip on it.

"Get down!" she screamed.

"No!" I yelled.

I used my body to maneuver around her. Before I could trip her with my legs, Larisha and Ariena grabbed a hold of my arms, yanking me off the ground.

"Slam her against the wall," Marlene stated dryly.

Vigorously, they yanked me across the ground and my body collided into the cement wall. I tried to move out of their grasp but I couldn't.

"You think it's funny, huh? You think you're so wise and brave? You don't even know the definition of brave!" Marlene yelled. She walked closer to me with a sickening smile plastered on her face. "It was wrong of you to punch Leila in the face... You know that?" I glanced at Leila. She was on the ground with her hands on her face as she cried.

"She should know not to mess with me. I hurt people that try to hurt me."

"Well, you're in quite a vulnerable situation now. Aren't you?" Marlene said.

Larisha and Ariena adjusted their grip on me, making it to where my skin was bent that caused excruciating pain. Marlene laughed, punching me in the stomach with no hesitation. I felt the air escape my mouth and I bent over, trying to regain my breathing. The two girls lifted me up harshly while laughing. Marlene lifted her fist again, colliding it into my jaw this time. I watched as spit flew across my mouth and my head snapped back.

"Does it hurt?" Marlene asked. "Have you had enough?"

I didn't say anything. I adjusted myself, trying to take in all of the pain. I stared at her with eyes emotionless. "No."

She laughed, raising her fist once more. This time she collided it into my mouth. I felt my teeth skid across my lips and the taste of blood filled my mouth. I had an idea.

"Stop," I said, looking away in despair. "Please stop."

"Had enough already?" she laughed, coming closer to me. Her face was inches away from mine. "I guess you really are weak."

I turned my head to look at her. I gathered the blood in my mouth and I spat in her face. My blood soaked all of her features. Her friends, horrified, drew their attention to their friend. In a desperate attempt to get free, I used my strength to release myself from their grip. Once I did, before they had time to react, I socked both of them in the face. They fell to the ground.

I turned to Marlene, alarmed that she was ready to punch me. I grabbed a bunch of her hair, pulling it as hard as I could until I felt a wad loosely fall into my palm. I lifted my knee up as she groaned in pain, smashing it into her stomach. *I'm so getting suspended.*

"Stop!" a voice shrieked as I was about to punch Marlene again. I looked ahead, realizing it was a teacher. I dropped Marlene's body to the ground, slightly kicking it away from me. "All of you! Get up and come with me!"

"They attacked me!" I yelled. "I had to protect myself!"

"Come with me *now*," she said a little bit sterner. I watched as Marlene, Leila and their friends slowly pulled themselves

246

together, trying to get up. We all followed the teacher down the dark hallway. Well, I was sure what would happen next and it wasn't going to be good.

I sat in the detention hall, tapping my foot nervously against the ground. We had to come here so the principal could use some time to consider our punishments. Unfortunately, Mr. Sparks was our mentor. He had to watch us. Also, we were stuck in this place for hours on end. School was out but there was still a large number of students at various meetings and football practice too.

I avoided his eye contact as I did my school work. Luna and Rosa, for an unknown reason were also in the detention hall. Luna was probably here because she took the blame for Marlene. I glanced out the large windows to my left, tapping my pencil violently against the desk. Hopefully everyone realizes that I was just protecting myself from the people who attacked me. Slightly, I turned around in my chair, staring at Marlene, Leila, Ariena and Larisha. They were holding their faces with ice packs. I laughed silently to myself. I really screwed them up and they deserved it.

"Esther," Mr. Sparks growled, "don't even stare at your classmates."

"They're not even my classmates. They're ruthless *acquaintances*."

"You already wanna smart mouth me today?" he snapped.

"I was only correcting you."

"Do you know how long it's been in here? Huh? We were in here for most of the school period and *three* more hours after. It's nearly sunset! I'm in this situation because neither of you could behave yourselves."

I leaned back in my chair. "I'm sorry. You should probably tell those people back there not to mess with me. It's their fault we're in here." But not Luna and Rosa. I wasn't sure why they were in here.

"Esther, come up to the board. It's time someone talked some sense into you."

I groaned, sliding my hands across the wooden desk as I got up. I walked down the rows of chairs. The detention hall was the largest classroom in the school. It had large church windows on the left that let in kind, warm sunlight.

"My mother is probably wondering where I am," I said as I walked up a few steps and stood next to Mr. Sparks.

"All parents have been notified. Now, write 'I'm sorry' on the board in approximately twelve centimeters. Fill the whole board." He extended his hand, waiting for me to take the chalk.

Sighing arrogantly, I reached my hand to grab the piece of chalk. When I grabbed his hand, I felt an electric shock go through my body. It was nothing like Damion's electricity. It was something different. I looked up at him, my mouth nearly hanging open. I was waiting for a smile or some reassurance, but that never came. Instead, a dark smile slowly moved across his face. It looked unnatural—like he never smiled before. I stepped back a few feet, still holding the chalk in my hand. I was bewildered. I didn't know how to react. I wasn't sure what to do. He was from my world. Judging by the look on his face, he wasn't too happy that I found out. I wasn't supposed to grab his hand. I felt the chalk slip from my grasp. I heard it break once it reached the ground. *Shit.*

"Why do you wear sleeves, Esther?" he asked, stepping closer to me with the same sickening grin.

"I'm cold," I lied, staring down at my white blouse that had a very light, faded blue jean jacket over it. My jeans were black and long, tucked carefully inside my boots.

"Oh really?" He grabbed my wrist before I had time to back away. He lifted up my sleeve forcefully, quickly noticing the Mark. "Finally, after all this time..." I felt him press down on the Mark but no phrases appeared. Brilliance hadn't shown me anything in a while. "What do you see?"

"Nothing."

I felt a tingling penetration form on my arm. Suddenly, the penetration became hotter and stronger. He was burning me. I yelped, creating a steal force field to push him away from me. He flew back into the teacher's desk, falling onto the ground.

"Run!" I yelled at Leila's friends and the Windchester twins.

I leaped off the stage, collapsing into a row of desks. I heard Mr. Sparks' groans, indicating he was getting up. I watched as Leila and the others screamed their heads off. They looked at each other, trying to figure out what to do. The Windchester twins were still sitting at their desks, doing absolutely nothing but staring me down with their hollow eyes. Suddenly, Rosa got up and she stared passed me with freakish determination. She reached her hands out and simultaneously, the windows behind me burst and glass flew everywhere. I created a force field, shielding myself from the penetrating glass.

I turned around, my heart racing. Mr. Sparks was standing perfectly still on top of the stage. He opened his hands and looked up at the intricately designed ceiling. He yelled and I watched as large amounts of fire came out of his hands, burning the ceiling above us. I looked up, noticing the ceiling was burning and slowly crumbling from disintegration. I looked at the twins, focusing on Rosa. Was she disintegrating it?

"The ceiling!" I yelled, running down the rows of desks, trying to make my way to Leila and the others. "It's going to collapse!"

Leila looked at me, fear coursing through her eyes. "Look out!" she screamed.

I turned around, my hair whipping me in the face. I watched as fire hurtled my way. I brought up my arm, knowing I had to make a force field strong enough to withstand the large amounts of fire. I also had to make it twice as robust so I could protect the people behind me.

I created a forcefield, using all of my emotional strength to create a large, powerful one. I watched as the fire collided into the forcefield faster than I anticipated. I turned around, watching the fire totally bypass me and now it was hurtling towards Leila and the others. I screamed, trying to throw the forcefield around all of us... But I was too late.

I watched as the ashen bodies slowly crumbled to the floor and a large pit filled my stomach. I remembered Mallek from New York and how he was burned to death for standing up for something he believed in. He was burned alive by Darius. Just like how these helpless humans were burned alive by Sparks. I turned around, trying to fight the tears as the fire continued coming my way. Once it cleared out, the three Creators stood a distance away. They had sickening smiles plastered across their faces. *The time finally came. This is when I have to fight back.*

I ran out of the classroom quickly, releasing my forcefield so I could run faster. Students were still inside the school because of the after-school meetings. I heard a large noise erupt behind me and the ground shook. The ceiling fell, creating debris that spiraled outward all around me. I didn't have time to turn around to know the three Creators were coming for me.

"Go!" I yelled as students filed out of their meetings with bloodcurdling screams and cries of despair. "Run!" I screamed, my throat burning.

That was when I noticed a familiar face. Mason Knight. He had a math club meeting. He turned around, slightly confused until he noticed me. He smiled but then he realized my fearful expression.

"What's going on?" he yelled over the large amounts of yells. He ran over to me.

"You need to go! Go home!" I yelled.

Before he could respond, I saw some sort of black liquid coming our way out of my peripheral vision. Disintegration. I grabbed a hold of Mason's flannel, creating a forcefield around us as I pushed ourselves to the ground. The liquid hit a girl in the back and I closed my eyes. I could not afford to see her lifelessly crumble to the ground.

"What the hell was that!" Mason yelled, staring at me with wide eyes. I grabbed his face in both of my trembling hands, staring into his deep brown eyes.

"You need to go home. Try to make sure everyone gets out of here safely. I'm *counting* on you," I said eagerly.

He nodded his head, standing up. I stood up too, spinning around to notice Mr. Sparks shooting fireballs at students. I felt Mason walk out of my forcefield. I extended the forcefield on the group of students trying to pile out of the school. I lost interest in protecting myself and decided to make the field stronger on the students. None of the Creators in front of me could kill me. Only Dante could.

"Beautiful afternoon, isn't it?" Luna said with a large grin plastered on her face as they walked closer to me. I didn't know what her ability was yet.

I stared at her, my face contorting into fear. Was she dangerous or was she weak? Suddenly, the scene in front of me changed. Damion and I were sitting underneath our willow tree. He was tracing his fingers over my arms and he whispered to me sweetly.

"I love you, Esther," he said.

"I know. You don't have to remind me," I said calmly, staring into his bright blue eyes.

"I *have* to remind you. It's better that way." I smiled at him as he started to lean closer to me. He placed his hand on my cheek, turning my face to look at him directly. I watched as his lips parted and I began to close my eyes. Our lips connected and he kissed me softly and tenderly. Soon, he became rougher and more passionate. My heart fluttered and I followed his pattern and we kissed in sync, aware of our combination.

Suddenly, I heard him scream against my lips and I pulled away, opening my eyes. There was a tall man standing behind him and he had Damion by the hair. I watched as Damion's features became more intense and petrified with anger. His eyes transformed from a soft blue to a deeply-dark, menacing red. He lunged at me with claws and the man behind him laughed. I screamed, trying to push Damion away.

The scene changed and the three Creators were standing over me, smiling.

"Scary, wasn't it?" Luna asked gently.

I then came to the conclusion. She was the Creator that fed my mind dark images of fearful desires outside in my room each night. "You... it was you... You were the one outside of my house that one night...." My voice croaked. "You fed my mind."

"Amazing, isn't it?" she asked, bending down next to me. "I have the ability to show someone bliss and horror. That boy, you love him, don't you? Is that why he's in all of your visions?"

I stared at them, biting my lip. Now they knew my weakness. I looked at Mr. Sparks as I tried to remain calm. "Spontaneous combustion? That's pretty common, you know?"

"Let me hurt her," he said through gritted teeth.

"Don't worry, I have it covered," Luna said.

The scene in front of me changed and I was on a battlefield. The sky was yellow from the clouds of smoke. Everyone around me was biting their lips, trying to fight off their opponents. In front of me was a slender boy with black hair.

"Damion!" I yelled, running forward. I watched as the figure slowly turned around with a grin plastered on his face.

"Esther," he said. He reached his hand out, trying to reach for me. Our fingertips touched and the moment they did, Damion screamed, falling to the ground. His body was surging with electricity and he was crumbling into a ball. Heat rose in my face and I didn't know what to do. I wasn't sure how to react. What could I do?

"Damion," I whispered, dropping down on my knees. I pulled his black hair back from his face and his blue eyes were faded with pain. "What can I do?" I asked as the tears began pouring down my face.

"Get away," he breathed, trying to maintain himself.

"No—I—I don't want—to leave you!" The tears poured down my cheeks, dropping onto his skin, simultaneously making the tear sizzle.

He looked up at me and a groan escaped from his lips. "This isn't real."

"What? What are you talking about?" It felt real.

"Block your mind."

"But the children... I need to protect them."

"Just remember it's not real. Think peaceful thoughts."

I thought about Damion and I once again, sitting underneath our willow tree, while we listened to the birds' chirp. Almost spontaneously, I was greeted by the three faces once more. Luna stepped back, horrified that I stood against her power. I grinned while getting back on my feet.

"Don't screw with my mind!" I created a force field, pushing the three of them back. They fell into a pile of rubble, groaning as they tried to push each other up. I turned back around at the children trying to get out of the school. They were all trampling each other. "Go!" I yelled, pushing them with the forcefield I had originally put on them. They screamed as the force pushed them against the doors. I released the force field, using my ability to make myself invisible. I had to find another exit.

I felt the rush as I started to run passed the three Creators. I ran down the hallway, trying to avoid slipping on the ground from all of the rubble created by the detention hall. I proceeded down another hallway, running up the ramp that led to the doors to the parking lot.

"Esther!" I heard a familiar voice yell. "Where are you? Where's Leila?"

I turned around, realizing Acea was running up the ramp

blindly, trying to find where I was. He wore his football uniform but not his pads. He probably saw the school catch on fire from the outside. Behind him, I saw Rosa running up the ramp also. Oh god, she was going to kill him. I made myself visible as I ran midway down the ramp. He stared at me in bewilderment, wondering how I appeared in front of him.

I noticed Rosa pushing her hand back, trying to gain the energy to form her disintegration liquid. I grabbed Acea's hand and yanked him up the ramp. I turned around, creating a fiery forcefield and I whipped it down the ramp. The field hit her and she fell back, sliding down the slope. I watched Luna appear around the hallway with Mr. Sparks behind her.

"Ah!" Acea screamed, crumbling to the ground. "Get away! Get away! Don't hurt me!" I looked around frantically, trying to figure out what was wrong with him. I looked down the ramp and Luna was grinning.

"No! Get away from him!" I screamed, sending a forcefield that collided into both of them.

I grabbed Acea's arm, helping him to his feet. I heard him wheezing as he tried to accept what happened to him. I pushed open the double doors and we were in the back-parking lot.

"What's going on?" he asked, his voice quavering.

I shook my head, not wanting to tell him because he broke my heart. But I had no choice. I lifted my sleeve up, showing him the Mark. "They're after me because of this. They want to kill me." I watched as he traced his fingertips across the circles. He was mesmerized.

"It's beautiful," he whispered.

"We need to go."

I yanked him across the parking lot. I felt the ground rumble beneath me and I turned around, looking back at the school. The doors that we exited from burst open and fire surrounded the parking lot. One of the doors flew over to us, hitting a silver car next to me. I watched as Rosa emerged from the flames, moving her arms around, creating the disintegration liquid.

"Get down!" I yelled, pushing Acea to the pavement. The liquid whizzed passed me, hitting a lamp post. The liquid slowly ate away the metal and the structure that held the lamp up. The post began to fall over and was going to land on Acea and me.

I crouched down, allowing a force field to illuminate over us. The parking lot light fell onto the force field and I felt it crack. I let out a groan, trying to desperately make the field stronger.

"Let go!" Acea yelled. "We can run out of the way in time!"

"Go!" I screamed. "I have it."

"No!" he yelled, his green eyes penetrating with fear. "We can make it in time!"

Just as he said that, a pickup truck screeched into the parking lot. The door of the passenger seat opened up and I saw my mother sitting in the driver's seat, extending her hand to keep the door open. Her red hair whipped wildly in the wind. There was finally a new hope before me.

"Get in!" she screamed.

I glanced over my shoulder, watching Mr. Sparks, Luna and Rosa run my way. They weren't going to give up.

"Grab my waist!" I yelled at Acea. Willingly, he got up from the pavement and he wrapped his large arms around my waist. I released the forcefield, simultaneously creating another one that pushed us out of the way before the lamp post was able to fall on us.

I allowed the forcefield to take us to the car. I shoved myself into the middle seat and Acea followed, shutting the door. My mother stepped on the gas, backing up the truck. She put the car in reverse and stepped down on the gas again, making the truck lurch forward and we sped out of the parking lot.

I rolled down the passenger window, moving over Acea. I stuck my head out the window so I could see where the Creators were. I watched closely as Luna grinned at me and she began running out of the parking lot. Rosa and Sparks followed her at the same pace. Suddenly, they flipped in the air simultaneously, and each of them became a dark, black shadow. The three large, body-length shadows flew in the air, edging closer to us.

"Mom!" I screamed as they came closer.

"They're Shadows! It's another offspring of Ava's experiments!" She screamed, stepping on the gas harder. The truck lurched forward and she drove down the road at top speed. The road entered the forest and the setting became darker.

I still looked out the window, watching the Shadows. I saw a black, oozing liquid propel itself forward from one of them. I yelped, creating a forcefield before it could collide into the truck. A ball of fire formed from the Shadow next to Rosa. It hurtled our way and instantaneously, I created another forcefield.

"When will they give up!" Acea yelled, looking at me with a fearful expression.

"They won't stop until they get me," I stated, trying to pay attention to each Shadow.

"No!" my mother screamed and the truck screeched, spinning across the road. The truck turned sideways and I yelped, watching as my face came close to the pavement. I created a field, trying to put us upright. It worked. The tires shifted and waddled and before I knew what happened, we were facing the three Shadows that were coming our way. I glanced at my mother, realizing her eyes were in a daze. *Luna.*

"Move over," I yelled at Acea. "I need to go out there and stop her from hurting my mother." Just as I said that, the truck shook with my mother's screams.

"You can't go out there alone," Acea stated, his voice quavering.

"Then come with me dammit."

I pulled my head out of the window as Acea opened the door. We both stepped down on the pavement, readying ourselves for what was to come. The Shadows, aware of what we were doing, made themselves human again. They landed on the ground, taking their human form as they walked across the road towards us.

"By any chance," I whispered, "go after Luna."

"What about the people who shoot acid and shit?" Acea asked.

"Stay away from them. They have a better chance of killing you since you're mortal."

"And your immortal?" he asked.

"No. I'm not. We just refer to people from the human world as mortals even though Clockworks are mortals themselves. Come on, Acea. Use your head."

' "Oh, okay. Got you."

I watched each of my opponents carefully. I was waiting for one of them to raise their hands to gather energy. My eyes scanned the crowd until they landed on Rosa, whom was creating her disintegration liquid.

"Get down!" I shouted, immediately crouching to the

pavement. Acea followed my movement as the liquid zipped passed us. While we were in a vulnerable position, Mr. Sparks was creating a fireball as Luna destroyed my mother from the core.

This time, I had no choice but to create another forcefield. I felt weary from all of the energy I was using. The fire collided into the force field, inches away from our faces. I extended the field and pushed it out, creating a sphere that held the fire inside. I gritted my teeth, trying to adsorb the energy around me. I pushed the fire ball out and it collided into Rosa. I released the field and the fire started to burn her alive. She let out a scream as the fire melted her skin.

Luna gasped, losing interest in my mother and turning all of her attention toward her dying sister.

"Do something!" she screamed at Mr. Sparks.

"There's nothing I can do!" he yelled at her, staring at Luna with fearful eyes.

"Come on," I said, tugging on Acea's arm. Clumsily, we stood up and ran to the truck. We piled in and we closed the door behind us. My mother was staring at me with bewilderment.

"What happened?" she asked.

"Luna tinkered with your mind. She made you see painful thoughts. We have to go, now."

She nodded her head sheepishly and started to back up the truck. She put it in reverse and started down the road opposite of the three Creators.

"What now?" I asked as she drove down the road at the truck's fullest potential.

"We need to go back to the house, grab a few belongings and leave again."

I stared at her dizzily. "Where *do* we go from here?"

She shrugged her shoulders, glancing in her rear-view mirror periodically. "I have a few friends we could stay with in Ohio. It'll give us enough time to sort out our lives."

"What about me?" Acea asked.

My mother peered over me, widening her eyes like she just noticed him. "And why are you here?"

"Because I care about Esther," he stated.

She scoffed. "Sure you do. Why were you in love with Leila when you decided to care about *my daughter*?"

"Leila," Acea repeated. "Where is she?"

256

I stared at him. "Dead."

"I bet you're happy about that," he snapped suddenly, glaring at me.

"Why would you think that?" I asked.

"Because you hate her. I mean, you beat her up too."

I rolled my eyes. "I don't hate her, Acea. I get upset sometimes but I never hold a grudge for so long. It hurt me when I saw her die."

He licked his lips, taking deep breaths. "I'm just going through a lot right now."

"No shit," I said bitterly.

"Alvaro contacted me when you were in detention. He told me what he saw and I tried to get there as soon as possible," my mother stated as she drove.

"I wish you still had your abilities, Mom," I whispered.

"I know, honey. I wish I did too."

"How'd you get Dad's truck?" I asked, remembering we left it behind when we moved.

"In one of my fighting sessions, I was in Oklahoma so I wanted to visit the house. I decided to take his truck back with me."

I nodded my head as we turned down the road we lived on. I watched as the night sky started to make itself presentable. My mother turned the car and started going up our driveway.

In minutes, we were driving around our house. Before the car stopped, Acea opened up the door and we both jumped down and ran across the platform. I ran up the stairs and into the house. I knew what I was looking for. My father's letter and my mother's necklace. I hopped up the stairs, listening to Acea's heavy footsteps behind me. I turned the corner and ran down the long, winding hallway, passing doors I never ventured into. I made it to the end of the hallway and I threw open my door, immediately running to my desk. I opened up drawers, shuffling through piles of crumbled papers.

"Come on, Esther," Acea said impatiently behind me.

"I can't find it!" I yelled out of frustration. I closed the drawer shut and opened another one. "In my closest, Acea, get the royal blue book bag and lay it on my bed while I'm looking for this."

"Alright." I heard him cross my room and he opened my closet doors. "Big closet," I heard him murmur.

I continued shuffling through papers, trying to find my

257

father's note. Then I felt it; a shock that went through my entire body and I knew it was his. I grabbed the yellow-stained paper, folded it and shoved it into my pocket. I crossed my room, maneuvering around my bed so I could reach my dresser. I found the locket almost instantly. I grabbed the gold chain and attached it around my neck. I stared at myself in the mirror for a few moments. My jaw was bruised and I had a streak of blood across my cheek.

"Finally found it," Acea said, coming out of my closet.

"Thanks," I said, jogging into my closet to grab a few extra pairs of clothing. I grabbed shirts and jeans randomly off their hangers. I picked up two extra sets of shoes and ran out of my closet. I shoved the items into the book bag and I slung it around my shoulders.

"Are you scared?" Acea asked me.

I bit my lip, shoving my hand into my pocket to make sure the letter was still there. It was. "Yes. But I have my mother... She'll help me through this." He nodded his head. "You should go home. I don't want you to get hurt." I also didn't want him around me anymore.

He clenched his jaw the way Damion always did when he didn't agree with something. "No," he said sternly. "I owe you. I'm not leaving you alone with your problems like I did before."

"We need to go," I said, changing the subject. I ran out of my room, not even bothering to say goodbye to the room. I proceeded down the hallways and down the stairs. As I reached the floor, the ground shook and I almost lost my balance. A large, ear-wrenching sound occurred outside that I couldn't explain. My heart began to race and my palms began to sweat. I opened the door, closing my eyes at first so I didn't have to see what was in front of me.

"Who are *they*?" Acea asked, appearing at my side.

I opened my eyes gradually and then gasped. I walked down the marble stairs at a fast pace. I jogged across the lawn and stopped once I reached my mother. Three Exols stood in front of me. The two males were extraordinarily handsome and the woman was absolutely striking.

"I don't think you understand, Green. We *need* to take her with us," an Exol man said gently. He had white, spiky hair and intense blue eyes. Around the iris was a gold rimming that made each of them look exotic.

"They're coming, Icelos," the woman said, glancing at the man with white hair. She had waist-long, wavy blonde hair and extremely soft features.

"Castalia," the man with spiky black hair said impatiently, "tell them what they need to know in order to understand." Unlike Icelos, he had intense features and his eyes showed a hint of mockery.

"Phrixus, don't talk to her like that," Icelos said gently.

Castalia looked at me and smiled warmly. "We need you to come with us. Creators have taken seventy-five percent of the Clockworks. Unfortunately, there's only twenty-five percent of them left. A majority of them are powerless due to age and won't require much help to your journey. Most of them that do have abilities are at the safe house we plan to take you to. From there, you need to work together to save the remaining Clockworks before Dante kills them off."

I didn't know I stopped breathing until I began to feel dizzy. I was too mesmerized by their beauty. I played back what she said in my head again so I could understand everything. "Why was he taking Clockworks?"

"He already knew that you, Esther Green, was Chosen to protect Brilliance. As a threat for you to surrender, he had taken the Clockworks and imprisoned them," Icelos said.

I glanced at my mother, remembering the call she had from Alvaro that night. But why didn't she tell me it was a threat? "Why didn't you tell me?"

"Because I knew you would go after him and surrender yourself," my mother said, staring down at me.

"I don't have much of a choice now, do I?" I said bitterly.

"Intense," Phrixus whispered, "and hot-headed."

"Don't negotiate with him," Castalia said apologetically.

"What about my mother? Why is it me that only has to go?" I asked.

"Your mother no longer has her abilities. Therefore, she is no use in the quest," Phrixus said, crossing his arms.

"That's not fair," I said, crossing my arms to mimic him. "She's really good at fighting."

"Rules are rules," Castalia said.

"And obviously, some people don't like to follow them,"

Phrixus said, glancing at Icelos.

"You told humans about our existence," Castalia said, looking at me and then to Acea. "You also used your abilities for fun as a child."

I shrugged my shoulders, trying not to let my fear show. "It happens."

Suddenly, there were countless footsteps coming from the driveway. I looked ahead as the Exols turned to see what it was. I noticed twenty dark figures walking towards us in the darkness. I felt the blood rush from my face. They were here.

"Looks like we have to fight," Icelos stated meekly.

"You know fighting is not a part of our nature," Castalia hissed.

Icelos turned to look at her with soft features. "We have to if you want Brilliance to be in the hands of the Creators."

"That's why we have Clockworks," Castalia retorted.

"We only have *one inexperienced* Clockwork with us right now... We need to help keep her safe."

I gritted my teeth at the word 'inexperienced', glaring at Icelos for even saying that.

"You just made her mad. Nice." Castalia probably had empathy as her ability if she knew how I felt.

"Quit fooling around," Phrixus said sternly. "They're Shadows; beware."

Icelos turned around to look at me. "We can only do so much for you. I suggest you and the boy run."

I glanced at my mom. "What about you?"

"I have my weapons. I can help fight."

Suddenly, a gust of harsh wind swept our way and a Shadow was hurtling towards us. Acea grabbed my hand and yanked me away from the Shadow. We both fell onto our butts and we stumbled to get back up. My heart began to race as each figure transformed themselves into a black Shadow.

Phrixus turned around, glaring at me while gritting his teeth. "Run!"

I hesitated for a moment until I finally gained my senses. I took off running, knowing Acea was following behind me. I knew where we had to go and that was the woods.

"The golf cart! We need to get it!" Acea screamed at me in

the darkness.

I nodded my head and continued running. I was shocked to find out I was faster than Acea. It was probably because I was more light-weight.

"Watch out!" Acea screamed.

A black Shadow whizzed past my body and it stopped in front of me, taking the shape of a human. Sparks grinned at me, tilting his head to the side. I stopped dead in my tracks and I felt my heart beating against my chest, acting as if it wanted to jump out of my skin and run away.

"Luna isn't very happy with you," he taunted.

"Yeah. I wouldn't be happy either," I retaliated.

He pushed his hand out and I watched in shock as fire began to form in his hand. The thing about spontaneous combustion was that he could illuminate fire with his hands and not a source. It made him scarier.

I gritted my teeth, trying to use his energy to create a forcefield. The fire bounced off the field and I grinned.

"Artimis!" Mr. Sparks growled. "I need you!"

"I don't like the feeling of that," Acea said quietly as another Shadow flew around us, landing next to Mr. Sparks. The Shadow became a human, consisting of dark skin, a frail body and menacing brown eyes. He grinned, reaching out his fingertips. I still had my force field up so I couldn't understand what he was doing until his fingers touched it. The energy from my body faded quickly and there was no longer a force field protecting Acea and me.

"Shit," I whispered, staring at the Creators. He had the ability to wipe my abilities away. He instantly reminded me of Jeremy back in New York.

Another flame illuminated in the palms of Mr. Sparks. I gritted my teeth and began running towards the pool in the backyard. I heard Acea following behind me.

"Run!" I yelled.

"What did he do?" he yelled back as we ran side by side.

"He can take abilities away."

"How can you get them back?" Acea asked.

"I have to kill him."

A spark of light illuminated in my peripheral vision and I knew exactly what was going to happen next. I leaped into the air and Acea followed my movement. We crashed into the picnic table before the ball of fire could hit us. I groaned as I collided into the pavement, skidding my elbow on the broken bench of the picnic table. I glanced over at Acea, slightly worried about his condition. He was gritting his teeth, staring at his foot. I looked down and his shoe was melted and burnt skin surrounded a section of his foot.

"Agh," he screamed, throwing his head back in pain.

I saw another fire ball coming our way and we weren't in the position to move. I tried rolling to my side but my back sent bursts of pain throughout my entire body. *He can't kill me. He isn't the Wise. But he can kill Acea.* In a fury of panic, I pushed Acea over with all of my strength. He screamed in pain as he rolled close to the pool.

I watched as the fire ball was only feet away from colliding into me. I felt the heat from the distance and I prepared myself for the worst.

Spontaneously, before the bolt reached me, Icelos appeared in front of us. He held out his hands and ice seeped out of his palms, creating an arctic chill that soothed my pained body. But the ice wasn't for me, it was for the fire hurtling my way. The ice created a barrier and shockingly, it stopped the fire from hitting him and me.

He broke down the ice barrier with his elbow once the fire burned itself out. Icelos threw shards of ice forward, simultaneously hitting Mr. Sparks in his chest. Sparks gasped, clutching the piece of ice that was embedded into his skin. He collapsed onto his knees, glancing at me one last time before he died.

Artimis stood still, staring at Icelos fearfully. Icelos created another sharp piece of ice from his fingertips that pierced Artimis in the heart. He fell to the ground sideways while his eyes were in a daze. Once he hit the ground, I felt the energy regain in my body and I knew I had my abilities once more.

Icelos turned around, staring down at me with a smile. He held out his hand and waited patiently for me to take it. I reached out my hand and clasped it around his as he pulled me up, placing me back on my feet.

"You alright?" he asked kindly.

I nodded my head. "Yes." I looked at Acea and he was still on the ground with tears flowing down his cheeks. "He's injured."

"If we can deplete their forces with a minimum amount of

deaths, we can go through Phrixus's portal. There, in the safe house, there should be healers."

"What about now?" I asked.

He glanced at the golf cart that was on the edge of the forest. He held out his hand and with a simple flick of the wrist, the cart began to move towards us quickly.

In time, the golf cart was humming softly next to me. I looked up at Icelos, slightly confused on what his other ability was.

"It's slightly hard to understand, Esther... But basically, I can turn things to life, or start and end them when necessary. But sometimes the objects become so attached to life it's hard to end them."

"All you did was bring the golf cart over here," I stated reluctantly, trying to process what he described.

He smiled faintly. "I don't understand my ability either. Sometimes it's a gift and sometimes a curse."

"I think we all feel that way sometimes."

"Yes. Put him in the cart and drive far away from here as possible. We'll come get you when it's time."

I nodded my head. "Are you strong? I can't lift him." I glanced at Acea who was still on the ground, staring into my eyes dizzily. He was still in excruciating pain.

"Yes." Icelos walked gracefully over to Acea. He threw back the side of his royal blue cape before picking him up. He brought him over to the golf cart, placing him in the back carefully.

"Thanks," I said, securing Acea inside properly.

"No need to thank me," he stated.

I walked around the cart and got into the driver's seat. I stepped down on the gas and the cart lurched forward, adjusted itself and began speeding across the grass. I turned on the headlights so I could see in front of me.

I edged closer to the path in the woods. My eyes began to water at how fast I was driving the cart. I continued moving forward, entering the dark forest. The cart broke twigs underneath the tires and the wind wrapped around us.

"Esther," I heard a voice say faintly. "Some are following us."

I turned around, noticing two dark Shadows were moving in on us. I gritted my teeth, accelerating the chintzy golf cart. The

Shadows bifurcated, closing in on me from each side.

A ray of unknown light came from my right side and quickly, I reached up one hand and created a forcefield to block off the light. I could no longer form a forcefield all around us due to the loss of energy. The light repelled away once it hit the field and the shadow to my left threw a sizzling dark liquid. I created another field, blocking away the acid.

I stepped down on the gas again, noticing I wasn't putting enough pressure on it. The golf cart sped down the trail. I avoided hitting my head on stray tree branches as the speed accelerated.

"Give up," a dark, menacingly rough voice said in my ear. I looked out of my peripheral vision, noticing a Shadow was right next to me. "Don't risk anything more."

"Don't tell me what to do," I whispered.

"She'll kill everyone you know... We'll kill everyone you know. She looked inside your mind... She knows your weaknesses."

"Shut up," I said.

"She knows about Damion. She'll find him. And guess what?" the Shadow slurped. "*She'll kill him.*"

I felt the anger boiling up inside of me. No one could ever touch Damion. I would kill them before they land a single finger on him. "No!" I screamed, creating a yellow, electrifying forcefield that pushed the Shadow into a tree.

I made it to the meadow and there was still another Shadow on my trail. I had to wait before I could create another forcefield or even become invisible due to low energy levels. I wasn't prepared enough to fight.

"You killed him," a sweet, but sharp voice said next to me. It was the other Shadow. "I loved Sparks. And you ruined that."

"And you don't think you're ruining my life by chasing me down?" I taunted, keeping my eyes on the forest. I drove passed the meadow. Icelos said to keep driving until they came to get me.

"*You* didn't have to kill him," she hissed.

"Icelos killed him. Not me."

"An Exol?" she asked, slightly amused. "Exols couldn't kill anyone."

"They had to so they could protect me."

"It's all *your fault.*"

Suddenly, a force yanked me out of the cart. I flailed my

arms around as I soared through the air. I tried creating a force field to protect myself from hitting the ground but one never came. My energy was still low.

I landed on top of a twig, scratching my arms against the pine needles. I yelped out in pain from the impact. I landed on my wrist.

"Ooh, oh," I whispered, trying to move my wrist. But it didn't work. I think I broke or sprained it. I pushed myself up with my other hand. Slowly and gradually, I got up, balancing myself on a tree trunk. I looked up, noticing the cart hit a tree and Acea was still in the back. The figure of a woman walked calmly and gracefully forward with a dark, sizzling liquid forming in her palm. She was going to kill Acea during his most vulnerable moment.

I ran forward despite the pain I felt. I had to save him. I knew he hurt me but I still shouldn't let him die. "Acea!" I screamed. Before I could reach him, another Shadow whizzed passed me, grabbing my arm as it went.

"No!" I screamed, batting at the gassy Shadow. It didn't work. My hand went through the misty substance.

The Shadow dropped me to the ground. It took its form of a man and he grinned demonically. A flash of light formed in his hand and he shot his palm out as the flash of light hurtled my way. I rolled to the side, allowing the light to hit a tree. I felt the sticks pinching into my palms as I tried desperately to roll away in the dark. I heard Acea's scream. The scream came and went as another one happened. She was torturing him.

"Does it hurt?" the same man that talked to me before asked. "Does it hurt to know that she's playing with him?"

He shot another flash of light my way and I rolled away again, sitting behind a tree before it could hit me. I heard my own breaths. It'd be nice if my abilities could regenerate at the moment. My heart raced quickly and a lump formed in my throat as I heard another set of Acea's screams. I had to do something.

I glanced over, watching as the man walked calmly around the trees, trying to find which one I was hiding behind in the labyrinth. I looked to my other side and quickly, I noticed a decent sized stick that could probably do some head damage. I picked it up, making a few twigs snap. I heard the man turn around and I watched as he grinned, moving closer to me but not staring directly at me. He probably was still unaware of my exact hiding place.

I waited patiently for him to come near me. He walked around a tree, turning his head away from me to look behind it. His back was to me and it was the perfect time to attack.

I gritted my teeth and yelled, getting up to swing the stick into the back of his head. I swiped him hard and he stumbled a few feet forward, regained himself and turned around to glare at me.

"That wasn't very smart," he said, cocking his head to the side with a dark grin.

He reached his hand out, punching me in the gut. I toppled over, trying to regain my breath as the pain sunk in. He brought up his knee, hitting me in the forehead and I fell back onto my butt. I stared up at him with the stick still in my hand.

"Had enough yet?" he asked.

"I can't tell you how many times I heard that phrase."

I fought the pain inside of my head, knowing I probably had a concussion by this point of my day. He bent over me, forming the light inside of his palms. I wasn't sure what his ability was but I had a feeling it was something awful.

I groaned, throwing up the stick. I smacked it against his head as hard as I could. I watched as his eyes went unfocused, rolling back into his head. He fell to the ground slowly with his lips parted as the air escaped him.

I couldn't have killed him. It seemed impossible due to the lack of strength.

My thoughts were interrupted by Acea's screams. I groaned, pulling my injured wrist close to me as I stumbled to get up. My legs moved forward as I began running through the thick underbrush. I made my way quickly to the path, immediately noticing the lady hovering over Acea, burning him with her acid-like substance.

"Don't fail me now," I whispered, trying to gain enough energy to produce a forcefield.

I threw my hands outward, allowing the energy to surge throughout my palms. A small force field illuminated itself as it grew larger. I gritted my teeth, pushing it further into the woman. The force field slammed her into the tree and she screamed out in pain. I ran over to Acea, clutching my injured wrist to my chest.

"Esther," he managed a smile despite the wounds all over his body. His face was black with dirt smudges and exposed skin had bloody blotches taking its place.

"I'm so sorry," I whispered, extending my healthy hand out to stroke his face. It was my fault he was here with me.

"Watch out. She's getting up," he croaked.

I turned around, gritting my teeth with anger. I felt the venom boiling inside of me. I could feel the rage as it grew in my veins. She moved forward swiftly, ignoring the pain I had caused her. A large amount of dark liquid formed around her hand and carefully, managing my energy, I created a small forcefield.

The liquid smacked into my forcefield in the darkness. I could hear the liquid sizzling against my field. It was deteriorating it. I released the field, allowing it to drop at my feet along with the acid. I had to make them strong for this.

I held one hand out, keeping my injured one close to me. I closed my eyes for a brief moment, trying to think positively so I could create a strong, powerful field. I felt the energy surge through me and I opened my eyes. A yellow tinted forcefield surrounded my whole body and a blue forcefield was held out in front of me. Maybe that one was to throw at her.

Before she could regenerate her energy, I threw the blue forcefield forward, knocking it into her with all of my strength and she flew back, smashing her skull into a tree trunk.

I ran over to her, creating a new one that could be produced from fire. This one would kill her.

"Stop," she whispered, looking up at me from the ground. I had the fiery force field in front of me, readying to burn her.

"What?" I asked as venom coated my voice. Suddenly, the ground began to shake and a loud explosion came from the mansion. I looked up at the sky despite the fact I couldn't see the house. A large cloud of smoke was billowing from the trees, reaching the moon. Fire.

"Luna is going to get you where it hurts the most," she said, laughing as I moved the force field closer to her as a threat. "She's going to kill your mother... You better run. All Hell is going to break lose."

I closed my eyes and shoved the forcefield into her. She screamed as the fire melted her skin slowly. Once I was done, I released my concentration on the forcefield and I ran to the golf cart. I got in and backed the cart away from the tree it hit. I was surprised it was still running.

"You okay back there, Acea?" I asked as I sped down the trail towards the mansion. I didn't hear his voice, only a gurgle mixed with a groan. "Don't worry. Everything will be fine. We'll have to retreat in Phrixus's portal."

I drove passed the meadow and my heart ached. It was probably the last time I was going to see it. I continued driving the run-down golf cart. I had to make it there before Luna could reach my mother.

After a few minutes of driving quickly, I made it to my backyard. In front of me, the house illuminated with flames that reached higher than the trees. Around the mansion, Shadows soared through the sky, shooting more fire down on the house. I looked down as the heat from the fire surfaced across my face and I tried to fight the tears. I had to remember this was only a temporary home. It wasn't something worth crying over.

I saw Phrixus in the distance as a metal man. The surface of his body only looked bronze from the fire that shadowed the darkest parts of the lawn.

I sped closer to Phrixus, watching as he grabbed a Shadow by their collar, raising his metal fist to punch the man in the face. The Shadow fell onto their back as I approached.

"What are you doing here?" he spat as I stepped out of the cart.

"We need to gather everyone up and go to the safe house," I stated. "Luna is going to kill my mother and I want to leave so it won't happen."

Phrixus's features hardened against the blaze of the fire. "Okay," he said. "Icelos!"

Icelos swooped in on a front of ice, staring at Phrixus intently. Castalia and my mother ran across the yard, trying to fight off a few Shadows as they ran. They approached us, nearly out of breath.

"We need to go," Icelos stated. "All of us. No one deserves to stay here alone." He stared at my mother. "I'm sorry for underestimating you."

My mother smiled warmly. "All is well." I smiled at her as a warm feeling grew in my heart. All of this time, her and I had been arguing over nonsense. I had forgotten who she really was, how her smile formed and how she had a slight gracefulness I would never be able to understand. She was kind, even when she didn't want to be.

"Your hand, it doesn't look right," Icelos pointed out. "Does it hurt?"

I was about to respond until Phrixus cut me off. "Shadow overhead! Dunk!"

Simultaneously, we all crouched down but my mother wasn't fast enough due to her old age. The Shadow clutched onto her shoulder, taking her high above the ground and around the corner, entering through the front door with a large crash.

"Mom!" I screamed, running forward until a large, hard hand clamped onto my shoulder.

"We need to go through the portal," Phrixus stated. "She's done for."

I shook my shoulder away, glaring at Phrixus. "She's the only family I have left. I'm *not* going to let her *die*." My lip curled as my anger boiled.

"Esther," Acea said, "please... don't."

"My mother would go after me if the same thing happened," I stated dryly. I stared at all of the eager faces around me and I knew what I had to do.

I ran around the bend of the house, my feet slapping against the platform. I ran up the stairs, stopping at the fiery doorway. The door wasn't there anymore.

The fire circled the outer rim of the door, making a tiny space for me to go through. I gained the momentum steadily and I leaped through the small space, fire barely grazing my ankle. I held my hands in front of my face as I landed on the hardwood floor next to the staircase. I screamed when my wrist began to throb due to the impact.

"Esther!" I heard a voice behind me. I turned around, getting up off the floor as I clutched my wrist close to me. It was Icelos. "I'll try and freeze the fire. Go get your mother back."

I nodded my head. I heard a bloodcurdling scream come from upstairs. I turned around, hopping up the large steps. My heart raced as I rounded the corner, unaware of what room she was in.

"Mom!" I screamed, kicking down the closest door next to me. No one. I ran to the other side of the hall, using my leg to kick down the door. I had powerful soccer legs from when I was younger. No one.

I continued kicking down each door until I found a door already open. I took deep breaths as I turned the corner, entering the room. The room had gold fringe and burning couches. Paintings hung loosely from the walls. The curtains on the window were scorched with fire. I scanned my eyes in the room until I found my mother against the wall, her body slumped over. I screeched, running over to her, fearing for the worst.

I crouched down beside her, taking her head in my hands. There were multiple stab wounds in her stomach that bloodied her shirt. I felt a sob arose inside of me and all of the emotions I held in for such a long time finally started to pour out. Gingerly, I reached my fingers out, placing them on her heart. Her heart was still beating.

"That will be you in a moment," a chillingly calm voice stated from behind me.

I clutched my mother's hair with my good hand before I stood up. I still kept my back towards Luna. "You're not wise."

"We knew about you after the attack in New York. We knew all about your notions. A Tracker followed your movement after you left Erin Springs." She laughed. "And you thought we were fooled."

I never heard the term Tracker before, but I assume it was a category. "So why did you destroy my hometown?" I asked, my voice strong.

"We wanted to hurt your heart first. Dante said the only way to get to you is by destroying you from the core." I heard her movement behind me, coming closer. "Just wait until I tell Dante about Damion. We know, other than your mother, he's the one you care about the most." She moved closer again. "I looked inside your head, Esther. He taught you kindness. He taught you how to be strong. He showed you how to be happy even in the darkest of times. And most importantly, he showed you something you always wanted to feel." This time, she was closer, nearly standing directly behind me. "*Love.*"

I licked my lips, readying to hit her. "You won't be able to inform Dante."

She laughed. "It sucks I'm not wise enough to kill you, but I can't wait until I hurt you—physically."

I turned around as she thrust her knife forward. Quickly, I created a force field, blocking her blow.

She frowned. "No abilities. I want us to fight normally."

I laughed. "Sucks for you. I never go by the rules." I created another force field, pushing her into the wall. I watched as the wall crumbled around her. Luna growled, getting up drowsily. She stared me directly in the eyes and I felt everything around me shift.

I was standing over Damion, my mother, Becca and Alvaro. Their skin was pale and they resembled wax figures. They were all dead. I felt as if a hurricane swirled inside of me and all of my emotions were seeping out of my eyes. *No. Protect your mind. Protect your mind. Shield it.*

I opened my eyes and Luna was standing over me. She brought down her knife and her eyes were hollow. I yelped, rolling over quickly. I used my strength to pick myself back up and I was still unsure how I was on the ground.

Luna looked at me and smiled. "You're blocking your mind. Therefore, due to low energy, you can't make yourself invisible or use any more of your force fields."

I gritted my teeth, staring at her. My wrist throbbed from all of the movement. "You definitely know your facts."

"Yep." She lunged at me, grabbing a hold of my hair. I yelled, trying to pry her hand off of me with one hand. She brought up her knife, slashing me across my stomach. I screamed out in pain as I felt blood starting to seep out of my wound. She didn't cut me too deep, only enough to cause me pain.

I turned around, ignoring the pain from my hair as I did so. I brought up my knee, kicking her in the gut. She doubled over and I brought up my good fist, knocking her in the jaw. She released me, falling onto the ground to collect herself.

I ran out of the room, holding my injured hand close to my chest as it throbbed. I proceeded down the hallway and quickly down the stairs. I made my way across the dining room, pushing open the kitchen door with my foot. I proceeded around the island, grabbing a knife out of the knife holder. I needed an extra weapon so I could fight back and allow my abilities to gain their power again.

I heard the kitchen door open behind me and my heart began to race.

"Why don't you just give up now?" Luna taunted as I turned around. "Save the people you love from getting killed." She was clutching her face.

"There's a reason why Brilliance Chose me and not any of you."

She growled, throwing her knife at me. I moved out of the way, trying to remember what Acea taught me about knife throwing. In a hurry, I scrambled to grab her knife off the ground.

I threw her knife first without giving it much thought. She moved out of the way in time, picking it up off the floor before I could throw another one. Luna threw her knife at me and quickly, I spun out of the way, throwing my knife forward once I faced her again.

The knife hit her in the shoulder and she screamed, clutching it. I smiled, getting up on the island and jumping down, spontaneously smashing her in the face with my good hand. My fingers throbbed from hitting them against people's faces so many times today.

She snapped her head back and her mouth was full of blood. Luna grinned, grabbing my shirt while simultaneously pinning me against the wall. She extended her arm, readying to punch me. I tried to move out of the way but pain engulfed the right side of my face. I groaned, trying to lift my good hand to hit her back but she hit me again before I could move a muscle.

Luna grabbed my collar, throwing me against the ground. I held out my hands before I fell, smacking them into the hard tile. I screamed as my injured hand snapped back unnaturally. She walked towards me, kicking me in the ribs. I screamed out in pain and I remembered the time when Becca used to bully me.

Luna picked me up off the ground, holding me in the air. I brought out my knee, kicking it into her abdomen. She released me and I fell to the ground again. I crawled across the ground, trying to make my way to the knife. I reached out my bad hand and tried to grab it as pain surged throughout my body. The shoulder on my good hand didn't allow me to move.

Suddenly, a large, booted foot stepped down on my injured hand. I heard the bone crunch and I screamed, allowing the foot to penetrate my hand. Luna grabbed my jacket, lifting me off the ground. Once I stood up fully, she brought her leg up, kicking me into the island. The corner of the island buried itself into my back and I stumbled over as my vision became blurry. I fell onto my butt, trying to keep my eyes open. I couldn't let her win. I had to get my

272

mother some place safe.

Luna grabbed the knife off the ground, walking near me. She smiled as she crouched down, putting the knife against my throat.

"It sucks, doesn't it?" she asked. "Everyone you know will be killed."

I looked up at her dizzily, trying to focus my eyes. "Can you tell... me something?"

"What's that?" she asked.

"If this hurts." I brought up my leg, kicking her in the head. The knife bit into my throat as she fell backwards onto the floor. I plied the knife out of her hand, using the island to help me stand up. I focused on where her body was on the ground and I threw the knife, making it penetrate her heart. "Where it's supposed to hurt the most."

I limped out of the kitchen as my body throbbed. I made my way around the table and up the grand staircase. I released the block on my mind, knowing I didn't have to use it anymore.

After a few minutes of trying to get up the stairs, I finally made it. I limped down the hallway and entered the room where my mother was. She was still propped against the wall and I saw a faint smile spread across her lips when she saw me.

"Mom," I said weakly, limping near her. I grabbed her head gently with my good hand and my shoulder screamed at the slight movement. I allowed her to lay on my lap. She smiled up at me, taking short breaths.

"We need to get to the portal," I said quietly, stroking her soft hair. "There's a healer."

She shook her head, reaching her hand up to stroke my face. "No."

"Mom, you'll make it," I said. I felt a lump form in my throat and the tears began to well up in my eyes. "There's a healer."

She smiled, wiping my tear with her thumb. "Ju—just stay wi—with me."

I swallowed the lump and my throat was raspy. "Okay Momma. I'll stay with you." I paused, sniffling. My voice was incredibly hoarse and I could barely make out any words. "I'll stay with you until the end."

"I knew yo—you wou—would be special on—one day."

I smiled despite the achy feeling in my chest. "Did you know about your death?"

"No—not right now. I d—idn't kn—ow I was goin—going to so so—soon. Alvaro tol—told me."

"Save your breath, Momma." I stared down at her green eyes.

Memories flooded through my head, making the tears fall more freely now. I remembered how she would make me mad and then act kindly to me. I acted like I was annoyed with that but I really wasn't. I knew she really cared about me. My vision was blurry and I thought back to the time when I had a nightmare and she would always set Mr. Slithers next to me. She knew he would keep me safe but it was really her keeping me safe. "I love you."

"Be strong," she whispered weakly as she tugged on my jacket.

"I'll be strong for you. For Daddy." What was worse was the fact that I was watching the love and soul of my life dying right in front of me. My father died peacefully and not in front of me, only in the hospital.

"I love y—you, Est—her."

"Please, Momma, stay with me. Please." I couldn't help but scream.

I smiled, tasting a few tears that landed on my lips. Her breathing slowed and I heard her last intake of air before her head went limp in my arms. I stared down at her and my heart sunk into my stomach.

I choked and frowned as the tears continued to flow down my cheeks. I couldn't see anything in front of me. I screamed a bloodcurdling scream as all of the emotions inside of me erupted like a volcano. I continued on screaming as the agony was too strong to simply bare. I held her in my arms like she had done when I was a small child. Everything inside of me continued to pour out like a waterfall. Losing the one that propped you up your entire life due to foolishness of another was truly a traumatic experience. *So, this is what they wanted. This is how they were going to destroy me. And sadly, to say, it was working.*

I no longer had parents. I no longer had a family. All of my family members either died or disapproved of our ways. I looked down at the locket my mother gave me earlier. With a clumsy hand, I held the locket in my palm, trying to suck in the tears. Why wasn't anyone here to help me save her? The Exols could've helped me. But they didn't. And that was what made the fire burn inside of me.

I heard the fire crackling around me and the floor beneath me began to sway. I had to leave or the house would collapse. I used my fingertips to close my mother's eyes before I started to get up. I wrapped my arm around her one last time, wishing I could feel her strong grasp around my waist one more time. I waited patiently for her to extend her arms but it never came.

"Esther," Phrixus said, appearing in the doorway. "Are you done yet?"

I turned to look at him and the anger began to surface. "Where were all of you when Luna killed her?" I screamed at him as the tears began to poor rapidly down my cheeks.

His features hardened as he came near me. "Push away your feelings. We have work to get done."

Phrixus grabbed my body but I pulled away from him because of the pain.

"Can you walk?" he asked. I stared at him stubbornly, wanting to desperately rip his throat out. He sighed, bending down to pick me up bridal style.

Phrixus carried me out of the room and I stared back at my mother's lifeless body. I hoped her and my father would get to see each other again.

"How bad are you injured?" Phrixus asked, staring down at me as he walked down the crumbling stairs at a fast pace.

"I don't know and I don't care," I lied, ignoring the stabbing pain throughout my whole body.

"How is your energy level?"

"Low. Very low."

He nodded his head as he reached the bottom of the stairs. Ice was frozen around the doorway. Icelos probably did that so we could enter and exit without being burnt.

Phrixus stepped over the ice so he wouldn't slip and he carried me down the once beautifully crafted steps.

"What about my mother's body?" I asked quietly, remembering it doesn't feel right to leave her body behind.

He shrugged his shoulders as he walked around the platform. Remaining Shadows shot unknown abilities at Castalia and Icelos. As we rounded the corner, Acea was still in the golf cart with his head thrown back. "It's not worth it. She's dead. Her soul is what travels."

I wanted to reach up and strangle him but my body throbbed too much.

"Icelos!" Phrixus screamed as Shadows began to surround Castalia and Phrixus. "We need to go! I have her!"

Icelos nodded his head, jabbing his sword into a Shadow. I watched as Castalia spun around, her blonde hair drifting through the air as she did so. She stabbed another Shadow, making them take their human form.

"Come on!" Icelos yelled, gesturing for Castalia to run.

"I can't," she yelled back. "My leg was cut and I can't run quickly."

Instantaneously, Icelos grabbed her waist, keeping her close to his side. He iced the ground beneath him and further on. He lurched forward, sliding across the ground with Castalia in his arm. He reached us and he let go of her. Phrixus extended me and Icelos took me carefully. I felt a sharp shooting pain go through my stomach and I moaned quietly. Phrixus turned around and picked up Acea. He gave him to Castalia and she held his arm around her shoulder.

Phrixus stared at a certain section in the air and he raised his hand. He opened them widely, staring at the ball of purple flame wildly, extending it carefully. Swirls of black and purple electrified with energy as the portal reached its final stage.

"Go! Hurry!" he yelled, staring passed us. I turned my head, noticing a Shadow hurtling our way. "Shadow! Move!"

We all jumped into the portal and a large screeching noise echoed throughout my ears. We moved in the purple darkness blindly as our bodies tossed and turned. Suddenly, excruciating pain engulfed my right side and I looked over, noticing the Shadow was swarming through with us. Phrixus yelled and Icelos reached his hand up to freeze blindly at the figure attacking us. In the short distance, I could see light and what looked to be wood.

We landed on a tile ground, sliding across the slippery substance. Each of us slammed into a wooden wall and I yelled out in pain as did everyone else.

Icelos released me as the Shadow moved towards us in the bright lighting that affected my eyes harshly. Phrixus and Icelos moved forward, gritting their teeth. Phrixus transformed into a metal figure, slamming his hard fist into the Shadow. His fist went through the figure and he growled angrily.

"Stand up and fight you coward!" he yelled.

Icelos studied where the figure was heading and it was hurtling towards me. I lifted my hand weakly, trying to shield my face. Icelos lifted his arms, closing his eyes patiently, creating a large block of ice in front of me. The Shadow shattered into the ice, sliding across the floor and it transformed itself into human form. It was a man in his early twenties and his hair was bright red.

I started to notice that if we were patient with our abilities, we could make the Shadows human.

The ginger stood up, staring Icelos directly in the eyes. A ray of yellow light shot out of his eyes and instantaneously, Phrixus jumped in front of Icelos. The laser hit his metal body and boomeranged back to the man. The yellow ray sliced the ginger open and his eyes rolled back in his head. His remains crumbled to the ground. I closed my eyes tightly, trying not to remember my mother. Her eyes rolled back inside her head when she died.

Suddenly, clapping filled the air, making me open my eyes. A boy that was probably fifteen, but looked eighteen, stood behind a bar that led into the kitchen. He was smearing peanut butter across his sandwich after he was done clapping.

"I never knew Exols could kill people," the boy said, staring at a jar of jelly. "Well, anyone but themselves."

"We already broke the rules enough. Why not do it some more?" Phrixus said, staring at the boy.

He shrugged his shoulders. "Well. It's good you do break the rules. But not the rule that Icelos broke." He gave a little laugh.

Icelos hardened his features. "I wish we didn't save you, cocky child."

He chuckled. "Anyone want a sandwich?" He glanced to Castalia who was sitting next to Acea, then to Acea and then he rested his eyes on me.

"No," Icelos stated. "We need Sapphire for medical attention, Phoenix."

Phoenix smiled. "She's too busy coaxing her brother to talk to us."

Icelos rolled his eyes impatiently. "We *need* medical

attention or this boy will die."

He glanced at me. "What about her? She seems pretty beat up. Almost death-like."

"She can't die," Phrixus said.

"Ohhh," Phoenix said, clapping his hands together. "You have one of those abilities?"

"No. She doesn't," Icelos said.

"Well, who are they then? They seem pretty useless to me. Probably not worth saving." He picked up his paper plate, walking calmly towards the small dining table. He pulled out a chair that squeaked loudly, sitting down instantly. "Come on, Exols. You should spend your time trying to find that Esther Green chick. Hopefully it's not too late."

I gritted my teeth, wanting to get up and punch him in the face. But I couldn't. I was in too much pain to move and my wrist was absolutely broken.

Phrixus laughed. "You're funny, kid."

Phoenix grinned, leaning back in his chair, staring at Phrixus with his golden eyes. "I know." He glanced back to Acea and me. "What are all of your names?"

I glanced at Acea whom was drooling and staring blankly up at the ceiling. I groaned, grabbing onto the wooden wall to steady myself as I got up slowly. I stared Phoenix directly in the eyes. "I'm Esther Green."

He opened his mouth, dropping his moist sandwich onto his plate. "Wow. We're doomed."

"Shut up," Castalia said, finally getting up. She adjusted her royal blue dress, staring at the boy. "Don't underestimate her. She killed many Creators today. I'm surprised at how strong she truly is. How she can maintain herself so fluently."

"I'm sensing a little bit of envy here," he said, putting his feet up on the wooden table.

"Can you please go get Sapphire. They need to be healed," Icelos stated.

"In a few days, you guys have to take out another Creator base and free the Clockworks inside." Phrixus stared at the boy.

"Ugh," Phoenix groaned. "I liked it better when we were in hiding. I can't do all of this fighting stuff."

"Sucks for you," Phrixus said. "You guys are the only

Clockworks left that could take out the Creators easily."

"Okay." He got up, walking down an unknown hallway. "I'll go get her."

I stared up at Sapphire as she shifted the water through the air, swiping it back down at me and onto my wounds. The water sizzled against my arm and the pain slowly faded in that area where the ginger flashed me in the portal.

"That's awful," she stated, staring into my eyes with her dark brown eyes. She was Asian and extremely beautiful. Her black hair laid perfectly passed her shoulders in a wavy form. Her face was round and she wore a ruby sapphire necklace.

"What's awful?" I asked, sitting up slightly.

She smiled warmly. "I have not only the ability to heal with water, but the ability to see the past in objects with a single touch."

"So, you've seen my past," I stated meekly, trying not to remember my mother but it was poking at my mind continuously.

"I lost my parents a year ago due to the Creators," she stated softly, rubbing the water against my wrist next. She was trying her best not to touch it but it wasn't working. I bit back a scream as the bone started to shift back into place underneath my skin. "They thought my mother was the Chosen one for some unknown reason. My father tried to protect her but they were both killed."

"I'm sorry," I said quietly.

She smiled slightly. "It happened at night in our house. My brother and I were upstairs, listening to the feud. Next thing we know, my mother was screaming and a thump hit the floor. It fell quiet and we heard another thump." She paused, examining my arm, trying to heal all of the bruises. "Not a day goes by where I don't think of that night. And I think my brother is the same way. After their funeral, he quit talking. Cadoen only says a few phrases to me once in a while but no one else." She paused again. "I miss his voice."

I looked up at her. "I couldn't imagine having to go through that."

"Well, you can imagine because you went through the same thing. You haven't heard Damion's voice in a year."

"It's amazing how you are able to know so much about me."

"It's quite fun actually," she said with a smile. She applied the last bit of healing water on my face. I felt the water going deep into my skin, erasing the cuts and bruises from the fight with the Creators and the fight with Leila's crew. I felt a stab in my heart when I remembered I couldn't save Leila in time.

"Don't regret, Esther," Sapphire said quietly as she touched my face gently. "Some things happen for reasons."

I looked out the window in the corner of the wooden, cozy room. The trees swayed violently in the wind. A storm was coming. "I don't think I can believe that."

"Sometimes it's the best way to think. You won't drown in your own sorrow," she said, finishing up.

I sat up slowly, feeling the power that surged through my veins. I was glad to have my abilities regenerated. I hung my legs over the hospital bed, jumping onto the hardwood floor. The cabin was extraordinarily large and clean. It felt cozy and vibrant.

"Don't get used to it," she said, "we won't stay here for long."

"I'll enjoy any minute I can," I said, walking out of the room with her. She was only a few years older than me but she was still slightly short.

We walked into the wooden hallway that smelt like cinnamon and it was only lit by one lamp but it was enough. A figure strode down the hallway towards us.

"Cadoen," Sapphire beamed, "meet Esther Green. She's the one that was Chosen!"

I smiled at the dark figure, extending my hand in the dim hallway. The figure ignored my hand, walking passed us with a harsh wind. "Is he always that rude?" I whispered once he rounded the corner.

"Yes," she said and we continued walking until we reached the kitchen. A girl and Phoenix sat next to each other, eating soup.

"Electra, how was practice?" Sapphire asked, reaching up to open a cabinet. She took out a white square bowl, dishing herself some soup from the pan.

"It was very good. I finally mastered the bow," a girl with bright red hair said with a laugh.

I moved quickly towards Sapphire, trying to make it to where I wouldn't be the center of attention. "What kind of soup is that?" I asked, looking at the bubbling stew.

"Oh," Sapphire said calmly, "would you like some? It's

Electra's famous recipe."

"What does it have in it?" I asked, looking into her dark, but radiant eyes.

She smiled kindly. "Why not keep it a surprise?"

I shrugged my shoulders. "Alright. Dish me up." I grabbed a white bowl, holding it out in front of me. Sapphire picked up the spoon, scooping it into the slimy liquid. She poured it into my bowl and she gave me a plastic spoon from a drawer.

We walked over to the table, sitting across from Phoenix and Electra. She had bright green eyes that resembled Acea's but they coruscated more. Phoenix's hair was cropped black and he had a few piercings in his lip and on his eyebrow. Underneath his black, leather tunic, tattoos surfaced across his biceps, making intricate designs. He caught my eye and I quickly looked down, stirring my soup around.

"So, Esther, we heard what happened," he said, leaning back in his chair.

I looked up too quickly. "What do you mean?"

"Your mother. Father. Damion kid. Acea kid. All of your life events." He glanced at Sapphire and she looked down. She probably informed them somehow without me knowing.

"Where is Acea?" I asked. "And the Exols?" I tried changing the subject so I didn't have to think about my mother. Images surfaced through my mind. Her smile flashed before my eyes and I felt her embrace. I shook my head, trying to push the thoughts away.

"Acea is resting," Sapphire said. "The Exols, I suppose, are having a meeting somewhere in here."

"So, Esther," Electra said eagerly, "what are your abilities? I bet they're extraordinary since Brilliance Chose you."

"Um... Force fields and invisibility," I said.

"Wow," Phoenix said. "Those are awful."

"They kept me alive this long," I stated dryly, staring into his golden eyes as he smiled coldly.

"Phoenix, she's been through a lot," Sapphire stated. "Give her some slack."

"I just think it's stupid Brilliance would Choose her; a girl afraid of her own shadow, to protect humanity and all of us, really. It should've Chose me. I could protect it from harm better than anyone else."

I gritted my teeth. "If you're going to be so *rude*, what are

281

your abilities?"

He laughed deeply. "Acid and portals."

"I already met people who could do that. Therefore, your abilities aren't that unique," I said.

"I think mine are unique," Electra spoke up. "Electricity and melting."

"Melting is new," I said quietly, drinking my soup from the spoon.

"Esther was electrocuted and burned nearly to death," Sapphire spoke up. She knew me better than anyone due to her abilities.

Electra's mouth dropped open. "Whoa. You have been through a lot. All we've done was save a few Clockworks. We never got hurt that badly."

"Plus, Phoenix, Esther might save your life some day with her abilities. You should treat her with some respect."

He shrugged. "I can save myself."

Chapter 12: The First Rescue

I sat in the bedroom I was assigned after dinner. It was a decent size and it had a small window that showed the garden. I wasn't sure where I was—what state—but it definitely didn't feel like I was here before.

I was waiting for Sapphire to lend me some clothes. I had some in the bag I brought but she insisted.

"Esther?" she asked quietly, knocking twice on the door.

"Come in," I said.

She came in with a large duffel bag full of clothes. She laid it gently on the quilt, taking out a night gown. "It's nearly after one in the morning. I'm sure you're tired."

"I am, actually," I said, taking the silky material from her.

"Well, I'll leave you alone. Try to rest up for a few days. We're leaving on Friday to save another Compound."

I nodded my head, hoping I'll be ready for another fight. "Okay. Thanks for healing Acea and me."

She smiled warmly. "Anytime." She turned on her heels, slapping her bare feet against the polished wood flooring. She shut the door behind her without another word.

I took the duffel bag off the bed, dropping it on the floor next to my book bag. I undressed from my bloody, dirty clothes, walking into the bathroom in my room. I turned on the shower and the water flowed out of the faucet. I stared at my reflection, noticing my face was absolutely cut-free and bruise-free. I looked like a normal person.

But the thing was, I wasn't even close to normal. Normal people don't have people wanting to kill them any chance they get. Normal people don't have special abilities. And most importantly, normal people don't have to worry about keeping their world safe from destruction.

I felt the tears welling in my eyes once more. I saw my

reflection and I appeared to be absolutely broken. I had no one. Not a soul. I gritted my teeth, smashing the glass with my fist. The mirror broke into many pieces. I grabbed one of the pieces of the mirror, crying at what I was about to do.

I'm a Soul. I can kill myself. I don't want to be the Protector of Brilliance. I don't want to fight in this War. I just want to be dead. I want to join my family. I can't do this anymore. I just can't. Maybe if I kill myself, Brilliance would disappear. I am not a hero. I'm a selfish girl that only cares about myself. Hell, I'm selfish enough to kill myself so I don't have to protect the world.

"I don't know what you saw in me," I whispered.

With meek hesitation, I brought the shard of glass up to my throat. I watched my tears trickle down my freckles in the remaining parts of the mirror. I gritted my teeth, allowing the glass to bite against my throat. I exhaled, feeling the excruciating pain of the blade. But I kept going, I sawed my throat. Back and forth. Back and forth. Back and forth. Blood oozed out of my neck, pouring onto my shirt. I felt myself getting dizzy and the bathroom was spinning in circles. But I wasn't dying. I should've died by now. I shrieked, continuing to saw at myself. I saw my neck bone in the remains of the mirror but I wasn't dead. I could feel all of the pain and I began screaming in treacherous amounts of despair. I dropped the shard of glass, gripping the sink, watching my blood pour into the sink.

"Oh my god, Esther!" I heard Sapphire scream.

In seconds, I passed out.

"Esther, I can't believe you would try to kill yourself. I had to heal your wounds again." I heard Sapphire's voice drift in the walls of the wooden room.

I got up slowly as black dots swarm in my eyes. "I didn't die."

"No shit, Esther. It has to be *another* Soul. I can't believe you would do that. Do you understand how many people are looking up to you, thinking they're our savoir in this War? You can kill Dante."

I shook my head, instantly regretting what I tried to do. Tears began streaming down my cheeks. "I'm just so broken... My mom was murdered."

Sapphire sat down beside me, taking my hand in hers. "I

know, Esther. It's going to hurt. It's going to hurt for a long time… But we all lost people. We all don't have our families anymore. It's a War, Esther. It's one that we need to fight. Together. You're not alone. We're here for you."

I nodded my head. "Please don't tell anyone about this… I promise you I won't hurt myself like that ever again." I took a deep breath. "I just need to remember why Brilliance Chose me and what It saw in me."

Sapphire smiled warmly at me, squeezing my hand. "You'll find out, honey."

I was in the bathroom again, thinking. Normal people do lose their parents. Normal people do have a chance between life and death. Normal people do have their hearts broken every once in a while, to keep them sane. Maybe I wasn't so different?

The Mark throbbed against my wrist and I looked down at the intricate designs. My wrist was pulsing slowly and I knew then, I wasn't normal.

I jumped in the shower quickly, washing and scrubbing my dirty skin. Nothing in my body throbbed and I no longer had a broken wrist.

After a few minutes of showering in the hot water, I was finally clean enough. I got out of the shower, drying my skin. I wrapped a towel around my hair and walked into my bedroom. I lifted up the gown, sliding it passed my head and onto my body. I walked to my bed, lifting up the quilt and then tucking myself in. My mother used to always tuck me in.

"Mother!" I screamed, trying to run towards my mother in time. Luna was standing over her with in a knife in her hand. She was grinning as she plunged the knife into my mother.

I screamed as my mother fell to the ground. Her beautiful hair stayed weightless until she collided into the wooden floor. I felt a lump in my stomach as all of our memories resurfaced.

I saw her face over mine and she was smiling. She reached up her hands, tickling me and I laughed. I kicked and laughed in my bed and she laughed, hugging me against her soft chest. She picked up Mr. Slithers, tucking him in beside me. She leaned over, kissing my forehead gently.

"I love you," she said.

I stared at Luna as the anger began to boil inside of me. I screamed as loud as I could, throwing up multiple burning and sharp force fields. I continued screaming as I sliced her in every area I could think of.

"NEVER WILL YOU TOUCH HER AGAIN!" I screamed, continuing to slice Luna even though she was already dead. I screamed more as I crumbled to the ground next to my mother. I cupped my head in my hands as I began to cry wildly.

I woke up to bloodcurdling noises. My throat felt raw and I soon came to the conclusion that I was the one making the noises. I was screaming. I looked around my room, noticing force fields placed in every corner and section of my room. I glanced down, realizing my body wasn't actually there. I was invisible.

The force fields were cracked and jagged with sharp edges. They glowed a variety of colors.

"Esther," a gentle voice said. I looked up. Sapphire, Phoenix, Acea, Electra, Icelos, Phrixus and Castalia were standing in my doorway. They couldn't reach me.

"Esther, calm down. Think happy thoughts," Icelos said gently.

"There are no happy thoughts," I mumbled.

"At least try to calm down. Take deep breaths."

I groaned in anger, lifting my hand to take down all of the force fields. They disappeared and I reappeared again.

"Will she be alright?" Sapphire asked.

"Yes. Go back to bed. I'll try to talk to her."

"Can I stay?" Acea asked, staring me directly in the eyes. He acted like everything was normal again. He acted like I still liked him but I didn't. I didn't think I ever did.

"No," Icelos answered finally, noticing my expression. "Everyone go back to bed. Exols, patrol the ground."

"Make her feel better," Castalia said, gently placing her hand on his shoulder before she turned away.

"She needs to learn how *to grow up*," Phrixus stated impatiently as he scurried everyone out of my doorway.

"Shut up," Sapphire stated dryly. "She's been through a lot of stuff."

They maneuvered out of my doorway, mumbling as they

walked down the hall.

Icelos smiled as he walked closer to me. He sat at the edge of my bed, continuing to stare at me.

"What?" I asked, growing impatient like Phrixus had.

"I'm trying to see if smiling would make anything better," he stated, losing the grin.

"Nope. Doesn't help at all." I laid back down, staring up at the ceiling. "I wonder if everything is my fault. I shouldn't have walked into the Rizzoli Bookstore. I shouldn't have been Chosen if I couldn't handle everything going on around me." I paused, trying to fight the tears that desperately wanted to pour out of my eyes. "I should have saved my mother when I had the chance."

"Esther, sometimes there's things we regret. Those things can never be fixed again... But you *have to learn* how to fix the emotions from those events."

I looked at him in the darkness. "What did you do? The three of you act like you've done something wrong."

Icelos's jaw clenched. "I lost two very special people, Esther and I regret what I created. It's known for its own self-destruction."

"What do you mean?" I asked, furrowing my brows.

"You'll figure it out soon enough."

"Who did you lose?"

"People I love."

"I don't think I'm understanding you," I said quietly.

He shrugged. "Because the three of us broke a few Exol laws; we're considered the Abase Exols. The high, mighty Exols that don't care much about the world are the Majestic Exols. They live off of this 'peaceful vibe' but they're causing more destruction by not doing anything.

"When I saw what was happening to the Chosen one through the Glass Transmitter in our Heavenly Castle, I realized that the Creators might have a chance. I quickly gathered Castalia and Phrixus, not knowing how they received their term and I asked them to join me.

"We set out quickly to find you and Phrixus allowed us to go in his portal. We arrived in your yard before the Shadows came. We, once again, broke another Exol law because we're not allowed to interfere with the Chosen one's issues. They said that you need to prove yourself without any help. We ignored the remark and we came anyways. Phrixus was upset that he joined because he was going to be crowned a few days from now. He was going to be a Majestic Exol again.

"Phrixus knew that you were more important. He was determined to save you but he promised me he wasn't going to be nice about it. I, of course, had to gather the remaining Clockworks a few weeks before I looked through the Glass Transmitter. Secretly, I gave them missions to free Clockworks. The freed Clockworks then went on their own to free others at the Creators' Compounds. Soon enough, it was time to save you."

"Why did you think I didn't have a chance?" I asked. "I was doing perfectly fine. I killed Rosa at that time."

"I saw what was coming your way. The Shadows were getting ready to come and attack you."

"Oh," I said. I thought I handled everything perfectly fine. "If you guys broke the law, why didn't either of you care when Luna took my mother into the house? And why did Exols take care of all of those Creator attacks last year?"

"At that time, I thought you should have handled everything. And about the Creator attacks a few years ago, you weren't Chosen then. Brilliance didn't have a host yet."

"Why did everything change when Brilliance did have a host?" I asked.

Icelos shrugged his shoulders. "I don't think the Exols agreed with Brilliance's Choosing."

"Why?" I asked, growing annoyed. "What's so wrong about me?"

"I don't think I can answer for them," Icelos stated quietly.

"Am I too young? Too weak?"

"Like I said, I can't answer for them."

I rolled my eyes. "And to think I looked up to you guys."

"Get some sleep," Icelos stated. "The Exols and I are leaving tomorrow. The Majestic Exols might have discovered our absences. From then, the fight will be your own. Allow the other Clockworks to help you now. Make friends with them."

"Okay," I said impatiently. I rolled onto my side so I didn't have to see him.

"Goodnight. I'm sorry for your loss." I felt him get up from my bed and I heard him shut my door.

"So much for making me feel better," I said quietly.

"Come on," a voice said in my ear. "Get up sleepy head."

I opened my eyes, rubbing the sand around them. My father always told me that a sand monster would come into my bedroom at night and when I would be in a deep sleep, the monster would carefully lay sand around my eyes.

"We need to practice," Sapphire said, throwing pieces of cloth onto my bed. "Two more days until we attack a Compound."

She walked around my bed, edging closer to the window. She opened the curtains and the sunlight burned at my eyes. I shoved my face into my pillow, groaning.

"Do you always sleep in?" Sapphire asked. "It's eight o'clock! We gotta' get cruising!"

"No," I groaned into the pillow.

She huffed impatiently. "Guess I just have to force you to wake up now..." Her voice trailed off mockingly. She yelled, jumping onto my bed, making the bed shake surprisingly with her small amount of weight. She grabbed my shoulders, shaking them continuously while laughing.

"Okay! Okay!" I yelled. "I'm getting up!" I laughed as I rolled off the bed sleepily.

"There it is!" She shouted, clapping her hands together. "You laughed!"

I got up while smiling. I grabbed my arm as if it protected me. "Yeah. I guess I did."

"You have a beautiful laugh, Esther," Sapphire said, sitting on my bed. "You need to laugh a lot more."

"Thank you," I said, picking up the clothes on my bed. I noticed they were black with thick texture in some places. I looked up at Sapphire, furrowing my brows. "What kind of clothes are these?"

"Fighting clothes. We wear them while we practice and when we go in the Compounds. It offers the best support and protection." She smiled. "Electra stitched them up. She's really good at creating stuff."

"That's amazing," I said, staring at the intricate stitching. I rolled the material over, noticing a rubber design across the breast plate. It was the mark of Brilliance. Brilliance's designs were inside a circle that had electricity forming around the edges. It looked slightly real. Almost like a drawing I suppose.

"It's a work of art," Sapphire said. "Besides our abilities, I think we all have an inner talent."

I looked up at her. "I never focused on a talent before."

"That's realistic." She jumped off the bed, standing next to me. "Most people don't have time to think about it."

I looked back down at the clothing. "I wish I had the time to."

She smiled sheepishly. "When this is all over, I'll teach you how to live again. No doubt about it."

I smiled as my heart fluttered. I was actually feeling happiness? Maybe it was best that she was able to see my life. "Since you can see what I've been through, can you see what Brilliance shows me?"

"No," she stated. "Brilliance leaves a block on my mind. It's like what that woman in the chamber told you; Brilliance protects you."

"Switching that subject," I said, "What is your talent?"

She smiled again, her dark eyes lighting up with happiness. "I'm an extraordinary painter. Maybe sometime I can take you back to my old house and show you."

"I'd love that." I paused, thinking back to last night. Everyone was outside of my bedroom besides Cadoen. "What are your brother's abilities?"

"Oh, well... He's a Spiritual Human. He's kind of upset about it. He wishes he was more powerful."

"I know how he feels," I said quietly. Wait. He was a Spiritual Human. I felt my eyes widen as I came to the realization. Cadoen had his own Prophecy.

"What's wrong?" Sapphire asked.

"Your brother, he has a Prophecy. He's supposed to help me during the War along with the Exol Child."

"An Exol Child?" she asked, her dark eyebrows coming together, making a crease in her forehead. "That's impossible."

"No, it's not impossible," I stated, growing excited that I found one person that's a part of the Prophecies. "It said it directly in Brilliance. One of the three of us is going to die... or get injured or something... And it was talking about a rebirth. It was slightly confusing but yeah...

"Two Exols had a strong enough love that was destroying the Exol Kingdom with emotions. They had to do something before they would start tearing everyone and everything apart. So, they had a child. But the thing is, Exols weren't allowed to have children. I never found out how Exols formed yet, but I'm sure I will if Brilliance decides to show me anything more. When Exols have a child, the child is so powerful and uncontrollable that it's incredibly dangerous. Soon enough, the other Majestic Exols figured out about the child and they knew they had to kill it before it learned about its abilities."

"So how did the Exol parents save the child?" Sapphire asked, listening closely.

"The father sent their child away to live with a mortal friend of his. The Majestic Exols killed his wife so he could experience the pain of losing the two things he loved very much, his child and wife." When I finished the story, an image flashed through my head from last night. Icelos told me he regretted losing the two things he really cared about.

"Wow... And how does my brother tie into this? And he better not *die*. You probably read it wrong."

"Maybe," I said. "But your brother is the first Spiritual Human I met. That makes him important."

I tried to think more about last night. Icelos was a Majestic Exol. When he sent the child away, what if he became an Abase Exol? "Oh my god, Sapphire," I stated once I came to the conclusion. "Where's Icelos?" Before she could respond, I ran out of my room and down the dim hallway. My bare feet slapped across the ground when I entered the kitchen. It was empty.

"Esther!" Sapphire said, running down the hallway as she tried to catch up. She stopped in the kitchen, noticing my blank expression. "They left already."

The words were like a stab to the heart. I was so close to figuring out the puzzle. "I guess I have to wait then," I said, trying to stay confident but my voice was quavering. "I thought Icelos was the one who committed the crime. If he did, he could probably tell me where he sent the child so I could find him." I paused, staring out the large glass window near the kitchen. "Then I would be ready for the War."

"But you're not ready yet," Sapphire said encouragingly. "Maybe some things happen for these particular reasons."

"I guess so," I said, turning around to look at her. "Let's get ready."

The outfit hugged my curves and it was a full body suit built with comfortable fiber pads, posing as armor.

"Here," Sapphire said, giving me a flat, metal square.

I grabbed it, staring at the straps on the back. "What is it?"

"You strap it around your torso. Sadly, it leaves your back exposed to pain. Only the fibers on your suit protect your back. Be aware of that."

I nodded my head, strapping the metal armor around my torso. She handed me a pair of metal shin guards. I strapped them around my shins willingly. "So, what are we doing today?" I asked, staring up at the beautiful bright sky. Trees surrounded the cabin, the green leaves thick with life. It was a striking sight.

Sapphire grinned. "You'll see."

We walked around the cabin and a few meters away was the start of the thick forest. There was only one cleared entryway and the rest was thick with underbrush. Beside the entrance was a large box of materials.

"We're allowed to use our abilities, right?" I asked.

"Yes. But we're going through a different part of the Maze. I want to teach you how to use weapons and not just your abilities, okay?"

I nodded my head, walking close to the materials. A loud scream of excitement came from the Maze and I instantly knew it was Electra. I smiled, excitement growing inside of me. I couldn't wait until I went inside.

"Here," Sapphire said, handing me a pair of black gloves. "They're fireproof." I grabbed them, sliding them onto my hands. "What weapon are you not good with in this box or you never tried to use?"

"The sword and the archery set," I stated.

"Okay. I'll give you the sword first so you won't get killed trying to figure out the bow and arrows." She grabbed the sword along with a sheath.

"Thanks," I said, wrapping the sheath around my waist. It

had multiple sword and knife holders. I placed the metal sword into the sheath and Sapphire handed me a few knives to fill the holes. I placed them in the sheath too. She handed me a shield last.

"I want you to keep in mind that this isn't child's play. Phoenix structured the Maze to allow us to have the best experience to fight. We get hurt in there... We'll fight together but keep in mind that it changes. You'll find yourself going around in circles."

"Is that Phoenix's talent?" I asked. "Structuring?"

"Yes. He built it but Icelos made it come to life."

I nodded my head, looking into the entryway at the blank trail before us. "Doesn't look that bad."

She laughed, grabbing her items as well. She had an archery set. "Let me use your shield once in a while. I have no protection."

We trudged into the entryway and the scene in front of me changed, leaving me perplexed. I thought we were going to walk down a trail in the forest. But no. We were standing behind a large tree. As close as I was, I could see all of the ants running up and down the tree trunk.

I took a deep breath, moving out from behind the tree. There was a ball of liquid hurtling my way and I heard Sapphire scream, pulling me back behind the tree before the substance could touch me.

"What the hell!" she exclaimed. "You could've gotten hurt!"

"I'm sorry. I just didn't know that was going to happen," I stated roughly.

"There's going to be mind games in the Maze too, okay Esther?" Sapphire stated. "You're going to see images of people who caused you trouble... Or you'll see faceless people. Be careful and stay near me. The objective is to kill anything you see. The images of you and me will never change. I'll never transform into a beast and you'll never be forced to kill me. We don't do things like that."

"Okay," I stated. "Seems intense."

"On three," Sapphire said. "One. Two. Three."

Quickly, we maneuvered around the tree and abilities were hurtling our way. I held the shield in front of me and Sapphire crouched down behind me so she wouldn't get hit.

"First person on your left!" she screamed.

I looked around wildly, noticing a faceless man was moving towards us quickly. Instantly, he he shot to the ground, an arrow sticking out of his stomach. I looked down at Sapphire, smiling at her good accuracy.

"Move forward and fight the one on your right and I'll fight the one on my left. Go!" she yelled.

I moved forward in a hurry, blocking the abilities with my shield. I jumped to each tree, hiding behind them for a few moments until I began running again. Sapphire followed closely behind me.

"Now!" she yelled.

I noticed a faceless figure coming my way and I brought up my sword. I clutched it with sweaty hands as the figure swiped at me with its sword. I jumped back, swiping the figure across the chest. The figure groaned, counterattacking. I held up my sword and they clashed together. I felt his force against my strength and I noticed the swords edging closer to my neck. I gritted my teeth, trying to fight the force back.

I brought up my knee, kicking the figure in the groin. He groaned, releasing his force and I brought up my sword, slashing at his head. I kicked the lifeless body onto the ground. His body broke the sticks underneath him.

I turned around, realizing Sapphire was having some trouble. More figures surrounded her and she was trying to fight them off with only the edge of her bow because they were too close for her to shoot at.

Frantically, I glanced at the tree next to me. It had great jumping distance and I could probably take out a few figures by landing on them. I gritted my teeth, lurching forward. I felt my feet land on the side of the tree and before I fell, I kicked off the tree, landing with my sword out in front of me. I slashed three figures, killing them instantly. A few figures moved my way and quickly, I brought up my shield, smashing one in the face then simultaneously turning to slash at the one behind me.

Sapphire smiled at me and I returned it with a grin. We stood back to back, turning clockwise to see all of the figures running down the hill in the distance. They ran around trees at a fast pace.

"How's it looking over there?" I asked.

"Rowdy," she replied.

I laughed, bringing up my sword as the first set of shadowed figures came at me. I fought each of them off with difficulty from the overflow of bodies. A figure slashed me across the back and I yelped in pain. I turned around, realizing Sapphire was a distance away, shooting her arrows at the approaching figures. I realized I was alone for the moment.

Another figured slashed me in the calf and I groaned as the metal bit into my skin. Instantaneously, I turned around, slashing my sword wildly while closing my eyes. I held up my shield in front of my throat so I wouldn't get slashed in the most sensitive area.

I opened my eyes, realizing I only killed a few figures. I yelled in aggravation, hitting the nearest shadowed figures with my shield, busting them in the face. Quickly, I spun, cutting the nearest faceless people with my sword. I finally made a path.

I looked ahead, realizing there was a tree that Sapphire and I might be able to climb. "Sapphire!" I screamed, running forward.

She turned around, trying to fight off her own set of figures as she did so. "What?"

"The tree!" I yelled, running closer to it. "We can climb it."

She groaned, deciding to follow me. I could feel the ground vibrating beneath me as all of the figures tried to run after us.

I ran forward, putting my shield and sword in the same hand. I jumped up, grabbing a hold of a branch with only one arm. I wrapped my arm around it, breathing heavily as I tried to pull myself up. In time, I made it on the branch. It was large enough for me to sit on.

I extended my hand to help Sapphire but she sprang up, grabbing a hold of the thick branch above me. My eyes grew wide in bewilderment. Wow.

"Climb higher!" I shouted. "You can shoot them from above."

She nodded her head, moving closer to the trunk so she could reach the following branches. I placed my sword in my sheath and I hooked my shield on my belt. I shinned up the tree, climbing as fast as I could. I followed Sapphire quickly until we reached a point where we felt safe enough.

"Whoa," I said, nearly out of breath. "I think I'm getting fat."

She laughed, rubbing her stomach. "I feel ya."

Sapphire positioned her fingers on the wire, pulling it back with the arrow lodged inside. She released and the arrow shot through two figures that were attempting to climb the tree.

I laughed, staring at her. "Nice one."

She grinned. "I try." She looked at the bottom of the tree.

"Slash at the ones near your feet."

I listened to what she had said, taking my sword out to slash at them. The figures fell off the tree, hitting the crowd of figures below. Sapphire continued shooting at them.

"Nothing better than doing this on a lovely morning," she stated, laughing as she shot down each one.

I laughed again. "You got that right."

Suddenly, the tree shook ferociously and I gripped onto the tree trunk with my sword still in the same hand. I watched as Sapphire began to fall off the tree. In a hurry, I reached out my hand, grabbing a hold of her arm as she swung forward, hitting the tree trunk. She held her bow in her other hand as I gritted my teeth, trying to pull her up. Figures grabbed at her legs and she screamed, trying to kick them off. I watched as my shield started sliding off my belt. I couldn't grab it because I was holding onto the tree and Sapphire. I watched as it fell into the group of figures.

"Swing me up," she said, "I'll make it."

I gritted my teeth, swinging her back and forth. I threw her up, hoping she'll catch the branch in time. She was too far away in the air for me to catch her again. Sapphire extended her arm, wrapping it around the tree trunk. She pulled herself up, breathing heavily.

"That would've been a long drop," she said, staring at the crowd of figures.

The tree shook again and we clutched onto the bark of the tree. I put my sword quickly back into my sheath. "What is happening?"

"I think the Maze is shifting."

The tree shook and the scene in front of me shifted into something else. I was sitting in a foggy forest with my back propped against a tree trunk. My sword was still in my sheath along with my knives.

I looked around, trying to find Sapphire in the fog but she was nowhere to be seen. "Sapphire!" I yelled, getting up. No one.

My Mark throbbed and something didn't feel right. My heart started to beat rapidly and my mouth went dry. In the distance, a shadow began to emerge from the fog. I watched as the shadow started gaining features. It was a man. The same man from my dreams.

He walked closer to me, his dark hair spewing around in the slight wind. The man had rough features with piercings in his ears. As he came closer, there was a piercing in his lip and he had dark, green eyes. I didn't recognize him.

"To believe we would meet like this," he said, his voice chillingly soft and exquisite.

"Who are you?" I asked, my hand gripped onto my sword.

He smiled, his piercing moving uncomfortably across his lip. "Don't play that game, Esther Green. You know *exactly* who I am."

I furrowed my brows, watching as he moved closer to me. I backed up surreptitiously until I touched the tree behind me. He let out a cold laugh.

"You always amaze me," he said, reaching out his hand to stroke my face. I moved out of the way but I felt a strong force on my body move me upright. His hand caressed my cheek.

I flinched under his cold touch, trying to move away but I couldn't. Was this happening inside my mind? "Who are *you?*"

"Don't be afraid when I tell you," he stated calmly. His hand moved down my cheek, onto my shoulder, down to my wrist. He grabbed my wrist furiously, pulling at my battle uniform greedily. The man made it to where my Mark was showing. I watched as a smile grew across his lips and his eyes illuminated with hunger.

"Don't touch me," I said, trying to move away but I was still planted on the ground.

"I can kill you," he said, rubbing his fingers across the intricate designs. No images appeared. "After all of these years searching for what I greatly desire... I found it..." He stared at me, frowning. "It's a shame I have to kill such a beautiful woman for Brilliance... But at least I'll know how to take control of this world."

"Dante Jett," I stated, coming to the fearful conclusion. But was this real?

He smiled. "I also brought a friend of mine."

In the fog behind him, another shadow protruded out of the darkness almost on cue. She had familiar white hair and pale features. Luna. I felt my blood starting to pump faster and my heart began to race. This couldn't be real. I killed her.

Dante laughed. "Luna, she's afraid of you. I can feel her blood pulse uncontrollably."

She stood next to him. The outline of her was heavenly.

297

White light surrounded her and she looked nearly transparent. "I did kill her mother." Luna laughed coldly.

Whatever Dante was doing to my body, I had to fight it. I moved my arm and I realized it was actually easy. Maybe he took it off? Quickly, I pulled out my sword, slashing Dante across the chest. He grabbed his chest while groaning out in pain.

I ran across the sticks, putting a force field around me, protecting myself from whatever mind tricks they were doing.

"Get her," I heard Dante say quietly.

I turned myself invisible, stopping to hide behind a tree. I tried to calm myself down as Luna moved in my direction quickly. I looked at the ground below her, realizing she was levitating. What the hell?

"I can't find her," Luna said quietly.

"Well, who else should I bring back?" Dante asked impatiently.

She smiled. "The Bloodsuckers. Jeremy and Darius."

I heard a large crack in the fog behind me. I turned around, noticing two more heavenly figures coming my way.

"Fire until you see resistance," Jeremy stated calmly.

"Finally, my revenge. If only the boy was here too."

Jeremy laughed. "It wasn't fair that I was killed by him."

Darius chuckled calmly. "You have to be stronger."

He looked in my direction, motioning Luna to stay away so he could burn everything he saw. I moved away quietly, trying to step backwards so I could see where Darius was positioning his fire. He held out his hands and fire spewed out, burning the nature around him. I watched as the trees had fire rolling up them, charring the trees as they swayed in the wind.

I noticed fire jolting my direction and I jumped out of the way so they wouldn't notice my resistance. I landed onto a pile of sticks and my force field broke every single twig, making loud cracking noises.

"Over there!" Luna yelled, pointing in my direction.

Darius smiled, spewing fire in my direction. My force field rejected the fire and I watched as Dante smiled.

"Get her Jeremy," Dante said.

Jeremy smiled as he walked forward. He trudged down a slight hill, coming near me triumphantly. I stepped back, trying to get away enough so they couldn't find me. *Oh, hell with it.* I took off running down a hill. I maneuvered around trees, raising my arms as I bounced down the hill, trying to balance myself. I looked behind me and Jeremy was running after me. He could hear every step I made.

I faced forward, continuing to run as fast as I could. I flicked out my hand, creating a fiery force field. It hit a tree next to him. I always had bad aim when I was running. I flicked out my hand again, creating a sharp force field that sliced down a tree on his other side. The tree came tumbling down, crashing against a few other trees. I felt the ground vibrate as the trees smashed against the forest floor.

I felt a force knock me down onto the ground and in a hurry, I flipped my body around so I could see what happened. Jeremy was on top of me, smiling. I looked down at my body, realizing it was revealed.

"Fine," I said. "You got me. You can get up now." I added humor despite my fear and surprisingly, he listened. Jeremy got up, laughing.

"Who wins now?" he asked.

"Definitely not you." I kicked out my leg, smashing it into his testicles. He screamed out in agony and I grabbed my sword, readying to slash him across the throat until I felt everything in my body shift. My hand released the sword and my head snapped back. My legs lifted calmly off the ground and I was levitating.

I heard Dante's laugh. "You think you're so clever."

I squirmed in the uncomfortable position, trying to free myself.

"Cause her pain," Dante stated. "Make her feel sorry for slashing me with her sword. Teach her *discipline.*"

I felt a cold hand grab my wrist and I heard an intake of air. I felt sharp, penetrating teeth clamp down against my skin and I let out a scream. I felt my arm losing blood rapidly.

"Not too much, Jeremy," Dante said. "I won't be able to control her."

The teeth released my throbbing wrist and I fell to the ground. Dante stood over me, smiling.

"Do you wonder *how* I was able to bring back your enemies?" he asked. "Ava Blacksmith and I are quite the close friends if you ask me. These hallucinations can only happen when

you enter places like this. Mazes. Things that mess with your mind."
He crouched down next to me, his mouth inches away from my ear.
"I guess you're wondering if I'm *real*."

Suddenly, there was a scream and the sound of a body
dropped to the ground. A figure dressed in black leaped into the air,
sliding a sword through Jeremy's heart. Fire spewed out of Darius's
hands, trying to keep up with the fast figure.

Quickly, the figure shinned up a tree with no hesitation.
Darius attempted burning the tree down with pursed lips. Dante
gritted his teeth, bending down as he wrapped his broad arms around
me. He tried to run but his wound was weakening him. I could tell
by his heavy breathing.

I heard another thump, indicating another body hit the
ground. The figure in black appeared behind Dante, stabbing him in
the shoulder slyly. The figure flipped over, his hands tightening
around me as he carefully took me out of Dante's arms. He carried
me close to his chest but I couldn't see his face. My vision was
beginning to blur due to loss of blood.

He carried me bridal style as he ran through the woods,
kicking up onto trees every once in a while, to give him a boost. We
came to a clearing and the sun shined on us. Despite my blurry
vision, I could see intense features with sharp cheekbones. His black
hair was matted on his head, sticking up in a few places. His eyes
were brown and slanted. Cadoen. It was the first time I saw his face
and just like his sister, he was also very handsome.

Cadoen continued running, not even breaking a sweat. He
looked down at me with an expression I wasn't expecting. *Hatred*.
After that, everything went black.

"She's losing blood quickly," Electra stated. I couldn't see anything;
I could only hear.

"Hurry, give me the Extreginishera. It gives her more blood,"
Sapphire said.

"Okay." I heard shuffling in a wooden box and then it
stopped. "I found it."

"Thanks." Sapphire took my head gently. "Esther, if you can
hear me, please drink this." I felt a cold glass against my lips. The air
wafted with the smell of baby barf and urine. I opened my mouth
slightly and I felt the warm liquid ooze over my tongue. I choked on

the awful taste.

"Swallow," Electra stated.

I allowed the liquid to slide down. I heard my stomach rumble once the acid started to break down quickly, almost faster than any type of digestion.

"Open your eyes," Sapphire said gently.

I allowed them to flutter open. I was sitting in an area that resembled a dentist's room. There were glasses of colorful liquids on a shelf next to a window. "What was that?" I referred to the event in the woods.

Sapphire touched me, feeding off of my memories. "Sorry," she stated. "Cado wouldn't tell me." She continued analyzing my thoughts. "I think it was a hallucination."

"It couldn't have been a hallucination," I stated. "I lost blood. Dante was *real*. Cado even had to fight them off."

Sapphire shook her head in disbelief. "How? How could he possibly get into *our* Maze?"

"He said he used Ava Blacksmith," I said. "You even saw what I saw. It was real."

"But people that are dead were there."

"I don't know, Sapphire. She has a point. Ava Blacksmith does some crazy shit," Electra said.

"Hello?" Another voice said. "Is she alright?"

"Yes, Acea," I stated. "I'm fine."

"You haven't talked to me directly since we got here."

I shook my head. "I don't want to deal with this right now, okay? Just please be happy that I saved your life."

"Just be happy that I'm here with you," he said, walking out of the room.

Electra stared at me with a grin plastered on her face. "Interesting. Boy troubles."

I rolled my eyes. "Trust me. We're not at all like that."

"Back on topic," Sapphire said. "Do you think that was the real Dante?"

I swallowed. "He seemed vague. But I do believe it was the real him."

"I think I know his ability also," she said. "Not only is he wise, he's also a Puppet Master. Only Ava could create such a rare ability."

"What's that? And how could she create it? Wasn't Dante born with it?" I asked, my curiosity sinking in.

"Puppet Master is the ability to bend someone's shape... To construct them by the blood," Sapphire stated meekly.

"That's explains why I couldn't move," I cut her off.

She nodded her head. "Since Ava poses as a Witch and she's nearly over a few centuries old, she could have created a potion, gave it to an individual and then that person carried it on through generations. Therefore, Dante could have been a part of that generation and he received the ability from blood. Just like how the Bloodsuckers were made. The Shadows. Anything else we haven't discovered yet."

"One strange place," I stated, shaking my head in disbelief.

Sapphire smiled slightly. "It sure is."

"Something that I'm still confused on is how Cado found Esther," Electra said.

Sapphire shrugged. "I guess he was at the right place at the right time. I could talk to him about it."

Electra laughed. "'Talk' to him about it."

"He's just having a hard time understanding his place, Electra, and you know that."

"Okay, Sassy Saphy." She laughed again and I couldn't help but smile.

"I want to practice again," I said once everyone calmed down. "Not in the Maze, of course. But don't you have practice ranges?"

"Are you sure you'll be up for that? I mean, you just didn't face your enemy or anything... And he hasn't killed you," Electra said.

I rolled my eyes. "Yes. I'll be fine with it. Trust me."

"Okay," Sapphire said. "Cado should be at the Range. Electra and I will go in the Maze. Phoenix is already in there."

I nodded my head. "Oh. And where did you go when I was transported somewhere else?"

"I was sent back to the beginning of the Maze. I realized you weren't with me and I thought that was odd."

"Geez."

I adjusted my uniform in the Range hut where the supplies were held. I grabbed a longbow along with the arrows. I slung the arrow holder across my back, keeping the longbow in my hand. In my peripheral vision, I saw a shiny black object. It was a grapple. I picked it up, connecting it onto my wrist. It was time to learn new things.

I walked out of the hut and was greeted by the sunlight. In front of me next to the tree line, stood three, large pillars. They were probably for grappling. Next to me was a red button that signaled the structures to make faceless people and willingly, I pressed it. A loud beeping sound rang in my ears and I took off running.

I held out my arm and I pressed the grapple. A large hook sprang out of its container, connecting onto a pillar. It took me up and I smiled as the wind smacked me in the face.

My feet slammed against the side of the pillar and slowly, I allowed myself to climb it. I made it to the top in one simple movement and I took out an arrow, loading it into my bow. Figures made their way around the pillars.

I scanned the area, focusing on only a few figures as my target. Taking deep breaths, I released the wire and the arrow shot out, penetrating none of the figures. Quickly, I loaded the bow again, aimed and then shot. I hit three in a row and I felt like I was getting use to the arrows now.

Suddenly, I felt something clamp onto my calf. I turned around, noticing a few figures climbed up the back of the pillar. Spontaneously, I smacked the figure in the face with the edge of the bow like Sapphire had done. The faceless man fell off the pillar, smacking into a few others that were trying to climb it.

My heart began to race as the figures were standing on the same platform as me. I smashed a few in the face with the edge of my bow. A figure clamped its cold, slimy hand on my wrist and instinctively, I pulled my hand down. The figure followed my movement and I kneed her in the face. A few more figures began touching me and I yelped.

"Are you serious?" I said aloud as my aggravation kicked in.

I lifted my leg up, kicking one in the groin. Quickly, I moved to the side of the pillar so I had a better view. I brought up my fist and I hit another figure in the face.

More came at me and I lifted my bow, loading it with an arrow quickly. I shot down four in one shot. I loaded the bow again and shot, killing two. More figures came and they were huddling around me. I had no choice but to stop the practice session.

My Mark throbbed and I looked down. The grapple was placed firmly over the Mark. I had an idea. I moved forward, beating the figures in my way with the edge of my bow. I gritted my teeth as I tried my best to punch each figure out of the way. I came to the edge of the pillar and I took deep breaths, trying not to let my fear overcome me. I jumped off the side of the pillar and my stomach did somersaults.

I shifted my body in the air, trying to stay leveled. Quickly, before I would hit the ground, I held out my wrist and the metal claw shot out, connecting onto a new pillar. I felt everything in my body lurch forward once I changed directions. My body sprang up, following the movement of the rope and gracefully, I landed on top of the pillar.

In the distance, Cado finally showed up. He was trying to climb up the pillar that had the figures on it with two knives. Every once in a while, he would stab a figure so he had a place to put his knife. He made it to the top quickly and I watched as he took out a sword. He stood still for a few moments and his chest heaved.

Suddenly, he lunged forward, attacking each figure that came near him. One by one, the bodies fell to the ground as he fought each one off with no difficulty.

"Well, seems like you have it under control," I said quietly. I allowed my grapple to take me back to the ground. I unhooked the claw and it slid back into its chamber. I glanced back up at the figures and I could only see Cado fighting. Nothing was near him. It was because I broke out of the circle.

"Thanks again for stealing my practice session," I said, shaking my head in disapproval. "Means a lot." He already had practice. He was a master at martial arts. I didn't see why Cado had to keep fighting. I threw the weapons into the large bucket angrily.

I laid in my bed, trying to block out the loud pots and pans clacking together in the kitchen. Images of Dante flowed back into my head slowly. Was that real? Did he really bring back my enemies only to have Cadoen kill them? And why was Cado such a jerk?

I rolled over and groaned. I missed my mother. I missed her looks of disapproval and her kind, sweet words. I loved it when she called me beautiful. I loved her and now she was gone. That's what the Creators wanted. They wanted to hurt the people around me so they could strike me in the heart.

Today was the last day for practice. I decided to spend it in my room doing nothing. Sapphire said it was best for me to receive rest so I ate ice cream and watched TV. I deliberately avoided the news and focused more on the cartoons. I didn't bother to dress out of my nightgown. I took a shower in the morning and threw the nightgown back on because I could. My mother wouldn't agree with it but I would.

There was a loud noise and I glanced up, noticing it was Acea. I looked back at the TV and I tried my best not to think about him. I didn't want him to die but I also didn't want us to be more than friends. Heck, I didn't even want to be friends. He proved his point. Acea only cared for me to let Leila know my weaknesses.

"Esther, we need to talk," Acea said, sitting on the edge of my bed.

"Did you know there's this magical thing called 'knocking'. You should try it sometime." I shoved some popcorn into my face.

"You're not even acting like yourself. What happened to the brave, heroic, beautiful Esther?" His green eyes reflected my appearance.

"Did you just say I'm not beautiful right now? Who cares? It's the personality that matters. Obviously, you wouldn't know what that means."

"I'm sorry that I hurt you." He reached his hand up to stroke my face but I moved away quickly, spilling my popcorn.

"Hurt me? You think you're the reason why I'm in here eating and relaxing?" I shouted. "No. It's not you. If you haven't noticed my mother was killed a few days ago. My dad died from cancer. I don't even *have* a family anymore. I saw Dante yesterday and he tried to kill me. I lost so much." I glared at him; my face was emotionless besides the tears forming in my eyes. "But even though all of this has happened, I'm still willing to stand up and fight back. *I'm going to make them regret what they did to me.*" I got up from the bed, staring him directly in the eyes. "I'm going to fight this War headstrong."

"Then fight it," Acea said quietly.

"You're not coming with us tomorrow. You're staying here

until we return."

"I want to come with you."

"You're just going to get killed," I stated firmly. "You're *staying* here or I'll have Phoenix take you home."

He gritted his teeth. "Fine. It's not like I have a part in this anyways."

"Phoenix!" I yelled.

"I didn't mean it like that," Acea said quickly. "I meant I'll stay here. I want to know that you're *not going to die*." He paused. "And you're not the only one who lost someone." He got up from the bed. "Leila... Friends from school that I saw burn alive... I even thought I was going to die." Acea stared at me, his face mirrored my expression. "But you saved me." He walked out of the room, passing Phoenix simultaneously.

"What's up?" Phoenix asked me, leaning against the doorway. "You dropped your popcorn?"

"N—well, yes. But that's not it. Never mind."

"I think it's awful you didn't practice today." He stared at me menacingly. "Those Compounds are awful. Anyone could die tomorrow. Including you if Dante decides to show up."

"I needed a break."

"Bad choice," he said. He turned on his heels and left my room without another word. I rolled my eyes, crossing my arms.

"Two boys left your room," another voice said. "Wow, Esther. You're really drawing them away." Sapphire smiled at me.

I returned it. "Well, I suppose so. It's better that way though." I sat back onto my bed.

"What about that one boy?" she asked. "Damion?"

I shrugged my shoulders, reaching up to grab my locket that my mother gave me. There had to be a reason why our initials were on it. Alvaro probably informed my mother about something. "I know we'll see each other again."

Sapphire smiled warmly. "Hopefully I'll be there the day you do."

"You will. How couldn't you?"

She shrugged. "I don't know. Oh, and tomorrow, wake up at five. Alright? We need to get our supplies. I don't have any abilities that are helpful in fights so I use weapons. Cado taught me."

"Does Cado hate me?" I asked, changing the subject.

"I wouldn't say he hates you..." her voice trailed off.

"So, you do know something?" I asked, raising my eyebrows.

She smiled slightly. "Shut up and get some food."

"I want to know what he said," I stated.

"He doesn't tell me anything, Esther. I swear." She placed a tray of food on my bed.

"Fine. I'll take your word for it."

"Eat this up. I expect you to be ready tomorrow morning. Good night."

"Goodnight, Sapphire. And thanks for everything." I gave her a smile and she returned it while walking out of my room.

I stood outside next to Sapphire and Electra. The wind whipped around wildly and my eyes felt like they were glued shut due to tiredness. A crack of thunder sounded overhead, making Electra jump beside me. We were all dressed in our battle gear and Phoenix was giving us an introduction to new weapons.

"Why do we use weapons?" Phoenix asked like he was a teacher.

"Because we could have a loss of energy or we are bid from our abilities," I answered.

He stared at me intently: expressionless. "Yes." He continued explaining each weapon he gave us. He never gave us a gun though. Not even Creators used guns. It could make things easier but it feels too useless.

I carried an archery set that was strapped across my back, a grapple, a sheath that circled around my waist that was filled with knives and a sword. I had a shield that was attached to my archery gear. I had fireproof black gloves on.

"Esther, you're going to walk in there invisible. You're going to get passed the Membrane because they can't see you. In the Compound, there should be a Nucleus that has buttons that could self-destruct the robots that guard the Membrane. Therefore, the four of us can make it into the Compound without fighting off their armed forces. Eventually they're going to discover something is up." He paused to make sure that I was listening. "From there we fight anyone who gets in our way until we make it to the area where the Clockworks are being held. We fight off those guards and we need to use their fingers to unlock the cells. From there, we lead the

Clockworks out of the Compound. Okay?"

I nodded my head, swallowing. "Okay."

"Don't screw this up, Rookie," Phoenix stated. "The four of us are happy that we don't have to fight to break the Membrane." He looked at everyone else. "Ready?"

We all nodded our heads besides Cado. He continued staring at me with twisted anger. So much for sharing a Prophecy with him.

Phoenix turned his back to us, molding a fiery, green substance in his hands. Phrixus's portal was purple unlike Phoenix's. In time, there was a crackling, green portal in front of us. We all jumped in and the portal swallowed us willingly. Green light shook us back and forth and, in the distance, I could see a dark, gray sky.

The portal spat us out and we landed on the ground. There was a slight sprinkle of rain and a crack of lightning once every twenty seconds. We all got up clumsily and hid behind a large rock in the empty field. In the distance was a large Compound that was created out of iron and bricks. It was shaped differently from any other buildings I saw.

"Try and hurry, Esther," Sapphire stated quietly. "Don't make any noises or they'll find us... Or you."

"Okay." I focused on a rushing, cascading waterfall and I could feel myself sway back and forth. I felt the sensation and I knew I was invisible.

"Good luck," she said. "Don't get hurt."

I walked out from behind the rocks and I ran across the field. Up ahead I could see the figures that took the shape of large, metal Bots. The Creators were getting fancy with their knowledge. I slowed down once I was twenty meters away from the robots. I moved quietly so my armor wouldn't crack or clank.

I bit my lip as I edged closer to the Membrane. I was only ten meters away now. The robots stared ahead blankly and I could see liquids and substances in tubes connected to their sides. It was probably the abilities that the robots were given.

I was only a few meters away from the large, ten-foot robots. They stared ahead and I knew they couldn't notice me. I bit my lip and I could taste blood in my mouth as I tried to shimmy myself between two robot torsos. I held my breath so they couldn't hear me. Suddenly, I heard a loud clank of metal and I noticed my shield touched the robot behind me. My heart began to race as the robot looked around, trying to find anybody. The robot shrugged its metal shoulders and continued looking ahead. I let out all of my air once I passed them.

I moved quietly down the dark facility, trying to figure out where the Nucleus could be. In the distance, there were a few Creators socializing. I wanted to wipe them out but I knew it would jeopardize the mission.

"Would you like to see it?" a woman with blue glasses and her hair tied up in a bun asked a man.

"Yes. I heard it's the best one out there," the man stated with a chuckle.

"It controls almost every setting besides the Clockwork Cells," the woman replied with a smile. She turned on her high heels and they walked down a hallway together. Hopefully she was taking him to the Nucleus.

I followed them down a dark hallway. They walked up a flight of metal stairs and willingly and quietly, I walked up the stairs behind them. The sounds of her clacking high heels washed out the noise my armor was making.

"When Mr. Jett checks out your Ratings, would he be impressed?" the man asked.

"Oh, yes, most certainly," she said with a cackle.

I followed them around a sharp bend and up another flight of metal steps.

"Ready to be amazed?" the woman asked.

"Yes. Of course."

We stopped at a set of huge double doors. She gestured her hand forward as she opened the doors. I followed them inside and I held my breath. The room was lit with blue lighting and there was computers and buttons everywhere. There were two visible floors and Creators were either working on a monitor or they were walking around. Everyone had dark gray uniforms on with the symbol of blood plastered across their breast plate. The symbol was a drop of blood that was going to fall into a body of water.

I walked away from the people I had been following. I trudged up another flight of metal stairs. I walked across the balcony, trying to find a button or section that controlled the robots. Suddenly I heard a set of feet running across the metal balcony. I turned around, noticing a woman was staring directly at me. Could she see me? I watched as a green substance formed in her palms.

Instinctively, I created a large, powerful force field. It probably wasn't a good idea that I was using up all of my energy now.

The green substance collided into my force field and I watched as it started to seep through it so I created another strong, thick force field.

"Roxe! Intruder! Come and bid!" the woman screamed.

"I don't see you and I don't see the intruder," a large, robust man said behind the woman.

"You're behind me and the girl is in front of me."

I was still confused but I couldn't stand and wait for something to happen. Before the woman and Roxe could get to me, I pushed out a force field that knocked them back into a wall filled with monitors and controls. Creators turned to look at what happened.

"Nania!" someone shouted. "Who is it? Who do you see?"

The woman fell from the wall and Roxe followed. She stood up, staring at the man.

"The girl has invisibility. I can see her because I have the same ability," Nania stated, staring at me. Well that made sense.

"Where is she?" the man asked.

"The balcony."

I turned around quickly, colliding into a man that was the size of an ape. I gulped. He reached his hand out and I backed away but he touched me. I felt the energy inside me dissipate and I groaned.

"Crap," I muttered. I turned on my heels, running across the balcony. All of the Creators quit what they were doing and they yelled and shouted, coming close to me. I was really sick of people that could bid abilities. It wasn't fair anymore.

Abilities flung my way and I screamed, jumping over the balcony so I wouldn't get hit. I held out my wrist and the grapple jolted me forward. There was a group of Creators in the way of my landing so I stuck my legs out. I released the claw, kicking the Creators down so I could land. I ran forward and I turned to look behind me. Creators were running my way and I felt my stomach churn with fear. I continued running, taking my arrows out so I could occasionally shoot a few arrows back.

I loaded the arrow into my bow and I turned slightly so I could run forward but still shoot the Creators behind me. I released the wire and the arrow shot through two people. I saw fire hurtle my way and quickly, the grapple swung me up into the air and my stomach did somersaults. I landed on a beam that held the ceiling together. I sat on it, aiming down at the Creators below me. Biting my lip, I focused on a group of Creators that were readying to shoot at me with their abilities. I had to find the man that bid me from mine and kill him.

I released the wire and the arrows penetrated a few Creators before they could hit me. I slung the archery set onto my back and I pulled out my sword. I positioned the grapple to take me back to the first level. It sprung me forward and I held out my sword as I hurtled to the ground. I slashed at a few Creators, cutting them across their throats. Suddenly, I felt myself hurtle to the ground faster than usual. I looked ahead, realizing a Creator disintegrated the rope.

I smacked into the tile floor and I slid across the ground, bumping my head against a Creator's foot. Next to the Creator was a monitor that showed a video image of the Membrane. Cado, Electra, Sapphire and Phoenix were trying to fight off the robots. I gritted my teeth. What were they doing? Did they have any patience?

The Creator picked me up from the hair and I groaned, trying to get his hands off my hair. His hand started to form an unknown substance and spontaneously, I swung my legs forward, kicking him in the groin. He doubled over, clutching his sensitive area. I brought up my fist and I smashed him in the nose. I looked around frantically for my sword but I couldn't find it. I grabbed a knife out of my sheath, stabbing the Creator in the gut. He fell over completely and his blood spewed out.

I turned around, noticing a ball of fire hurtling my way. I grabbed my shield, holding it out in front of me. The fire smashed into the shield and I could feel the heat of the flames on my face. Now I understood why we had gloves on. Our hands would burn if we didn't.

I found my sword a distance away and before the Creator could regenerate, I leaped across the ground, grabbing my sword. I continued sliding and I held the shield out in front of me as another ball of fire collided into it.

I stood up clumsily, staring at the Creator. I realized he was the one that bid my abilities. I threw the shield onto the ground and quickly, I grabbed my bow and an arrow. I loaded it and shot. The arrow zoomed forward and I stared at it intently, hoping it would penetrate the man. The arrow came close to him and I watched as it hit him in the chest. He fell to the ground and I yelled in excitement, feeling all of my energy coming back to me.

Creators ran forward, screaming at the top of their lungs. Series of blue, yellow, orange and purple abilities flew forward. I gritted my teeth, forming a large, clear force field that pushed all of the Creators back. With my hands, I molded the force field around the huge group of people, enclosing them. I smiled in relief that it worked. I only had to think about keeping it there until I left.

I turned around, staring at the monitor. The four of them were bloody as they tried to fight off the robots. I glanced frantically at all of the buttons, trying to find the right one that would demolish the metal structures. I turned around again, staring at all of the Creators that were trying to break my force field.

"Tell me how to destruct the robots!" I yelled. They all stared at me with smiles plastered on their faces. "If you don't tell me there will be consequences." The crowd erupted into laughter. In the first row of Creators, I saw a man and woman laughing, their hands clasped together. *Fine*, I thought, *I'll just destroy the heart like they did to me.*

A force field jolted out of my hands, breaking into the previous force field. I wrapped it around the woman, bringing her forward quickly. I held my sword out and it slid through the field. The metal was inches away from her neck and she stared down at me, slightly gasping with astonishment.

"I didn't know a Protector could be so powerful," she breathed.

"Tell me how the robots could self-destruct," I stated dryly.

"I'm not going to tell you." She had long blonde hair and round features.

"Fine. Then he will." I looked at the man she was once holding. "Tell me or she dies." He glanced at the woman fearfully and I watched as he started to shake. The man obviously didn't want her to die.

I pressed the sword against the woman's neck and I felt my heart become cold. I wanted to hurt anyone the best I could emotionally. I stared at her with no remorse. She quivered underneath the cold blade, breathing heavily.

"Yellow button," she said quietly. In my peripheral vision I saw the man relax.

I pushed the woman back into the other force field, returning her to the man. He pressed his body into her and he gave her a hug of relief. I shook my head as guilt began to form inside of me. That wasn't me? I wouldn't threaten someone just to hurt another emotionally?

I turned around and I noticed the yellow button. I pressed down on the cold surface and I watched the robots blow up on the monitor. The four Clockworks cheered as they ran into the Compound.

I smiled slightly at their cheering. Cadoen was the only one who kept moving. I ran out of the Nucleus, heading down the metal flights of stairs. I rounded a corner, eventually meeting up with the four Clockworks.

"What took you so long?" Phoenix shouted.

"Nothing is going to happen smoothly," I stated. "Somehow a woman that has invisibility saw me when she was invisible. I suppose it's a normal thing that I never heard of."

"We need to keep moving. The Clockwork Facility shouldn't be far from the Nucleus," Electra said.

We ran forward and our armor clanked together. Up ahead was a set of guards guarding a metal door. They stared at us, waiting for the right moment.

"Electra, you know what to do," Sapphire said with a smile as we continued running.

"Of course."

Electra held her hand out in front of her and a yellow, oozing liquid hurtled towards the men. They counterattacked by turning into a set of metal figures. Simultaneously, the men stepped forward and an electric blue liquid came our way. I held up a force field that was wide enough to cover us.

"Their metal only lasts for fifteen seconds," Sapphire said. "The metal relies on our abilities to generate it. If we hold still for fifteen seconds, they'll be powerless until we act again." She glanced at Cado and nodded her head. He returned it. Cado had to be the one to fight the men in fifteen seconds.

In my peripheral vision, blue, sizzling liquid jolted our way. I wanted to make a force field until I reminded myself I couldn't.

"Jump!" Phoenix shouted.

Sapphire and I jumped behind a brick wall. Cado, Phoenix and Electra landed on the other side of the hallway. I glanced at Sapphire and she smiled.

"If they catch us, I have a backup plan."

"What's that?" I asked.

"To keep you safe I decided to do something." She raised her sleeve, revealing the Mark of Brilliance on her wrist. It was obviously painted but it looked realistic.

"I don't need saving," I said. "I don't die unless Dante kills me. If they hurt you knowing you won't die, well, you will die."

"Esther, we're *friends*. I want to die knowing that I did something right. I will die as a hero."

"Let's just hope you don't die," I said, staring at her dark eyes. She was determined to save me. I only knew her for a few days but it felt longer.

"Why are their metal bodies still there?" Sapphire asked. "It's been longer than fifteen seconds."

"Is anyone using their abilities?" Phoenix asked over the loud noise of crackling blue liquid.

Who could be using their abilities? It would be known if they did. Wait... I still had the force field against the Creators in the Nucleus. I released my focus on the field and I watched as the blue liquid continued coming near us.

"Keep your legs behind the wall," I told Sapphire, noticing her legs were slightly sticking out. She pulled them closer to her.

Suddenly, there was a loud crackling noise and we all pulled our heads in the direction of the metal figures. Cado sprung forward, running quickly with his arms behind his back. He used the wall to leap up around the now human Creators. He held his sword out in front of him and one of the Creators with dark skin shot his liquid at Cado. I tried to retain my equanimity when Cado jumped over the man, rapturously slicing the lighter man's head off. The man with dark features screamed, throwing his sizzling liquid at Cado.

Cado yelled out in pain as he clutched his shoulder. My heart did somersaults and quickly, I ran forward, pulling out my sword and I held my shield close to my chest.

"No!" Phoenix screamed, running forward. A bolt of the liquid hurtled his way and he jumped behind the wall again. "Come back Esther!"

"Esther?" the man asked, cocking his head to the side. A sly smile grew across his face as he stared at me intimately.

I continued running forward, trying to stay brave. The sizzling liquid zoomed my way and I held up my shield. I felt the heavy substance smack into the shield and I felt my feet lift off the ground. I fell back onto the ground and clumsily, in a hurry, I got up, breathing heavily. I wiped my hair out of my face.

Cado stared at me a distance away. I saw pain reflecting in his eyes and I knew he was fighting to say something. I saw another bolt of the blue substance hurtling my way and I jumped out of the way, sliding into the brick wall. The man chuckled but he still stayed glued in his spot.

I got up, holding onto my elbow. The stitching of my uniform was ripped and there was blood pouring out of my wound from sliding.

"Esther is here!" The man shouted as the sounds of footsteps protruded behind me. I whipped around and all of the Creators that were in the Nucleus were standing a few meters away. Amusement lit up their eyes and they stared at all of us.

Suddenly, there was a scream behind me. Cado bent over the man with his sword lunged inside the man. Cado lifted up the heavy individual, using his finger to open the door. The door opened with a loud crack of metal.

"Hurry!" I screamed at the Clockworks behind me.

I watched as abilities rang out, trying to shoot us down. I held my hands out in front of me, moving them in a circular motion. A clear force field formed in my hands and I pushed it out, trying to block Electra and the rest of them from getting hit. I used my emotional strength to push it into the Creators. I screamed as a sudden sense of ennui swept inside of me. I had to be strong. I had to hold all of them off.

"Come on!" Electra shouted. "The door can hold them off once we shut it!"

I focused on the powerful force field so I could back up. I followed Sapphire and Cado into the metal room that held another set of guards that were ready to fight.

Once we were in, Phoenix slammed his fist down on a button that shut the door. I released the focus on the force field and slowly, I felt my energy regain.

"Spread out!" Phoenix shouted as a bolt of lightning zipped passed my head, hitting the door. I inhaled a take of breath, turning around to stare at the next set of guards.

"They're not metal figures," Sapphire stated. "We can use our abilities."

She huddled over Cado in the corner of the room, using her water to heal Cado's wound. I put a small enough force field around them so she could do her work.

Two bolts of yellow and silver thundering lightning hurtled our way. Phoenix leaped into the air, turning his body so the bolts wouldn't touch him. Acid sprung out of his hands and instinctively, the three Creators moved out of the way. More lightning regenerated in their palms.

Behind me, a sound of metal breaking arose from the crack of the lightning. I turned around and a shape formed in the metal. The Creators were breaking down the door. Why didn't they just use the man's finger?

"We have to hurry!" I shouted.

"Here!" Electra shouted, trying to block the lightning. "I have an idea!" Lightning formed around her arms, moving quickly down to her hands. "Release the force field on Sapphire so you can manipulate the lightning because you have low energy levels."

Lightning cracked out of her hands and spontaneously, I created a force field that held the lightning captive. I saw the force field slowly cracking as the lightning jolted wildly inside of it. I pushed the force field out and Phoenix jumped out of the way. I released the force field next to the Creators and the lightning burned each of them alive.

The door behind me burst open and I felt cold metal slam into my back, pushing me against Phoenix. I screamed in alarm, noticing we were going to be crushed into the next metal door. Phoenix tried to disintegrate the door but it didn't work. I held him close to my body, closing my eyes as I held my hand out. I used a force field that collided into the metal door.

"Think weightless!" I yelled.

I thought about the feeling of no gravity. I could feel my

body moving swiftly in the air and overturning slowly and gradually. I opened my eyes and Phoenix and I were clutching each other. We were laying on the ground with a clear blue force field around us. The metal door that burst open collided into the force field, shattering itself into millions of pieces.

I breathed heavily, shaking Phoenix. "It's alright. We're alive."

He opened his eyes, staring up at the force field. "I thought we were going to die."

"Me too," I said, nearly out of energy. "My energy. It's low. I used too much power already."

He shook his head in anger. "Why didn't you use it gradually?"

"Because I was too busy saving your sorry ass," I stated dryly.

"Guys," Sapphire yelled. "The door! Open that door!"

"Find Esther!" one of the Creators yelled. "Kill them all. The one that's alive is the Chosen one."

"Crap." I got up and Phoenix followed my movement. Series of oozing liquids, fiery explosions and any other ability hurtled our way.

"Use your last bit of energy for this!" Phoenix yelled.

I gritted my teeth, making a thick force field that was large enough to cover us. Abilities slammed into the force field and I heard a crack. "Open the door! Now!"

I heard the movement of metal behind me and slowly, I walked backwards so I could focus on the force field. Abilities repeatedly slammed themselves into the force field, cracking the surface even more. I didn't know I was in the next room until the door shut in front of me. I released my focus on the force field and I felt extremely weary. My feet gave way and I fell backwards. A set of strong arms grabbed my shoulders before my head could hit the ground. I looked up and it was Cado. He was absolutely opaque.

"Esther," Sapphire said, appearing over my shoulder. "It's alright... Everything is going to be fine." She caressed her soft hand on my cheek, trying to bring me back to reality. My vision began to blur. "Let's go save those Clockworks. Then we'll be done. Then we can rest."

I knew she was right. I couldn't give up. "Okay," I said with a nod. Sapphire grabbed my hand, helping me up. I swayed back and forth until I regained a little bit of my strength.

"We need to go up those stairs. It's only a matter of time before they break down the door," Phoenix said.

The five of us trotted up the metal flight of stairs. We walked across a narrow balcony that didn't have any railings.

"Wow, this sure is safe," Electra said.

Sapphire laughed. "True."

We stopped in front of a large, metal door that was more spacious than the others. I breathed heavily. We were close to taking down this Compound.

"Anything can be behind that door. Be cautious." Phoenix placed his hands on the door and slowly, he disintegrated it with his acid. The huge door slowly deteriorated and the sound of sizzling metal echoed throughout the room. This door was different from the others, almost easier to get in. That wasn't a good sign.

In front of us was a large room with metal pillars. It was the size of three football fields smashed together. In the distance, there was a dozen of Creators standing by another door. There were desks along the pillars that almost resembled a classroom.

"Something about these Creators doesn't seem right," Phoenix said.

"I have that feeling too," Electra said meekly.

We all shifted uncomfortably, wondering which side was going to attack first.

"Esther," Sapphire said. "We'll protect you." She nodded at Electra.

"Okay," I said.

Cado didn't wait any longer. He sprung forward, keeping his sword at his side. The Creators reacted quickly. I watched as their arms shifted strangely. Almost simultaneously, their arms transformed into a metal structure. They moved back as their metal arms shot out balls of fire at Cado. I held my breath as he jumped onto a pillar and then he kicked off of it, dodging each fireball.

Suddenly, a few Creators turned to the rest of us and shot with no remorse. Instantaneously, I lifted one of the desks, pushing it on its side before the fireballs collided into it. We all jumped behind the desk and we breathed heavily.

"What are those things on their arms?" I asked, keeping my

318

legs close to my chest. The sound of another fireball hitting the desk erupted into the air. We moved slightly further behind the desk so we wouldn't be burnt.

"I'm not sure," Sapphire stated. "It's odd."

"I don't know about each of you," Phoenix stated. "But I'm going to fight instead of hide." He stood up quickly before I could protest. In alarm, he swung his head in the direction of the Creators and I could hear the whizzing sound of a hurtling fireball.

"Phoenix!" I screamed, getting up expeditiously, wrapping my arms around his waist as I tried to bring him to the ground. I felt the ball of fire skim my back and my whole body engulfed in excruciating pain.

We landed abruptly on the ground, sliding across the floor. I released my grip on him, rolling onto my back and another wave of pain scorched my back. I gritted my teeth, trying not to scream.

"Why'd you do that?" Phoenix yelled, staring at me in disbelief. "I had it under control."

"Are you kidding me?" I snapped, trying to fight the pain. "You were *this* close to being killed." I held up my thumb and index finger.

"Why would you even risk your life for me?" he retorted, getting slowly up off the ground.

I gritted my teeth, staring at him with eyes full of venom. Why couldn't he just appreciate what I had done for him? "Remember, I'm the one that can't die."

He scoffed, reaching out his hand to help me up. "Sapphire, take care of her."

Another ball of fire hurtled our way and Phoenix willingly pushed me behind him, making me fall to the ground. He molded his hands together, quickly, in no time, creating a small portal in which the fireball went into. It disappeared into an unknown place.

"Esther," Sapphire said, staring at me with her back propped against a sturdy desk. "Come here. I'll fix that burn."

I nodded my head, crawling towards her in the chaos of fireballs and acid. Electra sat next to Sapphire, trying to maintain her breathing. I laid on my stomach next to her. I felt her soothing water gently caress my back and slowly, the pain began to dissipate.

"You feel better?" she asked, staring at me. I nodded my head. "I think the water may have given you some energy. I wouldn't rely on it though."

"Okay," I said. I glanced at Electra. "You ready? We need to help Cado and Phoenix."

"You're fighting too?" she asked with surprise plastered across her face.

"Off course. I'm not going to let all of you do the work."

She smiled. "Let's do it then."

We got up and two fireballs careened our way. I jumped out of the way and Electra followed my movement. We ran across the floor and I kept my eyes on the movement of the Creators. They laughed and joked but they stayed in place. They were guarding the door.

"Electra," I hushed. "We need to find a way for them to get away from the door."

She grinned wickedly, her pink lips pulling into a thin line. "I have an idea."

Electra sprung her hands out and bolts of lightning smacked into the door, making the Creators jump out of the way while screaming. A small smile spread across Cado's lips when he circled around two Creators, slicing at them with his sword while they were still on the ground. Phoenix darted acid at a few Creators and he laughed as the acid bit into their skin. I glanced back at Sapphire, making sure she was alright and unharmed. She didn't have much of a power to fight with and I knew she didn't feel comfortable with hand-on-hand combat in a time like this.

A few Creators were still guarding the door. They tried to focus on one of us to shoot but it was a mad house and they couldn't aim properly. I moved quickly, changing my direction occasionally so they couldn't lock onto me.

"Electra!" I screamed once we neared the door.

A bolt of lightning zoomed past my ear, striking down a Creator with gold hair. Another yellow substance shot out and it melted a Creator. I grabbed one of the knives in my belt so I could at least kill one of the Creators. I remembered how Acea taught me and I threw the knife. It spiraled through the air and it collided into a Creator's neck. I aimed for his chest but the neck was still good.

I ran towards the door. I grabbed the dead man's thumb, hovering it over a large desk with blue light that circled around its perimeter. Electra screamed a bloodcurdling scream behind me but I didn't look because I was too busy watching the screen boot up. A bolt of lightning zipped through the air and the sound of a scream erupted into my ears. She was fighting something back.

The screen reached 100% and I dropped the man's thumb. The humongous white door shifted its metal, turning knobs and wires counterclockwise. It slowly moved open and many dirty faces stared at me blankly. All of them were bewildered and malnourished.

"Okay," I said, taking a deep breath. "All of you need to come with us and we'll lead you out safely." That was the best I could think of.

"And who are you to tell us what to do?" asked an old man said with bright, yellow eyes. His mustache was white and he was bald but he still looked powerful and he surged with energy from his aura.

"Yeah. We only follow the Chosen," a girl said closer to the front, staring me down mysteriously. She had bright brown eyes and dark hair.

I rolled my eyes. It was obvious I had to show them the Mark. I rolled up my sleeve, revealing the intricate designs of Brilliance. Their mouths dropped slightly but they still remained strong with hope even though they had skinny complexions.

"Anyone can paint the Mark on themselves," the girl said.

"Just listen to me," I said eagerly, not wanting to sound too desperate. "We came here to save the rest of you so we can gather in the War to fight the Creators."

"Watch out!" a woman screamed, pushing through crowds of Clockworks.

I turned around abruptly, moving my hands through the air that created a clear and powerful, thick force field. The slimy substance collided into the force field, saving nearly all of the Clockworks in the front from death. At the other end of the chamber stood all of the Creators from the Nucleus. I turned around, staring at the Clockworks. My energy was weak.

"Please," I said, staring at their small, pale faces.

"Force fields and invisibility," someone from the group stated. "She already showed us the force field... The Mark... Her determination. I think she really is Esther Green."

"We don't have much of a choice now," the girl from the front said, moving forward. "If we want to get out, we have to fight our way out."

I released the force field behind me and I felt a small smile spread across my lips as all of the Clockworks cheered in unison. They lurched forward, passing me with harsh winds. The white scraps the Clockworks were wearing clashed with the gray uniforms the Creators wore. Series of abilities collided and a War of Freedom made itself known in front of me. Each of the Clockworks laughed as they joked with their inmates and killed off each Creator.

My heart skipped a few beats and I could feel myself choke on a slight laugh. I was filled with felicity. We had a chance to win the Final War. Everyone had a heart. Everyone knew what they were doing even if they didn't trust me.

Suddenly, I saw the first few bodies of Clockworks hit the ground. Before I even knew what I was doing, my feet were gliding across the floor. I glanced at the first few bodies and they laid emotionless on the ground, their wounds seeping blood. My stomach churned but I tried to move on. I had to use my abilities carefully.

I scanned the area, trying to find the four Clockworks. I spotted Electra fighting amongst the crowd of Creators. Cado gritted his teeth, using his martial arts to fight a group of Creators around him. Phoenix drilled holes of acid into each person in gray he encountered. I looked around, trying to find Sapphire. She wasn't anywhere in this mess.

I jogged quickly through the crowd of basic colors. A woman with dark hair and high cheekbones appeared in front of me, a red substance forming in her palms. Fear struck my heart and my fist instinctively collided into her jawbone. She doubled back but recovered quickly. I spun my legs across the ground, kicking her feet out from under her. I grabbed my sword from my sheath. I didn't remember putting it back in my sheath but it didn't matter.

I avoided looking into her minty green eyes when I brought the sword down. Blood spewed across the ground and the smell of metallic filled my nose. I ran across the ground, trying to find Sapphire in the mess. I slashed occasionally at the Creators in gray.

"I found the Chosen!" a voice yelled out. I whipped my head to the side. A man held Sapphire from the throat and her sleeve was rolled up. My heart began to beat rapidly. The Clockworks slowly turned their attention to Sapphire, furrowing their brows. They knew the Chosen wasn't described as Asian.

"I don't think that's Esther Green," a woman in gray said, walking closer to Sapphire and the man.

"Well, she has to be in this room," he said. "Radinusis said he saw her before he died. There was a group of five Clockworks that broke into our facility. This girl." He held Sapphire higher and she struggled in his grasp. "Was a part of that group. There were three woman and two men."

"She doesn't have the right features," the woman said.

"I am Esther Green!" Sapphire choked on her words. I stared at her—horrified. What was she doing?

"See. She could have dyed her hair and changed the color of her eyes," the man said with a laugh.

"If you're Esther Green," the woman said, stopping in front of Sapphire. "You can only be killed by Dante. Frankly, he's more intelligent than all of the Creators combined. There's only a few Clockworks that possess the *talent* to be wise. Such as; the Exol Child, the Spiritual-Human and of course, the Half-Blood." She stared Sapphire down, studying her reactions.

"And that is why you can't kill me," Sapphire stated bravely, staring the woman down also.

The woman smiled. "So, it wouldn't hurt you when I do this?" A black substance formed in her hands and she placed them greedily on Sapphire's chest. Sapphire screamed out in pain and my heart did somersaults.

"Stop!" I screamed. "Stop!" I pushed people out of my way, trying to get to Sapphire. "Stop!"

"Too late." The woman grinned, striking Sapphire in the heart. The man released her lifeless body, tossing it to the ground with a slight kick to her stomach. Black liquid poured out of her eyes.

"No!" I screamed, collapsing onto my knees. A rage formed around me, mimicking my feelings. Clockworks continued fighting against Creators. Cado lurched forward from the crowd, tears running down his tanned cheeks. He fell to the ground next to Sapphire and he clutched her body close to his chest as his sobs echoed in my ears. Tears ran down my cheeks too. She was the only one who understood my feelings, why I react the way I do. She understood me.

Electra came out of the crowd, followed by Phoenix. Anger

was plastered across their faces. Their lips were thin and their eyes were set. They ran forward, using their abilities to strike down the man and woman. Acid struck the man and he collapsed to the ground, screaming while clutching his wounds. Electricity hit the woman's back and she plummeted to the ground, unmoving. My heart throbbed too much to the point where I couldn't feel satisfaction.

I moved across the ground slowly, passing the dead bodies around me in the chaos. I crawled close to Cado and Sapphire. Tears continued streaming down his cheeks and he screamed out in pain. It was only Cado that was alive in his family now. Just like me.

I sat a few feet away from Cado, staring at Sapphire. Why did she do that? None of the Creators would discover me in the mess so why did they have to discover her fake mark? I glanced at the bland colors around me. We couldn't keep fighting or we would kill ourselves out. We had to get out of here.

"Cado," I said gently, staring at him. "We need to get out of here. Now."

He looked up at me. He was too sad to show any anger. But he did understand.

I stood up. "Move outside!" I screamed at the top of my lungs, my voice cracking. Clockworks glanced up and they nodded their heads. They finished fighting off whomever was in front of them and they began migrating out the large door. The room piled out and groups of Creators followed after them.

In front of me, a Creator formed boiling water in his hands, staring at Cado and me. The water hurtled our way but then a large figure jumped in front of me. Phoenix created a small portal and the boiling water disappeared before it could hit anyone. A strike of lightning shot the man and he fell to the ground. Electra walked over to me with a small smile, placing her hand on my shoulder.

"We stick together, alright?" she said.

I nodded my head. Phoenix walked over to Cado, shaking his shoulders. Cado stood up, wiping his tears away. He stared ahead and his arrogance began to shift into his persona again. This time he seemed stronger.

"We need to go," Phoenix said, running ahead of us. The room was still filled with a majority of Creators.

We ran forward and Electra caught up to Phoenix. I stayed

behind Cado just in case he ran back to Sapphire. We moved together and he fought off each Creator in his way, clearing a path for me. We made our way out of the room, entering the spacious chamber we came in before we fought off the Creators with metal arms. Electra and Phoenix used their grapples to jump off the metal balcony. My gut twisted. I didn't have one.

Cado's grapple shot out, latching onto a beam on the ceiling. He glanced back before he took off, studying my expression. He knew I didn't have one. Cado reached out his hand and I took it, wrapping my arms around his shoulders. We sprang off the balcony and I could feel his muscles tightening under my hands. We landed abruptly on the ground and we released each other. We ran across the ground, following shortly behind Phoenix and Electra. Behind us, the sounds of heavy footsteps filtered throughout the long, narrow hallway.

"Run in front of me!" Phoenix shouted.

Cado and I gained our momentum, catching up to Electra. I glanced back at Phoenix and he swung his arms out, shooting acid at the pillars that held up the foundation of the Compound. The ceiling above us began to crumble and collapse. Phoenix continued shooting at the pillars, trying to crush the Creators with the ceiling. We turned down another hallway and we could see figures ahead of us trailing outside of the Compound. It was the Clockworks. I glanced behind me again to see the ceiling fall onto the group of Creators. We ran out of the Compound, stepping into piles of wet mud. Rain poured down on us and cracks of thunder sounded overhead. We continued running with the other Clockworks until we stopped at the rock.

"What do we do now?" the girl from earlier piped up. There was blood splattered across her scraps.

"Raise your hand if you can create portals!" I shouted over the loud downpour. A series of bloody hands raised. "You're each going to get in groups no larger than ten. Find someone with portals and you're going to transport yourselves to Compounds. You're going to overthrow just like we have done and expand your groups. Continue on until the War is known to be ready. Save as many Clockworks as you can." I stared at the group, watching the rain pour down on everyone. They stared at me blankly but they understood what they had to do. "Find someone that can heal and allow them in your groups."

"Together we can stop what the Creators have done," Electra spoke up. "We lived in peace for too long... Now it's time to fight back."

The Clockworks began breaking up into groups and they found the required people that could form a healthy team. Portals were created and the number of Clockworks began to decrease. I turned to look at Electra.

"I think it's time we go back to the cabin," I said, avoiding Cado's eyes.

Phoenix, without a word, created a large, electrifying portal with frayed edges. Willingly, each of us hopped into the portal, leaving the collapsing Compound behind. The image in front of me contorted and shifted until I could see the kitchen in the distance. The portal spat us out and we landed perfectly this time.

"What happened?" Acea asked, sitting at a stool in the kitchen. He stared at each of us. "Where's the other girl?"

I glanced back at Cado but he acted like he wasn't paying attention. "Some of us can't make it back after we *risk* our lives protecting the ones we love." Acea nodded his head. His face slowly collapsed but I had a feeling it was faked.

"I'm sorry, Cadoen." Acea looked around and he acted confused. I turned around again but this time Cado wasn't there.

"Great," Electra stated. "He's gone."

"Where did he go?" I asked.

"Go see for yourself," Phoenix stated. "We have Compound battles every day of this week so make sure you shower and you're ready."

I nodded my head. "Where is he?"

"Outside. By the pond." Phoenix stared at me. "And when you're done, meet me in the front. I need to talk to you."

"Okay."

"Don't be late."

"I won't."

Chapter 13: Maybe It's Time to See Him Again

I sat on a wooden bench, watching Cado levitate in the air. His eyes were shut and he didn't even flinch a muscle. Maybe this was how he dealt with pain. He connected with his spiritual side.

I remembered when Sapphire pushed me off my bed a few mornings ago and how she had my back in the Maze. I didn't even know her for very long but with how close we became, it felt like I did. Sapphire's smile reminded me of my mother's. I thought back to all of the times she tucked me in bed, read me bedtime stories and played with Mr. Slithers for my enjoyment. Whenever there was a storm, she reminded me that the sun was still shining behind the clouds. Even my father taught me that.

I glanced down at my locket. My cold fingertips slowly picked it open and I saw the picture of my parents. We were all so happy. There wasn't a care in the world. We were free then. I felt the tears starting to well up in my eyes and my heart longed for them. I missed them so much. I missed what we used to be. Cado probably felt the same way with his family.

"I know, Cado." I wiped the tears off of my cheeks and my throat felt hoarse. "I know how it feels... It hurts."

"Esther," Phoenix said, walking around the side of the cabin. His face had hard features and his hair was spiked. He wore all black with his arms exposed.

I wiped my tears off my face, trying to regain myself. "Uh, yeah. Um, what's up?" I tried my best to sound casual but obviously it wasn't too convincing.

"Were you crying?" he asked with a hint of mockery.

"No. Of course not." I gave him a slight smile.

"Don't lie to me. There's water streaked across your face."

"Okay... Then fine. I was. How else am I supposed to control my emotions?"

Phoenix was standing next to me and his features were intense. "You're not the only one that cared about Sapphire. So, I suggest you quit crying your little ass off and show some respect for the rest of us."

I stood up off the bench, looking up at Phoenix. "I know that. I don't know about you but I deal with my emotions by crying... For you, you handle it like a pissy pants."

"That was a lame comeback."

"I don't care, Phoenix. You say I'm not showing any respect but I'm not the one trying to pick a fight with a helpless person."

"I don't think you understand, Esther," he said through gritted teeth. "*You're* the reason *why* she's dead."

I stepped back, almost hitting the back of my calf on the bench. I stared up at him with a horrified, sickening expression. "It's not my fault she wanted to protect me! I tried to tell her to take the paint off her wrist!"

Phoenix gritted his teeth and he pushed out his arms, making me fall onto the bench. "You could've stopped them! You could have given yourself up!"

I stared up at him as the anger started to boil up in my face. "I didn't have the energy to save her and you know that!" I screamed as the tears started to well up.

"That's your problem, Esther! Brilliance Chose you to protect it when you can't even protect *yourself!*" His dark eyes pierced at me menacingly. "You can't even protect the people that care about you."

I gritted my teeth. Images of the fiery, blazing house coursed throughout my head and my ears echoed my mother's screams. I stood up. "Shut up!" I laid my hands on him and I pushed him with all of my force. He stumbled backwards and quickly, he regained himself.

"We were fine before you came... We weren't even worried that one of us was going to die until you came here. You *practically* killed Sapphire... You haven't been through a single thing and you think you have the right to feel sorry about yourself!"

"I don't think you understand, Phoenix."

"I do understand. Sure, your mother died. Sure, your father died. But you need to get over it and stop thinking about what *was* and think about what *is*. If you cared about your mother, you wouldn't have let her get killed by Luna. If you cared, you would have gotten there in time."

"You don't know anything about that night," I stated through gritted teeth.

"If you cared about Sapphire, you would have said that you were the Chosen one and not her... But you didn't... Because you're a *coward*."

"I was too lost with words to do anything at that time and I couldn't fight back. I didn't have any energy. I wouldn't have made it... And I do care about my mother, my father and Sapphire. I care about them and to have you say I don't pisses me off."

Phoenix turned away, staring passed Cado to look at the pond. "You have an energy problem, Esther. Your energy is the weakest out of all of us."

"I used my abilities too much as a kid. My body just can't keep up with it," I said. At least he wasn't screaming at me anymore.

"I just can't..." He paused and I saw a tear form in his iris. Slowly and gracefully, the tear fell passed his jaw. "I can't live with myself knowing what I'm doing."

"Phoenix, what are you talking about?" It felt so strange to see him so vulnerable due to his tough guy image.

"A month before Icelos rescued me, I was attacked and I lost someone very important to me." He looked up at the dark sky and more tears welled up in his eyes. "Her name was Paris Franco and she was my little sister." Phoenix closed his eyes as if he was replaying the events inside his head. "We grew up as foster children. We switched many houses until we came to one very different house. This house was when I discovered my abilities through my foster parents. They were Clockworks and they wanted to see if we were like them.

"We were but my sister couldn't figure out her abilities. She was a Clockwork due to the charge but her abilities never surfaced like mine had. I tried to tell her that they will come and all she had to do was focus. But, like I said, they didn't come.

"Paris and I had a very healthy and inspiring life at this house until a month ago we were attacked by Creators. They were Shadows and they destroyed everything. I remember picking up my sister while our foster parents told us to leave before anything happened to us. I ran down the stairs but the staircase collapsed underneath my feet due to the disintegration ability. Our parents ran to the side where the stairs were destroyed but before they could react, Shadows picked them up and another Shadow did something to them that I can't understand. They died.

"I stood up weakly, trying to fight them off but it was no use. I wasn't powerful then. They took my sister right from underneath me." He choked on his tears. "They threatened me with a deal and they would give her back to me: unharmed... But obviously, I didn't get her back."

"Do you think she's...?" I couldn't find myself to say the words.

"She's not dead," Phoenix said firmly. "I know she's alive because I think they're waiting for me."

"Waiting for you?"

"They're waiting for me to get her back."

Phoenix sat down on the grass, continuing to stare out at the pond. The clouds disappeared slowly and the rays of a sunset formed in our eyes. Cado levitated without a single flinch. I moved my body slowly so I could sit down next to him. I laid out my hand close to his and I watched as another tear fell from the corner of his eye.

"Sometimes I wonder why bad things have to happen to good people," I stated, watching the sunset. "I believe the bad things make us into bad people." I glanced at him for a reaction.

"I feel like I have changed since I lost Paris... I feel like I became darker on the inside." He turned his head to stare at me. "I feel bad for every time I pissed you off... And I suppose I should say sorry for all of the times that are coming."

I felt a grin creeping up on my face. "I might just have to punch you in the face the next time."

Phoenix laughed. "Yeah. If you can reach me."

"Phoenix," I said, changing the subject, "I will help you get your sister back. I'll do anything I can to make you feel whole again."

"Thank you. That truly means a lot to me. I just wish I can help you with your needs too... To make you whole again but I think you can't be fixed."

I bit my lip as I stared out at the falling sun. "I can find a way to fix myself."

This whole week consisted of devious plans to take out Compounds and save Clockworks from their doom. Cado hasn't moved a muscle since Sapphire died. He was still sitting outside as water from the pond surrounded his body, levitating with him. I brought food to him every single day but of course, it went spoiled. I would sit down and tell him about my life and how I felt in certain occasions and positions. I didn't think he could hear me so I told him my feelings. Tomorrow we had to attack the last Compound on our list before the War. The thing was, I haven't even found the Exol Child yet. I had to see Icelos soon before it was time to face Dante.

I stood in the kitchen with my blue velvet nightgown on, making a plate for Cado. We got done with a Compound a few hours ago so I decided to change into my pajamas because I needed the comfort.

"Esther, let me bandage that up for you," Acea said, pointing to the long, deep gash on my forearm. I got it today when a Creator slashed me with their sword. Other than the cut, I didn't have very bad cuts and bruises.

I sighed, stirring the pot roast and carrots. "Fine, but do it gently please." Of course, Acea and I haven't been talking for a while. It wasn't the same anymore and he knew that. I wanted him to leave here before he got hurt.

He grinned. "You know I'm gentle." Acea walked over to the First Aid kit on the table and he grabbed a few trinkets.

"I think I should sit over there. It wouldn't be sanitary for Cado if you did this over his food," I said with a small smile.

Acea laughed quietly. "Well, come here then."

He grabbed my healthy arm, pulling me gently to the kitchen table. He pulled out a chair for me and I sat down. Acea took out his tools and I looked away as he started cleaning my arm. I gritted my teeth as he became fiercer with his tugging and pulling.

"I'm sorry, am I hurting you?" he asked quietly, his green eyes showing regret.

"Just a little."

Acea concentrated as he sewed my wound together and carefully, he wrapped a large bandage over the sickening cut. I got up from my chair once he finished to turn off the stove. I stirred Cado's food around and then I put it on a plate with corn.

"Thank you for fixing me up," I stated as I worked with Cado's food. "You should be a doctor."

"I actually do want to be a doctor someday. I feel like I can put my past of selfishness behind me and put people first."

"Yeah. I think that's what most people want." I walked

331

around the small bend of the kitchen counter, edging closer to the door. "I'm going to give Cado his food."

"Why do you give him food if he's not going to eat it?" Acea asked, rolling his eyes.

"Because I hope he will eat it one day."

I walked out of the cabin and I made my way to the meditating Cadoen. I sat down a few feet away from him, avoiding the swirling pond water around him. In the distance, I could see the battle pillars and the Maze. I put his food down next to my leg and I felt the rays of the fading sun behind the thick forest.

"Cado, can you please wake up?" I asked quietly, wishing he could actually be here, in this time, awake and alive. "I know you're hurt... But you just can't run away from your problems. You have to *face* them headstrong." I took deep breaths as I thought back to the time he saved me from Dante in the Maze and how he swept me off my feet in the Compound when I didn't have a grapple. Even though it seemed like he hated me, he was still there for me and he still didn't want me to die.

"Sometimes we can't choose if we get hurt but you still have to stay strong and fight it back. Come back to us, Cado. I *need* you. You're a part of the Three Prophecies. If I can't find the Exol Child, you'll be my only hope in this War. Hell, I don't even understand why there's a war. I don't understand why we have to fight over this thing that courses through my veins... The Creators want to make themselves known so they can destroy the structure we have. The thing is... They don't know how. But this thing inside me does. It's stupid, really. The Creators still need someone to hold their hands before they do something awful."

I paused to stare at Cado. His eyes were shut and his features were hard as the water spun around him. The water wasn't there the first time I noticed him in this stage but after each visit, I noticed the water piling up around him. Somehow, someway, the water that circled around Cado reminded me of Damion. I remembered how rocks would spin around him whenever he was troubled. I could never fully understand why he was vulnerable all of the time. He never fully explained to me what his fights with his parents were about.

I guess it would be hard not to be understood by his very own parents. It could make someone feel lost in this world. I couldn't imagine what was going on with his parents at this moment. I always wondered if Damion was anywhere to be found. Where was he?

"Cado, honestly, I think life sucks," I said, thinking back to everything that had happened to me this year since I received Brilliance. "I feel like I have to be the one that has to be the hero. I feel like I'm too immature to even handle this huge responsibility that was placed in my hands." I could feel my throat starting to get dry. "Everyone around me dies. Everyone I care about and all of my friends have these terrible lives because the Creators took away the only family they had. It's like we all have to find a place in this world and go from there. But how? How do we find a place? And most of all... How do we survive?"

I stared up at Cado, watching him peacefully levitate in the air. "We're going to have to fight for what we love soon. And in that Prophecy, it said something like one of us was going to die. The Exol Child, the Half-Blood or the Spiritual Human. It described that one of us had the key to a new beginning or something like that and honestly, I hope you're the one that receives a new beginning. You are so strong... But weakened by emotions. But those traits create a hero. I want *you* to be the hero, Cado. I want you to move on with your life once all of this is over. I want you to find yourself." I forced a smile as a few tears began to stream down my face.

"You just have to wake up first before any of that has to happen," I said with a laugh. "So please, get your lazy butt up and wake up so you can show everyone what you're capable of. I know there's something special about you. You just need to show it. Remember what Sapphire would do."

I waited patiently for him to move a muscle. I watched him but as more time passed, the more the excitement started to fade. I sighed, standing up. I dusted the wet grass off of my nightgown. I left the plate of food where it was and I started walking away. "I guess a hero doesn't live inside of you," I said solemnly, walking towards the large cabin.

"You're an ass," I heard a loud, grumbling but beautiful voice say.

My heart did somersaults and a huge grin spread across my face. I turned around and I started running barefoot across the wet grass to Cado. He stared at me with opaque eyes but I ignored it. I wrapped my arms around his neck, feeding him my happiness. I was filled with felicity now that he was awake. Slowly and gradually, I felt his arms wrap around my waist.

"Cado, I'm so sorry about Sapphire... I'm just so happy you're awake," I continued to ramble on until he laughed.

"Sometimes we need to take a break from this menacing life," Cado stated.

I pulled away from him to stare at his face. His eyes were finally filled with life. "You're talking too... That's amazing!"

Cado gave me a small grin. "Like you said, I can't run away from my problems. Plus, I think I could save more lives with my voice. I probably could have saved Sapphire if I said something."

"Don't regret the choices you didn't make, Cado. It makes it unbearable to live if you do. I mean, after all, we are human."

"We are indeed, human." He looked up at the sky as the moon began to peek behind the trees. "We should probably go inside. I need to eat a lot of food." Cado picked up the plate of food I gave him and he started to walk inside. I followed him until we got inside. Electra and Phoenix were standing in the kitchen and their mouths dropped open when they saw Cado.

"Hey," Cado said.

"Cadoen!" Electra yelled with excitement. She and Phoenix ran across the floor to pile him with hugs.

Acea walked in with a smile on his face. "Wow, you're finally awake."

I grinned as the dark atmosphere lightened with happiness. I finally realized that you had to fight off the darkness with light. You had to remember to be the light in the darkest of times. It was the way to live and it was the way to keep all of us alive.

I walked around in my bedroom, picking up my dirty clothes and putting it into a small hamper. I was still smiling about what happened an hour ago. I couldn't believe Cado heard everything I told him and he was finally awake. I heard him talk for the first time too.

Suddenly, a strong sensation swept over me and I lost my balance. I fell to the hardwood floor, smacking my head into my bed. I groaned in pain and I couldn't see anything around me. Words filtered my vision and I knew what was happening.

The Overwhelming Death

We cannot choose the life we live. The life is already chosen and that method is called your destiny. Each and every one of us has something to fulfill in our lives before we are meant to die. It's a part of our nature, the very reason we even live.

In the Prophecy, unfortunately one of our fellow heroes has to die a horrific and painful death, fulfilling their destiny. Their destiny was to keep Brilliance safe and they have done very well, but it will be the time of the new Protector. The Half-Blood will die in the upcoming War for Freedom due to the ending of their destiny. But when they are killed from the Wise, one of the two Prophecies has to be the last to kill the Half-Blood so Brilliance will flow into their veins.

Heroes are always meant to die after they complete what they are meant to. It, unfortunately, is best for everyone else.

Sorry, Half-Blood. You are meant to die. You were born to die.

The phrases disappeared as quickly as they came and I was left hyperventilating on the floor of my bedroom. So, this was it? I was the one that had to die for everyone else? I felt the tears starting to well up as the thoughts started to consume me. I would never graduate, get married, get a job or have any kids. I wouldn't have a life that I always wanted. I always wanted to live until I was too sick to move. I *vowed* to make my life worth living.

All of the things I wanted to do wasn't going to happen now. I had to give up my life so everything would be okay. I had to accept the fact that my death could save everyone from harm. I hoped it would help save everyone or I would basically be dying for nothing. When I die, I want a purpose to die. Just like my mother, just like my father and just like Sapphire. I wanted a reason.

I threw my head back on the side of my bed. The tears started streaming down my face. I couldn't tell anyone or they would want to protect me. If they protect me, then they have a chance of dying as well.

"I don't want anyone to die for me," I whispered while choking on my words. I wanted to hear it to make it more final. "I only want my soul to move on." And then, I knew my purpose of dying. It was so I could save the people I love. Dying in the place of another person was the greatest way to die. I could die peacefully knowing I did the right thing.

Cado, Electra, Phoenix and I stood around a glowing portal that leaked green liquid across our legs. We all felt the tension. We were going to the last Compound assigned to us and anything could happen. One of us could die. I swallowed the lump in my throat and I shifted uncomfortably on my feet. Maybe it was going to be me. What if Dante was there?

"So, is everyone ready?" Phoenix asked, glancing at each of us.

"Yes," Cado stated firmly. "The quicker we get this done, the faster we can end the War."

"For all of us," Electra said, staring at me with a smile. "And Sapphire."

"Let's go then," Phoenix said. "There's no time to wait. Everyone knows their positions."

Cado walked over to me and he grabbed my hand. I looked up at him with shock plastered across my face. I glanced behind me to see Phoenix and Electra holding hands also.

"It's to ensure safety," Cado said. "It could be the last time we see each other. This may be the biggest Compound we ever ventured to."

"To ensure safety," I said quietly with a smile. He returned it.

Cado and I leaped into the portal and Phoenix and Electra followed. Swirls of green circled around us until I could see a set of trees in the distance. My stomach began to churn as we went faster through the portal to the point my eyes were watering. The portal spat us out, making Cado and I slide across the thick underbrush. Once we stopped, Electra and Phoenix landed at our feet.

Groggily, we all stood up and we stared at the Compound ahead. I glanced at Phoenix, waiting for him to repeat the mission.

"Cado and Esther, you'll go in underground. Electra and I are going to go to the back entrance where there aren't any Metal Men. This time we're going to hit them all at once."

I nodded my head and Electra gave me a smile.

"No one is going to die today, alright?" Electra said. "You've been unsettled lately."

I shrugged my shoulders. "It's just a big Compound."

She smiled. "You have Cado with you. He'll help you when you lose energy."

I tried to show bravado but I didn't think it was concealing my fear. Anything could happen. "Okay. I know I'll be safe then."

"We have to go," Phoenix said. "Sector B is on their lunch break."

"To think they would even have lunch breaks since they like punching puppies in the face," Electra said with a laugh.

"Okay," Cado said. "Let's go."

The four of us broke apart in the thick edge of the forest. Cado and I maneuvered around trees at a fast pace. My heart was racing as we edged deeper into the woods. The Compound was in the distance with smoke billowing out of the top.

"The wooden door should be around here somewhere," Cado stated. He stopped running to look around. I watched as he got on his knees and started scraping the dirt with his fingertips. "I can't find it," he gritted impatiently.

"Do you need help?" I asked.

"Does it look like I need help?" Cado said caustically. "Of course, I do!"

I rolled my eyes and I got on my knees. I started digging up the dirt underneath my fingers. I moved aside plants angrily. The thing about Cado was the fact that he had a short temper. Underneath my fingertips, I felt something hard and rough.

"Cado!" I said. "I found it!"

Cado moved across the ground gracefully and he stopped at my side. He brushed off the soil with his hand and he grabbed the latch. With a great amount of force, he pulled the wooden door back and I could see inside the facility.

"You first," he said. "It's not a far drop."

I nodded my head. "Okay. Remember, we have to find the men with the masks. They lead to the Clockworks."

I grabbed both ends of the trapdoor, slowly lowering myself in. I jumped down and my feet slapped against the wet floor. The tunnel was damp and dark. There was light at the end of the tunnel and that was where we had to go.

Cado leaped down next to me quietly and he started to run along the walls while pulling out his knife. I moved with him and I could hear voices at the end of the tunnel. They were aware that we were here.

"Esther!" Cado screamed. "Something purple is coming our way!"

I moved around him and I held my hands out in one simple movement. I created a force field and I molded it around the unknown purple liquid, bursting it forward, killing a man ahead instantly. Cado moved forward, decapitating a few men that were coming our way.

Suddenly, I saw water hurtling my way in my peripheral vision and quickly, I leaped to the side, creating a sharp force field. I killed the man before he could attack again. In front of Cado and I stood ten men and women, waiting to kill us.

"Someone ring the alarm!" A voice called out.

Cado ran forward with his sword held close to his chest. He followed after the woman that was about to pull the alarm.

"Cado, hurry!" I screamed.

A man with shaggy long hair came forward with a sickening grin plastered across his face. "Why are you here, young lady? Why get yourself into so much trouble?" The man spontaneously was at my side and I blinked wildly while my heart was racing. "Atomic speed," he said, his face inches away from mine. The men and women in front of me laughed while a few others went to go fight off Cado.

The man rushed around me and my hair flipped wildly in his wind. He stood in front of me, staring me down with wicked green eyes. I pushed out a sharp force field and quickly, he dodged it, moving to an unknown area. The force field sliced a few people in front of me and that's when the fun was over.

The men and woman moved forward and a rush of abilities shot out at me. I yelped, turning invisible while keeping a force field around me. I pulled out a few of my knives and I ran forward, attacking a man with red hair. He screamed while I stabbed him in the stomach. I closed my eyes as the smell of metallic filled my nose and I heard a body drop. Screams echoed in my ears and then I felt a force knock into me from behind. I turned around and a woman stared up blankly.

"I think I found her!" she shouted.

I leaped forward, using my leg to kick her in the face. She fell onto her butt, staring up blankly. Someone from behind touched me and I could feel all of my energy drain. I gritted my teeth as my anger started to boil up inside of me. I really hated the people that could bid abilities.

A flood of abilities came forward and I screamed, jumping out of the way. I felt something bite into my ankle and I yelled out in pain. I backed up against the wall while breathing heavily. Men and women in gray uniforms started surrounding me. I looked amongst the faces, trying to find the man with blonde hair. I finally spotted him. He was in the back behind the crowd.

I moved my hand, grabbing the shield that was attached to my back. I held it out in front of me and I pulled out my sword. *I don't want to get hurt today.*

I stood up weakly as my ankle throbbed. I looked down and there was blood pouring out of my wound. I gritted my teeth as another sharp pain went through my leg.

I shook off the pain quickly, noticing a ray of blue, glowing light come forward from the crowd. I held up my shield quickly. I ran forward, slicing the few people I could get before having to jump back and hold up my shield again while abilities flew at me. I had to get to the man with blonde hair.

I looked up, trying to find Cado. He tackled a man to the ground before the man could pull the alarm.

"Whoa!" I yelled, coming up with a decoy. "Look over there! What is that?"

The men and women looked in the direction I was pointing and spontaneously, I ran forward, slicing people in the stomach. Flashes of abilities rang out but they only hit the people around them. Finally, I stabbed the man with blonde hair in the chest and I watched as he fell helplessly to the ground. I felt all of my energy regenerate and I screamed out in excitement. I created a force field, trapping two Creators that were yelling and screaming. I pushed the force field out and they flew into the back of the tunnel. I turned around, simultaneously sliding across the ground to kick someone that was coming my way with a knife in their hand. I grabbed her knife and I closed my eyes while driving the knife down on her body.

I placed my shield on my back. I turned invisible and I shielded myself with a thin force field around my body. I glanced around me, noticing there were only three Creators I had to fight. They clumped together while looking around frantically. I sprung out my hands and a sharp field cut them across their bodies and they fell to the ground. I turned around and Cado was fighting off a woman as gently as he could. He wasn't a fan of hurting women.

Suddenly, something made my hair lift up into the air and a breeze coated my body. I saw a flash of gray and I instantly knew it was the man with the super speed. I watched as the gray came close to Cado.

"Cado, watch out!" I screamed.

Cado leaped out of the way with his sword in hand, accidentally slicing the man and woman. He gently landed on the ground and he stared at the dead bodies next to him with wide eyes.

"I think we're done here. There's no one else left to kill," he said, getting up and he came towards me.

"Now we just have to find our way through this thing," I said.

"Is your ankle alright?" he asked.

I glanced down at it. "Yeah. It'll be fine." I ignored the pain.

We continued moving forward at a slight speed. We finally reached the inside of the Compound and it had bright lights that contrasted with the dark metal.

"We should go up those metal stairs over there," Cado whispered.

I looked ahead, noticing the Creators standing around the metal staircase. "Do we fight or do we hide?" I asked.

"We distract them," Cado said. "And when we do, you need to use all of the energy you can to make us both invisible. If you lose your energy, I'll protect you, okay?"

I nodded my head. "Okay. I'll make us invisible now so we can distract them long enough to get up the stairs."

I placed my hand on him and I closed my eyes. I thought of everything that was swirling around inside my mind. I tried to change the dark thoughts into peaceful things. Instead of dying, I thought about being alive. Instead of dwelling on my parents' deaths, I thought about all of the times we had fun together.

I opened my eyes and I couldn't see Cado, I could only feel his arm. We both stood up simultaneously. I grabbed a knife from my belt and I threw it across the floor, getting the Creators' attention. They piled away from the stairway and I screamed, trying to make them come in this direction.

They started coming close to us and slowly, we moved quickly but quietly away from them. We made our way to the stairs and slowly, we climbed them as quietly as we could. Each step was as quiet as a mouse scurrying across a floor.

We reached the top and we slowly made our way around a bend, entering a different atmosphere with white, metal walls and a dark, metal floor. I released my focus on making us invisible. I took deep breaths as I tried to regenerate my energy.

"Are you okay?" Cado asked.

I nodded my head. "Yeah. I'm fine. I just don't think I can be invisible anymore."

"Use the rest of your energy wisely."

We moved down the long, white corridor. I turned my head, realizing there was something peculiar that branched off into a different section of the Compound.

"What does this corridor lead to?" I asked quietly.

"I don't know... But we should probably stay on track. When we meet up with Electra and Phoenix, they'll be expecting the Clockworks to be freed."

We continued moving down the long hallway until we reached a huge, white door. I noticed on the side of the door was a panel.

"Press your thumb on it," Cado said.

I pressed my thumb onto the panel but the phrase, "Access Denied," echoed throughout my head. I looked at the panel, realizing it had dried blood on it.

"I think you access it from blood," I said with a shiver.

"I'll do it," Cado said, instantly pulling out a knife.

"No," I said, putting my hand on his so he could lower the

knife. "I can. I have a wounded ankle." I bent down and gently, I placed my thumb on the oozing blood. I pressed my thumb into the panel and the panel said, "Identification please."

"Uh, type in a random name," Cado said.

I typed, *Phil,* into the panel and the large, white doors moved open. Ahead of us stood five guards with masks that blocked off another set of white doors.

"Hey, they're not supposed to be here!" one of the men yelled.

"Hit the alarm!" another said.

I glanced frantically around the room while the set of white doors behind us closed. I spotted the alarm and it was midway in the room. I sprang forward, throwing up a force field, simultaneously knocking down a man that leaped for the alarm. I gritted my teeth as I tried desperately to consume my energy.

Cado sprang forward with a long, sharp sword at his side. He jumped on a man and he slashed his neck. A man behind Cado was readying to kill him with his abilities, so quickly I threw a sharp force field up and it slashed the man across the stomach.

A ray of yellow light hurtled my way and I didn't have time to make a force field so I leaped out of the way while slamming my back into the wall. Another ray of light came forward and I grabbed my shield, sticking it up in front of my face. The yellow light smacked into the it and I gritted my teeth as I slid across the ground. Once the light stopped, I glanced down at my shield and it was nearly eroded. I threw it to the ground angrily and I pulled out my knife.

I ran forward, dodging all of the abilities that came my way. One by one, the men started to die as Cado killed them off.

"Here," Cado said quickly, extending his hand for me to grab. "Grab my hand."

I grabbed his hand and he swung me forward. I kicked out my leg and I smashed a Creator in the face, sending him to the ground. The Creator looked up at me with fear plastered across his face. I closed my eyes and brought down the knife, screams echoed throughout my ears and then it was quiet. I opened my eyes and I noticed all of the Creators were dead.

"You okay?" Cado breathed heavily.

I nodded my head. "Yes."

Suddenly, the white door behind us slid open and the sound of an alarm went off. I turned around quickly to find Electra and Phoenix in the doorway. Creators ran up the stairs, screaming and yelling.

Electra and Phoenix ran inside and the white door closed behind them before any of the Creators could catch them. The sirens began to ring more loudly.

"Crap," Electra breathed. "We didn't know how to get passed the Creators guarding the stairs."

"We need to hurry... They all know we're here now," I said.

Cado ran over to one of the dead Creators and he grabbed the man's thumb, placing it over a panel. The white doors opened smoothly, revealing a new set of Creators.

"Electra and Phoenix, go fight them off and Cado and I will drag in these bodies so the other Creators can't get passed this door."

"Yeah," Cado said. "This door only opens if one of the dead men touch the panel."

They nodded their heads and they ran across the floor while abilities rang out. Carefully and cautiously, Cado and I dragged the dead bodies out of the first white room into the next. Once we were done, the doors closed behind us. Electra and Phoenix killed off the last Creator and we used one of their thumbs to open up the next door.

"We need to hurry," I said. "We can't drag these bodies in."

Right on cue, bursts rang out on the white door behind us. We ran into the next white room quickly and simultaneously, the door behind us closed again. This time there were about ten Creators waiting to attack.

"Go! Go! Go!" I screamed.

We all started running spontaneously, taking different directions and angles. Phoenix used his portals to make his opponent's ability disappear and he used his acid to kill his victims. Electra used her melting and lightning to destroy whomever was in her path.

I heard a petrifying scream and I glanced to the side. Cado was being electrocuted by a Creator. I yelped, running forward to attack. I had my knife at my side and I came up on the Creator's back and forcefully, I stabbed him in the lower part of his ribs. He screamed out in pain, moving to slap me across the face.

343

His hand electrified my face, sending tingles and odd sensations across my cheek. I got up while gritting my teeth and I stared at the man viciously. My anger was starting to boil across my entire body and it was getting to the point where it was hard to breathe.

I started walking towards the man until I realized Electra started melting the door with her abilities. As I was watching Electra, I felt a petrifying pain surge throughout my chest. I moved my eyes to the side and the man was electrocuting me. I let out a bloodcurdling scream as the pain grew more intense. Suddenly, I felt my body collapse to the ground and I got a glimpse of Phoenix disintegrating the man.

"Cado, you alright?" Phoenix yelled over the loud commotion of the new Creators filing in from the next room. "Can you carry her?"

"Yes," I heard Cado say.

I felt a set of strong arms lift me up and all I could see was the lights above me as Cado ran into another room. The sounds of Phoenix's screams coursed throughout my head. I heard Electra melting the next door and Phoenix was the only one left to fight. I had to get back in the fight. I couldn't let anyone get hurt.

"Set me down," I said quietly. I stared up at Cado and he had tears welling up in his eyes. I wasn't sure what he was thinking about at that moment but I had a feeling it was Sapphire.

"What, why?" Cado asked, finally staring down at me in his arms.

"I've been electrocuted before way worse than this... Don't worry about me. I stay alive until Dante kills me."

"No," Cado said sternly. "You stay alive forever."

Reluctantly, Cado set me down and I felt another wave of pain wash over my body. I gritted my teeth and stared up at the ceiling. I had to be stronger than I was before. I had to fight the pain just like how Cado was managing.

I gritted my teeth and I started walking which soon formed into a run. I glanced at the battle of masked Creators around me. Viciously and violently, they attacked Cado and Phoenix while Electra continued melting the white doors. I ran across the floor, dodging all of the harmful abilities that soared through the air. I stopped at Electra's side.

"We made it passed four doors already... This one I'm melting is the one that holds Clockworks inside. Hopefully we don't die before I get this damn thing open," Electra stated with aggravation.

"Alright, I'll watch your back, okay? I'm going to use my last bit of energy for this."

"Okay, be careful. It's about to make a dent in the metal."

I stood in front of her, watching the Creators break out in front of me. A majority of the Creators wore white masks with drops of blood on it to symbolize Dante. In the near distance, Creators started running in our direction. I stood strongly in front of Electra, waiting for their attack. I pulled out my bow and I loaded it with arrows. I pulled back the string, not taking my eyes off my targets. I shot an arrow and missed. My fear started rising to my throat and they were coming closer. I couldn't shoot properly because I was afraid.

I loaded an arrow again, focusing on one of the Creators. I shot and missed once more so I put my bow and arrows away. This time, the Creators were ten feet away. Rays of blue, yellow and red hurtled towards me and instantaneously, I focused on my ability to create a force field. I locked into my Spiritual Side and before I could process what was going on, a force field shot out of my hand, knocking down two Creators.

"How's it coming?" I yelled at Electra while focusing on the next herd of Creators.

"I'm starting to see Clockworks behind the door!" she shouted back.

I held out my hands, creating a large force field to block Electra and the Clockworks that were behind the door. Creators forced abilities at us but my force field boomeranged the powers back at the Creators. The more I held the force field, the more I felt ennui. I couldn't keep the force field strong enough to last the melting phase.

"Electra!" I screamed. "I can't hold it anymore!"

"Don't worry! I'm almost done! The Clockworks might be able to jump out of the hole."

I glanced behind me, noticing all of the dirty faces through a large hole in the door. All of the Clockworks were malnourished and they wore white and gray scraps, similar to previous Compounds. I

345

felt a pang in my heart, realizing they sat in there, waiting for a hero to come and rescue them for the longest of time.

I turned to look back at the Creators starting to break down my force field. I gritted my teeth as I felt all of my energy release from my body. I watched as the force field slowly decayed around the edges.

"Electra!" I screamed. "I can't do this!"

"Here, you convince the Clockworks to come out. I'll fight now!" Electra yelled back at me.

I released the force field and swiftly, we switched spots. This time she was protecting me and I was facing the Clockworks. I jumped into the hole in the door, standing in front of many men, women and children.

"I know for the longest time you have been waiting for a moment to escape. Now, it is the time," I said, my voice becoming hoarse. "I am the one that was Chosen by Brilliance and my friends and I have come to help everyone escape. After you escape, build teams with Clockworks that can heal and create portals. Stay in a safe place until notified that the War has come. When the War comes, we will take back the freedom that we had. Who is with us?" I yelled.

Reluctantly, the Clockworks yelled and cheered. I moved out of the way so the first few rows of Clockworks could file out of the door and begin fighting. Row by row, Clockworks retreated from the cell. I started to move out with the last row of Clockworks.

"Everyone retreat out of the Compound!" I yelled over the commotion. "Fight whomever is in your way!"

I glanced around as white and gray fought against each other. I couldn't find any black uniforms.

I ran with the gray uniforms, scanning the area to find Phoenix, Cado and Electra. My heart started racing as I became more anxious. If I couldn't find them then I might be stuck here.

Suddenly, a hand latched onto my arm, pulling me to the ground. A Creator with a mask got on top of me and he wrapped his hands around my throat. I struggled underneath his grasp as the air started to escape my lungs. I used my hands to grab onto his wrists and I dug my nails into his skin. He screamed out in pain, releasing my throat for a second, giving me a chance to attack.

I lifted up my knee, kicking him in his groin. He fell to the side, clutching himself while I moved on my side, grabbing a knife from my belt. I brought it down on his chest and he didn't make a noise again.

I turned around while standing up. The Clockworks around me started running down the chamber and I was the only Clockwork left in the area. Creators with masks started walking closer to me slowly while others followed after the Clockworks.

I grabbed my bow again, loading in an arrow. I focused on a set of targets and I shot, killing three Creators. I loaded the bow again and killed a few more. I continued shooting a few more until abilities came my way. I shot one more while a bolt of lightning hurtled my way. The bolt electrified the arrow, creating a spark that danced around the corridor.

"That was pretty cool," I said underneath my breath.

"There's only one reason why you stayed back to fight," a Creator stated dramatically. "You are the one whom was Chosen by Brilliance itself."

Actually, I thought, *I was just lost in the crowd.*

I loaded the bow again and shot at the man but I missed. The crowd of Creators burst into laughter and angrily, I threw the bow to the ground. I pulled out my sword and I watched them closely.

Abilities flew at me all at once and I screamed, jumping to the side of the corridor. My heart started pumping very loudly and all I could hear was my blood pulsing from fear. More abilities hurtled my way and I jumped to the other side of the corridor. When I leaped into the air, I felt a biting sensation in my thigh and I created a bloodcurdling scream as the pain engulfed my whole thigh. I collapsed onto the ground, smacking my face into the white wall while my sword dropped a distance from me.

"I don't want to die," I whispered as I stared up at the ceiling as tears flew down my cheeks from the pain. I couldn't walk.

A group of Creators circled around me. One of them with a mask on bent down next to me, gently putting his hand on my wrist. With his other hand, he ripped open my sleeve and my Mark was conspicuous.

The man's lips smiled underneath his mask. "We found her. Dante should be arriving soon. He was informed about the attack."

"What should we do with her now?" another man asked.

"Put her in the Reveal Cell for now. Today may be the day

we get what we need."

I gritted my teeth, jumping up to attack the Creator that ripped my sleeve. I punched him in the jaw and he doubled onto his back. Other Creators grabbed my arms and legs while I screamed viciously, struggling against their grasp. I tried moving my arms and legs but they used their abilities to calm me down. As pain surfaced across my body, the more I screamed.

I stared up at the ceiling, watching it move with every step of the Creators. The atmosphere changed and I was in another bright hallway. It was narrow.

"Set her down," the Creator I attacked stated.

The Creators sat me down and at first, I started falling to my knees from my inability to walk from the pain. Two masked men held me up and they dragged me down a hallway with rooms that had blue glass covering the doorway. I had a feeling this place wasn't good.

The men continued dragging me until they stopped at a glass door at the end of the hallway. Another Creator with a mask stood patiently next to the door with their arms crossed.

"Dante would want to see her," the Creator I attacked said.

The Creator next to the glass door nodded his head. He turned his back to me, punching buttons on the levitating panel. The blue glass door slid open and the Creators holding me pushed me into the man that was guarding the door. The masked Creator grabbed my arms, sending sensational vibes throughout my entire body. This touch was more than a shock that each Being receives when touched by another Being. The touch was almost familiar. It was vibrant as it still coursed throughout my entire body.

I glanced up at the masked man, waiting to see a body reaction. There was nothing but when I looked at his lips that were revealed behind the mask so he could speak, they held a tight line and I knew he felt it too. The masked man pushed me into the room and I fell to the white ground. I felt air escape my lungs and the air in the room was heavy. All of my human energy escaped me.

"This room," the Creator I attacked said, "takes away all of your abilities; even your human energy. The Creator turned to look at the one particular masked man. "Dante Jett should be coming soon. For the meantime, stand your ground. I'm leaving Jox with you too, okay, Rivil?"

348

Rivil nodded his head without speaking.

"Esther Green has no way of escaping. If her friends come to rescue her, kill them all."

Rivil, once again, nodded his head.

The Creators left, leaving Jox and Rivil guarding the blue glass door.

I stared down at the ground as all of my thoughts started to consume me. *This is it. I am officially going to be killed in moments.* This wasn't supposed to be the way I was going to die. I wanted to die with a heroic purpose. I wanted people to remember me for what I did for the humans and the Clockworks. But now I wasn't going to have a chance. I wasn't going to have a chance to see my friends again or even outside of this Compound. I wouldn't know what it would be like to grow up strong and independent. I wasn't going to experience the love of being a mother. I wasn't going to fall in love. I wouldn't get a job. I would have nothing. No experience of being alive.

I stared up at the Creators standing outside of the door. The masked man was staring at me and once he noticed I was staring back at him, he shifted uncomfortably. He glanced at the Creator standing next to him and his legs swayed back in forth. I was trying to remember where I felt the shock from and who gave me that shock. Or, in that case, why did I feel that way from him?

Suddenly, a noise from outside of my cell erupted my thoughts. Fire burst outside of my door and I watched as the two Creators began fighting. The masked Creator pushed the other Creator out of view. Suddenly, the Creator turned to glance at me. He looked away and started typing in numbers on the panel. The glass door slowly slid open.

The Creator ran inside the room and slowly, I moved out of reach, fearing for the worst. I was too weak to move all of the way and he finally reached me. He held out his hand and I stared up at it, furrowing my brows. What was I supposed to do?

Reluctantly, I grabbed his hand and he hesitantly pulled me up. My body throbbed but I was okay enough to walk slowly. We moved out of the cell that bids our abilities and we started moving down the narrow hallway. Up ahead, Creators started moving down the hallway, laughing and joking around, unaware what was going on.

"Stay here," the masked man said with a dark voice. He ran forward and all of the Creators in front of him were pushed out of the way. The man kept fighting and he became out of view.

I leaned up against the white wall, breathing heavily from my lack of energy. Suddenly, shouts were coming down the hallway. A group of unmasked Creators started running my way while screaming and yelling. Fear started to embrace me.

"Make sure you don't hurt her! Dante wants to make sure she is the real Esther! Don't disfigure her face!" a Creator yelled.

One of the Creators came up to me, grabbing my arm forcefully. I gritted my teeth, using my strength to punch him in the jaw. I kicked out my leg and I hit him in the knee. I heard a crunch and he fell to the ground. Two Creators came my way, both of them grabbing my shoulders. I shook their hands off, using my elbow to hit one in the throat and I used my fist to knock the other man out. They both fell to the ground, trying to straighten out their bearings. My fists started to ache from punching.

One last Creator ran my way, screaming out unknown words. He brought up his fist, punching me in the cheek. The impact made me fall to the ground and I clutched my face, staring up at him. The Creator grabbed my hair and started forcefully picking me up from the ground. I screamed out in pain, trying to dig my nails into his hand.

"Let go of her!" a familiar voice screamed.

Suddenly, the Creator that was holding me from the hair was thrown into a wall and I fell to the ground once he released me. The masked man ran over to me, pulling off his mask. I stared into his bright blue eyes and familiar face, gasping.

"Damion," I whispered.

Damion stared down at me, grabbing my hand to pull me up. But the thing was, we didn't hug, we didn't truly acknowledge each other because I was sure we both knew things were different now.

"Can you run?" he asked me.

Even though I couldn't run, I nodded my head. I ignored the pain as we started running down the hallway. We made our way into the corridor that had dead bodies everywhere. I turned around, realizing the hallway that I noticed before with Cado was where I was locked up.

"Dante is coming. I need to get you out of here before then,"

350

Damion said with a hint of distress.

"I need to find my friends," I yelled over the slapping noises our feet made.

"How are we even going to find them, Esther?" Damion asked.

"Clockworks wear white and my friends and I wear black. Easy find," I said.

"They're probably in the main section of the Compound. That's where the large battle is to kill off Creators."

"Oh, and by the way, I'm pissed at you too," I yelled.

"Understandable. We can talk about it later though because right now we need to hurry."

We came out of the corridor and now we were standing in the entrance where the Creators use to be guarding the doors. Abilities sprang out everywhere amongst the white and gray uniforms.

"Clockworks!" I screamed. "Hurry and get in groups and leave!"

In the chaos, I managed to find a black uniform in the crowd. It was Phoenix. Off in the distance was another set of black outfits: Cado and Electra.

"We need to get to them," I said.

Clockworks began to form into groups and most of them began to retreat.

"Hold onto me," Damion said. I stared up at him, furrowing my brows. "Now!"

I grabbed a hold of his torso and he placed his hand in the direction of the ground. We levitated in the air, moving off the balcony and below to the battle. We landed on the ground next to Electra and Cado.

"Why the hell is a Creator with you?" Cado exclaimed.

"I'll explain later," I stated.

"Esther, I'm afraid you're not thinking straight," Electra said, staring at Damion.

Phoenix ran over to us, eying Damion suspiciously. "Where were you, Esther? We were trying to find you in the crowd."

"I'll explain everything later but we need to leave now," I said, my voice cracking.

"Why?" Cado asked.

Almost on cue, the wall closest to us exploded open and

351

Dante with an army of Creators started to pile in. Damion pushed out his hands and Dante flew to the other side of the wall. Creators turned to look at us and abilities started flying our way. Damion used his telekinesis to push the abilities back at the Creators. I watched as he bended the abilities powerfully, using them against the Creators. Damion stood in front of us as he fought them off and I felt myself being mesmerized by his abilities.

"Esther," Dante said quietly in my ear. I turned around, noticing he was standing in front of me. I brought up my fist, knocking him in the jaw. Before Dante could react, a hand grabbed my arm and my vision clouded with green, fiery gas. The next thing I know, we landed in the cabin, all of us breathing heavily.

"Whoa," Electra breathed. "That was intense."

I held myself up against the wall, staring at Damion with wide eyes. All of it started to hit me now. Why was he a Creator? Why didn't he just come and see me if he was so upset about me moving? And why the hell was he standing right there in front of me without a damn explanation?

"Now, Esther, why is there a Creator with us?" Phoenix asked.

I continued staring at Damion while he glanced at the scenery of the cabin. "I'm sure Sapphire told you what she saw about me. And this, this is Damion. I'm still confused on the situation as well."

Damion turned around to stare at me. I looked into his blue eyes and I couldn't believe those blue eyes acknowledged me.

"Well, we're not going to take care of him. He is your doing and you take care of him," Cado said. "You also need to take care of Acea. He has to leave before the War begins. I have a feeling the Creators aren't going to wait for you to find the Exol Child."

"Acea?" Damion asked. "Who is that?"

"A person," I stated.

"Well, I suppose I'll leave everyone alone now.... To gather themselves since this whole situation is... Well..." Electra said.

"Awkward," I said firmly, continuing to stare at Damion. He still held his slender composure but I could tell he gained muscles.

"I'm going to go get Acea," Phoenix stated. "You need to tell him to leave because I'm afraid he is going to hold us back."

"Okay, yeah, okay," I said, still staring at Damion. He was staring at me back and I knew all of our memories were resurfacing in his mind.

"Alright, well, I'm going to go too," Cado said while walking out with Phoenix.

"I don't even know what to say to you, Damion," I said dryly.

"Well, that's a surprise. I mean, after all, we haven't seen each other in quite a few months," he said caustically.

I rolled my eyes and I crossed my arms. "Whatever."

After a few moments of awkwardly standing in the center of the living room, Phoenix came into the room with Acea. Acea walked in with a smile but I knew Phoenix already told him that he had to leave.

"Hi," Acea said calmly.

"Hi."

"I'm very proud of you and what you have done for your people," Acea said as he stood in front of me, staring me in the eyes.

"I can finally say that I am proud of myself too," I said with a smile.

"Promise me, Esther, that after this all ends, you'll come back to see me?" Acea asked with calm eyes. "I don't deserve a friend after everything wrong I have done... And I have done a lot of bad things to you... But please, promise me." I noticed a few tears welling up around his irises.

"I promise, Acea. And after all of this time, I do forgive you. People mess up. We make mistakes. But it's all a part of being human," I managed a smile as I looked into his soft, plush face. I remember the time where we were in my meadow and he poured out his soul to me. I knew there was truth behind the phrases he said even though he played the game with Leila.

"You're always going to be my dawn in my darkness, Esther," Acea said.

I couldn't hold myself back anymore. I reached up and placed my hands around his neck and embraced him. He wrapped his arms around my waist and I gently put my face on his shoulder.

"I'll come back to you, I promise. But don't you dare screw up again," I said with a chuckle. I released him and I felt the tears welling up in my eyes too. I felt bad I didn't notice how good of a person he was before. He was only clouded with the thoughts of school.

"I'm going to take him back home now," Phoenix stated.

"His parents are probably worried sick. While I'm gone, I'm going to check on the Clockworks and tell them to prepare for the War. Alright?"

"Okay. Bye Acea," I said.

"Bye Esther," Acea said with a smile.

The two of them engulfed in a green, fiery blaze and they left without another word.

"You couldn't have been more dramatic?" Damion asked.

I turned around, giving him a glare. "Where were you then? Huh? I'm allowed to move on *without* you."

Damion and I sat at the kitchen table and I watched him eat his soup. He slurped every piece of corn and broth. I continued watching him, trying to think of harmfully mean things to say to him.

"So why did you become a Creator? Huh? Why did you join forces with the people that are after me?" I asked, trying to keep the venom in my voice to a minimum.

I watched as Damion licked his lips, staring down at his bowl of soup. "Esther, I hope you know how much things can affect people."

I rolled my eyes. "If me leaving you hurt so bad, why didn't you just come to visit me? Why did you choose to become a Creator if you could still see me? You *didn't* try and you *didn't* understand."

"I know I didn't understand, Esther. I was foolish then. I was arrogant. But you don't understand either."

"What are you talking about? I do understand. You were just a butt hurt kid that was desperate to feel happiness," I said, staring him down.

"That's it," Damion said, standing up while slapping his hand against the table. "I don't see why I should stay here if you can't understand."

I crossed my arms over my chest while rolling my eyes. "K, I'm all ears. I'll listen."

Damion sighed, sitting back down. I knew he couldn't fully walk away until he said what was needed to be said.

"Before I met you, Esther, everything in my life was awful. I was an outcast at all of the schools I've been to. Everyone looked at me strangely as if they knew I was different. We moved countless times so everywhere I went was known to be a temporary home. It was never ending. I didn't have a dad to play sports with and teach me how to become a man because he didn't want nothing to do with me. He called me an alien and I was known to be their mistake. He said after me my mother couldn't have any more kids.

"My dad used to beat me in my younger years because I would blow something up or simply break something valuable. I didn't know how to control my abilities as a kid. But when I started to learn, the more I began to fight back. I broke his back one year and that's when he decided to work his life away so he didn't have to see me. I only had my mom but then she started to become my dad. She started to hit me and she told me if I hit her back, she would send me away to a juvenile camp." Tears started to form around Damion's irises.

"My aunt was the only one that taught me true kindness. I lived with her for a little bit before I moved to Oklahoma. But unfortunately, she became busy with a man so she sent me away to live with my parents again. When I came back into their lives, they didn't welcome me. They got a big house so they wouldn't cross paths with me. Yes, I did have a big house and nice things, but honestly, money doesn't matter to me. Love does. I wished I had a family that could teach me about life. I wish I had a mom that could teach me how to stand up for what I believed in. I wish I had a dad that could teach me how to be brave." Damion looked up at me. "But you taught me how to be brave and how to be rebellious. Obviously, I still need to work on more aspects of my personality... But no one is perfect. We all make mistakes in the long run.

"But when I said the things I said to you after Becca's grandma's funeral... I thought you hated me. I thought you never wanted to see me again. I fought with my parents so they could take me to Pennsylvania but they told me that you called and you never wanted to see me again. I don't know if that was true or not, so I tried calling you. But before I could press Talk, my mother came into my room, punched me hard enough to make me drop my phone. She smashed it with her foot and walked away without another word."

"I never called your family and said that, Damion. I thought you hated me. After all, you did say you did," I stated.

"One of the biggest mistakes I made was on that very day and I am sorry for my careless, reckless and arrogant self, Esther.

But anyways, I was shut off from the people around me. My parents didn't want me to leave the house and they wanted me to stay in their sight. Since I was locked away in my own confinement, I felt myself not wanting a single place in the world. I wanted to be a Creator to see if I could feel happiness again and I wanted to see if I could find you by being one too. I didn't have a phone to call you and I didn't know exactly where you lived. So being a Creator was my last choice. I felt like Alvaro and Becca wouldn't accept me either if I was to reach out to them."

"They would've accepted you, Damion."

"Yeah, well, like I said. I wasn't thinking too straight then."

"Damion, I can't tell you how sorry I am that all of that has happened to you. I wish I was there for you," I said what I truly felt.

"Esther, where's your mother? I would expect to see her by now," Damion asked while furrowing his brows.

I swallowed a lump in my throat. My hands started to tremble and memories of the knife wound to her gut resurfaced. "She died protecting me."

Damion leaned back in his chair, starting to shake his head in disbelief. "Esther, I'm so sorry... I know a 'sorry' won't fix anything... But... I just can't believe..." he trailed off.

"Its fine," I said, getting up from the table. "She died for a purpose. She knew what she was doing."

Damion shook his head. "Things will never be the same again."

"I know," I whispered, leaning up against a wall. "I know they won't."

"How do we act the same?" he asked.

I shrugged my shoulders, unsure on why things should be the same. "I think it was just puppy love, Damion. We were both unhappy. We were both desperate for a spark of happiness."

Damion stood up, walking his bowl to the sink. "You're right. We probably weren't meant to feel that way about each other."

I took a deep breath. "Yeah. I agree."

"So," he said, taking a deep breath. His hands gripped the counter. "We are only friends now?"

"Yes, Damion. It was only puppy love," I stated. "It wasn't real."

"Well," he breathed. "I'll still stand by you in the War."

I swallowed, crossing my arms. "Okay. Cado is the Spiritual Human in the Prophecy. He is supposed to help me in the War. I couldn't find the Exol Child and I know I don't have any time to. In the Prophecy..." I trailed off, realizing I was about to mention the part about my death. I couldn't tell anyone. I especially couldn't tell Damion.

"Yes?" Damion asked, arching a brow.

"Well, you know... After Dante dies everyone lives in harmony." It wasn't technically a lie.

"Well, I suppose that's good." He paused. "I'm going to go to the room assigned to me now... See you tomorrow."

"Yeah, uh. See you tomorrow," I said, trying not to be awkward. I watched as Damion left the kitchen and made his way into the hallway. Once he was gone, I let out a deep sigh, resting my head on the wall. *I hope I made the right decision. On letting go not only Acea, but Damion as well.*

It was the next morning and the sun was shining brightly overhead. The air was slightly humid but bearable. Electra was tending to the cabin's gardens. Cado, Phoenix and Damion were practicing battle strategies together and I helped them with a few moves myself.

I was walking across the yard with a box full of battle equipment. My legs were buckling underneath me because the box was absolutely one of the heaviest things I ever carried. I walked a few more steps until I laid it gently on the grass, taking a few breaths. I wiped the sweat off my brow, picked up the box again and continued making my way towards the Maze.

Up ahead, I saw Damion walking out of the Maze with a sword in his hand. He was slightly sweaty and he had a large gash above his beautiful blue eyes. I shook my head angrily, wondering why I even thought that.

"Do you need help carrying that?" Damion asked me once he reached me.

"No. I got it." I adjusted the box in my arms to make it seem like I had it under control.

"I mean, Esther, your legs are shaking... Here, just give me the box," he said.

"No, it might be too heavy for you," I said.

"Um, I do have super strength," he said with a chuckle.

I sighed, handing him the box of supplies. I felt our hands graze each other and the electrifying spark swept over my body. I pulled my hands away quickly and he stared down at me. I knew he felt it too. It was always a stronger spark than with any other Being.

"I guess the spark isn't going away," I whispered, putting my hands in my jeans. I felt my flannel rustle in the slight breeze, making the humid day slightly comforting.

"Yeah," Damion said, holding the large box in his arms. "It's just a spark."

I watched as he walked away back towards the Maze. I sighed again, wondering what even happened.

"Esther," Electra said, appearing next to me. "Why are you guys acting so awkward? You guys obviously like each other."

"We don't like each other, Electra. Maybe back then but not now."

"Ugh, whatever. Can you help me tend to the gardens? You've been practicing enough," Electra said.

"Okay. I'll go get some gloves."

"When do you think the War is going to begin?" Electra asked me as we pulled out the dead plants and put in new flowers.

"I don't know. Why are we even fighting?" I asked.

She shrugged her shoulders. "I think we're fighting for freedom from the Creators."

"All because of one damn section in a book?" I asked, angrily digging up an old flower.

"Well, the Creators want to know how to gain more power over the humans and the Beings. I suppose that section describes the steps."

"If Icelos did create Brilliance, why would he put things like that in it?" I asked, my curiosity growing stronger.

"Like I said, I don't know. You need to ask him or an expert," Electra said.

"Well, if I could talk to him I would. He left me with so many questions."

"Ask somebody else, Esther. I don't like hearing talk about Brilliance. That thing changed everything in everyone's lives."

"Yeah," I said, looking down at the yellow, coruscating flower. "It changes everything."

There was noise coming from the Maze so gradually, I glanced up, noticing Damion, Cado and Phoenix laughing and joking with each other. Damion was in mid-laugh when he looked at me. I felt my blood rise to my throat and quickly, I looked back down at the flower. I still couldn't believe he was here with me. The boy who saw me before everything changed: before my dad died, before I was Chosen, before my mother was killed. I didn't know what life would be like after everything was over.

"Hey, Esther and Electra, want to go inside and eat dinner? It looks like it's about to rain anyways," Phoenix said.

I glanced up at the sky, noticing the swirling dark clouds rolling in. I felt a single raindrop fall onto my nose.

"Yes," Electra said, getting up while dusting off her dirty knees.

I stood up with her, noticing Damion was watching me. I gave him a small smile and followed Electra into the cabin. Once we entered the cabin, we were greeted with nice, cold air that made all of us sigh with relief.

"Feels nice in here, doesn't it?" Cado asked with a small laugh.

"Does this feel nice?" Phoenix asked, putting Cado into a headlock. They laughed jokingly but then Cado used one of his MMA moves on Phoenix, making him fall on his butt.

"I don't think that was very fair," Phoenix said, creating a ball of acid while laughing.

"Knock it off," Electra said, "before you disintegrate the whole cabin."

Almost simultaneously, Damion and I let out a laugh. We glanced up at each other but then I looked away quickly. I stood awkwardly against the counter, watching as Electra began making cold sandwiches for all of us.

"Mayonnaise and tomatoes, right Phoenix?" Electra asked as she pulled out ingredients.

"Yes, please," Phoenix gave Electra a small grin. I glanced at Electra and she quickly looked down at the sandwich while smiling.

"When did you two become so friendly?" Cado asked while raising a brow.

"What are you talking about, Cado? I'm acting the same way," she retaliated.

I laughed. "I don't know... There are more smiles and blushes in the air."

Phoenix shook his head angrily while staring at the ground. I frowned slightly, wondering why he was upset that we noticed his feelings. Slowly, Phoenix moved across the living area and he stared out the window.

"What are you looking at?" Damion asked, arching his eyebrows. I saw tingles run up his body and he was instantly covered in goose bumps.

A loud rumbling came from outside and the front side of the cabin went completely up in flames, making Phoenix fly back. Screams rang out and another boom sprung out, sending me off my feet as waves of pressure engulfed my body. I flew into the air while shards of wood followed my movement. I hit my head against the back of the cabin and I fell to the floor. My body began to erupt into a series of awful and agonizing pain. I screamed, trying to look around for my friends. Dark pieces of wood surrounded me and I knew I was trapped.

I used my hands to crawl across the ground but shards of glass and pieces of wood pierced my skin.

"Esther!" I heard Damion scream. "Where are you?"

"Agh!" I gritted my teeth as another wave of pain surfaced across my legs. "Ov—ver here!" I tried to manage my muffled words.

I fought the pain and the ennui. I had to be strong and get my friends out of this mess. I felt my air starting to escape my lungs. I was suffocating underneath all of the planks. I had to make it out of here. I couldn't pass out from an explosion. I screamed, using all of my energy to create a force field. The force field repelled against the pieces of wood. The wood lifted up off of me in a heap. I looked up and I could see the dark sky along with sections of the cabin going up in flames. Shadows danced across the skies like black ghosts floating in the air. We were being attacked.

I used my strength to lift myself up. Gradually, I stood up. Most of the cabin was gone and at the front entrance stood Creators that swirled fire and other powerful abilities around the cabin.

"Stop!" I screamed as flaming ashes floated down from above. I gritted my teeth and I created a force field, pushing it out at the men. They yelled while flying back into a set of trees outside. Up ahead, I could see Dante with a group of Creators circling around him. I felt my blood rise up to my throat and I dropped down in the mess of wood quickly. I glanced at the remains of the long, winding counter ahead. I had to hide behind that before Dante could find me.

I crawled across the planks as they cut up my hands and knees. I groaned while setting my back against the counter. Everything around me was a mess and I didn't know where anyone was.

"Esther," I heard Damion whisper my name. I glanced around the area, noticing he was hiding behind a few cabinets.

"Dante is here," I whispered.

He shook his head and he held up a finger to his lips, motioning me to be quiet. I could hear footsteps stepping on shards of glass on the other side of the counter. I held my breath and I could feel my eyes starting to water from fear.

"Find them!" I heard Dante scream. "I'm in charge of when the War begins and it begins now!" I could tell Dante was outside due to the distant sound of his voice.

I inhaled a deep breath, staring at Damion with large eyes. His eyes widely stared back at me and I knew he was scared. Suddenly, Damion opened his mouth to scream but I felt the pressure hit my back before I could react. I found myself flying through the air and my body crashed onto the kitchen table, breaking it in half. I rolled off the remains and I could smell charred skin. I glanced down, noticing my flannel was ripped and had ashes all over its red texture.

"Esther!" I heard Damion yell. Another scream protruded and the sound of a body hitting the ground filled the air. In seconds, I felt a set of strong hands grab onto my arms, pulling me up. "You okay?"

"Yes," I breathed, sucking in all of the pain. "What was his ability?"

"He's still alive but I believe he has combustion. He can blow shit up," Damion said.

"No, kidding."

"Get down low. We need to crawl to the hallway that leads into the bedrooms. We have a better chance of possibly finding your friends there. They could have ran."

We got onto our hands and knees and stayed down low so the

explosions wouldn't knock us off of our feet. Everything around us was completely destroyed. In the distance, I saw Dante's head move quickly passed a window. I knew he was looking for us.

"Do we fight or do we hide?" I asked Damion, looking at his serious features. His lips were pursed into a thin line and his blue eyes scanned the area of Creators outside of the cabin. To the side of us, behind the cabinets, we heard footsteps cracking the pieces of wood.

Before Damion could respond, another explosion blew out next to Damion and I could feel my body lift up into the air and quickly, we fell back down, landing on top of each other.

"Go! Go!" Damion screamed.

We crawled across the ground while explosions went off behind us. I could feel slight pressure grazing across my ankles as we crawled at a fast pace. I felt myself struggling across the planks and my heart was beating rapidly. More explosions went off on either side of us, making us jump.

"I don't know where he is!" Damion exclaimed.

"We can't keep crawling!" I yelled at him.

Suddenly, I felt the pressure hit my leg and I screamed out in pain, knowing I was hit.

"Come on!" Damion yelled, tugging onto my arm.

I gritted my teeth as I crawled across the ground. I knew I had to do something to get us out of this mess. I had to use my energy to fight back. I latched onto Damion's wrist and I closed my eyes. I began to think about peaceful thoughts such as my mother's smile and my father's eyes. I felt the sensational rush and I opened my eyes. I couldn't see Damion but I could feel his wrist. Our hands slid into each other's' and we got up while the explosions were going off. I moved my hand around, creating a force field around us. We ran across the cabin and I felt my feet sinking into the planks.

"Fight!" Damion yelled.

I glanced behind me and I saw the Creator with combustion trying to locate us. Suddenly, the Creator flew back into the side of the cabin that had the couch up against the wall. The wall crumbled onto the Creator and he screamed underneath the weight. I knew Damion used his telekinesis to push the man and the wall. Spontaneously, the wall exploded off of the man and he stood up slowly. He grinned blankly at his surroundings as if he knew where we were. One by one, he threw balls of explosions at each corner of the living room.

One ball of fiery explosions hurtled our way and I yelped, knowing my force field wouldn't hold it off. I let go of Damion's hand, simultaneously creating a force field and I molded it around the explosion. With all of my strength, I pushed the explosion back at the Creator, releasing the force field once it reached him. The ball hit the man completely, blowing up each of his limbs.

"How'd you learn to do that?" Damion yelled.

"I don't know! It just came to me one day!" I yelled back.

Our hands met each other and I could feel the warmth of his skin on mine. We ran across the living room, making our way into the demolished hallway. Up ahead, I could see Cado in his bedroom tending to Phoenix's wounds.

"There they are," I said. I released the force field and invisibility on us and we made our way into Cado's room.

Cado glanced up at us with eyes full of worry. "In the explosion Phoenix lost half of his foot. He's losing too much blood and he can't walk. What do we do?"

I swallowed, noticing Damion and Cado were looking at me for an explanation. "Where's Electra?"

Cado shrugged his shoulders. "I don't know. I can't find her!" I could hear the panic in his voice. "I thought Phoenix and I were the only ones alive."

I glanced down at Phoenix and he was groaning in pain. My heart sunk and I knew we had to find Electra and find a way out of here.

"Damion and I will try to find Electra. In the meantime, use Sapphire's medicine to tame his pain." I grabbed onto Damion's arm. "Come on, let's go."

Together, Damion and I ran back down the demolished hallway. We stopped behind a wall before we went back into the open-concept living room and kitchen.

"I need to save my energy for force fields to keep us safe. Invisibility takes too much of it," I whispered. I could hear footsteps entering the cabin ahead.

"Why do you have ennui now? It's so much worse now," Damion whispered, staring down at me with his acknowledging eyes.

"Things change. I used them too much," I said as a sense of guilt washed over me.

"Your burns, on your back, are they okay?" he asked.

"Yeah, they're fine."

"Are you ready to fight?" he asked, placing his hand on my shoulder. I felt the spark tingle my entire body again. Every time he touched me I could feel the spark.

I nodded my head and gave him an encouraging smile. "As long as you are."

"That's the Esther I know."

We ran out behind the wall and a few Creators ahead noticed us. Abilities starting hurtling our way and quickly, I created a force field, blocking each ability from hitting us. Damion clenched his jaw, pushing his hands out. He mentally picked up two Creators and smashed them together, killing each of them instantly. The other two Creators continued firing non-stop blows that weakened my force field. Damion pushed out his hands once more, making the Creators fly back into a few trees outside.

"Did you here that?" a Creator asked.

"Yes," I heard that familiar voice that added in a chuckle. "I can only imagine who they are."

"Dante," I whispered to Damion. "He's around the corner. Outside of the cabin."

I could hear footsteps on the porch and in seconds, three Creators were standing in front of us.

"You ready?" Damion asked with his usual goofy grin.

I smiled reluctantly. "Yes. This time we attack from the front. Not from a distance."

I dropped my broken force field right before abilities started to come our way. I moved out my arm, using my hand to create another one that was long enough to cover Damion and me. We ran forward while the force field blocked the abilities. I could see the fear that surfaced across the Creators' eyes once they noticed us coming at them full speed. I dropped the force field while Damion jumped onto a Creator. I lifted up my fist, punching a man with dark hair and dark eyes in the face. The Creator beside him wounded up her abilities but I used a force field to push her off the porch before she could hit me. The man in front of me watched her fly back and hit her head on a rock with dark, menacing eyes. He created a gooey substance in his hand but I punched him again, making the man drop the substance onto the floor of the cabin. The gooey substance began to eat at the floor of the cabin at a rapid pace.

"Don't let it touch you!" I yelled at Damion, jumping over the affected areas. "Hurry! Get out of the cabin!"

I used a sharp force field, slashing the man before he could create more of the substance. I glanced over at Damion and he finished killing his Creator.

"We need to warn Cado!" Damion yelled. He grabbed my hand and he pulled me close to him. I wrapped my arms around his neck and he placed his other hand in the direction of the melting floor. We levitated up in the air and he pushed us off of the porch. We landed on the grass next to each other, watching as the substance devoured the remains of the entryway. It started to reach the area in the hallway.

"Cado!" I screamed at the top of my lungs, loud enough that anyone could hear. "Get out of there! Now!"

The green, gooey substance ate away the cabin and I could see a dark figure run out of the small remains of the cabin with a body in arms and a bag across his back.

"He got out in time," Damion said. "He's running towards the Maze."

Shadows began chasing after Cado and they disappeared once they all entered the Maze.

"So nice to see you again." I glanced up, noticing Dante walking casually over to us with a flock of Creators and Shadows surrounding him. Dante still had his piercings and tattoos.

"Esther!" Damion screamed. "Run!"

Without hesitation, I got up and began running across the yard, edging closer to the small pond where Cado spent a week when his sister died. Before I could continue moving, my body automatically stopped and I knew I was in Dante's spell. I felt my spine shift and pain washed over my entire body. I let out a bloodcurdling scream and I felt my body fall to the ground.

"No! Stop!" I heard Damion yell.

"Attack him," Dante simply said, flipping his wrist and I felt another series of pain engulf my body. I let out another scream while my spine shifted once more. My body was in an awkward position. I glanced to the left of me and I watched as Damion started to run while Shadows chased after him. They swirled around him and he tried swiping them away but he didn't know the true way to fight a Shadow.

"Damion," I whispered barely audible to my own ears. I felt a single tear starting to stream down my cheek as the pain began to subside.

Dante started walking over to me and I tried desperately to move away but my body wasn't cooperating. He knelt down beside me with a small, sickening grin plastered on his face.

"The mighty Esther in love with a stupid boy," Dante said with a chuckle.

"Shut up," I said through gritted teeth. "You don't know what true love is."

He let out a harsh laugh while leaning over me. "So ignorant."

"Esther, watch out!" I heard Electra yell.

I grinned up at Dante. "You lose."

A bolt of lightning shot Dante in the back and he screamed out in pain. He fell onto his side and I felt all of my energy come back to me. I stood up and ran across the pond to Electra.

"Where were you?" I asked.

"When the explosion happened, I flew out of the cabin. I was knocked out for quite some time until I woke up right next to the cabin that was being eaten away slowly by that stuff. I heard screams and I tried to get up. Now I finally did enough to save you," Electra said, giving me a warm smile.

"We need to go save Damion and find Cado and Phoenix."

"Fricken assholes destroyed my flowers!" Electra screamed after we started to jog.

We ran across the yard, trying to find Damion. There were two Creators ahead of us and simultaneously, Electra shot one down with a bolt of lightning and I sliced one with a force field. In the far distance by the tree line, I saw Damion trying to fight off the Shadows swarming around him.

"Patience Damion!" I screamed.

He glanced up for a moment, acknowledging that I was okay and then he focused on the Shadows again. I watched him take a deep breath and then chaos sprung out. Shadows screamed and their form started to weaken. Bodies began falling from the sky and

Damion caught them with his telekinesis. He slammed the bodies into trees and rocks, killing most of them instantly. We finally reached Damion when he killed the last Creator.

"We need to go into the Maze and get Cado and Phoenix," I stated.

Damion glanced at Electra and then to me. His eyes were filled with bewilderment. "How do we get out of here? Creators are everywhere." He motioned towards the sky. There were Creators swirling around Dante's body in the distance.

"Uh... I know. We can visit Alvaro. He'll help us with our wounds," I said.

"Alvaro? Who is that?" Electra asked.

"An old friend of ours," Damion stated.

I heard commotion coming from behind us. We all turned around realizing Dante was walking across the yard with a small army of Creators. I created a large enough force field that wrapped around us. Abilities started hurtling our way and they smashed into my force field with small explosions. We started running towards the entrance of the Maze and I could hear all of the abilities smacking into my force field. I tried to keep it strong but I had a lack of energy.

We ran inside the Maze and the scenery around us changed. There were tree trunks everywhere. Figures started making their way around the trees and they added more abilities onto my force field.

"How do we find Cado?" I asked.

"We each have to think of them and the scenery might change! I don't guarantee it will work but it's worth a try!" Electra yelled over the ear-wrenching noises.

I closed my eyes and started thinking of Cado. I thought of his facial features and his personality traits: young and afraid, but wise and strong. I felt the atmosphere change around me so I opened my eyes while taking down the force field. Cado was in the distance fighting off Shadows and Creators while Phoenix was on the ground with his eyes rolled back inside his head. Electra screamed, clutching her chest. She ran over to Phoenix and knelt down next to him while holding his hand.

"Cado!" I screamed.

Damion and I ran forward at a quick speed. I reached a Creator while punching her across the face. I brought up my leg and kicked her to the ground. I created a sharp force field and ended her life quickly while Cado was trying to fight back many at once. Another Creator with a dark mustache and light eyes came up to me. He slapped me across the face and I felt the petrifying tingle sizzle across my cheek. I looked up and he spontaneously shot a red liquid at me. I tried to create a force field fast enough but the liquid bit into my shoulder. I screamed out in pain while clutching part of my shoulder. Blood started to pour down my arm. I glanced up again and the man shot the same red liquid at me but this time I created a force field fast enough. Angrily, the man created the substance again but I blocked it with another field. I laughed, creating a sharp force field that sliced him open.

Suddenly, I felt arms wrap around my throat from behind. I grabbed a hold of the cold hands but the person started turning my neck to the side. I felt my neck starting to crack and I yelped. I kicked out my leg, kicking the large man in the groin. He let go of me and Damion killed the man before I could.

"Are you okay?" Damion asked with worried-filled eyes.

"Yes. I'm fine. We need to get out of here though. We can't fight all of them off and who knows when Dante will know the mystery of the Maze," I said.

"Okay," Damion said. "Cado! We need to go!"

Cado flipped over a man, slicing him across the back in one simple movement. Cado ran across the underbrush, meeting Damion and me. We all ran over to Electra that was hunched over Phoenix. His eyes were open but his breathing was beginning to slow.

"I'm so sorry," Phoenix whispered.

"I know you're in pain, Phoenix. But we need to get to a healer. His name is Alvaro and we have to go now. Can you make a portal?" I asked.

Behind us, a few Creators started coming but Damion pushed them back mentally. Weakly, Phoenix sat up with Electra's help. He closed his eyes and he began to create an electrifying portal that had frayed edges. In time, the portal grew to a size big enough for all of us to fit in. Cado bent down and picked up Phoenix while Damion grabbed my hand, giving me another spark. Electra went in first and then Damion and I went. Cado followed shortly behind. Whizzing noises filled my ears and, in the distance, I could see a dark room lit by candles.

The portal spat us out and we landed on a dark, hardwood floor. Each of us glided across the floor and we all yelped in pain. After a few seconds of coping, I glanced over at Damion on the ground next to me.

"Are you hurt?" he asked, staring at me with his intense blue eyes. He started to prop himself up.

"No," I whispered. I stood up gradually while Cado and Electra did the same.

Ahead of us, movement lurked about the curtains and distinctively I could see a shadow staring at us with cat-like eyes. The figure moved quickly in the dim lighting, passing beside me while making goose bumps trail across my skin. Light suddenly filled the whole room and Alvaro passed beside me again so he could stare at all of us. I watched as his eyes fell on Phoenix and his lips pursed into a thin line. His eyes began to scan Cado, Electra, Damion and then they stopped on me. A grin spread across his lips and he rushed over to me, wrapping his arms around me while breathing on my neck.

"I'm so sorry, Esther... About your mother," Alvaro whispered in my ear.

I wrapped my arms around him tightly while feeling his cold skin bring shivers down my spine. It felt good being in the arms of someone who understood everything about me. He knew a majority of the answers to all of my questions.

"She knew what she was doing," I told him so I could believe the words myself.

He embraced me with the love and compassion of a father. I could feel his body heaving every breath he took. Slowly, Alvaro pulled away reluctantly. "I'm proud of how strong you have become." He rubbed his hands down my arms while smiling into my eyes. I felt tears welling up around my irises as the memories of my mother and father glided into my mind as I stared into Alvaro's eyes. There was this peculiar feeling I received after losing both of my parents when I needed them most. I felt like waves were crashing upon me and I could never resurface. I felt like I need them to pull me out and save me. I needed them. I needed them more than anything right now. But slowly, I felt competent that I could be able to pull myself out of the waves crashing down on me.

"Don't cry, sweetie," Alvaro whispered, wiping my tears with his thumb. "A soldier doesn't cry."

I'm not a soldier then, I thought. "Phoenix needs help."

"Oh yes," Alvaro clapped his hands together and he lifted Phoenix out of Cado's arms. Alvaro gave Cado a nod and a smile and then he turned on his heel, exiting the room into his curtains.

"Will he be okay?" Electra asked, walking towards me with tears streaming down her face.

"He'll be fine, Electra," I managed a smile but I felt despair myself. "Alvaro helped me when I was electrocuted and burned. He can definitely help Phoenix."

"But you live until Dante kills you," Electra stated bitterly, sensing my own emotions. She stomped across the hardwood floor and she left out the front door while slamming the door shut.

"She just needs to cool off," Damion said, gently placing his hand on my back naturally as if he forgot we decided to not care about each other. I glanced up, wanting to give him a glare but I simply couldn't. My facial features softened and I allowed the electric tingle my entire body. Damion stared down at me as the familiar grin appeared across his lips. I knew he was enjoying the tingle too. I just couldn't let him care for me if I'm meant to die.

"Um, so what do we do now?" Cado asked, making Damion and I split apart quickly. "I mean, we were just attacked by Creators and the one who is leading them. They want the War to begin now." Cado and Damion were staring at me like they wanted me to answer.

I sighed. "I feel like we're not ready... We don't have the Exol Child. Without the Child, I know I'm going to di—" I stopped myself quickly so I wouldn't expose my death.

"Well, have you forgotten? The Spiritual Human is standing right in front of you. I can be as much as a help as the Exol Child... Unless Brilliance differed..." Cado trailed off, narrowing his eyes on me.

I bit my lip and I could feel my specious persona beginning to show. If I kept worrying about dying, they would eventually find out. "No, Brilliance doesn't say different. It's just... I don't feel complete without having the most powerful Clockwork in the world standing next to me while I fight off Dante."

"Oh? You don't think I'm *strong* enough to help you? You look down upon me, don't you? You think I'm *weak*." Cado glared at me menacingly. He shook his head angrily and stomped across the hardwood floor while pushing away strings that hung from the ceiling.

"No, Cado, don't go—" I yelled. He ignored me, opened the door, walked out and slammed the door shut just like how Electra had.

"Esther," Damion whispered with a tone I couldn't make sense of. "Is there something you're not telling me?"

I turned around slowly, quickly noticing his blue eyes that took my breath away every time I stared into them. I avoided staring into his eyes so I could easily lie to him. "No, of course not."

"Just know that I'll *always* be there for you. Whatever the circumstance, I'll be there for you... Because I c—" He quickly stopped what he was saying.

"Thank you. That means a lot. You're a good friend, Damion," I said, trying to keep the term only as friends. He nodded his head while clenching his jaw lightly.

"Yeah. You're welcome," he said with a nasty tone.

I rolled my eyes and scanned Alvaro's shop. It was completely the same with the original decorations. Across the room I spotted a calendar and I instantly grew curious on what day it was. I forgot the dates ever since I was attacked by the Creators in my school. I pushed away the thoughts as I walked up to the calendar. Old bookshelves filled with dusty books were slightly in my path but I slid through them to look at the date. It was May fourteenth. I gasped, remembering Damion's birthday was tomorrow. I placed my hands on a dirty desk while turning my head to look at Damion. "What day do you think it is, Damion?"

"Uhh, I don't know. I haven't looked at a calendar in months," he replied bitterly.

"Well," I said while walking out from behind the bookshelves so he could see me. I wiped my dusty hands on my jeans. "Today is May fourteenth. Your birthday is tomorrow."

Damion shrugged his shoulders, avoiding my eye contact. "I don't care. It doesn't matter."

I was about to protest until Alvaro called me into the curtains. I felt very vexed with the way Damion was acting but I was competent to ignore it. I walked into the curtains, quickly noticing Phoenix holding his leg with tears streaming down his eyes. He stared up at the ceiling with desolation.

"Phoenix," I whispered, running to the side of the bed. I grabbed his hand that wasn't clutching his leg while Alvaro worked on it. His hand was entirely warm to the point I felt his sweat trailing down my fingers. I frowned slightly, watching him thrive in pain silently. "What's wrong with him?"

"I gave him a strong sedative that comes from the Mighty Oliver's Tree in the Exol's palace. It froze him in that position so he doesn't show us that he's hurting... But he is on the inside," Alvaro responded in sorrow.

"I'm so sorry, Phoenix." I bent down and kissed him on the forehead. His eyes remained opaque but that didn't fool me. He was writhing on the inside.

"In the explosion he lost two toes and patches of skin were blown off on both of his legs. I gave him medication that will help him grow back his skin within twenty-six hours. His toes will take thirty hours but he'll be able to get up and walk again in three. He will survive. The sedative will wear off in an hour."

I nodded my head while biting my lip. "I'll tell Damion the news."

Chapter 14: It All Comes Down to This

Damion went outside to inform Cado and Electra the news about Phoenix. I was sure all three of them were pissed at me but I had to push those thoughts out of my head and come clean to something else that was bothering me. I had to ask Alvaro important questions and tell him about my death. I only wanted him to know. Phoenix was still under the sedatives so he wouldn't be able to know what Alvaro and I were talking about.

"Alvaro," I said quietly, while knocking on the side of the door frame in his medical office. He was sitting down with reading glasses on and a book in his hands. *Romeo and Juliet.* Phoenix was in the corner of the room, still in bed. "Can I talk to you?" I asked sheepishly. My heart was nearly thumping out of my chest and my palms were beginning to sweat. I had to ease my way into the conversation about my death.

Alvaro pulled off his glasses while setting the book down on an end table next to his potion's shelf. "Yes, please sit down. You may bring up the chair next to my desk."

I walked over to his wooden desk and pulled out the chair while sitting down across from him. I swallowed. "I think you know why I'm here."

He nodded his head, resting his cat eyes on mine. "You want answers."

"I want to know exactly why Brilliance is important and what is in that section of the book. I know you had a connection with Icelos. That's why you're so informed on what is inside the book." I felt the Mark tingle underneath my skin in excitement.

"You are correct. I did have a connection with Icelos. He, of course, has lived for a long time. I already told you how long I lived. It was a shorter period than Icelos."

"I want to know why we are willing to fight for this information and why Icelos even wrote it."

"Icelos wrote only a fraction of Brilliance. He decided to write it to record factual information of our Beings and to write material that will keep us believing in all of the beautiful things this world possesses. It is to remind us about how we use to be. How every majestic, inspirational actions that continuously kept this world at peace. Brilliance was made to remind us of our duties as Exols, Clockworks and Creators... Icelos, with the ability, received the support to make Brilliance a living factor. But once it grew its own thoughts and feelings, it began writing its own sections that were made from dark thoughts. Eventually, the darkness overthrew the light. Icelos didn't want to destroy this world, he only wanted to make it peaceful. Brilliance did this to itself.

"The darkness *always* overthrows the light. The Exols are changing. They weren't always like the way they are now. They are starting to label themselves as a government instead of peaceful Beings that help create Clockworks and help them in their time of need. The Abase Exols are examples of how they use to be. The so-called 'Majestic Exols' are false. They live to a high standard. They're starting to become selfish. Also, if you haven't noticed, groups are starting to be labeled amongst us. Such as, the Militants, Boundaries, Elements etc. Before you know it, they'll start dividing us based on our abilities."

"Yes, but for now, we need to focus on what's currently happening with the Creators. Why haven't I saw anything about the beautiful things? I mean, I've seen things about the Spiritual Humans and the Exol Child but that's about it. Brilliance doesn't care to show me anything."

"Esther, that's because you don't let Brilliance in. You have to have a connection with it and truly let Brilliance know what you need to know. When you get passed that stage, Brilliance will begin showing you more. But always remember that the darkness overthrows the light," Alvaro stated.

"How can I get it to be the opposite?" I asked, leaning in while staring into his eyes.

"Do what most of us can't: believe."

"The section that the Creators want; about, you know, controlling Earth and all of its systems, do you know why they want it?"

"Well, it's quite explanatory actually. They're Creators—

374

they've felt isolation and desolation their whole lives. They *want* a feeling of power and control. They're just too stupid to know how to do it. They're too busy wanting all of the knowledge of Brilliance instead of sitting down and focusing on how they can pull off a diabolic plan."

"I also question the fact that Dante is the only one that can destroy me. He was given the ability to be wise—yet he can't come up with a plan without using Brilliance? I find that hard to believe. Brilliance also stated that the Exol Child and Spiritual Human can kill me too? But how? Humans are wise. Exols are wise. Clockworks are wise. Why is it that only those three people can kill me when we're surrounded by intelligent forces?" I asked while arching my eyebrows.

"Ah, I see your confusion. When the universe was being created, all four of your atoms were juxtaposed. As the atoms came together to create all of the planets, including Earth, all of your atoms stayed beside each other during the whole process. Therefore, making all of you Soul Mates. When our images were being created, all of your souls always came back together. The Wise, the Exol Child, the Spiritual Human and, of course, the Half-Blood. This only happened to all four of you. Brilliance was attracted to you all because of your Souls. One is meant to be your enemy, the other is supposed to be your lover and the third is meant to be your friend. The order may be explanatory or not. You disregard the fact that you were Chosen... but do you see, Esther? Your life was played out to happen the way it does. Everything happens for a reason," Alvaro said eagerly.

I nodded my head, coming to all of the conclusions of my existence. "And that's why I'm meant to be killed. I understand now."

Alvaro frowned while staring deep within my eyes. "You knew that I know."

"Of course I knew. You can see passed anyone," I stated while biting my lip.

"I'm sorry, Esther." He reached across, placing his hand on my knee.

"I think I already accepted it. I lived the life I wanted to. I wanted to be important. I received my wish and the wish is going to kill me."

"Is that why you want the Exol Child so much? So he could protect you."

"Yes. At least I know for certain that the Child is a he."

"Which one? Do you love Cado or do you assume he's your friend?" Alvaro asked, bringing up the topic of the Soul Mates.

"Cado is my friend. I know that for a fact. I just don't receive any... feelings from him. You know?"

Alvaro smiled. "Yes, I know."

"Since you knew Icelos... You must know who the Exol Child is for certain, huh?" I asked, growing more curious. With Alvaro's help, I might be able to win the War.

"Yes... I assume you want to know the story?" he asked. I nodded my head. "We were close friends before I was banished to live in Erin Springs for the rest of my existence. We went through daily life finding love, friends and hope. I soon became in love with Calypso and our friendship went downhill after that. After I killed her husband and his men, I was banished to only live here. Icelos didn't talk to me until he needed my help. I was the one that helped him relocate and protect the Exol Child."

"Can you please tell me who the Exol Child is and where I could find him?" I asked.

A grin appeared on Alvaro's lips. "I already told you way too much stuff that you should have figured out on your own. The Exol Child is closer than you think... Just open your mind instead of keeping it closed all of the time."

"Alvaro... Please."

"No. You need to learn how to open your mind to figure out where the Exol Child is."

I leaned back in the chair with aggravation. "Fine then. Why is there even going to be a War? I want to know the exact reason why."

"Tell me something; would you want to hide, or would you want to fight for your life before it's too late?" Alvaro asked me with an arched eyebrow.

"Fight, of course."

A smile pulled at his lips and his features relaxed. "That's why there's going to be a War. The War is to not live in fear but rise up against the Creators. The War of Brilliance will be known to mark a huge section in our history books." He paused, searching my eyes for more to say. "There's a warrior inside of you Esther... Don't disregard the faith in yourself or you'll lose your heroism. Remember you are in control of your life. Make terms with Brilliance and you'll know more than you bargained for."

I nodded my head, trying to stay positive but there was fear knocking at my heart's door, waiting to be let in. My blood rose to my throat and I felt like a coward.

"You and Damion... What's going on?" Alvaro asked.

I shrugged my shoulders. "After everything that's happened, we decided to stay just friends."

"Even though you still feel for him? Wouldn't that be hard to ignore all of the beautiful, enchanting things your heart and mind is telling you?"

"Well," I said. "We're not meant to be together anyways. I guess I'm supposed to fall in love with the Exol Child... And you won't tell me who that is... So..."

"How are you so intelligent but so youthful at the same time? Open your eyes and all of the answers will be in front of you."

I sighed, getting up from the chair. "Thanks for answering a majority of my questions." Alvaro gave me a small smile as I started for the curtains. "Oh, can you buy us come clothes and an ice cream cake? It's Damion's favorite. His birthday is tomorrow."

He grinned. "Most certainly."

I informed Electra and Cado of Damion's birthday. Hesitantly, we all came to the conclusion to have a party to see the light in some of the darkest times. Electra cooled off from her outburst but Cado's trust in me failed. Sometimes I wished that I could tell my friends why I was so afraid but it would make them risk their lives for me. I didn't want anyone dying for me.

It was Damion's birthday and Electra told Damion and Cado to pick up a few items from the drugstore so we could set up the party materials. Phoenix sat in the corner and he was very much awake. The casts were still around his legs so I couldn't see the growth of his toes and skin. He continued to sit even though he could walk around a little bit before he became too tired.

Alvaro tended to the large, two-foot ice cream cake that had blue and green frosting plastered in beautiful designs around the edges. Electra set up the food and drinks while I hung decorations from the ceilings. I had a silky lavender dress on while Electra had a smooth yellow floor-length dress on. Alvaro, of course, wore a tux. Damion was turning eighteen now.? I watched him grow into an extraordinary person but I had to refrain myself from loving him. Trying to forget an edging feeling that picks at your heart nonstop was one of the hardest things to do in life.

"Alright," Alvaro said. "Is everyone done with their decorations?"

I stepped down from a stool while wiping my sweat from my brow. "Yeah." I started to think slightly while I was staring at all of the decorations. I had to go see Becca so she could be a part of us too. "I have to see Becca."

"No!" Alvaro shouted spontaneously, making me jump out of my skin. "You cannot bring her into this! Not until the War is over and Dante is dead."

I stared at him, perplexed in absolute horror. Someone who never lost his calm persona just screamed at me for no reason. "She's my friend... Alvaro."

"Yes, but she is your mortal friend. She can't handle our world. Not just yet. She's happy in Alabama."

I crossed my hands over my chest while biting the inside of my cheek. Maybe he was right. I promised Acea that I would see him after the darkness ended and mentally, I made a plan to see Mason too.

The door opened from behind me and I turned around while Electra and Alvaro screamed out in triumph, "Surprise!"

Cado and Damion stood in the doorway with bags in their hands. A huge smile spread across Damion's lips and his eyes lit up with happiness. His bright blue eyes scanned the party equipment until they landed on me. I noticed I still had my arms crossed and a pissed off look on my face so I quickly gave him a little smile.

"Wow, thanks, I don't even have words..." Damion trailed off while he scanned the food on the counters and the large cake.

"To believe we would have a birthday party in the beginning of a War," Electra said with a little laugh. She skipped towards Damion and grabbed his hand. She tugged him across the room, showing him all of the food and decorations while describing their origin.

I watched the both of them stare at the party space with

excitement until I got bored. I turned around slowly, noticing Cado was walking across the room. I gave him a small smile to see if he was still disappointed in me from yesterday. He stared at me menacingly with dark, brown eyes. He walked passed me with a harsh wind and he bumped me angrily in the shoulder. I watched him with narrowed eyes. I had the urge to punch him in the jaw so he would know not to piss me off after all of the storms that were rolling around inside my head. But I decided not to. It was Damion's birthday and he deserved it to be a good one.

It was an hour after the party supposedly started but all we were doing was sitting down, eating sloppy sandwiches as the rain tapped gently on the windows of Alvaro's shop. Phoenix had been quiet the whole night and he wasn't engaged with his surroundings. I watched him as he gingerly picked at his salad and occasionally nibbled on his sandwich. I glanced at Alvaro and with his cat eyes, he was staring Phoenix down. Was Alvaro worried about Phoenix's health or something else? I felt an awkward tension between all of us. No one spoke a word since we sat down to eat our food on benches.

Damion sat across from me and gradually, he would look up at me after he took a sip of his sparkling cider. I wondered if he was waiting for me to start a conversation but I was too lost in my thoughts to even say a word. The War still rummaged throughout my mind. It was getting to the point where I couldn't breathe from fear. The fear tightened at my chest and my lungs would begin to close up.

"Okay, well. I'm going to get another glass of cider. Does anyone want some?" Damion asked while standing at the quiet group. Electra looked around the room while she drank at her cider but she wasn't finished with it. Phoenix was staring at his shoes and Cado was picking viciously at his salad. Alvaro was still transfixed on Phoenix.

I shrugged my shoulders as Damion stared at everyone. "I'll take some more," I said, trying to make conversation. A small grin appeared across his lips and he walked over to me. I held up my glass and he took it from me, grazing my hand softly with his fingers. Healthy shivers went up my spine and I refused to enjoy the feeling. I crossed my arms over my chest protectively as he walked over to the juice table. I watched him as he picked up the container of sparkling cider and poured an equal amount into each glass so delicately and carefully.

When he was done, he walked around the benches and bookshelves to get back to the small area we were in. Triumphantly, he walked down the aisle of benches where we all sat, feeling satisfied with how well he poured the juice. He headed straight towards me while smiling at the glasses. Suddenly, I saw his pant snag on a floorboard that was slightly propped up and before I could react, he began falling to the ground. The sparkling cider spilled out of the glasses and it poured all over me, soaking my entire lavender dress and my skin to the bone. Damion used his telekinesis to hold him up so he wouldn't fall to the floor. He brought himself into an upright position and he stared at me with wide eyes filled with terror. His cheeks began to flush and so did mine. I felt a revenge of anger that boiled up inside of me.

"Esther... I'm so sorry... I didn't mean to. It was an accident..." Damion trailed on.

I stood up while trying to hold back my stressful anger. I glanced down at Alvaro's glass of cider that was barely touched. "Give me that," I stated, grabbing it out of Alvaro's hands. He glanced up at me with furrowed brows. I ignored his bewildered expression and I walked over to Damion with the glass in my hand.

"I'm so sorry," Damion whispered.

"It was a new dress," I said through gritted teeth. I stared him down even though he was taller than me. He stepped a foot back so I wouldn't punch him. Instead, I threw the glass up and the cider spilled all over his suit. He stared at me with large, wide eyes as if he still was unsure on what happened. I couldn't help but break a small smile because his face was absolutely clueless. Acknowledging the smile, Damion let out a laugh.

"Oh yeah? That the best you can do?" he stated with a huge grin.

I placed my hands on my hips. "Yeah, why? You think you can do better?"

"Oh, I can definitely do better."

Damion turned on his heel and began walking to the table that had the large birthday cake placed on the top. He grabbed the table and pulled it back without effort so the cake would be closer to us. Cado, Electra, Phoenix all watched to see what he was planning to do. Suddenly, making Electra gasp, he shoved his hand in the perfectly-baked cake made by her. Alvaro was too busy to buy one. He grabbed a handful greedily and he turned around.

"I like cake," he said with a goofy laugh.

"Damion... What are you doing?" I asked, arching an eyebrow while also stepping back a little bit.

He quickly threw the large ball of cake and frosting across the room and it hurtled straight towards me. The ball of cake smashed directly into my face, making my eyes go blind with all of the frosting that covered them. With a huff, I wiped a majority of the cake off my face and I shook my hands, making the cake slap onto the ground. My eyes narrowed as I stared at Damion.

"Oh, shit just got real," Electra said, beginning to stand up.

"Damn right it did," Alvaro said with a bit of sass. I looked back at him, noticing the remains of the cake ball splattered onto his tuxedo. I couldn't help but break out a laugh. He stood up. "This is war."

Damion laughed, turning around to grab more. He threw a ball at Cado, making him stand up and get involved. He then threw a piece at Phoenix, finally making him notice his surroundings. Hesitantly, Phoenix stood up.

I glanced at everyone around me and we were waiting for someone to make the next move. My legs took off running across the wooden floor without giving them the command to. I shoved Damion out of the way and everyone else followed. We stuck our hands in the cake. The cake was cold and moist but it could easily be made into a ball of thick frosting. We were all laughing as balls of cake flung out everywhere. I was hit quite a few times but my true target that I wanted to receive revenge on was Damion. I ran around the bookshelves, chasing him like a wild lion that chases its prey.

"Come back here!" I yelled as I carried the glob of cake in my hand.

"Never!" Damion yelled as he ran behind a bookshelf.

I decided to cross paths so he wouldn't assume the way I would attack him from. I maneuvered around a different path of bookshelves filled with potions and crafts. Suddenly, Damion came out right in front of me because he didn't know that I took the shortcut. I grabbed firmly on his wrist and pulled him back, slamming the cake into his face. He stopped in his tracks and he tried to make sense of what happened. He looked down at me with a face full of cake and he flashed a set of white teeth.

"Clever," he said.

I shrugged my shoulders while smiling. "I always am."

He placed his hand on his face, wiping off some of the cake. "Maybe not as clever as me." He chuckled as he smeared some of his cake onto my face with his hand.

"Hm. Very clever indeed," I said, using my finger to get some frosting off of his face. I placed my finger in my mouth and my taste buds were instantly filled with a sweet, rich flavor.

"Was that good?" Damion asked with a chuckle as his bright, blue eyes stared down at me.

"Of course." We were inches away from each other and my back was pressed against the bookshelf. I felt his breath tingle my skin and I knew I wanted to care about him. There was just something about him that I was so addictive to and I knew he felt the same way. But how was I able to grow to love him if I was meant for the Exol Child?

"I know what you want Esther," he whispered.

"I know what I want," I said, my voice cracking slightly.

"But you're afraid of it and I understand that. I can wait for you. I will wait until you're ready... This feeling between us—I feel like it's supposed to be this way."

"I feel like it is too... But logically, it's not. Alvaro told me that my destiny is with the Exol Child, my friendship is with Cado and my enemy is Dante. That's how my life is supposed to play out."

"You can always change your destiny," he said gently.

I nodded my head slightly while contemplating. "I need to figure out who I'm supposed to be on the inside before I start changing what I am on the outside." I couldn't let him in because I would die and that would break him. I had to make it easier on Damion because I truly do care about him.

He nodded his head and he gave me a lopsided grin. "I understand, Esther. And that's why I care about you so much. You're independent and you do what's best."

I smiled slightly. "We are missing a cake war right now. Let's go hit them hard."

He chuckled. "Okay."

I ran out from behind the bookshelves and I stared at the cake war going on in front of me. I grabbed pieces of cake and began throwing it wildly, not even caring who I had hit. Globs of cake would smash onto my dress but that only encouraged me to throw more. I threw each ball of cake one by one.

Suddenly, I felt familiar hands wrap around my waist and he spun me around, pulling me into the middle of the cake war. Damion and I continued to laugh as balls of cake hit us across the face and everyone would laugh. We all continued laughing until or stomachs began to cramp up and the cake wasn't on the table anymore.

Damion and I pulled away and all of us stopped once we realized there was no more fresh cake left to throw. We all looked at each other and we began to smile. It was the first time we felt felicity in a long time. It was like all of the stress vanished into thin air and positive vibes filled each of our souls. Having fun was the best way to relieve heartbreak and stress. I mean, after all, we were children. We needed to have fun.

"That was the best time I had in centuries," Alvaro stated, sitting down on a desk chair while putting up his legs that had splatters of cake all over them. He carefully picked up the remote and he turned on the small TV that hung on the wall in between two shelves. Sounds of a news reporter speaking hysterically filled the whole room. The camera man was panning across a small town in Tennessee and figures in gray ran across the streets while buildings exploded, sending fiery balls of black, thick smoke spiraling up in the dark sky.

"We need to get out of here," the lady with thick, blue eye shadow stated eagerly to the cameraman. Behind the woman, police officers attempted to shoot at the Creators, believing they were humans. The Creators ignored the bullets and the groups of Creators ran into the exploding buildings. Inside the windows, I could see rays of electricity bouncing off against the shadows. The Creators used a portal to find a different location to terrorize. I knew they were looking for me.

"They're gone!" A policeman yelled out.

"We just received word that the men and woman that may pose as terrorists disappeared," the woman stated.

Spontaneously, a huge ball of darkness broke out and the camera fell to the ground as more explosions went off and the only thing I could see was the woman falling to the ground with blood pouring down her head and her pale, lifeless green eyes stared into the camera. The camera suddenly shut off and the news channel panned back to the discussion room.

Alvaro was about to turn the channel when something else caught my attention.

"Don't change the channel," I stated.

"Esther... You shouldn't be watching that crap," Phoenix stated, attempting to stand up. I ignored him and I continued to focus on the news.

"I... We are at loss of words right now," the anchor stated quietly while staring down at his papers. "Our reinforcement units haven't even received a lead on this case and I do not know when they will finally catch these terrorists."

"Yes," the lady that was sitting next to him with short blonde hair stated dryly. "The school that was attacked in Pennsylvania strikes us with the most despair. So many children died in that attack. Innocent children."

The hair on the back of my neck rose and I felt everyone in the room stare at me as I continued watching the news.

"Esther, you shouldn't see this," Alvaro said with a hint of distress.

"Alvaro, please change the channel," Damion said while clenching his jaw.

Alvaro picked up the remote again and simultaneously, before he could change the channel, I used a force field to smack the remote out of his hand. I made the force field wrap around the remote and slowly, I brought the remote towards me while I was still transfixed on the television screen. I held the remote firmly in my hand.

"Let's take a few moments to acknowledge the many young lives lost in the school bombing." It wasn't a bombing; it was supernatural abilities that destroyed the school.

"Veronica Bres, Jake Miola, Frankie Nera, Elizabeth Syers, Brendon Jacu, Luna Windchester, Rose Windchester, Phillip Wade, Daton Rows, Esther Green, Lola Pierce."

My ears discontinued listening to the names of the dead students and it focused on my name and the Windchester twins. *Did I hear it correctly? Everyone thinks I'm dead? Even Mason?* I couldn't stop thinking about all of the possibilities that rummaged throughout my head. Now I knew why Alvaro didn't want me to see Becca. It was because Becca thought I was dead. Mason also believed I was dead. The anger began to boil up inside of me. Slowly, I turned to look at Alvaro. He propped up his face with his hand and he was staring at the ground with a defeated look plastered across his face.

"Why didn't you tell me Alvaro? Wait, let me guess. You wanted me to figure out the world on my own?" I snapped at him. My entire body was filled with dark venom and all of the thoughts about felicity were immediately washed away.

"Esther, I couldn't tell you because I knew you would've wanted to go see your friends and let them know that you were alive... Therefore, making them apart of your issue with Brilliance."

"Alvaro!" I yelled. "They think I'm *dead!* I know Becca is not handling it well at all and you continue to let them live in... sadness? Is that how you want people to feel?"

"Eventually they'll figure out you're not dead."

I turned my back to Alvaro while crossing my arms. I bit my lip and I knew all eyes were on me. "So, how do they think I died?"

"In a house explosion. They found your mother's charred body but the investigators couldn't find yours. They figured your remains just blew in the air so they labeled you dead. I'm sorry."

I felt my throat beginning to tighten and I couldn't breathe. Thoughts of all of the dead children I was unable to save began to haunt me. The students at my school needed a hero and I couldn't save them in time. I felt the first tear beginning to stream down my cheek. I clutched the remote tightly but I still couldn't breathe. Even worse, I couldn't even save my mom. With that thought, I lost it. I slammed the remote down on the ground and I heard the plastic break in half. I ran passed Damion and Electra while slamming the back-patio door open. I ran across the field, moving away from the stores that were clustered together. The high grass tickled my ankles and I continued running until I reached a small expanse of forest. I walked throughout the forest silently, breaking a few twigs occasionally. I made a small force field the size of my hand, using a special air technique to turn the force field into a ball of blue light. I heard a smooth rush of water nearby so I followed the sound until I could see a small river. I sat at the edge of the river and I discarded the force field.

My mother's smile blinded my eyes and she was the only one I could think of. I couldn't save her. My heart was beginning to fall back into my stomach where it shouldn't be. I felt the darkness slowly creeping at the corners of my thoughts again. I was weak. I wasn't strong enough to save my own mother. If my mother still had her abilities, she would've saw when her death was approaching.

"Why do the Exols take away our abilities!" I thrashed out, splashing my hand vigorously into the piercing cold water. More tears began streaming down my cheeks. I remembering seeing the dead students at school when they were alive. They enjoyed their lives and they always had smiles on their faces. I was the reason why they were dead. I wasn't strong enough to save them. Everyone tells me Brilliance Chose me for a reason but I couldn't understand the reason why. I was a weakling. I felt like I couldn't even stand on my two feet long enough before another terrible thing happened to the people I loved the most.

"Esther?" I heard a voice ask quietly behind me. I turned around, recognizing the familiar outline.

"What do you want?" I asked with a hint of venom.

"I wanted to see if you were okay," Damion stated, walking quietly and calmly closer to me. He sat down next to me and he stared silently at the rushing river.

"Well, I'm fine. You can go now."

"Why are you such a bitch to the people that actually care about you? Me? Your mother? Alvaro?" Damion asked with an attitude.

It felt like his words were a slap to the face but he was right. "I was such a jerk to my mom before she was killed by Luna." I stared into the dark, deep, rushing water. "I'm sorry."

"I know," he said, his voice rumbling.

"I feel like I'm too childish to handle the world around me. I hate myself, Damion. All of the people I killed and all of the people I let die."

"You needed to kill those people, Esther. And it wasn't your fault they died. You tried everything you could. You're the strongest person I ever came to know. The whole world is on your shoulders so you absolutely deserve to be stressed out. I know you don't understand why Brilliance Chose you, but I see something inside you too that I'm sure is what Brilliance saw."

"What is it?" I asked quietly. The moonlight glittered against the trees and everything was easier to see. "What do you see inside of me?" I was unsure of who I was on the inside.

"Will. You're filled with dauntless in the worst scenarios, you touch the world with your light, you're filled with optimism and you fight for what you believe and what you love. You're going to change this world, Esther. You're going to turn it back to the way it was before the Creators took over and before when the Exols began to abuse their power."

"You think we're going to win the War?" I asked.

"Yes. Don't you?" he asked.

I wouldn't be alive to see if we did win the War but I couldn't tell Damion that. "Yes, of course. I was just making sure if you thought we would."

"You're awful at hiding your emotions. You've obviously been skittish about thoughts of the War. You can either tell me the truth now or lie straight up to my face like how you've been with our friends," Damion stated firmly all of the sudden.

"What are you talking about? Yes, I have jitters. But that's nothing. Everything is okay." It was obviously a lie.

Damion laughed coldly. "You are a good liar but I know the truth. If I hadn't known the truth, I would've believed you."

I felt goose bumps beginning to graze my body and my hairs on the back of my neck stood up. He knew, but how? Did Alvaro tell him? "How did you know?"

"No, Alvaro didn't tell me if you were wondering. Phoenix did. Alvaro thought that he gave Phoenix enough medicine to knock out his senses but it didn't knock out his hearing. He heard you talk about everything. He heard you and Alvaro talk about your death."

I stared at Damion, watching the moonlight reflect in his icy blue eyes. "I didn't want to tell anyone because I didn't want anyone to try and save me. That's why I wanted the Exol Child so he could protect me with his powerful abilities. I knew I should've told you... It's just... I didn't want you to blame yourself that if I died, you didn't protect me enough."

"I know why you did it, Esther," Damion said, his soft voice coming back slowly. "But I will try to protect you no matter what. I don't care if I die trying. I care about you enough that I will risk everything for you. You deserve to grow up, fall in love, and have cute little children... I want you to be happy. That's all I ever wanted."

Gingerly, I reached across the grass that tickled my wrist and I gently entwined my fingers in Damion's. "If you died that wouldn't make me happy. That would haunt me for the rest of my entire life."

"Why though?" Damion asked. "I died for you. That should show you how much I care."

"I don't need for you to show me, I already know. You don't need to die for me. It wouldn't change anything. If the Prophecy states that I am going to die then that is what needs to be done. I accept my death. At least I can see my parents again."

Damion's face fell and his eyes were beginning to lose their beauty. He didn't want me to die. "I don't know what I would do without you. My life sucked until I met you. It was like I found out who I was by you. I'm still trying to figure myself out but I know enough to live."

"It's just a bad day," I said, picking up a rock and I skipped it across the river. "Not a bad life."

Damion stared blankly into the river as if his thoughts were visible by the water. "Everything would be different. I just can't see a world without Esther Green."

"And I can't see a world without Damion Storm. You need to stay alive. You're the one that has to grow up, fall in love, find a place in the human world and have cute babies that have the same blue eyes as you."

"How about none of us die? Wouldn't that be a better thought? Live each day like it's your last?" Damion asked with a hint of anger.

"Let's just pretend that I'm not going to be killed by Dante... It would be a better thought."

"Yeah. I agree," he said.

"Do you ever miss your parents, Damion?" I asked, changing the subject.

He sighed. "Yes. I'm always going to miss them. They did help me in terms of life. They helped me learn that you have to be strong enough to put up with the darkness. That is the only thing I miss about them."

I bit my lip. "Do you want to see them again?"

"I don't want to see them to where they see me."

I stood up while wiping the dirt off of my dress. Annoyed with the length of my dress, I ripped it off to where it was slightly above my knees so I could move easier. "Then let's go. I'll make us invisible. I wanna see my old house too."

Damion stared up at me. "You sure?"

"Yes, I'm sure. Come on. Let's go."

Damion and I stood outside of his house in complete darkness. Only the moon lit up our path. He grabbed my hand and instantly, I thought of beautiful, enriching thoughts that wanted to be released. I felt the satisfying rush and we were invisible.

"I find it odd that they don't have any lights on in the house," Damion said. "Usually they would still be awake at this time."

"Peculiar."

We walked up the large porch. All of Ella's plants were dead and they no longer smelled pretty. The door in front of us suddenly opened but I assumed Damion was the one that opened it because I couldn't see his movements.

"They would have the door locked, Esther... But they didn't."

We moved quietly and quickly into the house. We were instantly greeted with a harmful odor that made my stomach churn uncomfortably.

"Gross," I said with a short shriek.

I heard Damion laugh but I could tell he was nervous. I felt Damion tug on my arm gently and I heard a flip of a switch but the lights didn't turn on.

"The power isn't working," he said.

I created a glowing force field the size of my palm. Instantly, I noticed that furniture was overturned and there was a red, sticky substance splattered against the walls. I inhaled a sharp breath when I saw a body on the ground with long, flowing black hair.

I made us visible again so I could read Damion's facial features. His jaw was tightly clenched and his eyes were narrowed as he stared at his dead mother's rotting body. I peeked my head around the wall and his father's rotting corpse was sitting in a desk chair with his blood and guts splattered on the ground.

"Damion," I said, grabbing his arm while staring into his eyes worriedly. "I'm so sorry."

He didn't say anything, he only stared at their dead bodies

with an utterly straight face. He grabbed my waist and he pulled me into a strong, but gentle embrace. I laid my head against his chest and I wrapped my arms around his waist. He placed his chin on top of my head and I could hear him swallow.

"I don't want to go to my old house," I said quietly. "I'm not ready after what I saw."

"I understand. Let's get out of here before we become a part of a crime scene."

It was the next morning and I felt the aura was slightly gloomy. I had to apologize to Alvaro. He was right; it was safer for Becca and Mason to know that I was dead. Damion's quirky side vanished last night after he saw his parents' rotting corpses. I allowed him the time to grieve.

I walked into Alvaro's office and he was still reading _Romeo and Juliet_. I knocked on the wooden door frame and a small grin pulled at the corners of his lips.

"Good morning, Esther," he said cheerfully like nothing had happened.

"I wanted to apologize for last night... I was being selfish. It is better for them to know that I'm dead until everything has washed away," I said.

He smiled at me with gleaming cat eyes. "I'm glad that you have reasoned."

"And," I licked my lips. "I think I'm ready to fight. I can't live in fear; I need to fight the fear."

He closed the book and stood up while walking over to me. "When you make this decision there's no going back."

I stared into his eyes and I made it known what I wanted. "I want to _fight_," I said through gritted teeth.

"I'll inform Phoenix to set out and tell all of the Rescued Compound Clockworks to gear up and meet at a certain location."

"Where is that location?" I asked.

Alvaro swallowed. "The Creator's main Headquarters. It's in the middle of a vacant field where there's no civilization. Their Headquarters is located in Idaho."

"With that type of information, why didn't anyone bother to attack?" I asked.

"Oh, Esther. It's their main Headquarters. There's no way in

Hell people are that stupid to attack their Compound. It's heavily guarded and that's where 3/4ths of the Creators are."

"Oh..." I said, feeling stupid. "Wouldn't we be considered stupid for attacking their Headquarters?"

"Yes, but it is logical to do it at this point in time. My impression is that Dante is going across the United States to find you and destroy places that he thinks you could be. He may even come back to Erin Springs."

I nodded my head. "We need to work quickly then."

"Yes."

I nodded my head. "Okay. Now, what about us knowing who is a Creator and who is a Clockwork?"

Alvaro laughed. "I'm always one step ahead of you. Creators are going to wear gray and we wear black uniforms; the one's that Electra created."

"How is she going to sew uniforms for almost all of the Clockworks in the United States?"

Alvaro turned around quickly, staring at all of the potions on his shelf. He tapped his finger to his chin vigorously while searching for a potion. "Ahah!" he exclaimed, grabbing a royal blue liquid from the shelf. "I put a thread from Electra's uniform in this bottle. I experimented with different potions and I finally found one that would work. You place a drop of this liquid in the field outside and instantly, uniforms are created by the threads of grass."

I laughed slightly. "You definitely know how to create new technology."

"I believe I am the Scientist of the Beings," Alvaro said with a sly smile.

"Yeah, you sure are." I stood with my arms crossed and I began thinking. "Alvaro... Can I ask you a favor?"

"Yes, please commence," he said with a delighted grin.

"I'm going to die in the War, I know that. But I want something that could keep my abilities strong enough to fulfill some things I need to take care of in it."

"You want a steroid to make you stronger and more affective with your abilities?" he asked with a raised brow.

"That's what I want. I need to know that everything is going to be fine before I die. I know my abilities will give out some time in the War."

"I think I know a combination of potions that will fulfill your needs." Alvaro quickly handed me the potion in his hand. "Go outside and began growing the uniforms. None of the shopkeepers should notice at this time of day. You're safe along those lines. While you're doing that, I'm going to work on the combinations." He rushed to the corner of the room and began grabbing multiple potions eagerly.

I turned on my heels, pushing through the curtains with the potion in my hand. Phoenix was sitting on a desk chair with his arms crossed over his chest and he was wearing a black tunic. Ever since the Safe House was attacked, he hasn't been himself. He hasn't directly spoke to me like he would. I rested my eyes on him until he gradually looked up at me, avoiding staring into my eyes.

"Is everything okay?" I asked hoarsely, afraid he would snap at me in anger.

Phoenix's face hardened and he continued to stare at me. "I believe my little sister is dead. I didn't do the task the Creators wanted me to do."

"What was the task?" I asked, feeling sorrow for his young sister.

"It's nothing," he said, standing up. He picked up a glass and slammed it into a bookshelf, making the glass shatter everywhere. He paced back and forth with his hands matted in his dark hair.

I walked up to him, placing a hand on his shoulder. "Phoenix, it wasn't your fault. You tried to do everything you could."

He moved away from my touch, staring at me with eyes full of despair. "No. I didn't. I could've saved her if I did what was requested of me... I just—I just couldn't do it because I'm a *weakling*."

"Phoenix, you're not a weakling. You're strong and independent. I know losing a loved one is a hard thing to comprehend—"

"I think I need some time alone... I need to get ready to venture out."

"You overheard Alvaro and me?" I asked.

"Yeah. I always do."

"You also told Damion something I didn't want you to."

"I had to tell someone that could protect you," he said.

"Why can't you 'protect me'?" I asked, rolling my eyes.

"Because I'll be busy killing Dante," he said, his eyes illuminating with hatred. I was silent for some time until he spoke. "You should go make the outfits with Electra."

"Electra!" I yelled, continuing to stare at Phoenix as he trotted away into a dark room.

"Yes?" she yelled, coming from a different room. She walked over to me with a smile on her face and her green eyes glowed with happiness.

"What's up with you?" I asked once Phoenix completely left the room.

"I found something new about my abilities. When I melt and use electricity, I can target multiple enemies instead of one, therefore killing Creators easier and faster."

"That's fascinating. I've been discovering a few new things about my abilities as well. I can create glowing anomalies that help me see at night and an old one I learned was warping the force field around objects."

"Yeah. I think it's amazing how our abilities can create new things."

"It's not about having unique abilities; what makes them unique is what you can do with your ability."

"So, what did you want me for?" she asked.

"This." I held up the potion. "It creates uniforms for the Clockworks since all of the Creators are going to wear gray."

She snatched it out of my hand, staring down at it eagerly. "What are you waiting for? Let's do it now!"

I laughed and gave her a pleasant smile. "We have to drop it in the field."

We walked out the back door of the shop simultaneously. We walked casually into the field, looked around to make sure no one was around then Electra dropped a single drop of the potion into the field. In seconds, euphony sounds of grass entwining, slowly sewing together recreations of the armor that Electra had made. The uniforms sprouted out of the ground section by section, stretching across the field beyond the woods.

Electra dropped down onto her knees, clutching the black uniform similar to our battle gear. "They're exact replicas!"

I chuckled. "Now the hard part is picking all of them up. Phoenix is going to have a lot to carry once he sets out."

393

"I'll go with him and help him out."
"Great idea."

"Esther, I combined the correct potions together. I believe these cylinders will help you in the War," Alvaro stated. He handed me cylinders filled with an electric green liquid. "There's only two that I could make for tomorrow afternoon... Hopefully you don't mind. Phoenix and Electra should be back around midnight so they can receive sleep."

"Two is fine. They'll keep me alive long enough." I grabbed a green cylinder out of his hand. "Do you have a sample for me to use right now? I don't want to use up the cylinders."

"Yes, I do." Alvaro turned around quickly, grabbing a large cup that held the same green substance. "Follow me. We'll do it outside."

Alvaro and I pushed through the curtains. Cado and Damion perked up their heads from watching TV, their eyes scanning us as we crossed the room.

"What's going on?" Damion asked, standing up while Cado turned off the TV.

"We're fixing my energy crisis," I stated meekly. I stared into Damion's eyes and I felt my heart clench together with fear and admiration. I wished so desperately that I didn't care about him because when I leave this world, it'll be the hardest thing that I ever had to do. I would be leaving behind the people that counted on me the most.

"Can we see?" Cado asked, his face set but his eyes showed amusement.

"Of course," Alvaro said, opening the backdoor.

We all made our way out of the door and the chill of the spring air wrapped around our warm bodies. Stars hung in the clouds, dancing along with the beautiful moon. It was going to be the last moon that I would ever see in my entire existence. I stared up at it and I felt butterflies in my stomach as I was infatuated with the absolutely stunning crescent moon that lit up the field with rays of blue light. I felt like I was admiring everything I took for granted because soon, everything would be washed away and my soul would be blank. I believed that the thing I feared the most about death was dying and never existing again. My soul would be gone; my memories of the life I desired so much would be gone. Everything about me would disappear. I didn't want that to happen.

"Here," Alvaro said.

"Drink up, Green," Damion said with the edges of his mouth slightly raised in a lopsided grin.

I took the cup in my hand, lifted it to my soft lips and I allowed the oozing, but electrifying liquid slide down the back of my throat. I drank as much as my stomach allowed me and when I was done, I crushed the cup and gave it back to Alvaro.

"How did that taste?" Cado asked with a raised eyebrow.

I was silent for a few moments. I felt something strange moving in my stomach. I looked down at my skin and it illuminated with green and gold in the night sky. My whole body was changing spontaneously and I felt my body growing with exuberance, essentially to a state that I was gradually filled with liveliness.

"Great," I said, wiping my mouth of the green substance. Damion and Cado chuckled.

"Most importantly, how do you feel?" Alvaro asked.

"Alive."

"Show us that you're alive," Alvaro said.

I closed my eyes, allowing the energy to leisurely cascade throughout my entire glistening body. I took three deep breaths and mentally, I could feel the satisfaction of a force field growing.

"Oh my god," I heard Damion say in awe.

"Powerful," Cado said hushed.

I opened my eyes, quickly noticing a golden force field expanding at a rapid rate. The edges of the golden force field were frayed with an electrical field. It continued expanding all around us with such an extraordinary flaxen color that lit up the entire sky.

"It is unbreakable," Alvaro said with enthusiasm at his own creation.

"It feels so... good," I said with a laugh as the force field continued to dance around us, creating more force fields behind each one. The grass and the trees were illuminating with the sparkly golden color. "This was the color my force fields originally created before I began to notice a lack of energy.

"It's absolutely beautiful," Damion said.

"How am I going to sleep tonight with all of this energy?" I asked, discarding the golden force fields. The only thing that was lighting up the area was the crescent moon.

"I guess I didn't think that one out," said Alvaro.

"Well, that was a pleasant thing to see for the night," Cado said. "But I think I'm going to go get some sleep. Who knows, maybe I'll see Sapphire tomorrow." Cado turned on his heels and headed towards the door. Quickly, I grabbed his arm and yanked him back with an unusual amount of force.

"You're *not* dying tomorrow," I said, staring deep into his brown eyes. "Sapphire wouldn't want that. I wouldn't want that. None of us do, Cado. The only way you can die tomorrow is if you lose faith in yourself. Stay alive; don't meet the painful truth of death."

Cado stared at me, searching my eyes for any hidden lies about his death. He thought he was the one that was going to die. He didn't know it was going to be me.

I shook him in my arms. "You're not going to die."

"Okay," he said, believing in my words. "I'm not going to die."

I released my painful grip on him and slowly, he turned around and walked back into the shop.

"Are you afraid of his fate?" Damion asked, wondering if Cado was going to die too.

"He's not going to die," I said, continuing to stare at the shop.

"But why are you the one that has to die?" Damion asked hoarsely.

Alvaro stood uncomfortably next to us. "I'll let you two be alone... I suppose you have to say your goodbyes tonight. The morning will be too hectic." I watched as he too, walked back into the shop and he shut the door behind him, giving us privacy.

"Why?" Damion said again, but this time with more pain.

I turned around to stare at him. His face was set but his beautiful blue eyes had fallen into despair. "We all have to die someday."

"But why *now?*" he asked, his shoulders hunched as he began to crumble slowly.

"I never wanted us to say goodbye like this," I stated as the tears began to well up in my eyes. It was hard for me to look at him.

"You didn't want to love me because you didn't want me to lose myself when you died... But we could've had a forever even if it didn't last that long. I don't care about the time; I care about the moment. Either way, your death is still going to affect me the same way." I watched as the first tear poured down his cheek.

I wrapped my arms around his waist when I saw his first tear. He wrapped his strong arms around my waist, holding me as I started to cry in his shirt. I did wish I spent more time with him. My last night was not how I pictured it to be. As a child, I pictured me as an elder the last night before I was meant to die. That night, as an old woman, I ventured the best amusement park in the world and rode rides to receive thrills that could last a lifetime. But instead, I'm crying in the arms of an eighteen-year-old man that I should've had a forever with.

"I remember the day I first saw you in that classroom with Mrs. Banks. I acted like I didn't notice anyone in that room but I *did* notice you. I felt like I've known you forever... Almost like we were soul mates. I felt connections that I never felt before in my entire life. I knew we were going to have a future... But not this short of one."

"Me too," I whispered in his chest. I felt him lower his head as he placed his chin on the top of my head.

"I'm not going to say goodbye yet... I still need to believe that I can protect you from your death."

"I'll say goodbye to you when I'm writhing on the ground and the air is beginning to escape my lips. It'll be the second to last thing I'll say to you." The last thing I would say to Damion was that I love him.

"You're not dying. I can't afford to think that you are."

I pulled away to look at Damion. A few tears were streaming down his cheeks. "When I do, promise me you'll put the world back together."

"I promise, Esther. I promise I'll make this world a better place."

My hands trailed along a dusty stair railing as I made my way up a staircase that was caked with ash and debris from what looked to be a fire. A few images were resurfacing in my memory and this place grew to be familiar. I finished walking up the staircase but there was nowhere else to go. All of the rooms upstairs fell to the first floor. I looked down, continuing to hold onto the railing with a tight grip. I noticed a burnt-up skeleton and my heart sank into my stomach. *Mother.*

"Come downstairs, honey." The hair on the back of my neck stood up and chills went down my spine, making goose bumps coat my skin. It was my mother's voice. The skeleton with black eye sockets was speaking to me without moving its mouth. "It's about Damion."

"Wh—what about him?" I asked with a shudder.

"It's almost like we were soul mates," Damion's voice suddenly filled the air.

"Remember what Alvaro told you, child?" my mother's voice asked.

I looked around the area, trying to figure out where the voices were coming from because I knew skeletons couldn't speak. "Uh yes."

"The Wise, Spiritual Human, Half-Blood and the Exol Child are all Soul Mates. All of these spots are filled but the Exol Child. Do you understand?" my mother asked.

"Damion said that it was almost like we were soul mates... Damion is very powerful but I don't think he understands the great power he possesses. He never had a connection with his parents... And I believe I love him."

"Damion is the Exol Child, Esther. Sometimes you're way too blind and listen to what your thoughts tell you, not your heart."

"So, Damion will be the one I need to transfer Brilliance to?" I asked, staring all around me, still trying to figure out where my mother's voice was coming from.

"Yes. Remember Esther, on that battlefield, you'll discover something very important about your fate. You are in control of your own life. You make the decisions that benefit to your needs the most." My mother paused. "And quit looking around. I am your heart speaking to you. Your father and I will be there for you. We've always been here."

"I love you, Esther," I heard my father's voice.

I felt the tears welling up in my eyes and I was at peace. "I love you both. Thank you for being there for me. I promise I'll make you proud."

"I love you Esther," I heard my mother say until everything went black.

Brilliance by J.G. Lynn

Chapter 15: I Promise This Won't Be the End of Us

I woke up the next morning without any emotions. I was too numb with emotions at this point that I just had to go through the motions. I heard the sounds of metal smacking against wood outside of the shop and I knew they were practicing with weapons just in case their abilities gave out during the War.

I walked down the dark hallway, my bare-feet smacking against the dusty wood.

"Good morning," Alvaro said with a small smile. I could tell he was scared but he didn't want to show it.

I had to make my last hours the best. I couldn't dwell. "Morning," I gave him a pleasant smile.

"They already have their uniforms and armor on. They said you guys are leaving in an hour."

I nodded my head. "I'll have some breakfast and then put on the uniforms." I started to turn around to get some milk from the storage room until I felt Alvaro grab my arm.

"Have you noticed something strange about Phoenix or is it just me?" Alvaro asked.

"Well, can't you see why he's acting that way?"

"No. For some odd reason I can't see anything. I feel like he used something to block his thoughts from me... Which is slightly peculiar unless he has something to hide?"

"He believes his sister is dead... But I don't see why he would block anything from you? Do you think you're just not focusing on him as much as you would want to?" I asked, disbelieving he had anything to do with the fact Alvaro couldn't read him.

"I don't know. Just don't get too close to him. I don't know if he's a threat."

"I doubt he's a threat, Alvaro. He's just having a hard time. All of us are."

"I noticed you discovered who the Exol Child is. Did you realize that Brilliance did that? Brilliance allowed you to hear what your deceased parents wanted to tell you. Work on your relationship with Brilliance so it can show you more."

400

"I don't need a relationship with Brilliance. I'm going to be dead soon so it doesn't matter. And yes, I did notice. I miss my parents but I won't have to today. I'll see them again."

"Are you going to tell Damion that he's the Exol Child?"

"I want him to know during the War when he's about to have Brilliance transferred to him. I want Damion to have Brilliance embedded in his skin."

Alvaro smiled. "Now you see why I don't want to tell you things... It's a lot better when you find out on your own."

I nodded my head. "At least I know he can protect me as much as he can."

"Well, go eat some breakfast and get your battle gear on. You only have an hour."

I stood in front of the floor-length mirror, staring at all of my battle gear. I wore the same uniform as before with Brilliance's Mark on the breastplate. I held a shield in my right hand, a bow and arrows on my back, knives in sheaths around my belt and a sword in a sheath connected to my belt. In an hour I would be covered with my own blood as I attempt to fight for the freedom Clockworks deserve and put the Creators out of their own misery.

I walked down the hallway as my armor clanked against each other. I walked outside, noticing Phoenix was away from the group, stabbing blown up figures with a sword. Electra was trying out a new technique that she learned. Cado was using his martial arts to take down the wooden figures and Damion was throwing knives into the center of the figures. Something that I had to work on was archery. I was decent but I wasn't as good as I wanted to be. I dropped my shield on the ground that had Brilliance's design painted on it in purple. I took out my bow and loaded it with an arrow. I aimed at a single wooden figure and shot. The arrow landed in what would be the figure's shoulder. I tried again. I loaded the bow and shot, this time hitting the figure's chest. I loaded the bow again and the arrow hit the figure's heart. I did it one more time, making the arrow hit the figure's head.

"A bit rusty, are ya?" Cado asked, appearing at my side with a smile.

"Just a little but I'm usually better under pressure."

"That's because you're a procrastinator," Electra said, joining

401

in on the conversation.

"Hah, maybe," I said. I noticed Damion and Phoenix weren't in on the conversation. They were the ones that knew I was going to die. Each time Damion threw the knife, he threw it faster and harder. I observed him differently now. His parents weren't even his parents. Exols were his parents. He would've been an Exol if he stayed in the Land of the Exols. I suppose everything happens for a reason though. If he hadn't been sent away, then I never would've met him. I hated the idea of not meeting him. He couldn't be immortal though because he was born naturally, not in the waterfall of Innocence.

"Esther," Alvaro said behind me. "It's almost time." Suddenly, he wrapped his warm arms around me. "I watched you grow into becoming a brave character. Continue to be that character today. You are in control of your fate. I need you to be strong. Everyone is counting on you." He gave me the pouch that held the green liquids inside. I put the pouch on my belt.

"I know. All of us are going to be strong. You don't have to worry. I love you, Alvaro and I'm happy you were there for me."

He smiled, pulling away. "Go kick some ass."

I laughed. "I will, trust me."

Cado and Electra laughed. I heard Damion give a short laugh because it was funny. Phoenix walked over to us.

"It's time. Dante shouldn't be at the Headquarters because he's searching for you. His next stop is here. Be careful Alvaro. Stay alert."

I picked up my materials and put them back in the designated area. Damion stood at my side as Phoenix began creating a huge portal. He stared straight ahead with opaque eyes but I knew he was afraid on the inside. I slowly reached out, grabbing his black glove that was meant to keep his hands from burning or freezing when an ability touched his shield. He closed his large hand around mine and I could feel his warmth and our electrifying spark. He looked down at me and gave me a small smile.

"You're so beautiful in the sunlight," he said gently.

"Thank you, Mr. Storm," I said, bringing back old memories.

"Is everyone ready?" Phoenix yelled over the crackling noises the portals gave off.

We all cheered and simultaneously, we leaped into the portal. We spiraled around the mixtures of green, blue and purple electricity. In the distance I could see a forest and groups of Clockworks huddled together.

We arrived quickly, this time landing fluently instead of clumped together on the ground. Clockworks began cheering once we arrived and Electra smiled enthusiastically, enjoying the attention.

"Esther!" a few Clockworks yelled out, wearing our uniforms.

The last of the portal occurred closer to the back of our army. There was about four thousand Clockworks with us in the moment. It was a good amount for it only being Clockworks from the United States.

"Okay!" I yelled over the amount of Clockworks talking. "Listen up!" I screamed. Only half of the Clockworks in the front stopped talking. Damion put his fingers up to his mouth and whistled sharply, making my ears cringe. That stopped everyone from talking.

"EVERYONE UNDERSTANDS WHY WE ARE HERE, AM I CORRECT? IT'S TIME WE TAKE BACK WHAT THE CREATORS TOOK FROM US. THEY TOOK OUR FAMILIES AND FRIENDS AWAY: OUR LOVED ONES. THEY STOLE OUR LIVES AND HOW WE USED TO LIVE IN PEACE UNTIL THE UPROAR OF BRILLIANCE BEGAN. TODAY WE MUST FIGHT TO GET BACK WHAT ONCE WAS OURS. WE ARE COMPETENT OF SPLICING TOGETHER WITH CAREFUL DILLIGENCE TO END THIS WAR." The crowd cheered with enthusiasm at my words. "NO MORE FEELINGS OF SORROW. NO MORE TEARS; FOR TODAY IT MARKS A NEW IDEA OF A REVOLUTION. A REVOLUTION FILLED WITH LIGHT AND NO DARKNESS."

"NO DARKNESS," all of the Clockworks cried out.

"CLOCKWORKS IN THE FAR BACK, YOU'RE GOING TO BE ONE GROUP. YOUR GROUP IS GOING RIGHT NEXT TO WHERE THE MOUNTAINS BEGIN. THE HEADQUARTERS IS RIGHT IN FRONT OF THE MOUNTAINS AND THAT IS THE BACK OF THE HEADQUARTERS. THEY WON'T BE EXPECTING YOU FROM THERE. THE CLOCKWORKS IN THE MIDDLE, YOU'LL BREAK UP INTO TWO GROUPS AT EACH SIDES OF THE FOREST RIGHT NEXT TO THE FIELDS. GROUPS IN THE FRONT, WE WILL MARCH TOGETHER AND

BEGIN FIGHTING IN FRONT OF THEIR HEADQUARTERS. REMEMBER, DANTE ISN'T HERE YET. GROUPS IN THE BACK, TRY TO GET IN UNNOTICED AND START DESTROYING THE HEADQUARTERS FROM THE INSIDE OUT. GROUPS AT THE SIDE AND FRONT, WE'LL FIGHT OFF A MAJORITY OF THE CREATORS BECAUSE THEY THINK WE'RE COMING IN ONLY HEADSTRONG. ELECTRA WILL LEAD THE BACK GROUP. CADO WILL LEAD ONE SIDE GROUP AND PHOENIX WILL LEAD THE OTHER. DAMION AND I WILL LEAD THE LARGEST GROUP, THE FRONT. IF YOU HAVE ANY QUESTIONS, ASK THEM AND ONLY WAIT FOR THEIR CUES. SIDE AND FRONT GROUPS, WE SHOULD MEET IN THE MIDDLE OF THE FIELD AND BY THAT TIME, THE BACK GROUP SHOULD HAVE BROKEN INTO THEIR HEADQUARTERS. DON'T FORGET WE'RE A TEAM AND WHY WE ARE HERE TODAY! COMMENCE!" I screamed. The entire Clockwork Army roared with cheers and cries; they screamed louder than the demons in Hell and stomped the ground repeatedly.

"Esther," Damion said, grabbing my arm, staring me directly in the eyes.

"The Structures are already set up. They mark the beginning of the War."

I nodded my head. "Okay."

Phoenix, Cado and Electra jumped into a portal that would take them to their designated locations. The Clockworks in the middle and back began to disappear as they too, went their separate ways. Soon, only the front Clockworks stood in front of me with determined expressions.

"WHO IS READY TO TAKE BACK THE LIVES THAT WE HAD?" I screamed.

"YES!" the army yelled.

Damion and I turned around, facing our backs to the army. In front of us was the large battlefield that had dead, yellow grass with large blue mountains standing patiently in the background. Damion and I trudged through the thick underbrush of the forest, maneuvering our way onto the battlefield. The army behind us cheered and yelled enthusiastically but their enthusiasm did not shield the true fear I was feeling.

We positioned ourselves in rows on the battlefield. Damion

and I stood in the front with twenty other Clockworks. Behind us, there were a thousand Clockworks. Their Headquarters were quite a distance away in this large wasteland of a valley. On each side, I could see Cado's and Phoenix's armies hiding in the thick forests.

"Load the Structures!" I yelled at the groups of Clockworks that controlled the structures. "FIRE!"

Balls of illuminating golden spheres of fire flew out of the Structures. The fiery golden ovoid soared through the air, smashing into each side of their Headquarters. Everyone cheered with felicity at the start of the War. Almost instantaneously, Creators swarmed out of the Compound and abilities began whizzing through the air.

"Charge!" I screamed.

The Clockworks from all directions began running and abilities flew through the sky, lighting up the trees with illuminating shadows. All of us sprinted across the field and Damion stayed at my side the whole time. We continued charging until the Creators met with the Clockworks. Screams protruded in my ears as the first few Clockworks dropped to the ground with blood pouring out of their wounds. Fear tightened around my throat and I came back to reality, knowing that I had to protect as many Clockworks as I could from death.

In my peripheral vision, a glowing ball of blue acid hurtled in my direction. Spontaneously, I created a force field, blocking the acid from hitting me and the people at my side. I discarded that force field and created another one, pushing it out at the Creator who had thrown the acid. He flew back halfway across the field, hitting all of the Creators in his pathway, killing a majority of them on impact due to speed.

Beside me, I felt wind gaze my skin and I saw the grass sway violently underneath my feet. I glanced to my right, noticing Damion taking out six Creators at one time. He pulled them apart mentally, making them scream at the top of their lungs. Behind Damion, a Creator had made her way around him. She created an unknown substance in her palms and instantly, I screamed out. I threw a force field forward at the woman and I wrapped it around her tightly until she was squeezed to death. Damion wiped out the next set of Creators hurtling his way and he turned to look at me with a small grin.

"Thanks," he said.

"No problem."

Ahead, a man zipped through the Clockworks, killing each of them with a sword while using his intense sonic speed.

"Heads up!" I yelled at the Clockworks around me.

Suddenly, the Creator flashed beside me and I felt my body overturn and I landed on all fours. The Creator flipped me over. Quickly, I stood up before he could slash me. I wrapped a force field around me and pushed out multiple ones, trying to catch him. He was always faster than me. I yelled out in frustration and I pulled out my sword, slashing blindly at my surroundings. Finally, I felt an object smack against my sword and blood splashed across my palms. The Creator slowly fell to the ground, staring up at me with eyes full of sorrow while clutching his wound. I closed my eyes and stabbed my sword into his stomach. I heard his body fall to the ground and then I opened my eyes without staring at the dead body. I looked around me, noticing Clockworks and Creators dropping to the ground due to ricocheted abilities.

"Esther!" Damion yelled, kicking down a dead man while pulling his sword out of their chest. "We are 1/4th to the Headquarters. We're about to meet Cado and Phoenix's armies also."

I didn't have time to respond because I felt someone yank the back of my hair and I screamed out. I did a cartwheel backwards, pressing my hand on the woman's shoulder. I landed behind her, pulling out my sword again and I stabbed her in the back before she had any time to react. She screamed out in treacherous pain but I had to ignore her cries of agony and pursue what I had to do. I pulled out my sword, keeping it close to me.

I charged amongst the crowds of black and gray, slashing my sword at any Creator who stood in my way. I brought up a force field when I noticed bubbling liquids hurtling my way. I wrapped the force fields around the substances and then threw them back at the Creators, killing them with their own abilities.

I glanced back at Damion and instantly, I admired his strength and how powerful he was. He took out ten Creators in an instant with only his mind. He would occasionally lift up a few boulders and throw them at Creators that would smash in their skulls. He would glance up at me to make sure I was okay.

In front of me, I noticed a mass of Clockworks beginning to die by an unknown force. Oddly, Clockworks in front of me would fall to the ground. Suddenly, I felt a sharp pain hit my thigh and I fell to the ground while holding my injured thigh. I glanced around me wildly, trying to find the source of what had hit me. I felt the same pain again bite into my shoulder and that was when I came to a conclusion. I closed my eyes quickly and thought about peaceful thoughts in the midst of dead bodies that circled around me. I felt the rush and I knew I was invisible. I opened my eyes and I saw a man forming boiling water in his hands. He was invisible. That's why I couldn't see him until I turned invisible also. I flipped my leg around, tripping him before the water could reach me. He fell onto his buttocks and I used my leg to kick him across the face. His tooth flew out of his mouth and blood began to pour down his lip. I grabbed him by his shirt and slammed my fist into his face. I heard his jaw crunch and he yelped. He held up his hands with tears streaming down his face.

"Please... Stop... I didn't ever want this life," he said, sobbing.

My heart instantly grew a place for compassion. "Then why are you fighting?"

He looked up at me and his eyes darkened and the sorrow vanished. "To kill you of course."

Suddenly, I felt a force grab the back of my throat and heat began to surface underneath their muscular fingertips. I screamed, bringing back my leg to kick the man behind me in the groin. He dropped me to the ground and I instantly brought myself back up. I was dealing with two men that had the same ability as me but luckily, I could see them. I brought down my sword, slashing the man with the broken jaw first and then I slashed the other but it looked like it didn't affect him at all. He stood back up with an awful grin plastered across his face.

"To be in the presence of Esther Green is amazing but sad enough, we are not on the same sides. I know I can only injure you but I want to be the one that will bring you to Dante."

Quickly, I created a sharp force field, slashing his bicep but then I noticed the slash instantly healed. My eyes widened and I created a force field around me.

"Afraid of me?" he asked, coming closer to me, stopping in front of my force field.

I created another sharp field that sliced through his arm,

cutting it clean off as the blood sprayed onto my force field.

"Still won't kill me," he taunted.

I created another sharp force field, this time using it to decapitate the man. His body dropped to the ground as well as his head. I discarded the force field. I looked behind me, watching Damion fearfully look around him as he continued fighting. He didn't seem like he was concentrating on fighting, but trying to find something. I made myself visible and instantly, abilities soared my way and I created a force field, repelling the abilities.

"Esther!" Damion screamed, fighting off the group of Creators that surrounded him. I noticed multiple abilities careened at him from all different directions. He held up his shield trying to block all of the abilities that whizzed through the air but I knew eventually he would become weak and wouldn't withstand the pressure. Suddenly, he moved too slowly and a red, thick ability grazed his shoulder. He winced but he tried to continue fighting.

"Damion!" I yelled, running around a bend of dead bodies, trying to make my way towards him. I pushed out three sharp force fields, cutting each of them into the Creators. I pushed out a force field that wrapped around Damion, protecting him against all of the abilities. I came up beside him, morphing my way into the force field with him.

I yanked out my sword, not remembering that I had put it away. I swiped at the useless Creators, killing each of them off.

"Back to back," Damion stated. "Discard your force field so you save energy for now and use the serum with Dante."

I discarded the force field, pressing my back up against his. Creators scurried my way with foam hanging from their mouths and their love for death could no longer save their humanity. I held up a force field, blocking out the abilities from reaching me. Spontaneously, a bolt of electricity hurtled my way and I held up the same force field. The bolt of lightning collided into my force field, shattering it into pieces. Damion and I flew up in the air due to the impact of pressure. We landed beside each other. My breath escaped my lips and I tried to get my breathing under control.

"Get up, get up," Damion said, nudging my arm. He scurried to get up while grabbing my arm. Once we were in a crouched position, another powerful bolt flashed our way. We each leaped into different directions and I felt the pressure of the bolt gently graze my foot as I got out of the way in time. I did a somersault and then stood up quickly. My eyes scanned quickly and wildly until I found Damion struggling to get up. Another bolt of lightning hurtled his way and I yelped.

"Damion! Run!" I screamed at the top of my lungs.

Damion was in the situation where he couldn't run in time. As the bolt careened his way, he lifted up his hand and the bolt moved in a different direction, hitting a huge group of Creators. I stared at Damion in awe, realizing he just deflected an ability with his telekinesis. He stared down at his palms in bewilderment. I ran over to him quickly, jumping over bloody bodies. I grabbed his arm, pulling him up. I realized the side of his foot was burnt and his shoulder still had a large gash in it.

"You okay?" I asked, tugging him along, trying to get him away even though we couldn't.

"I'll be fine. Only my shoulder hurts."

Suddenly, I heard the same crack and I whipped around, staring at the bolt of lightning. Damion stopped the bolt, turned it around and then soared it back at the Creator, killing him instantly. I looked up at him and gave him a small grin.

A scream protruded in my ears and I looked behind me, realizing a little girl Clockwork had an ability strike her in the leg. I watched as she fell to the ground and blood began to pour down her mouth. The young male Creator casually walked over to her, forming his ability in his hands.

"No!" I screamed out, running over to the man. Before his ability hit her again, I smashed my whole body into him, knocking him over. Angrily, he pushed me off of him and he began forming the same substance. I created a sharp force field, cutting off the arm that had the ability forming. He screamed out in pain. I created another sharp force field, cutting open his chest. He fell to the ground, landing his torso on his lanky legs. I crawled over to the little girl. She had the most beautiful sea green eyes that I ever saw before. Her hair was a dirty blonde and she stared up at the sky as blood poured down her mouth. She was breathing heavily and the beating of her heart weakened. I stared down at her stomach, realizing she had another wound.

"Hey," I whispered gently, picking her up in my arms. "Look up at the sky? Isn't it pretty? Now, just think, if you could paint the

Brilliance by J.G. Lynn

sky any color, what would you make it?" She smiled up at me and before she could say anything, her heart stopped beating. I felt a frown come upon my face and a few tears streamed down my face. She was too young to be in this mess and then die.

Another scream filled my ears behind me. I got up quickly and turned around, realizing Phoenix disintegrated a Clockwork woman.

"Phoenix, what the hell did you just do?" I exclaimed.

Phoenix turned around, staring at me with wide eyes. "I don't know."

"What the hell? Are you colorblind? She was a Clockwork!" I screamed.

"I'm sorry... I wasn't thinking... I just..." he trailed on.

The ground around began shaking underneath our feet before I could respond. I looked around, realizing there was a Creator that had the ability to control the earth. He created a huge boulder and attempted throwing it at me but Phoenix created a portal in front of me, sucking up the boulder before it reached me. I pushed out a sharp force field, cutting the Creator in half. I glanced around the battlefield, watching each body drop every five seconds. The field was still clustered and we were close to their Headquarters. Damion was a distance away but he wasn't that far. He was fighting off Creators and their abilities easily.

Spontaneously, I felt strong arms wrap around my waist tightly and the sound of a portal opening up filled my ears. I wasn't sure what was going on so I couldn't help but scream.

"Damion!" I yelled. Damion turned around, staring at me until he noticed what was going on. His eyes reflected fear into mine and he screamed because he was unable to help me. His beautiful blue eyes showed absolute fear that I would never forget.

The strong arms pulled me into the portal and we flew through it at an atomic speed unknown to me. We landed on the harsh, cold cement floor. Before I could process what was going on, I felt a sharp needle pierce into my neck and all of my energy vanished. I glanced up fearfully, noticing Phoenix had a syringe in his hands and he was staring deeply into my eyes with regret and hatred.

"What the hell are you doing?" I yelled. I looked around, realizing we were in a large room with generators and large, 20 foot

410

gears. Noises of despair and abilities whizzing through the air could be heard outside of the factory walls. "How did you make it through the Creator's defense system? No one could ever get into a Compound with a portal. It's impossible."

"Shut up," Phoenix yelled at me, pulling on my arm. He pressed me into his body so he had a better grip on me.

"What are you doing?" I yelled, trying to pull away from him but he only vigorously pulled me back into him.

"Ahh, the beautiful Esther Green here to meet her fate." I felt the hairs on the back of my neck stand up and I glanced up. Dante was standing in the huge doorway of the Generator Room. We were in the Headquarters. My heart dropped into my stomach and I instantly knew this was going to be the end. This was where I was going to die due to a betrayal of what was supposed to be my friend.

"I trusted you!" I screamed out at Phoenix, trying to break free from his inseparable grasp.

Phoenix ignored my comment and began stripping off my armor and weapons. He tossed them to the other side of the factory right next to the largest generator. He took knives out of secret places I kept them and tossed the knives with my other weapons as well. The only knife he didn't retrieve was the one in my boot but I couldn't blow that cover just yet. I had to weigh my options.

"Yes, yes. I want to make this as easy of a fight as possible," Dante stated with a deep, grim voice. I couldn't stare into his eyes. I couldn't even glance at him due to the fear I was experiencing.

"Where is she?" Phoenix yelled; his voice dark.

"Oh, Paris? Is that who you're asking for?" Dante asked.

"Don't play games. I did what you want. Now give me my sister back."

"Or what?" Dante taunted.

"I can easily create a portal and get Esther out of here."

"You can't, Phoenix. I already switched off those possibilities. The only time you could get in here with a portal was now."

"You promised me," Phoenix said darkly, still holding me in his arms.

"Bring out Paris," Dante stated angrily. The doors slammed open and Creators threw a girl that looked a couple years younger than me into the room. She fell on dirty, cut up knees and she looked slightly malnourished. Her hair shined a beautiful blonde and from the distance, I assumed her eyes were a chocolate brown.

Phoenix, in a hurry, tied my hands and feet together, letting me fall to the ground as I lost my balance. He ran over to Paris, giving her a warm hug as a few tears streamed down his cheeks.

"I missed you so much. I love you; I love you Paris," he stated as they both cried together in each other's arms.

"I love you too."

"Now, the both of you are in time for the show," Dante stated with a sickening grin.

"No, we're leaving," Phoenix said, standing up along with Paris.

"No. Lock the doors, gentlemen!" Dante yelled at the Creators that were standing behind the double doors. "You're not leaving until she is dead. That was the deal also. You choose your sister over the hero, nearly the most important person in the world and your sister that still hasn't had her abilities yet. Wow, what a mistake that was," Dante said grimly.

"Don't watch, Paris," Phoenix told his little sister. He avoided my eyes and he stared down at the ground. I heard Dante's footsteps approaching me and my throat tightened.

Dante bent down next to me, staring me directly in the eyes. He had small gauges in his ears and a few nose and eyebrow piercings with a buzz cut. He gave me a small smile. "You have gotten away too many times, Esther. Because of this, you will *die* painfully, slowly and traumatically. Hopefully you told that boy you loved him because he won't be here to save you this time and nor will that Asian."

I gritted my teeth and pulled back my lip, staring into his eyes. "You can kill me, Dante... But you'll never kill my heart and the legacy that will continue on in my name. You'll be known as the great ass that never had a life to begin with and I'll be known as the hero that died for something that I grew to believe in. Brilliance is me: not you. You'll never have a connection with it in the ways I do. I am the Light and you are the Darkness."

Dante chuckled coldly. "Oh, Child, the darkness always overthrows the light."

I closed my eyes, waiting for the pain that was going to soon begin. I felt my bones shift underneath my skin and I knew he was turning me into his very own puppet. I screamed out in pain as the first wave of agony washed over me. I felt my foot snap in an unnatural way, making me screech in anguish. I heard Dante chuckle as he cut open the ropes on my hands and feet so he could control me more. I felt my body raising off of the ground and I stopped in midair, levitating high above the ground. Suddenly, I felt my back snap and my head touched my feet for a split second. I wailed with a bloodcurdling scream.

"Stop!" Phoenix said. "Just make it quick."

"There is no fun in that," he said.

I opened my eyes and I glanced at Phoenix. He was shielding his sister's eyes from the horror but he couldn't shield her ears. He stared at the ground, trying not to look up at me. I knew he didn't want to turn me over, but he did want his sister more than anything. The love for a family member is unconditional while the love for a friend is temporary. I didn't blame Phoenix; he was put into a terrible place. I wasn't going to hate anyone in this world before I died. I wanted to die with peaceful thoughts, not dark menacing ones. The only two people that I would hate was Dante and Luna.

"How does it feel?" Dante said through gritted teeth, lowering my body so he could see my face.

"Amazing," I said, losing my breath.

Dante chuckled coldly. "You always cease to amaze me with your fearless persona. But I can feel your blood pulsing underneath my fingertips with fear. You fear death you stupid child." He levitated me even more closely to him so he could whisper in my ear. "But why?" He sent another wave of shivers up my spine.

I turned my head and I stared him directly in his dark, menacing eyes. I laughed with a harsh bite to my spine. "I do not fear death; I fear that my death will affect the people I love. That is what I'm afraid of. Not you. Never will I be afraid of a coward."

Dante gritted his teeth and he sprung my body outward, making me soar across the room. My body smacked into a metal generator and then I landed on the concrete with a loud smack. My spine erupted into a series of pain but I ignored it. I had to fight back. I couldn't just let him throw me around. I felt my blood overturn inside of me and I was abruptly pushed forward, gliding above the ground. I passed Dante and he was laughing at how stupid I looked as he controlled every single movement I made. I slammed into the bare factory wall and my nose cracked against the metal. I fell to the ground and I clutched my nose as blood poured out onto my hand. I turned around, getting up slowly. I stared Dante in the eyes and I felt my lip curl back.

"How does it feel to have no control of your own body?" he asked, pushing me back to the other side of the factory again. I collided against the ground, landing near my weapons. Quickly, before he could move me away again, I grabbed my sword. He pushed me back to the other side of the factory. I passed him, reaching out my sword far enough to where I slashed him against the collarbone. He screamed out in pain, hurtling my body quickly back into the metal wall once again. I dropped to the ground, this time my body erupted into a series of uncontrollable pain. Dante trotted over to me in indignation. He glared at me in resentment. Once he reached me, he picked me up by the throat. Dante gritted his teeth and his large hands clasped around my throat. I felt my lungs beginning to weaken at the lack of breath. I opened my mouth, trying to breathe. I had to get out of this situation. I couldn't die from being suffocated. I reached out my hands as Dante was too busy trying to squeeze my throat and I shoved my thumbs into his eyes. He screamed in pain, dropping me once again to the ground. I felt my knee shatter as it cracked against the concrete. I grabbed for my sword and I stood over Dante that was fearfully tending to his eyes. I was about to slash him against the throat until I heard a section of the Headquarters closest to the Generator Room explode. I grinned, knowing it was the Clockworks that finally got in.

Suddenly, Dante grabbed my hand, digging his nails into my skin. I dropped my sword and briskly, he levitated me above the ground once again. I screamed, thrashing about as I wished that I had control over my own body. Loud explosions and clanks came from outside of the Generator Room's doors. I watched as Phoenix pulled Paris away from the doors and tears streamed down both of their cheeks. Phoenix glanced up at me as I levitated in the air. His eyes had regret plastered all over them. I looked away quickly so I didn't have to look in anyone's eyes when I died. I felt my back snap back the way it did before. I bit my lip, trying not to scream out. I didn't want Dante to feel the satisfaction. I didn't want him to feel any sort of dominance over me. Dante shifted his hands and I could feel my blood shift underneath my skin. He did a strange motion and instantaneously, I felt my blood literally rising up in my throat and I screamed out in excruciating pain. Blood poured out of my mouth and my thick, red metallic blood circled in the air around me. I let out a bloodcurdling scream and I could hear cries of anguish outside of the room's doors.

Spontaneously, a loud explosion occurred and the doors of the Generator Room flew open, smashing against the metal walls with a loud bang. Damion and Cado stood in the doorway along with Clockworks that fought off Creator's behind them. I reached my hand out towards Damion, wishing I could reach him. His face fell and his eyes erupted into anger. He threw out his hand, making Dante fly back into a wall. He fell to the ground as well as me. Damion stopped me midair, gently placing me on the ground with his telekinesis. A battle slowly maneuvered into the Generator Room. Cado ran over to me and Damion charged towards Dante.

Cado bent down over me, gently placing his hand underneath my head, prompting me up with his strength. "Here, drink. It'll heal your wounds quickly." He looked at my face and his eyes were solemn. He stopped and stared at my neck where I was injected. He placed his fingers on whatever mark was there that indicated I had serum inside of me. "Your abilities should be back in about thirty or more minutes. The serum that Alvaro gave you can't help you now with that stuff in you."

I nodded my head and drank a huge gulp of the liquid. Almost instantaneously, I felt my nose snap back into place and my shattered knee mend itself back together. My back aligned slowly and I felt some of my human energy come back to me.

"Damion?" I asked, beginning to stand up. I glanced around the factory, noticing Clockworks and Creator's fought against each other. I saw Damion in the distance trying to fight off Dante. Both of them controlled each other making it hard to contrast them. Each of them would fly back simultaneously and each of them would scream out in pain each time.

"I have to help the Clockworks," Cado stated, staring me in the eyes. "Please be careful. We need to try and get out of here before the rest of the Headquarters falls apart."

I nodded my head. "I'll be fine. Go help them. I'm going to help Damion."

We both went our separate ways. I ran across the factory,

pushing Clockworks and Creator's out of the way so I could retrieve my armor. I ran over to my armor, realizing everyone took my weapons, leaving me with only my shield. I grabbed the shield and darted across the factory, holding my shield out in front of me so I wouldn't get hit by abilities. I found my sword on the ground so I picked it up, holding it close beside me. I watched as Damion flew up onto a catwalk because Dante controlled his blood. I gritted my teeth, taking the metal flight of stairs so I could get up onto the catwalk. Dante levitated himself by controlling his own blood. I hurried up the stairs as my heart thumped out of my chest. Dante was going to kill Damion if I didn't reach him fast enough. I reached the top of the metal stairs and I had two catwalks to choose from. I was twenty to thirty feet up in the air, the highest part of the factory. I felt the air ducts brush my skin with cold air. I decided to choose the left path. I raced down the catwalk, watching Damion and Dante fight on the catwalk that was five platforms over from where I was at. I reached another point where I had to choose where to go. I chose left again, making my way passed three catwalks. There were two more catwalks I had to cross in order to make it to Damion and Dante. I charged down it, watching as Dante pushed Damion backward. Damion lost his balance and fell off the edge of the catwalk. My heart dropped down into my stomach as he caught hold of the metal floor and hung loosely off of it. Dante stood over him with a satisfied smile plastered across his face.

I held my sword out in front of me as I charged down the catwalk they were on. Dante looked back at me and before he could react, I collided into him with my shield, stabbing him in the hip. He fell to the floor, clutching his wound. I glanced over at Damion and he gave me a small smile as he helped himself back onto the catwalk. I grabbed his hand and he gave me a short embrace until Dante recovered and pushed us apart. Each of us flipped over either side of the catwalk. I dropped my sword but kept my shield close to me as I struggled for the metal edge. I missed my grasp and I began falling. I screamed as Damion also couldn't get his grasp on the edge of the metal. We both fell quite a distance from each other and the ground was quickly approaching. Damion used his strength, pushing across the air, trying to use every part of his abilities to reach me in midair. Finally, his arms wrapped around me tightly and we held onto each other. He used his telekinesis to slow down the speed of our fall. We floated closely to the ground and we landed gently. Damion released me but still held my hand. I looked up and Dante jumped off the catwalk and he too, fell midair, trying to reach us. He controlled his own blood and landed on the ground ten feet away from us.

In vexation, he pushed out each Clockwork in his way, staring the both of us down with gritted teeth. I held onto Damion's arm and I pulled him along viciously.

"We gotta' go!" I yelled.

Damion and I sprinted across the battle within the factory. We could feel each person's blood closest to us flip out of the way as Dante struggled to push his ability closest to us.

"Where did your sword go?" Damion yelled over the noises of abilities whizzing through the air as we ran.

"I dropped it somewhere! I have a small knife in my boot though!" I yelled back at him.

"Come on. We need to get behind those gears. There probably won't be any stray abilities there. We need to kill Dante there too," Damion said.

We charged through the crowd and I held up my shield in front of me, blocking out all of the abilities as we hurried. We could feel Dante close on our heels. We turned around into the large mess of gears. They stood nearly twenty feet high and they were in rows, spaced apart by five feet beside each other and ten feet away from each other.

"Run between them so Dante can lose sight of us!" I yelled.

Damion and I ran down the row and then we cut between two gears into another row. A loud crack filled the air and the gears began moving all around us.

"Run!" Damion screamed as the gears began turning in different directions and each of them grinded together.

A gear turned behind me and I could feel it on the back of my heel. I leaped between two gears before they began to shift. Damion followed my movement and we both landed on the concrete ground, sliding across it until the gears stopped shifting.

"Why the hell did they move?" Damion asked, staring at each circular gear.

I could hear the clacking of footsteps in the distance and I instantly knew who it was.

"Dante," I said quietly. Once I said his name, he appeared out from behind a set of gears with a small remote in his hand. Damion, instinctively, pushed me behind him and stood in front of me. I glanced up at his facial features and his jaw was tightly clenched. There was dirt smudged all over his face.

"Amazing, isn't it?" Dante said, stopping a few feet away from us. "I built it myself. You see, these gears don't control the electricity or whatever they're used for... I built them to play a small game with my victims. I find it funny that the both of you fell into the trap, thinking this was the safest place in this part of my Headquarters. This is the most dangerous part of this factory."

"We can handle anything thrown our way," Damion stated dryly.

"Anything?" Dante chuckled. "Then you'll enjoy this little game."

Dante controlled our blood and violently pushed us away from each other. I flew into the next row of gears and Damion flew into a different row. Dante laughed as he pressed the button and all of the gears slowly began to move and rotate. The gears closest to me shifted and they were beginning to close in on me. I screamed, pushing myself up and I ran down the row as all of the gears turned clockwise behind me. I leaped in between the last two gears, getting to a safe place that had no gears. Damion ran out from the maze of gears and he came over to me, trying to catch his breath.

"Are you okay?" I asked, staring at him.

"Yeah. I'm good. What do we get ourselves into?" he asked, giving me a small smile.

"I don't even know," I said, returning the smile.

"Glad we're out of that gear maze. It was intense."

"Very intense."

Clapping filled our ears and the atmosphere instantly changed as Dante walked casually over to us.

"Wow, I can't believe Esther is still alive... I always have a great time playing with my food, but eventually I'll have to eat it. I believe it is that time, sadly."

"If you touch her, I'll rip out your organs and grind your corpse in those damn gears," Damion said through gritted teeth.

"Ah, interesting. Tough words: weak mind. How sad," Dante said with a wicked smile.

Damion used his telekinesis and pushed Dante into a gear. The gears weren't moving so he was only injured from the impact. Dante fell to the ground and quickly stood up. He controlled Damion's blood, lifting him into the air. Damion began choking on his blood and his blood began to flow out of his mouth like how mine had.

"Stop!" I screamed. I pulled out the knife that was in my boot and I dropped my shield finally. "Stop, Dante!"

Dante dropped Damion to the ground while laughing obnoxiously. Damion stood up, limping over to me weakly. He lost a lot of blood already.

"How amazing would it be to kill the both of you? I'll have to kill that little Asian next and I would be free to do as I please with Brilliance," Dante rambled on.

I stared up at Damion, holding the knife tightly in my hand. "Trust me." He nodded his head.

I remembered how Acea taught me how to throw a knife and the best time to do that would be now when Dante least expected it. I gritted my teeth, trying to connect to my Spiritual Side so I had the strength to hit him perfectly. I threw the knife and it spiraled through the air. Damion used his telekinesis to push the knife further and we both watched as the knife slammed into Dante's chest. He doubled over, laughing mockingly at our attempt to hit his heart. He pulled out the knife as blood poured out of his wound. He gritted his teeth and whipped the knife through the air. Damion and I opened our mouths and before Damion tried to jump in front of me, the knife spiraled closer to me in slow motion. I felt the knife penetrate me below my heart. I could hear Damion scream out as I slowly fell to the ground. I smacked my head against the concrete and everything was swarming around me in a distant haze. I didn't focus on the pain at all. I only focused on how I breathed one less breath each time.

I heard Damion scream once again and the floor shook underneath my body. I heard Dante yell and I heard a body drop to the ground. In the distance, I could see Phoenix and Paris running from a few Creator's that chased after them. There was a flash of acid as my eyes had a haze over them and the three Creator's dropped to the ground. Phoenix stopped in his tracks once he noticed me.

Damion's face came over me clearly, considering I could

only see what was closest to me. Tears were streaming down his cheeks and he was breathing heavily while making odd, choked noises.

"Damion," I whispered, my voice barely audible as my breathing began to slow.

"Esther, please... Please stay with me," Damion cried out. "Don't leave me. I don't want to lose you. Please, Esther... Stay awake," Damion screamed as tears flew rapidly down his cheeks. He turned his attention to Phoenix. "You did this! You led her to her death! She trusted you! All you are is a coward! A coward!" Damion screamed.

My eyes faded in and out as waves of felicity strangely washed over my body. I could feel the Mark of Brilliance tingle underneath my skin and slowly, I felt each circle glide off of my glistening wrist. A few designs began trailing across the cement, making its way to Dante. I felt my eyes open clearly and I knew I couldn't let Brilliance reach Dante.

"Damion," I whispered, reaching up to wipe off a tear on his face. "I need you to do me a favor."

Damion chuckled slightly, rolling his eyes. "You're dying and you want me to do a favor? That's your last request?"

"Yes," I felt my heart beginning to slow even more. I had to hurry. "You're—the Exol—the Exol Child. I didn't tell—you. I know. Sorry. You—need to—stab me—in the heart, Damion. Brilliance needs—to transfer—to you."

"I can't do that, I can't," Damion said as more tears began to flow out of his eyes.

"Don't let Dante... Take over," I said, my voice beginning to weaken.

"I can't," he said.

"You have to. If you—can't—then get Cado. You won't—find him—in time."

My eyes began to blacken around the edges and I could only see a portion of Damion's face. I felt the knife slide out of my skin and I winced slightly but then again, I was coated with warmth and happiness for some unknown reason. I thought death would be dark and cold, but it was the opposite. It was refreshing and soothing, making it to where it wasn't that bad.

"I love you," I heard Damion whisper and I smiled slightly

before my eyes completely blackened. I felt the blade penetrate my heart and Damion collapsed over my body, pulling out the blade and throwing it across the ground. I could tell Brilliance changed its course and began maneuvering its way towards Damion. Eagerly, it reached him and Damion screamed out as Brilliance began to Choose him. I remembered the electrifying pain that Brilliance caused when I was Marked. That was the same pain Damion was experiencing.

The sounds of Damion's screams slowly vanished and in the far distance, I could see a ball of large, white light. I looked down, realizing I was wearing a beautiful white gown. Winds refreshingly wrapped itself around me, making my hair and dress flap lightly. Images suddenly circled around me and memories danced in the air.

A memory of my father throwing five-year-old me up in the air when he was perfectly healthy. Each time when he threw me, he would catch me and we would laugh together. Another memory came upon me and I saw me sitting on top of my father's shoulders. I always use to think I was Queen of the World, sitting on top of the highest peak of a mountain whenever I sat on his shoulder.

A memory of my mom snapping pictures of me on Christmas day came back to me. I was seven years old and it was my first Christmas present due to harsh economic times. I remembered being incredibly happy and we all took cute little pictures that day. I remembered a time where both of my parents were teaching me how to ride a bike and when I pushed off for the first time and rode the bike alone, they ran beside me yelling and cheering with happiness. I continued racing on, a huge grin plastered across my face as I continued riding perfectly. I wanted to ride to where the colors of the sunset touched the earth but I soon came to the realization that I wouldn't be able to reach it, because it was impossible. My parents still encouraged me to ride and so I did. It was one of the greatest memories I ever had.

Another memory came into mind when my mother was protecting me in Pennsylvania after I had been Chosen from Brilliance. She loved and cared about me and I wished I saw it then instead of being a jerk to her. I hated that but my mother still loved me no matter what. I remembered when I was first born and my mother and father held me in both of their arms and they were crying with joy because they had a baby. I remembered when my mother gave me the locket that had our beautiful family portrait in it and mine and Damion's initials were engraved in it. I wore that locket every single day and I still had it on my body and Damion continued to scream as he was being Chosen.

"Esther," my mother's voice filled my ears.

"Mom?" I asked, looking around. She appeared from the big ball of light and she was absolutely stunning. She wore a long, white dress and her hair was long and shining beautifully. She stopped floating once she reached me. My mom had a glow all around her body.

"Please," she said eagerly. "I need you to remember something Alvaro told you. It was when he told you that darkness always overthrows the light, do you remember?" she asked.

I nodded my head. "Yes, Mom. I remember." I looked around me, realizing the light was overthrowing the darkness and I felt a small smile creep upon my lips.

"Do you remember the part where he said you are in control of your own destiny?" she asked.

It took me awhile to remember but then I heard his voice say the phrase in my head again and I nodded. "Yes, I remember."

"Don't let the Prophecy tell you about your own life. You are in *control*. You make the decisions about your life." Her beautiful green eyes stared me directly in my own and I felt my heart warm. "That means you are in control if you stay alive or if you want to stay dead."

"Okay," I said, nodding my head. I knew what I wanted to do.

"What do you want to do?" she asked.

"I want to stay alive... I am in control of my own Prophecy. No one writes out my life for me."

She smiled, reaching her hand up to touch my face gently. "I am so proud to call you my daughter." I felt a tear fall from my cheek as I felt my mother's warmth radiate against my skin. She wiped off the tear with a little grin. She wrapped her arms around me, embracing me with love and compassion. I wrapped my arms around her and this was the first time I ever got to touch my mother again after her death. "I love you, Esther. Stay strong and never lose yourself."

My father emerged from the light as well with a smile

plastered across his face. He instantly embraced all of us and we all sank into his warmth.

"I'm proud to have a daughter as strong as you, Esther. And I know you will succeed. I love you," my father said.

"I love you too."

Instantaneously, my eyes fluttered open and the Creators and Clockworks migrated their way in this area. Damion was laying on the ground with half of Brilliance's Mark on his wrist. I lifted up my wrist and I noticed I had half of a Mark as well. Slowly, I sat up, turning to look at Dante beginning to wake up from being unconscious. His eyes adjusted to his surroundings and then he noticed me staring at him. He blinked in bewilderment and he began to stand up. I felt like I had my abilities back but I had to be stronger in this moment. I grabbed the small pouch from my belt. Thankfully Phoenix didn't take that off when he stripped me down. I pulled out the serum, opened it and then drank it until the last drop. I felt everything inside of me grow with absolute vigor. Dante stood up, readying to fight me again.

"Some people never know when to *die*," Dante said through gritted teeth.

I laughed coldly. "The Light always overthrows the Darkness. I *am* in control of *my* life."

I thrust out my hands, making a force field illuminate a golden color around me. I pushed out another force field, slamming it into Dante. He flew back onto his side. He got up quickly, trying to control my blood but he was unsatisfied. I created a sharp force field, planning to cut him into pieces. He jumped out of the way in time and the sharp force field shattered into the gear. I thrust out another sharp force field and he jumped over it, making the force field shatter again. He controlled the Clockworks' blood around me, making them use their abilities all at once to weaken my force field around me. It didn't work. I was too powerful for Dante. I threw out another sharp force field and Dante dodged it again. He ran over to a Creator that had the ability to create portals. Simultaneously, they both jumped into the portal so I threw out another sharp force field. The portal closed in time, sucking up the sharp force field with it. One of them had to die since I threw in a sharp force field. My hope was for Dante but I doubt it hit him. He probably used the Creator as a shield so the force field wouldn't hit him. A rage formed inside of me at how childish he was.

"You coward!" I screamed at the top of my lungs. Dante wouldn't even fight me.

"Esther," Cado exclaimed. I turned around and watched as he ran over to me as the battle continued. He gave me a short embrace and then he pulled away. "We have to get all of the Clockworks out of here and retreat. The Clockworks outside already burnt down the other side of the Headquarters. They won't stop for us, I know it. We need to go."

I licked my lips and nodded my head. "Dante got away."

"We always have the chance to fight another day but for now, we need to get out of here. I heard what Phoenix did. We should just leave him here."

"We need him to get back home," I said.

"Are you kidding? We're leaving him here. I'm sure him and his sister are going to become Creators even though the Creators haven't accepted them yet. We can just ask a Clockwork to get us back there."

I nodded my head. "Okay. We need to get Damion and find Electra."

"Okay."

I pushed through Creators and Clockworks, trying to get to Damion. I wrapped a force field around Cado and me. We charged through all of the people until we reached Damion. I discarded the force field and I bent down next to Damion. I shook him gently until his eyes fluttered open. When he saw me, he shot up with his mouth slightly hanging open. He furrowed his brows and then a small smile crept across his face.

"We need to go. Clockworks are going to begin blowing up this side of the Headquarters," I said.

Damion nodded his head, beginning to stand up. Suddenly, he stared down at his wrist, noticing the Mark. Cado noticed it too.

"We both have Brilliance inside of us," I said. "We can't think about it right now. We have to go."

"Okay," Damion said. Across the battle, I noticed Phoenix create a portal and him and Paris jumped into it. They weren't going to be a part of either side. They wanted to go their own way and I understood that. He wanted what was best for Paris.

"CLOCKWORKS! RETREAT! NOW!" I screamed.

Each Clockwork looked up, nodded their heads and began evacuating the factory section. Cado stopped a few Clockworks, asking them if they could create portals. Finally, we found a Clockwork that could. She had short brown hair and dark eyes.

"I can only take you home and then I have to leave back to my Clockwork group," she explained.

"That's perfectly fine," I said.

Together, we all ran out of the factory doors, down a long series of winding hallways. The sounds of explosions could be heard from outside and the electricity no longer was on. We ran through the darkness until we found a ray of light down one hallway. We ran out into the field, quickly noticing metal Bots.

"Bots!" Cado screamed out.

One Bot noticed us and it swung down with its large fist, making all of us dunk. It whipped around, creating a boulder in its palms. The Bot threw the boulder down on us and all of us did somersaults, trying to get away from the Bots. We continued running across the battlefield and people were still fighting. In the distance, Clockworks lined up and the Structures were filled with balls of fire. They unleashed the balls of fire and the Clockworks in the rows created their own explosions once they noticed we were out of the Creators' Headquarters.

The balls of fire soared through the air, each one colliding into the Compound with loud explosions. With each explosion that smacked into the Compound, the structure began to slowly crumble into ruins. In the distance I spotted Electra.

"Electra!" I screamed and we all raced over to her. We ran across the battlefield, passing heartbroken Creators that stopped fighting to watch their home fall apart. There was a side of me that felt bad for them but they already killed way too many people to begin with. They deserved their heartbreak.

Electra stopped directing her side of the Clockwork army and she greeted us with a huge smile. Her eyes scanned my face and then they dropped down to my chest.

"Were you stabbed in the heart?" she exclaimed.

"Slightly below the heart. I decided I was the one in control if I was to die or live another day."

Electra gave me a huge hug and then she pulled away, scanning the group. "Uh, where's Phoenix?"

"I'm sorry, Electra..." Cado began.

"Phoenix gave Esther over to Dante. He was the reason she almost died," Damion stated bitterly.

Electra gasped. "He couldn't have done that... I don't believe you. I can't."

"He did it so he could get his sister back. He left the War with her and I don't know when we're going to see him again. I'm sorry, Electra," I said compassionately.

"We should leave. The Creators will try to fight even more since we destroyed their home," Electra said, ignoring the information about Phoenix.

"We need to fight another day. Dante left already," I said.

"RETREAT!" Damion screamed.

The Clockworks began breaking up into groups and they created portals. Group by group, the Clockworks began to disappear.

"This is Sopha," I said, addressing the girl that offered to take us home. "She'll take us home."

"Where we belong," Damion said, grabbing a hold of my hand while smiling down at me. The sky made it seem like it was early evening and the rays of the sun illuminated his beautiful blue eyes. I smiled up at him as Sopha began creating the portal.

Sopha's portal was a bright yellow with frayed edges dancing around. Simultaneously, we all jumped into the portal. Sounds of electricity engulfed my ears and, in the distance, I could see wood and Alvaro sitting at his desk, waiting for us to come back. The portal spat us out and we landed perfectly on the ground. Alvaro's eyes glowed vibrantly when he saw me.

"Esther!" he yelled, running over to me. He gave me a strong embrace and I could tell his breathing was choppy. He was crying. "I love you so much, Esther. I'm so happy you're alive. I knew you would figure it out. I knew you would discover that you can write your own Prophecy."

I pulled away from Alvaro, smiling up at him. I was filled with felicity to be alive. "Dante wasn't killed. He ran away."

"It's okay, Esther. You'll have the chance to kill him another day," Alvaro said. He looked around at our group, noticing Sopha. He smiled. "Don't worry, you can go back to your group now."

"Thank you, sir." She quickly created a portal and then left.

"I see you guys lost a fellow group member. Don't tell me, I know the reason why as I look into your memories." Alvaro stared at the wound on my chest. It didn't hurt at all due to my rebirth. "There are potions lined up for each of you and your injuries."

We all formed into a line and each of us picked up our cylinder and we drank the serum. Instantly, our injuries began to vanish. Damion glanced over at me and he gave me a small smile. I felt the heat on my cheeks and I had the urge to talk to him alone. Electra and Cado gave me hugs of reassurance and I began to walk to the back door. Damion followed behind me and we both walked down the field together as the sun began to lower. He grabbed my hand and we simultaneously walked into the forest, making our way to the rushing river.

"How do you feel taking a small boat ride down this river?" Damion asked, vigorously breaking a thick, seven-foot-tall tree. He ripped sections out of the tree so we could sit inside of it while being comfortable at the same time. He grabbed a few smaller trees and broke them in half, making small, imperfect paddles.

"How elegant," I said with a chuckle. I felt like we were younger again and just the thought of that warmed my heart. Memories of how we acted before I was Chosen resurfaced and I couldn't help but smile.

"Get in, Esther," he said.

Carefully, I stepped into the small, wooden canoe. I grabbed a paddle and Damion pushed the small canoe into the river. Quickly, he jumped in before the boat left without him. He let us follow the movement of the river before he started to paddle. Willow trees hung all around us as we gracefully floated down the river. I stared into his eyes and I couldn't help but smile.

Damion stared at the thick expanse of trees that surrounded the water with an unreadable expression.

"Your parents, how does that feel?" I asked, referring to his Exol parents.

"I knew I didn't belong with two mortal parents. Everything makes sense now... I just wish they didn't get rid of me."

"Your father wanted to do what was best for you. The Exols would've killed you, Damion. He saved your life and your mother loved you so much that she died for you."

"I wish I knew them. I wish I could hear my father's laugh and feel the touch of my mother. I want to know what a true family is supposed to feel like."

I swallowed, staring into his eyes. "I met your father—Icelos. He wrote the Light section in Brilliance. And eventually, Brilliance wrote the Dark section. Your father is a good man. He saved my life but unfortunately, he couldn't save my mother's."

"I need to meet him one day."

"Damion," I said after a long pause. "I need to tell you something."

"Yes?" Damion asked, beginning to use his strength to glide us over the large rocks that rocked our canoe back and forth. The canoe was small enough to where we were only a foot or two away from each other.

"I'm not going to stay away from my feelings... I can't ignore them anymore. I *have* to care about you or it doesn't feel like I'm living at all."

I saw a small grin creeped upon Damion's lips as he continued paddling the boat. He rested the paddle on his lap when he was done. "When I saw you die, I fell to pieces. I felt like there was no more hope left in the world because I—," he cut himself off.

A smile pulled at the corner of my lips. "Don't worry, Damion. You already lost the game."

Damion laughed. "Yeah, but I won at the same time."

I giggled. "You always know how to make me feel radiant... With your beautiful blue eyes... Quirky little lopsided grin... I just... I love everything about you, Damion. I always have." I said as a tear streamed down my cheek as my emotions began to pour out faster than my mouth. "We've been through so much and you still helped me through everything."

"Even though having the entire world on your shoulders, being a Clockwork feels like a gift with the feelings that come with it. Feeling love is the most beautiful emotion in the entire heart of our emotions. It feels like you're angry, or in despair when you see your lover in pain, wanting to protect them with every fiber of your being. The constant butterflies and the cold sweats you receive whenever I touch your skin or look into your beautiful, hazel eyes. There are too many emotions that happen all at once that it's unexplainable. I love you, Esther Alexis Green. I always have and I always will. I will protect you from the darkness that comes our way because you're the brightest light I ever saw."

I wiped a tear that had fallen from my eyes. "I can't contain my love. This love demands to be known."

"Then let it be known," Damion said.

Damion leaned in and this time, in this moment, I knew it was going to finally happen. I closed my eyes gently and leaned in. Damion's hands found my hips and my arms wrapped around his neck. I felt his cold, tender lips reach mine and my heart erupted into a series of beautiful butterflies that danced around inside of me. Everything inside of my body relaxed and I never felt such happiness before in my entire life. To share a moment as beautiful as this was rare and the beauty of being a Clockwork washed over me. He kissed me passionately and I returned it, wishing the moment could last forever. I wanted to feel this forever. I wanted this moment to last for an eternity. I was glad that I stayed alive because life was such a remarkable and enchanting thing. To leave it behind would be a stupid, reckless decision. I couldn't possibly leave behind the people I loved. I couldn't leave the things I had to complete in life in order to feel satisfied enough to greet death as an old friend. Sadly, our lips locked together one more time and then we pulled away, staring at each other while breathing heavily. Our hearts wanted to pump out of our chests because the feeling was too extreme for our simple little hearts to handle.

"I'm going to protect you, Esther. I don't want you to die. Ever. Again."

I nodded my head, reaching my hand up to touch his face. "I won't leave you again. I've done that too many times."

"We're almost oddly the same now. Brilliance lives inside the both of us," he said.

"I know. Hopefully you'll enjoy the throbs and images Brilliance gives you," I said with a chuckle.

"May be too much for me to handle." He paused, staring deeply into my eyes. "So, what's next?"

"I already think I know what's going to happen next. I want to go to the Land of the Exols."

"Why?" Damion asked.

"My mother died because she lost her abilities. I'm going to demand for our abilities to last until death. Every Clockwork. Not just us. I want to feel like I accomplished something to avenge my mother's death in a positive way. Another thing is I want Alvaro to be free from Erin Springs."

Damion nodded his head. "I'll come with you on the journey. We need to start planning it."

"Before we start planning it, let's visit Becca, Acea and Mason." I grinned. "I need to let them know I'm alright and everything is going to be fine for a while."

"I understand. I do miss Becca a lot."

"Me too."

Damion looked at my neck, noticing the locket. He reached over and he pulled the chain out of my Clockwork uniform. He turned it over and his eyebrows raised as he noticed his initials.

"My initials?" he asked, opening the locket. He stared at my family picture and his face fell slightly at the fact that both of my parents were dead.

"My mother engraved our initials. She knew we had a future together. Everything with that locket represents the family I have."

"We're family," Damion said, smiling with a grin.

"Forever."

Damion and I paddled down the river and I watched as the sun began to set with rays of orange, pink and red. As we continued paddling in the vibrant rays of colors, I quietly pretended that we were going to touch the rays of light. I stared into Damion's blue eyes and my heart wanted to burst out of my chest. He gave me a grin and I returned it. We continued paddling down the quiet part of the river and I knew we already had reached the light. We were Light.

Epilogue

The only thing he could hear was water dripping in the black expanse. The room was cold and exceptionally dirty, making Acea fear for unknown. The only thought that rummaged through his mind was Esther. He surely believed she would soon discover his disappearance and come to rescue him. There was also a cataclysmic side to him that had occasionally disregarded his optimistic thoughts. He would conjure up the idea that Esther hated him and wouldn't come to his aid in this crisis.

Acea had strong sentiments toward Esther even though he was caught up in Leila's game. Everything he told Esther was genuine and that was the only hope he needed.

Acea sat on the dirty cement floor. The only thing he could see was scorpions gradually walking amidst the ground, ignoring Acea in the darkness. Suddenly, after a week of sitting in absolute darkness, a spotlight switched on, lighting up the cell. Instinctively Acea got up quickly and simultaneously, he fell back to the ground due to lack of nutrition. He had drunk from the dripping water and that was what kept him alive this long. Gradually, he stood up, using the damp brick walls to hold his balance. Across the cell he could see a mirror with a sink he hadn't known was there before. He slowly carried himself along the perimeter of the cell, finally reaching the sink.

Acea stared into his own reflection and he couldn't recognize himself at all. Dirt and grime were splattered all over his face along with cuts and beats he had taken from Phoenix when he transported him there. After Phoenix was meant to take Acea back home, he actually brought him to this dark cellar. Acea had tried to fight back but he was unsuccessful due to Phoenix's brute strength.

Eagerly, Acea turned on the faucet and he shoved his mouth under the thin line of water that trickled slowly into his mouth. He slammed his fist on the sink and screamed for more water due to dissatisfaction. The water abruptly turned off and Acea recoiled, staring at the faucet in agony.

"No!" he screamed as tears began to flow down his cheeks, burning his gashes.

Acea gripped each side of the sink and he stared into the mirror with dark, menacing eyes. In exasperation he brought up his fist, colliding it into the mirror. The mirror shattered into tiny little pieces.

A long, ear-screeching sound drew Acea's attention away from the broken mirror. He noticed two dark shadows walking towards him, avoiding the direction the spotlight was pointing. As they walked underneath the light, their features lit up. There was a woman with long, pitch black hair and she had bright green eyes. The man next to her had a series of pierces and tattoos all over his body. His eyes illuminated green as well.

"Who—who are you?" Acea asked fearfully, backing up against the sink.

"We are not here to hurt you in any way, young child. My name is Dante Jett and this is Ava Blacksmith," the man said gently with a deep, dark voice.

"How do I know you won't hurt me? Why am I here?" Acea asked as the questions flew out of his mouth.

"We need you," the woman said, approaching him slowly. "We need your help for a very important task."

"Have you ever admired the abilities of the Clockworks?" Dante asked, furrowing his brows.

"I admired them but..."

"Being a human is pitiful," Ava stated darkly, coaxing Acea into believing every word she said. "You are weak. Frail. Unintelligent. *Worthless.*" Ava carefully and collectively glided around Acea as he never wanted to feel worthless before.

"And Esther," Dante stated. "She isn't who you think she is."

"What? I care about Esther," Acea snapped.

Ava trailed her long fingernails across Acea's cheek. "She hates you... She hates what you did to her. She cares about someone else... She *loves* someone else."

"You meant nothing to her," Dante stated darkly, staring in to Acea's eyes.

"Nothing," Ava whispered in his ear. "She used you to get over the heartbreak with the boy... Nothing more. Esther is a stupid child that believes she is a hero when she is not." Ava trailed her cold fingers across Acea's skin. "You have a chance to be something if you decide to take on the encouraging offer to be one of us."

"You can show Esther that you *are* something, not a toy," Dante said.

"Tell me," Ava said quietly. "Tell me that you hate the girl... She never cared for you."

"I uh—," Acea said, unsure on his decision.

"SAY YOU HATE HER!" Ava screamed, using her ability to manipulate Acea.

"I hate her," Acea stated firmly as his whole demeanor changed.

"Now, Acea, tell us that you want to destroy her," Dante said, smiling wickedly.

"I want to destroy Esther Alexis Green," Acea said without a single thought of his original self.

"Ava," Dante said, "you know what to do."

Ava smiled freakishly. "Finally."

Ava Blacksmith shoved her long, black nail into Acea's skin, tearing deep down until she hit his bone. Acea screamed out in treacherous pain as the chromosomes and DNA inside of his body began to abruptly change. He began to gain multiple abilities a Clockwork would receive. He continued to let out bloodcurdling screams and Ava grinned wickedly as blood poured out of Acea's wound. Dante stood still, transfixed on what Ava was doing. Suddenly, Ava pulled out her nail, allowing Acea fall to the ground.

"Now, Acea," Dante said, walking around his body, "you are no longer a weak human; you are a Creator that will follow all of my commands and instructions. You are our instrument to destroy every single fiber left in Esther and now, unfortunately the boy as well. Everything in your past life has been swept away. Your parents, your sister, pleasant memories with Esther and all of your emotions that held you back from what you are meant to be are gone. The only emotion that lives inside of you is rage. Every feeling of love and remorse is unknown to you.

"You possess the abilities of electricity, control of the elements, increased strength, increased speed, twin creation, disintegration, shape shifting to an abnormal size of a raven, breathing underwater, manipulation of the gravity around you, knowledge of hunting your victims, possession and last but not least, you have the ability to be invincible. You cannot be killed but you can be seriously injured."

433

"You will be the best creation I ever constructed," Ava stated.

Acea stood up slowly as he adjusted to the power that surged within him. "This feels—amazing." He admired the strength that made his blood vessels pop.

"Do you understand what you must do?" Dante asked. Acea turned his head slowly to stare at Dante.

"Yes. I will destroy the weak, Esther Alexis Green."

The End

Brilliance

By J.G. Lynn

Brilliance by J.G. Lynn

Acknowledgements

Huge thanks to my mother, father, brother and Cameron and his family for supporting
me on this journey.

Huge thanks to all of my friends that showed excitement and gratitude about the novel.

(You Know Who You Are)

And huge thanks to all of my colleagues that helped me and showed excitement to the
novel as well.

Brilliance by J.G. Lynn

Brilliance by J.G. Lynn

Made in the
USA
Columbia, SC